The Cyclops Effect

By CJ Williams

The Cyclops Effect

By CJ Williams

Copyright © 2019 CJ Williams

ISBN: 9781673444575

English Edition

Table of Contents

Chapter 1 – The Accident

Chicago, Illinois

Asha leaned against the headboard and gazed at the gray skies over Lake Michigan. The dreary atmosphere matched her mood. The only silver lining was that the hospital had finally moved her out of the Intensive Care Unit into this luxurious private room. At least in here, she had a view.

For twenty-two days, she had lain comatose in the ICU. She woke up almost a week ago, yet recalled none of her first 72 hours of wakefulness.

Although her physical condition steadily improved, Asha could not tell the doctors her name or where she was. When she looked in a mirror, even though only part of her face was covered with bandages, she did not recognize herself.

A neurologist was called in, and he subsequently recruited a psychiatrist, Doctor Christina Browning. After a two-day evaluation, the psychiatrist concluded that although Asha retained her mental faculties, she had lost all of her *episodic* memories; in other words, her entire life history was gone. The clinical label was Severe Retrograde Amnesia.

During the sessions, she learned her name was Asha Riddle. She was the newly married bride of the wealthy industrialist Kenneth Riddle.

Mr. Riddle's personal attorney had confirmed her identity, taken from the name bracelet found on her wrist. He also verified that Kenneth had updated his will, making Asha his sole heir, prior to jetting off to Las Vegas for a private wedding ceremony.

Tragically, coming home from the airport, their car was involved in a terrible accident. Mr. Riddle remained in ICU and had not yet regained consciousness.

Asha felt no particular grief about her husband's condition because she had no memory of him. What really depressed her was that, aside from her memory, she had lost her right eye.

The psychiatrist visited once a day, but Asha found the sessions useless. Although Christina meant well, the psychotherapy was irritating. It amounted to little more than saying, "Cheer up! Maybe your memory will return."

A male voice interrupted Asha's musing, "Mrs. Riddle?"

A middle-aged man stood in the doorway. His rumpled business suit had the cheap look that said public servant.

"Yes?" Asha replied

"I'm Detective Lon Harding with Chicago PD. Are you up to answering a few questions about your accident?"

"I guess, but I won't be much help. I have amnesia."

"Amnesia?" Harding was surprised. "I didn't know that."

"Welcome to the club."

"Well, you might want to see this, then. It's a video of the accident. Maybe it will jog your memory."

Although Asha had heard about the recording, the shrink would not share it. She felt viewing it would be detrimental to Asha's recovery.

"I would very much like to see it, Detective," Asha said.

Harding pulled a tablet from his jacket and brought up the video. "This is from a traffic camera at the intersection," he said. "I'll play it in slow motion."

The display showed a silver-colored SUV entering the intersection from the right. A worn-out dump truck, speeding from the bottom of the screen, T-boned the SUV against the driver's side. The impact drove the vehicle through an empty bus stop on the far corner and into a utility pole. The SUV spun about and came to rest with the passenger door torn off its hinges. The truck backed up and drove off, hurrying away from the scene.

"We found the truck," Harding explained. "The company said the driver hasn't shown up for work since that accident. We have lots of prints, but none of them match anything in our system."

Asha wasn't listening; her eyes were glued to the recording. She had gotten out of the vehicle and was pulling on the driver, trying to drag him across the seat through her open door.

The only passerby was a young man, maybe in his early twenties. He squeezed in close to Asha. When she leaned into the vehicle to pull Kenneth from the wreckage, the man reached into the passenger side and grabbed her purse. Holding it against his chest, he tore off down the street out of the camera's view.

"We found that bastard," Harding said. "Guy named Eddie Becker; long rap sheet. He had already dumped everything by the time we caught up with him. We'll keep looking but don't hold your breath. Anything you had in that handbag is long gone."

Asha didn't care about the purse; she was more interested in the utility pole. Weakened by the impact, it wobbled precariously overhead while Asha struggled to free her husband. She got him to the door and put her shoulder under his as a crutch to help him move to safety. He was conscious but obviously in great pain.

They made it about two steps before the utility pole gave way. One of the cables snapped, and the loose wire whiplashed, striking Asha and Kenneth across their shoulders amidst a shower of sparks.

The electrical discharge was like a hammer blow, vaulting them ten feet through the air where they landed like rag dolls in the broken glass and other debris of the crushed bus stop. The vehicle's leaking fuel tank exploded, sending flames everywhere, and lifting the back end of the car fifteen feet into the air.

The injured couple lay unmoving.

Harding muttered, "Can't believe you two survived that. I don't know if you saw that God-awful spark between your skulls. That's probably what zapped your memory. You have to be watching pretty close to see it. Want me to play it again?"

"Play what again?" a loud voice demanded from the hospital room's doorway. It was Christina with a very angry expression. The detective introduced himself and explained he had a job to do, but the psychiatrist didn't buy it. She got in his face, forcing him to back up until he had literally retreated all the way into the hall.

3

Asha didn't watch Christina's protective performance. Instead, she mentally replayed the video in her mind. The detective had been correct. How both of them had survived not only the crash but the impact of those power lines, was a miracle.

Her heart thudded against her chest as she touched the bandages around her face and the side of her head. The so-called spark from the power line had passed through both of their skulls.

"That must have sent a million volts into our brains," Asha said to Christina, who had come to her bedside.

"I agree it looked bad," the psychiatrist replied, "but it obviously didn't, or it would have killed you. That's why I didn't want you to watch that recording. It's impossible to understand what happens with electricity because it shunts around all over the place. The important thing is you're getting better. And so is Ken."

..*.*

Beijing, China

Major Wong stood out as an anomaly in the Second Department of the Chinese Army's military intelligence operation. Rather than the harsh stereotypical officer who shouted at subordinates in frustration, Wong enjoyed his work. As an analyst, he didn't have a thousand underlings to keep in line. Instead, he had a small staff of brilliant assistants who, like him, enjoyed the intricate attention to detail that made their work successful.

One of Wong's talents was to sift through the accumulated output of the US media empire and spot those nuggets of information that had military significance. And no one could match his ability to imbue that same competence in his people.

Lieutenant Soong was one such protégé. She had distinguished herself on more than one occasion, and her reward was an ever-growing team of intelligence assistants. She had just provided Wong with a report and waited patiently for his answer.

"Give me a summary," he said, skimming through the three-page document. She had stapled several clippings from the *Chicago Tribune* to the package.

"It's a privately owned company, a relatively small player in the defense industry. They manufacture seeker heads and camera modules for the US military. The corporate name is Riddle Systems Group."

"I remember reading about them," Wong recalled. "They are considered an up-and-coming organization and generally well managed. What's new here?"

"The CEO was in a car accident recently and is in a coma. His recovery is uncertain."

"Ah. So perhaps the employees have let their guard down?"

"Yes, sir. It's a common pattern among American companies. Rather than working harder to pick up the load, they see it as an opportunity to slack off. The company is relatively low priority, but we could add it to the schedule for our people in Pudong."

Pudong, the eastern-most district of Shanghai, was home base for a particularly capable cadre of Chinese army hackers. Several of the teams had made headlines in the Western press after successfully stealing trade secrets from Lockheed Martin.

It made sense to have them go after Riddle Systems. According to Soong's report, the small firm sub-contracted to Lockheed, and if Pudong could penetrate the company's network, they might find a new backdoor to the giant defense contractor.

Recent guidance from above had emphasized a thorough investigation of all potential leads.

"Good job, Lieutenant," Wong said, signing the request form. "Let's find out what's new inside Riddle Systems."

* * * *

Saint Bernadette's Hospital

Asha frowned at the morning news on the television. A distinguished-looking anchor informed his viewers that a Chinese navy vessel had *accidentally* rammed a Japanese fishing boat, sinking it with all hands. The two nations' respective foreign ministers were outraged. The broadcaster put up video clips showing China accusing Japan of illegally intruding into Chinese sovereign

5

waters while the Japanese official condemned the provocation, saying it threatened world peace. The anchor explained such occurrences were becoming common.

I was better off asleep, Asha thought and turned off the TV.

Her door opened, and Doctor Combs entered. Combs was her assigned physician. He had a brusque manner and offered none of the upbeat platitudes that most of the medical staff routinely peddled. Instead, he gave her forthright assessments that she had come to trust. Today, instead of the usual nurse, Combs was accompanied by a man Asha had not seen before.

"Good morning," Combs grumbled. "This is Doctor Raphael Acosta. He is the Director of the Medical Technology Division within Riddle Systems."

Asha assumed that meant he was part of her husband's company. "Hello, Doctor Acosta," Asha said.

"Mrs. Riddle," he said. "First, let me express my utmost sympathy for you and Ken. It is such a horrible thing to happen. I'm so sorry."

"Thank you," Asha replied. She gave Combs a questioning look. "And?"

"Yes," Combs said hesitantly, as though unsure of his message. "Rafe has a proposal for you."

"Concerning?"

"A prosthetic eye."

Combs' words confirmed her worst fears. She had secretly hoped that when the bandages came off, it would not be as bad as she feared.

"It's really gone?" she asked.

"I'm afraid so," Raphael said in a kindly manner. "The oculus dexter, that's your right eye, was damaged beyond any repair, including the retina. The orbit, that is, the eye socket remained essentially intact, and will give us a good starting place."

It sounded gruesome. It meant she had a giant hole in her head, an empty cave that needed to be filled up to make her look human.

"All right," she said. It was difficult to keep her voice from wavering. "Do I have to get fitted or something?"

"Well, I would—"

"It's more complicated than that," Combs interrupted grouchily. "I guess I should tell you that although I have no problems medically with Doctor Acosta's approach, you should be aware it is unorthodox. I don't have any experience with the device he is proposing other than the FDA has approved it for human testing."

"Human testing?" Asha asked. "For a glass eye?"

Raphael put a hand on Combs' arm to forestall any misinformation. "Mrs. Riddle," Raphael said, "your husband and I have created a rather advanced prosthetic eye. One that can restore your vision to some degree."

The revelation caught her off guard. "Really?" she said. "I never imagined such devices were even possible."

"Yes, ma'am, they are. In fact, several universities are engaged in the research. Companies in the US, Europe, and even in Australia have developed vision-capable replacements. Human testing has been ongoing since MIT performed the first trials in ninety-eight."

"And they work?"

"They do, to a limited degree, and the technology is progressing rapidly. I believe our model is a breakthrough."

"In what way?" Asha asked.

"Kenneth believed the human brain is more flexible than generally accepted, and that it could be taught to understand digital signals. We developed an advanced protocol that connects an optical sensor directly to the optic nerve and then teaches the visual cortex how to decode the image."

"That is amazing," Asha said carefully. She wondered if the scientist's concept of vision was the same as hers. His carefully worded phrase, *to a limited degree,* did not sound that promising.

Raphael continued, "The catch is that we can't wait too long. Over time the optic nerve deteriorates. As with other models on the market, and under the right conditions, our device can restore a degree of vision after a traumatic eye injury such as yours."

There it was again, another caveat, *a degree of vision*. Asha wanted to believe in Raphael's proposal, but she had no idea what he was actually offering.

"You said my husband developed this?" she asked.

"That's correct. Kenneth is rather a remarkable man, but of course, you know that." Raphael spoke with sincerity.

"I'll take your word for it," Asha said. "I have no memory of him."

Raphael blushed slightly. "Of course. Forgive me. Doctor Combs mentioned that. I can't speak for Ken since he is still unconscious, but if he were awake, I am certain he would urge you to move ahead with this option."

Asha didn't comment on the assurances. It was easy to make a promise that could not be tested.

"Any risk to my good eye?" she asked.

"None whatsoever," Raphael said. "And let me add that if you wish to consider the procedure, I will formally go over all the risks. I'm required to do so by the FDA."

The concept called for a significant leap of faith on her part. She didn't know any of these people and wasn't knowledgeable enough to understand the medical considerations.

"When do I have to decide?" she asked.

"The sooner, the better. I discussed it with Doctor Combs, and he believes that you will be healthy enough for the surgery within the next few days. The entire process, from the time you say okay and Doctor Combs gives his approval, to you being able to use your new eye is about ten days."

"And that's it? I'll be able to see with it forever?"

"More or less. We will provide you with medical support for as long as you stay with the program. Additionally, we will monitor your progress on a twenty-four seven basis for at least a month afterward."

"How would you do that?" Asha wasn't interested in living in a laboratory.

"Electronically," Raphael replied. "The unit is equipped with wi-fi capability. You won't even know we're watching."

"What do you mean watching? You would see what I see?" She had a mental glimpse of herself standing nude in front of a bathroom mirror while geeky technicians looked on from some laboratory.

"No, no," Raphael said quickly. "I mean, we would be watching your vitals and the signal processing between the camera and your brain. It's more of a monitoring process."

"Can I think about it? Do you have any literature I could read?"

"Yes, of course," Raphael said. "Quite a lot, actually. I'll send it over, or would you prefer a link?"

Asha looked noticeably confused.

Combs glanced at Raphael and said, "Amnesia patients often have issues with technology. For now, it would help if you could just print out the material."

Raphael nodded. "I understand. Mrs. Riddle, I shall do as Doctor Combs suggests. You will have the literature this afternoon."

"Thank you, Doctor Acosta. I'll let you know as quickly as I can."

Raphael repeated his good wishes for her and Ken's recovery, and the two men left the room.

Asha watched them leave, frustrated by the many topics that hovered at the edge of her consciousness. She must have been familiar with modern life, but couldn't pin down exactly what that meant. Her condition left her with knowledge but no experience.

She didn't *feel* mentally disadvantaged. In fact, she considered herself reasonably intelligent. It was more a sensation of emptiness that she had lost something, but what or how much, it was impossible to tell.

* * * *

An hour later, Christina put in an appearance.

"I want to see my husband," Asha said before the shrink could start in with her cheery clichés. The proposal from Raphael had left her curious about the type of man she had married.

"Good idea. Let me get a wheelchair, and I'll take you myself."

A few minutes later, Christina pushed her into the circular room that was the core of the hospital's Intensive Care Unit. A nurse at the central monitoring station nodded toward one of the patient rooms.

With her first glance of her husband lying in bed, Asha let out a sigh of relief. Thank God, he wasn't a burn victim. After seeing that video with flames shooting into the sky, that was one of the things she had worried about it.

Christina helped her to stand so she could get a closer look.

Kenneth was a handsome man except for the many cuts across his face. They were similar to her own, but for him, people would say the scars gave him character, that they added to his good looks. Still, it was like looking at a stranger.

Christina said, "The neurosurgeon said his MRIs are good, and he has plenty of encephalographic activity. The neurologist believes he'll definitely wake up, we're just not sure how soon."

"I don't recognize him," Asha said quietly. "Is that bad?"

"Considering the circumstances, it's neither good nor bad. But since you are newlyweds, you have plenty of time to get to know each other again. You should talk to him. He may be able to hear your voice, and it would be good for both of you."

"What would I say?"

"Anything. Talk about the weather. And remember, you two had just gotten married in Las Vegas. Tell him you love him. You need to get used to saying the words."

Feeling awkward, Asha took Ken's hand in hers. "I'm here, Kenneth," she said. Christina gave her an encouraging nudge. Asha sighed and added, "I love you."

* * * *

The next morning, Asha had Raphael's colorful brochures spread over the bed covers. They depicted smiling families gathered around a husband or wife whose face was bright with excitement. It all looked a little staged. The back pages were full of medical disclaimers in small print.

A man she had not met before knocked on the door and came in. He was immaculately dressed in an expensive business suit. He gave her a cheerful wave.

"Hi again. Any more trouble from family members? I warned Aunt Erica to leave you alone after the last time. She can be difficult."

He walked up to her bed and gave her toe a little tweak. His overt familiarity put her off.

"Who are you?" she asked severely, drawing her legs back out of his reach.

With a little bow, he said, "I am Cody Anderson, the General Counsel for Riddle Systems, and your husband's personal attorney. And as long as you guys are getting along, that makes me your attorney too."

"My attorney? You know who I am?"

"I know exactly who you are. You are officially Asha Riddle, and don't let anyone tell you otherwise. In fact, I thought it best to get a judge's ruling on that subject to forestall any action by the family."

"A judge?"

"I showed his honor that traffic cam video of the thief," Cody explained. "That, plus your medical record. Plus, Ken changing his will to designate you as his sole heir. It was enough to convince the court."

"So then, who am I? Who was I before I married?"

"Sorry, I don't know your maiden name. Your husband wouldn't give me any details. I assumed you were a tech rep or something. He had me put a new will together before he left for Vegas. I thought it was a little rushed, but his mind was made up."

"I must have a name."

"You do. That's what I'm saying; the court ruled you are officially Asha Riddle and gave me papers to prove it." He put an envelope on her bedside table and looked proud of himself. "It's a credit card and a copy of the ruling. Enough to get you started. When Ken wakes up, he can tell us about your background. I know you must be worried about your family, but we haven't had any inquiries. The police took your fingerprints, but nothing came back. I have to say, I'm kind of curious."

No inquiries from her family? Did she not have any? She stared at Cody for a moment as a feeling of loss once again settled across her shoulders. Maybe Christina's upbeat attitude wasn't such a bad idea, especially compared to the stark reality Cody had just delivered.

She gathered Raphael's literature into a stack and placed it on the bedside table. Ignoring Cody's envelope, she lay down with her back to the man.

"Go away," she said.

It was difficult enough to move forward with Raphael's fancy artificial eye. The idea she had no family, no past, no nothing, in her history, did not help.

"Sorry," Cody said apologetically. "I'm leaving. You get well. Until then, I promise to take care of your paperwork."

Asha ignored him and a moment later, the door closed, leaving her alone in a room much emptier than before he arrived.

* * * *

That evening, the staff had just taken away Asha's dinner dishes. The sun outside was setting and cast a rippled glow across Lake Michigan. Raphael appeared in the doorway and knocked lightly.

"Come in, Doctor Acosta," she said. "Sorry I was so late getting back to you."

"Not a problem, Mrs. Riddle. So, you're ready to go ahead with the surgery?"

"I guess so. I read the literature you sent over, but honestly, it was pretty much over my head."

"Can I explain any of it to you?"

"That's the problem, Doctor. I'm sure you can, but anything more complicated than ringing for the nurse just doesn't register. I'm trying to understand, but…" She opened her palms in surrender.

"That's all right," Raphael said. "Let's try it this way. I'm required to explain to you in layman's terms what the device is and how it works. Ready?"

"You need to keep it really basic."

"I can do that." Raphael took a one-page graphic from his briefcase; it showed a stylized eyeball and a mechanical socket. "This is the ForSight Eye. It's a two-part device; the eye socket and the camera module. The most important of these is the socket. With me so far?"

"Got it," Asha said.

"We surgically implant a titanium receptacle into your existing eye socket. The medical breakthrough for our model is the connector between the socket and the optic nerve. Research into genetic recombination has shown that bound enzymes are not present at the same levels during all stages of growth. In fact, they are contrary to the normal autolytic process that…" Asha stopped him by drawing a thumb across her throat. "Yes?" he asked.

"Layman's terms, you said?"

Raphael glanced at his diagram and nodded. "Right. Sorry. Well, we discovered a better way to connect our socket to the optic nerve."

"Okay. That's plain enough."

"Indeed. By using cell-based therapies, we apply regenerative molecules directly to the optic nerve sheath, fusing multiple fibers to the end-connectors for the eye socket. That means we can send detailed images straight into your brain from the camera module."

"So, it's like a TV camera hooked up inside my head?"

"Sort of. The optic nerve includes over a million individual fibers; that's thousands of times more than commercial fiber optic bundles. What we can't predict is how many and how well those nerve fibers will come together with our biosynthetic connection."

"So, it might not work?" Asha asked.

"It might not," Raphael agreed. "But in the last twelve months, all our tests have succeeded to some degree."

"What does that mean, realistically?"

"Some people have better vision than others."

"If I wind up with a lousy connection, can you try again?"

Raphael shook his head. "The risk would be too great. The optic nerve is incredibly fragile. If we get a connection at all, we just stick with that. It would be dangerous to try and fine-tune it."

"So, I cross my fingers and hope for the best?"

"That's not how I would phrase it, but yes. I can't make any promises, but I am confident we will restore your sight to some degree. And our research shows that when it comes to regaining their vision, most people believe a little is better than nothing."

"What if it is nothing?"

"Then you have a very expensive socket for a standard glass eye. If that happens, and I don't think it will, I promise that we will make it look real. I am fairly confident that at the very least, we can give you partial vision." Raphael considered his words and added, "But I am not allowed to make promises. You must understand there is some risk entailed."

"I realize that. But let's say it does work out, at least to some extent, as you said. In that case, when I look at things, do I have to use one eye or the other?"

Raphael smiled, preferring to talk about a positive outcome. "No. For the user, it's automatic, just like a real eye. The brain will receive the signal from the camera and seamlessly merge it with the other eye. We even had a few cases where the patient reported improved vision."

"What are these wiggly lines?" Asha asked, pointing at the diagram.

"That's the wi-fi. The camera module includes wireless technology so we can monitor your health. We also use it to track your brain activity and how the unit is operating."

"Do I have to replace batteries for it to work?"

"Not day-to-day. There is a tiny battery built into the socket as a backup that has to be changed annually. It's a five-minute process on an outpatient basis. The camera's main power source is an internal unit that recharges at night. You'll sleep with a wireless charger under your pillow."

Asha sighed, completely lost with all the futuristic terminology. If it weren't for the fact that her husband owned the company, she would never do it. But she didn't want him to wake up and find she had ignored the only chance to restore her vision.

"All right," she said. "When does all this happen?"

Raphael pulled a sheaf of papers from his folder. "I have several places for you to sign. Cody reviewed the documents; he wrote most of them, actually. I can call him if you have questions."

"No, I'll just sign."

"Here's a pen. Your surgery is scheduled for tomorrow morning. That's why you had soup for dinner. Don't eat anything else tonight."

Chapter 2 – The Surprise

It was not reassuring. Raphael stood by Asha's bed with a concerned expression on his face. Three days had passed since he had surgically implanted her new titanium eye socket. Raphael's scowl made her wonder if she should be back in ICU.

"You're making me nervous," she told him.

He immediately brightened. "Sorry. Professional demeanor. I get criticized for my bedside manner."

"Because you have bad news?"

"Oh no, not at all. But I have to follow medical protocol. This is when I remind you that your eye socket will require time to heal. I have to warn you, it won't be pretty when we take off the bandages."

"It can't be any worse than the last time I came out of surgery," Asha said.

Raphael grimaced just slightly.

"It can?" Asha asked unhappily. "It's going to look worse?"

"A little. But only temporarily. That's the point you should understand. You've got a few more scars, and the area is swollen again, but from a medical perspective, the surgery went extremely well; that's a factual statement. You have to be patient."

"Will I ever look normal again? Ken will think he married a freak."

Raphael made calming gestures with his hands. "Listen to me. Movie stars go through a lot worse than this, and they do it to make themselves beautiful. I promise that in time, you will return to your normal gorgeous self. I repeat, you must be patient."

"For how long?"

"A month or two. When you talk to Lee, he can give you a better idea." Lee Emerson was the plastic surgeon that she had previously consulted with. "He'll wait for the swelling to go down before he touches you. After that, it will be one, maybe two more surgeries."

"All right," she said. "I guess I'm ready for the unveiling."

Each morning the nurses replaced the bandages to ensure the healing process was proceeding as planned, but they didn't offer her a mirror before bandaging her up again.

Raphael carefully unwound the gauze bandage, murmuring from time to time. Then he stepped back and scrutinized her face like an artist examining a troublesome painting.

"Well?" she demanded after a moment.

He straightened up. "It looks good," he said sincerely. He gently touched Asha's cheekbone a few times and pushed the skin above her eyebrow. "Does any of that hurt?"

"A little," she said. "Like you're touching a bruise."

"That's to be expected. Any fullness or pressure on your sinuses? Anything giving you a headache?"

"Not really."

"It looks good. I'm optimistic."

"You weren't before?"

Raphael chuckled. "No, I was always optimistic. I'm just not allowed to tell you so beforehand. Do you want the mirror?"

That was the question Asha had been dreading. She had planned to say yes, but now that she had a little good news, she didn't want to take a chance on ruining the mood.

"I think I'll pass. I have this image of a steel bowl bolted inside my skull, and I'm not sure I'm ready for that."

"That's fine," Raphael said with a nod. "In that case, I'm going to switch it on." He pulled a tiny jeweler's screwdriver from his shirt pocket. "Be still for a second. I just have to flick one little microswitch."

She felt his fingers on her eyelid. "Will it hurt?"

Raphael stepped back with a grin. "Nope, it's all done. Now, we're going to train your brain to process digital signals. For the next few days, the socket will transmit simple images of geometric shapes into your lateral geniculate nucleus and from there into the primary visual cortex. As your brain learns how to deal with the digital format, those geometric shapes will start to appear in your mind. Don't worry when that happens; it's a good sign."

"Like a cube?" Asha asked.

"That's right. Or you might see—"

"A triangle?"

"Right. They sequence—"

"Or a cylinder? Now it's a circle. There's a star. Ooh, there's a valentine. Now it's a pentagon."

Raphael's eyes grew wide. "You're seeing those right now?"

"Isn't that okay? You said they would come up."

"Well, yes. But it normally takes a few days. At first, most people see fuzzy images like a screen full of static."

Asha shrugged. "I did there for a second. But now I'm seeing the shapes cycling through. I have to look at these for four days?"

"I'm not sure," Raphael murmured in surprise.

"It's like you just opened a door," Asha said.

"How do you mean?"

"It's weird. As soon as the images started appearing, it was like my mind knew there was something else. What's an ASRAAM?"

"Seriously?" Raphael asked, now completely astonished. "That stands for Advanced Short-Range Air-to-Air Missile. Why are you asking?"

"I'm not sure what I'm seeing. It's like old computer code or something? It's like…Whoa!" A bombsight appeared in her mind and instantly vanished. "What was that?"

"Are you okay?"

"I'm fine. I think I can read part of my socket if that makes any sense; from the inside, I mean. It's like there is an interface to…" Her voice trailed off.

"It's probably best you don't fool with it, Asha. It sounds like you are sensing deactivated software. One of the CMOS chips inside your socket is from one of our military projects for an air-to-surface missile. I am amazed you can see that. I'm not sure how that's even possible."

"Does that mean my eye doesn't work?"

"I wouldn't say that. But this is certainly unusual. I wonder if it's a result of your memory loss. Perhaps your brain is compensating by reaching out."

"What does that mean?"

Raphael shrugged. "Hard to say. But if your mind adapted that quickly to the digital format, it can't be bad."

Asha flinched slightly. "I think I activated something. I saw something strange, but then it went away."

"What kind of strange?"

"Like a schematic diagram? It's gone now."

Raphael grew thoughtful. "This is unexpected, and it opens up a thousand questions. I'm blown away that your mind interacted with the old software. Of course, the goal was to teach your brain how to deal with digital information. I'd like to investigate further, but that's not what we're trying to accomplish here."

"Is it a problem?" Asha asked.

"I'm going to say no because there's nothing we can do. The chip in the socket is there to stay. Like I said, the installation is a onetime operation. If it's what I think it is, and I'll go back and check, what you found is either diagnostic software or the communication protocol, probably both. The original design was to allow the camera module to communicate with other aircraft systems. None of that will interfere with the eye."

"What should I do?"

"My advice is to just leave it all alone. The bottom line is, I see no reason not to move ahead with the camera module on schedule. Are those images going to be a problem for you? I can't really turn it off after the socket has been activated. Not until we install your new eye; that will replace the signal."

"They are absolutely not a problem," Asha said. "If this means getting my eyesight back, then I'll consider it part of the process. Besides…" Her eyes glazed over for a minute and she nodded.

"Besides what?" Raphael asked.

"I found an option in the software and already turned them off."

Raphael shook his head in astonishment. "Asha...aren't you the big surprise? We'll have to talk about this later, but I guess we can call the socket a successful implant. It's clear the electronics are functioning. I'm looking forward to installing the eye module. It's impossible to predict the level of visual functionality, but I'd say this bodes well."

"My fingers are crossed," Asha said, holding up both hands.

"I'll stop by tomorrow morning," Raphael said.

After he left, Nurse Becky Spears applied fresh dressings. The new bandage was much less bulky, more of a headband to hold a soft compress in place over her eye.

After the nurse was finished, Asha said, "I want to visit Kenneth, and let him know I'm doing okay."

"That's fine," Becky replied. "But you have to use a walker since you're still wobbly."

* * * *

Christina had been right; talking to her husband every day was beneficial. It improved Asha's mood, and she was actually developing feelings for him. She wouldn't call it love, more of a sympathetic connection to an injured friend. After talking to him for half an hour, she gave his hand a squeeze and encouraged him to get better.

Back in her own room, she found a stranger waiting for her, a young woman who appeared to be near her own age. Her blonde hair was pulled back in a ponytail, and she wore designer jeans with high-heeled boots. The sleeves of her white blouse were rolled up as though ready for work.

"Hi," the woman said. "I'm Maryanne. Sorry it took me so long to come by."

"Do I know you?" Asha asked. "Are you part of Ken's family? Cody said I shouldn't talk to you."

"Nope, I'm not a family member. Cody's my husband. He told me you threw him out of your room. Good for you. I have the same

20

impulse twenty times a week. I scolded him for not explaining your situation to me a little more clearly."

Maryanne chattered cheerfully as she helped Asha into the bed.

"I brought you some flowers," Maryanne said, waving at two big vases with colorful arrangements.

A nurse peeked in the door and said visiting hours were over.

"Thank you, Nurse Atkins," Maryanne replied without missing a beat. "I'll be here a few more minutes."

"Very well, Counselor," the nurse replied and left, closing the door.

"Counselor?" Asha asked.

"Forget that part. I'm a government attorney. It's nothing to do with my visit. Like I was saying, I didn't realize you don't have any family around, so I thought I would fill in. I brought you some decent pajamas, shampoo, and those essentials that hospitals never provide. I'm sorry you've had to wear a hospital gown this long. You should sue them for cruel and unusual treatment. Just kidding."

Maryanne's humor and good intentions were irresistible. After a feeble attempt at refusal, Asha gave in to Maryanne's pampering.

An hour later, she felt like she had a real friend. All showered, her hair clean and dry, and wearing soft silk pajamas, Asha let Maryanne help her back into bed.

"I also brought you some snack food—healthy stuff—but tell me if you want anything sinful. I'm as susceptible to chocolate cravings as anyone else."

The two women talked for another hour, avoiding any mention of the accident or uncomfortable topics. Maryanne was skillful in leading a conversation and keeping the mood light and cheerful. Asha was sad when the nurse finally came back and chased her out.

"I can't come back tomorrow," Maryanne said. "I'm in meetings all day, but I took Friday off, so we'll have three days to get better acquainted. See you then."

* * * *

21

The following morning, Asha had nothing on her schedule. The nurses agreed she could wander around the hospital. It would be good for her—just don't overdo it—and she had to use the walker.

The ground floor had a colorful gift shop filled with flowers, balloons, and get-well cards. Many of the clientele were wearing pajamas and slippers, often accompanied by visitors decked out in fashionable clothing.

Asha browsed through the shop but didn't buy anything. Instead, back in the main foyer, she braved the escalator up to the second floor. She wanted to walk around for exercise but was reluctant to go outdoors onto the hospital grounds. While shuffling down a corridor, she spotted a youngster in a small seating area off to one side. She guessed he was about thirteen. He appeared to be in a life and death struggle with his cell phone. Curious, she edged behind him and looked over his shoulder.

It was an animated cartoon car racing down a four-lane highway. He tilted his phone from side-to-side to control the steering. While she watched, the vehicle crashed into the back of another, and both vehicles burst into flame before disappearing.

"I'm no good at this anymore," he said, flicking a glance in her direction.

"Pardon?"

He held up his cell phone. "My coordination is shot these days. You wanna try?" He offered her the phone.

"No, thanks." Asha shook her head and sat next to him on the bench-style seat. "Thanks for the offer, though." She gave his pajama sleeve a little tug. "Is this why you don't have coordination?"

He nodded glumly. "Liver," he said. "What are you in for?"

Asha touched her bandage. "I lost an eye. They're going to give me a new one."

"I'm waiting for a donor too."

Asha stuck out a hand. "My name is Asha."

"I'm Chromite," he said, taking her hand for a perfunctory shake.

"Chromite? That's your name?"

"It's my username. Nobody calls me Scott except my mom. I thought Asha was your username; it doesn't sound like a real name."

"Nope, it's my actual name. Asha Riddle."

"What do your parents call you?"

Asha shrugged. "I have no idea. I lost my memory."

"For real?" Chromite looked interested. "All of it?"

"Pretty much."

Chromite considered her situation. "That's pretty lucky."

"Not really," Asha replied matter-of-factly. "I woke up in this hospital and didn't know anything. I still don't. Just that my husband and I were in an accident."

"Is he okay?"

"They say he will be, but he's still unconscious."

"Oh. Sorry. I hope he gets better."

The two patients sat there for a minute, sizing each other up when Chromite's stomach rumbled noisily. He looked embarrassed.

"Want to get something from the cafeteria," Asha asked.

"You paying?" he countered, hopefully.

Asha pulled a credit card from her bathrobe. "I got this a few days ago, so I need to try it out. Want to help me break it in?"

Chromite immediately assumed command. He advised her on the menu choices and guided her through the cash register transaction. Over lunch, he talked nonstop about video games. Asha found him enjoyable to be with. She didn't feel self-conscious about not knowing so much of what they discussed, and he loved the role of being her sensei.

"If I ever get out of here," he said, "I'm going to save up for a VR set."

"What's VR?" she asked.

"Virtual Reality. You know about that?"

"Not at all."

Chromite explained it in more detail than Asha cared to hear. All she really grasped was that Chromite desperately wanted something called an Oculus. According to him, it took the virtual cars she had seen on his phone to an entirely new level.

"I hope you like your new eye," he told her when they went their separate ways. He had been fascinated that she didn't have to wait for someone to die to receive the new organ.

"And I hope you get a donor." She liked the youngster. He was an engaging dinner partner.

* * * *

Nurse Becky Spears was changing Asha's bandage when Cody Anderson stuck his head in the room. It was Monday morning.

"Greetings!" he said cheerily. "I'm here because the judge said Ken's family has the right to see him, and they're here now. But he also ruled that I am allowed to be present to monitor their actions. Come in and say hi, if you like. Otherwise, I'll check in with you when they leave. Maryanne says you are a champion, by the way." Then he disappeared.

The nurse shook her head disapprovingly. "God doesn't give us a chance to pick our family. That's why I moved to Chicago."

"I've never met my husband's relatives," Asha said.

"Oh, yes, you have. And we would have called the cops if I had my way. Believe me, it's best you don't remember."

Christina had said something similar but had not gone into any detail. From the sound of it, in this case, perhaps ignorance was bliss. "Should I go in there?" Asha wondered aloud.

"I wouldn't," the nurse said. "The further you keep away from them folks, the better." She finished the bandage and stepped back. "There you are. All done. Not too tight?"

"Thank you, Becky. It's fine."

The nurse left, and thirty seconds later, she returned. "You might want to go after all," she said worriedly. "Augustina just called from ICU and thinks your husband might be waking up."

Asha scrambled out of bed and grabbed the walker. Becky walked with her to the elevator. Two floors down Asha entered the

ICU and went straight to Ken's room, Cody motioned her to his side of the bed. Five people were lined up on the other side.

"Why is *she* in here?" one of the men demanded.

Cody ignored the comment and spoke quietly to Asha. "Sorry they called you; it was a false alarm. Erica tried to wake him up, and I was too slow to stop her, so it registered on his monitors."

"Is Kenneth okay?" Asha asked.

"He's fine," Cody assured her.

Doctor Combs entered the room with Nurse Medina, who elbowed the offensive family members aside to make space. Combs took Ken's pulse and pulled out his stethoscope.

Cody used the doctor's examination to introduce the other visitors. "Everyone, this is Mrs. Riddle, whom you've met. Asha, the battle-ax on the left is Erica Townsend, Ken's aunt. She is the sister of Ken's father and a completely disagreeable person."

"Cody," Asha whispered, a little startled by his insulting remarks, made intentionally loud enough for the others to hear.

"It's okay," he replied. "They are well aware of my opinion. The man next to her is her current husband, Uncle Woodrow. The other three are scum-sucking attorneys; pay them no mind."

Erica was a formidable-looking woman, slightly over six feet tall, dressed in a business suit. Asha wondered if she was an attorney too.

"Hang on," Combs said sharply, cutting off any further comments. "I think he *is* coming around." He glanced at Asha and nodded toward Ken's hand.

She took it in both of hers and leaned close. "Kenneth? Can you hear me? I'm here."

Aunt Erica reached for Ken's other hand and in a shrill voice announced, "I'm here too, Ken," but Combs intercepted her grasp and pushed her away, forcing her down to the foot of the bed.

Asha gasped as Ken's hand closed lightly around hers. He moaned softly.

"I'm here," she said. "Don't hurry. Take a deep breath."

Ken's eyes opened, and his head moved slowly back and forth as though trying to recognize his surroundings.

"You're doing good, son," Combs said. "Take your time."

"Are you awake?" Asha asked. "Welcome back."

Ken tried to focus on Asha. His gaze moved over her body as though seeking recognition. He took a breath and tried to wet his lips to speak. The nurse had a moist cloth and gently wiped his mouth.

He took another breath and speaking to Asha, he said, "Who are you?"

Combs shook his head. "I was afraid of that."

The doctor's comments were drowned out by a screech of dismay from Aunt Erica. "Oh, my God. He has amnesia too. Now what?"

One of the attorneys by her side said, "In that case, he may not be competent to run the business."

"Don't even start," Cody said threateningly to his counterpart. He looked down at Ken and said, "Hey, buddy. It's me. You doing okay? Your wife has been worried sick about you." He nodded toward Asha.

"Who?" Ken asked in little more than a whisper.

Asha gave his hand a little squeeze. "It's me. We got married in Las Vegas. Remember?"

"Damn it," Aunt Erica complained loudly. "Now we've got two dummies to deal with."

"That's it," Cody said, stepping toward her. "Get out. I mean it, or I'm going straight to the judge for a restraining order."

Aunt Erica didn't argue. Without responding, she nodded at her attorneys and said, "Let's go. We need to strategize." The five of them stalked out.

Asha ignored the argument and concentrated on her husband. "You look good," she said, trying to keep a cheerful countenance.

"Wife?" Ken said, studying her face. His eyes flicked around her bandaged features as though trying to penetrate a disguise.

"She sure is, buddy," Cody said from the foot of the bed. "And she saved your ass too. Pulled you out of that burning car all by herself."

"Car?" Ken looked at Asha with confusion on his face.

"Don't worry about it," Asha said. "Just think about getting better. I'll help you."

"Not today, my dear," Combs said. "You seem a little pale to me. Sorry, son. Your wife is still recovering, too, so I'm keeping both of you in bed."

"Who…" Ken said, and then his eyes closed. His grip on her hand slackened, and his breathing slowed. He was unconscious once again.

Combs turned to Nurse Medina. "Margery, take Mrs. Riddle back to her room."

"Yes, Doctor."

"Don't worry, Mrs. Riddle," Combs added. "Those were excellent signs. He just needs time to recover. We'll keep an eye on him."

"Come on, honey," the nurse said. "Let's get back to your room. You'll want to rest up for Doctor Acosta's visit this afternoon."

* * * *

"Hello." Raphael smiled when he came in. "I hear that Ken woke up this morning." Raphael had two assistants with him.

"Not for long," Asha replied. "He was only awake for a few minutes. Everyone says it's okay, but I still worry."

"They say that because it *is* okay. The ICU said he was conscious and was able to speak."

"Doctor Combs assured me it's a good sign."

"I agree, but let's put that aside, I want you to focus on me now, or actually on you. Any new unforeseen issues with the socket?"

"No sir," Asha answered meekly. During the hours of boredom in the middle of the night, she had explored the device thoroughly but did not want to say anything that might delay getting her new eye. Her face was full of anticipation. "I'm ready."

"I can tell. Well, other than your advanced connection with the socket, our analysis is that everything is going to plan. My assistants here are Jack and Sam. They're going to help us get started. Sam, put the router over there on that table."

Asha exchanged hellos with the young men while Raphael removed her bandages, hopefully for the last time. If her appearance improved at all in the next ten minutes, she was leaning toward not having any plastic surgery.

Jack handed Raphael a square blue box that could possibly hold an oversized engagement ring. Raphael opened it and took out a soft cloth bag.

"This one is for you," Raphael explained. "It's a non-functioning eye for you to hold and get familiar with how it feels."

He held it over her open hand, and a gray porcelain object plopped into her palm. It was roughly round, with the back end flattened out where a row of metal dots provided electrical contact with the socket. The module was grooved along two sides, and the front third of it was solid white. There was no iris or pupil. She was surprised that it weighed almost nothing.

Until Raphael's briefing last week, Asha had imagined something like a golf ball, maybe with a black dot stenciled on the front.

"As you can tell," he said, "it's a pretty compact piece of equipment. Okay, now. Hold on to that for a moment."

He pulled on a pair of sterile gloves and took a second bag from the box, this one with a yellow diamond sewn into the cloth. Inside it was another porcelain orb. It looked exactly like the one she was holding.

"That's it?" she asked.

"Yep. Tilt your head backward just a bit."

She did so, and his hands pushed against the side of her face. It required more pressure than she anticipated, but then there was an audible *click*. Raphael stepped back.

"Is it in?" Asha asked. She wanted to touch it but restrained herself.

"It's in. Any discomfort?"

"No, but I can't see anything. Does it have to warm up?"

Raphael smiled. "No, we haven't turned it on yet." He glanced over at Sam, who was sitting in the visitor's chair, examining his laptop. "Tell us what you've got."

"Good signal," Sam said. "Diagnostic checks out." His face brightened as he added, "Strong link with CN2!"

"That's what we want to hear," Raphael said calmly. "That means the eye is talking to the socket and has a solid connection with the optic nerve." He glanced up at Sam and nodded. "Activate the cosmetic setup."

Raphael opened his own laptop and placed it on the portable meal table at the foot of her bed. He pushed it closer to Asha so he could see the screen and her face at the same time.

He handed her a hand mirror. "Here you go."

Asha examined her reflection with her good eye. Her face looked reasonably normal, literally for the first time that she could remember, except that her right eye was solid white.

"All right," Raphael said. "Just like we talked about, we're going to match your real eye." He pressed one of the keys on the laptop, and while she watched, her new eye came alive. In the middle of the white space that Raphael had called the sclera, a blue iris appeared with a large pupil.

"Oh," Asha said, breathlessly. Involuntarily she blinked several times. Both eyelids operated in tandem. "It looks like a real eye!"

"Let me adjust it now," Raphael said. "The pupil is a little too big…there. Is that better?"

Both of her pupils were now the same size. Raphael then had her move around on the bed to alternately face away or toward the window. He made an adjustment each time she moved, so as the ambient light changed, the artificial pupil would match the real one.

"Okay," Raphael said. "Now, I'm going to bring up the camera slowly. It will appear scratchy for a minute, and then you'll see two images until your brain works out how to merge the signals from both eyes. Because it worked so well in the training phase, I don't think it will take too long." He pressed a key on the laptop.

Like he said, at first, it was a hazy image, hundreds of horizontal gray lines that flickered. But after a few seconds, a picture began to emerge.

"I see it," she said, "but it's all gray."

"That's okay. I'll bring up the color in a minute. Just stare at Sam for a minute so your brain can stabilize. Tell me when the images come together."

"They are now, pretty much."

"Okay, then here comes the color."

Asha adjusted her gaze to focus on the larger of the two flower arrangements that Maryanne had brought in. The gray in her vision slowly disappeared until the colorful bouquet was rich and vibrant.

"Does that look right?" Raphael asked.

"It looks beautiful."

"Try this. Too much color or too little? Which one looks best, A or B?" As he spoke, the color saturation in her eye changed.

"I think A was better."

"How about this one, C or D?"

Raphael repeated the process several times until he was satisfied that the camera module was in sync with her real eye. He then performed a similar exercise to establish focus. She noticed that both of her eyes moved in tandem.

"How does it move?" Asha asked.

"It doesn't. The socket senses ocular muscle movement and adjusts the placement of the iris to keep it synchronized with your other eye. It only looks like it's moving around."

When he finished with his fine tuning, she stared at the mirror to admire the final result.

"This is amazing," She said, moving a fingertip in front of her camera eye. "I never imagined it would work this well, but my world is so beautiful now. Thank you, Raphael." She leaned over and gave him a hug.

"I'm glad you like it. We're going to keep an eye on it, so to speak, for a few days. Jack is installing a wi-fi router in your room so we can connect to the device from the lab."

"What does that mean?" Asha asked.

Raphael turned his laptop around so that the screen faced her. The display showed inset windows with constantly changing graphs and histograms.

Asha peered at the charts and colorful representations that were being generated, based on the data stream going from her eye to the laptop. After staring at the screen for a moment, she gasped as a wave of vertigo rolled through her mind. It seemed like she actually traveled inside the laptop. "I think I can see the data transfer taking place," she said uncertainly.

"Based on the other day, I'm not surprised," Raphael said, pointing to the different charts as he spoke. "The connection with your optic nerve shows us that your eye is working, and so are the health monitors. We'll keep track as your body adapts to the device. It appears your visual cortex has adapted perfectly; I'm detecting quite a bit of activity. How is it on your end?"

"I'm not sure how to describe it," Asha said. "It's like my consciousness is directly connected to the laptop. It's the same as it was for my socket; I guess I'm seeing programs." She found neat little bundles labeled with acronym-like words. One of them drew her attention as it was similar to Chromite, the young man she had met. The name was chrome.exe.

She mentally grasped at it, and it was like opening a doorway to another universe. It was as though her brain translated the confusing computer language inside into an understandable process in much the same way it had converted the digital signal from her eye module into an image that she could comprehend.

Asha couldn't find the words to describe it. "I'm not really connected to anything, but I can tell a data stream is there," she said.

"That's right," Raphael said, not catching her meaning. "Everything is wireless." He pointed to a list of strange words on the laptop's screen. "Those are the different wi-fi networks in the hospital."

"What do they mean?" Asha asked.

Raphael highlighted the first one. "BERNPUB is the public access point for the Internet that is available to patients. It stands for Bernadette Public. The others are for hospital use; visitors and patients can't see them. I can because I've got special access."

"I guess I do too since I can see them as well."

"Sure," Raphael said agreeably. "They're here on the screen because of the software on this laptop and the wireless router we just hooked up over there. Here. I'll show you how to log into the Internet in case you ever decide to use a laptop."

He clicked on BERNPUB, and a password dialog opened. Raphael typed in BERN1234. He gave her a humorous look and said, "It's not exactly the most secure link in the world."

"Does that mean everyone can see into my eye?" Asha asked, a little alarmed.

"No, no. The wi-fi router Sam just put in your room has a firewall with our own password, and it's quite a bit more difficult. Also, all the information between your eye and our lab is encrypted so no one could understand what it is, anyway. To them, it would just be a string of gibberish."

"Okay," Asha said, not really having any idea what he meant.

"Anyway," Raphael continued, "the public network, BERNPUB, is everyone else's gateway to the Internet."

"People keep using that word," Asha said with a frustrated shrug. "You have too, but it must be something I lost in translation. What is the enter-net?"

Raphael looked a bit surprised by the question. "The Internet? I guess I should have explained the first time we talked about your wireless connection. The Internet is the World Wide Web. The information superhighway."

"Superhighway?" A vision of Chromite's racing game flashed in her mind.

"That's right." Raphael's tone became professorial. "All the computers in the world, including the one in your eye, are connected electronically through a network. We call it the World Wide Web because it is so complex. So, whether I want to check on stock prices in New York or patient diagnostics here in Chicago, I log onto the Internet. That *highway*, as it were, takes me to the appropriate destination where I can access the information I'm after."

Asha nodded. "Superhighway," she said slowly. "I kind of understand that. So, the public access point, as you put it, is like an on-ramp? Once you go through it, you're on the highway?"

"Well," Raphael said with a shrug. "That's as good an explanation as any."

Asha glanced at the router as though peering at something in the far-off distance. "So that's what I'm seeing when I look past the router? It does look like a highway…and it has a lot of traffic." Superimposed in her vision, hundreds of automobile-like objects raced here and there. In a way, it was similar to Chromite's game.

Raphael chuckled. "Some patients experience minor hallucinations the first time they use their new eye. Those will dissipate in an hour or two." He beamed at her good-naturedly. "You're the first one to see the Internet, though. That's pretty unique. Any other questions?"

Asha leaned back against her pillows still holding the mirror, and studied her reflection. "About a million, but I guess they can wait. I copied some material from your computer into my memory. Maybe if I let my brain mull those things over for a while, it will make sense of everything." She spoke in a distracted voice as though deep in thought.

Raphael looked at her quizzically. "Are you serious? Or do you just have a very active hallucination going on there? Are you dizzy at all?"

Asha pulled herself back to the present. "No, I'm fine. I think I'm simply overwhelmed. Mostly, I appreciate the fact that I can see again." She looked in the mirror once more. "It's doesn't look too bad, does it?"

"Not at all! The original lacerations are all but healed. Honestly, the more time goes by, the less work I would say needs to be done. When do you see Doctor Emerson again?"

"He's supposed to come by tomorrow. I'm a little nervous about it. I don't really want him to do anything. Can I just stick with what I have?"

"If that's what you prefer. But talk to him first and let him explain the options. He knows when to do nothing. Sometimes, less is more. For now, try to relax and have a good night's sleep. We'll be checking on you, but you won't notice. If you experience any discomfort, tell the nurse, and she'll call me. Now that you can see with both eyes, you'll be tempted to walk around more than you have been, but be careful until your balance comes back. I want you to keep using the walker if you leave the room."

"Okay, I promise."

Raphael closed his laptop, and the connection between it and her mind terminated. The programs that her brain had pulled from his computer hovered in her thoughts like confusing puzzles.

"This has been a big day for you," he said, standing up and nodding to his two associates that it was time to leave. "Try not to stress out. Like we discussed, your subconscious will sort through all the new information over the next day or so, so just let the process happen." He laid a new batch of colorful brochures on her bedside table. "Go over these when you're up to it."

Asha wasn't sure Raphael actually understood that her eye was receiving more than just visual information, or that it had connected directly to his computer and beyond. But he seemed satisfied with everything she told him. After all, he told her the images would go away in a couple of hours.

"Okay," she said, following his advice. She would let the information percolate through her subconscious as he said, and let her brain treat it all as a challenging conundrum.

Most of all, she was grateful she had vision in both eyes again. Everything else took a back seat to that fact. "Thank you, Raphael. You are a miracle worker."

After Raphael and his team left, Asha moved to the window to enjoy the view. The sun was beginning to set and it was beautiful. *How many sunsets have I forgotten*, she wondered? Were they all this beautiful in her lost history?

She pulled on her robe and slippers and left the room, using the walker to stroll through the hospital. This time, the people she passed by didn't steal looks at ugly bandages that might be hiding a scarred face. Few gave her a second glance. That was a good sign. In its own way, the anonymity was comforting.

Although she looked for him, Asha found no trace of her new young friend, Chromite. She had hoped he could help her understand what she kept seeing beyond the real world. In the cafeteria, she stopped for a tray of food, missing his chattering companionship.

By the time she returned to her room, the sun was below the horizon. She wasn't in the mood to read the material Raphael had left for her, and the television didn't interest her either. She crawled into bed and pulled the covers up to her chin and tried to sleep.

After dozing for a few hours, she woke up, exasperated that her sleepiness was gone. She sat up and looked around her room.

On the small sideboard against the far wall, the green lights on Raphael's router blinked with tiny green LEDs. The network names that she had seen on his laptop hovered in the air, just above the lights.

She knew they weren't really there, but to be sure she got out of bed and waved her hand over the box. The labels were ethereal, untouched, and not disturbed by her movement.

She could see the network gateways that Raphael had described within the router. Her mind translated their individual properties into visual descriptions. The router's address was 192.168.1.1.

Asha had no idea what that meant and didn't really care. The bottom line was the BERNPUB network contained a doorway to the information superhighway.

Perhaps a brief investigation would make everything clear. And since she was wide awake anyway, it would give her something to do. She sat down on her bed and focused on BERNPUB label. When the password dialog box appeared in her vision, her mind inserted the word BERN1234.

Let's find out what this Internet thing is all about, she thought and pushed her conscious mind through the gateway.

It was like launching herself on a rocket sled, racing into the new world at blinding speed. She cried out and closed both eyes, holding her head in her hands, willing the crazy scene to stop.

And it did.

She held her breath, and sat motionless on the bed, waiting to make sure her consciousness would not take off again. Convinced the world would not spin out of control, and keeping her eyes closed, she propped herself against the pillows and allowed the mental picture to return.

The setting resolved into a coherent 3D environment. She was standing in the middle of a not-real highway while virtual cars, trucks, and buses whizzed by on all sides. *This is my brain's impression of the information superhighway* she realized, like Chromite's game but vastly more complicated.

It was the concept that Raphael had talked about and that Chromite had shown her. And thanks to the wi-fi module in her new eye, she was now a part of it. She could travel in cyberspace, out through the router they had installed in her room.

In a literal sense, the surreal world rapidly overwhelmed her senses. The highway was lined on both sides with hundreds of virtual signposts, like those above the router. They were place names, each one ending with suffixes like .com, .net, or .org.

It was too much. She wanted to go back to her hospital room, and the thought prompted movement within her mental environment. With a certainty of direction, the landscape whizzed by once again. At a speed she could not guess, the highway took her into the city, straight into downtown, and directly ahead, she saw the signpost for st-bernadette.org. She rushed into it at full speed, and the cyberworld vanished, both in front of her eyes and in her mind.

"Holy crap!" she cried out and pressed the nurse's call button.

A moment later, an unknown nurse entered the room.

"Are you okay?" she asked.

"I'm not sure," Asha said. "I just had some kind of out-of-body experience and it freaked me out."

"Probably a nightmare. I heard that you got your new eye today. Is it working okay?"

"You would not believe how well it's working!"

The nurse took Asha's pulse. "You want a sleeping pill?" she asked.

"That would be great."

"Let me check with the doctor and get his okay." The nurse made sure Asha still had some water in her plastic carafe and left.

The mundane interaction with the nurse was reassuring. It made the strange experience of going through the router not quite so overwhelming. In fact, now that she thought about it, dozens of questions came to mind. If she had this ability, she wanted to understand it.

Asha glanced at the sideboard; the network names still floated just above the device. She shifted her gaze toward the window, and the letters disappeared. *It's a matter of focus*, she realized. She turned her attention back to the router, and the names reappeared.

The first trip had been frantic, like getting into a car and stepping on the accelerator when you didn't know how to drive. She relaxed and let the browser process inside her head unpack into comprehension.

All she really needed was a name. Once she had that, an automatic lookup process returned the actual network address of the destination. The journey itself was actually through a series of routers similar to the one in her room, and each one in turn, pointed her down the appropriate path.

She focused on the public network label one more time and the highway again filled her vision. This time she was able to slow it down to a manageable speed and allow her brain to add the imagery to give context.

She needed a direction. *Show me my husband's company*, she thought. The name, Riddle Systems, appeared, and at a speed still beyond understanding, she reached the company's website that Maryanne had shown her over the weekend. She had explained that every website included multiple pages that linked to each other.

Behind the corporate homepage, Asha found an enormous repository of data available for public viewing, starting with a dozen years of annual reports. Reading them by hand would take hours, yet her digital mind sifted through all of them in what seemed like seconds.

The knowledge was there in her mind as though she had studied each document in detail. The firm had increased revenue and added employees each year. She idly wondered what their salary was and the question took her deeper into the corporate network. She found a digital ledger that included each employee's name, their personal information, and a list of all their financial transactions with the company.

While perusing the document, Asha became dimly aware that her presence had triggered an electronic watchdog, and it, in turn, had set off a series of alarms. She investigated and discovered the signal of a closed-circuit security camera. When she traced it back to the source, it was like looking out through a television screen. The view was of a control room with a half dozen agitated people clustered together. The camera had an integrated microphone, so she listened to the discussion. They were frantically investigating an intrusion into the corporate data center. Someone had executed an unauthorized breach of sensitive personnel files.

Asha realized they were talking about *her*. It might be a good idea to make herself scarce. The security team looked none too happy, and she didn't want them to know that their CEO's clumsy wife was the cause of the problem.

The thought of escape caused the virtual scene to disappear and she found herself sitting on her bed. The mad rush back to the hospital that she had seen earlier was not necessary. All she had to do was mentally cut the connection, and it was over. Only ten minutes had passed.

The door opened, and the nurse came into the room. "I'm back. The doctor said it was not a problem, so here is your sleeping pill." She handed Asha a thimble-sized paper cup with a blue pill and then poured her half a glass of water.

"Thanks," Asha said. She sipped the water and downed the pill.

"That will help you sleep now," the nurse said soothingly. "Hopefully without any more bad dreams. Goodnight."

Asha smiled at the nurse as she left the room and then pulled up her covers. In retrospect, it might have been better to skip the pill. Now she would have to wait until tomorrow to try that trick again.

* * * *

Beijing, China

Major Wong sensed someone hovering just outside his cubicle. It was Lieutenant Soong.

"Sir?" she said politely. "Excuse me for interrupting your concentration."

"What is it, Lieutenant?" He appreciated that she was always proper in her form of address.

"I just received a call from Pudong about Riddle Systems."

That was good news. Wong hadn't expected to hear back so quickly. "What about them?"

"It was from Captain Zheng; he supervises one of the intelligence teams. They were engaged in some preliminary reconnaissance of Riddle Systems when the team leader realized the American company was in the process of getting hacked."

Wong scoffed disapprovingly at the information. "Sounds like one of his men was a little overeager. Did they leave any evidence?"

"No, sir," Soong replied. "He swears that wasn't the case. One of his senior technicians, Master Sergeant Tang, was demonstrating how to observe when the hack happened. Tang described it as the most powerful attack he had ever seen. Whatever it was went through their firewall like it wasn't even there. He couldn't pinpoint its origin."

Wong put down his pen and leaned back in his chair. "That's interesting; I know Tang. The Master Sergeant is not one to carelessly set off alarms. How did they respond?"

"They withdrew and filed a request for further investigation. Captain Zheng said Tang's report was disturbing. He called to test the water about officially requesting an in-depth study on the incident."

Hmmm. Wong might not label it as disturbing, but it was certainly intriguing. What could startle Tang? His expertise in cyberwarfare was unquestioned.

"I would definitely consider such a request, Lieutenant. Please tell the captain to get started on the paperwork and emphasize that the approval will be above my pay grade. He should make the request as thorough as possible."

"Yes, sir," Soong said and returned to her desk.

In the meantime, Wong thought it might be worthwhile to do a little research of his own into this organization called the Riddle Systems Group. Something about it niggled at his mind. He had heard that name somewhere else.

American companies had the irritating habit of accidentally making technological breakthroughs and then, regardless of the original intent, rewarding the people who did it. He had seen it as a student when he lived abroad for his studies. In the United States, failure was considered a learning experience that eventually led to success.

That attitude would never work in the Chinese military. From Wong's perspective, people who highlighted themselves in the People's Liberation Army tended to regret it. An unsuccessful venture could quickly become a career-ender, and if you stepped on the wrong toes in the process, it might even be classified as subversive.

He would be careful while investigating whatever was going on in Chicago.

Chapter 3 – The Theft

"And a great Chicago morning to you!" Cody declared, entering Asha's room.

She was making up her bed. Cody had stopped in to say hello a few times, and now that she knew he was Maryanne's husband, she considered him a friend. His extroverted personality was growing on her, although it did not seem to match his corporate job title of General Counsel.

"Hi, Cody."

"I hear you have vision in both eyes now."

"Yes, I do. It's pretty amazing technology. I was just about to go tell Kenneth."

"Mind if I tag along? I decided to stop by on my way to the office and check on both of you."

"That would be great," Asha said. "In fact, I'm glad you're here; I have a question."

"Shoot."

"Do you know what an Oculus is?"

"The VR headset? Yeah. I have one. It's cool."

"Oh, good. There is a young patient here; his name is Scott Stuart, but he goes by the nickname Chromite. Would you buy him one as a gift from me?"

"Sure. Which one? They have several models."

"I have no idea. Just get him the latest and greatest."

When she compared the luxury of her own room to other hospital rooms she peered into as she walked through the hallways, being wealthy was a lot better than poor if you had medical needs. It didn't seem quite fair, especially when she considered Chromite and his dire condition. The gift might bring a little cheer into his life.

"Consider it done," Cody said. "I'll get him the kind that doesn't need a computer to go with it. That way, he can use it in the hospital to his heart's content."

"Thank you! Now tell me, how was your and Maryanne's weekend?"

"The weekend was okay, but last night wasn't so hot."

"Oh, no. What happened? Is Maryanne okay?"

"Yeah. Nothing to do with her. We had a security incident last night at the company. It's going to be a big deal."

"You mean someone broke in?"

"Not physically. We haven't figured out who yet, but somebody hacked the network. Since we're in the process of taking the company public, it means we have to report it."

Uh oh, Asha thought. He had to be talking about her activity the night before. It might be best to be upfront that she had caused the problem, especially since it was simply an accident.

"I'm so sorry," she said.

Cody didn't hear her apology. His grim expression indicated he was going through the incident in his mind. He shook his head and said, "But we'll find them. And one thing I can promise you is, they will definitely go to jail. The government comes down hard on corporations when this happens now days, and to protect ourselves, we have to make sure law enforcement nails those bastards to the wall."

"The police?" Asha squeaked, her throat tightening up. Perhaps honesty was not the best policy.

"Oh, yeah, for sure. Our IT guys said this had to be a targeted attack. It looks like they were after corporate and personnel files. They got the personal history of all our employees and even salary information. It had to be a pretty sophisticated group to get past all our security."

"Seriously? You had security in place?" Asha asked, surprised, and then bit her tongue. *Keep quiet!* she told herself.

"Absolutely! Although, that makes me wonder if it was an inside job. The IT Department was in the process of upgrading some of our network analytic packages when the attack hit." He glanced at the television where a news anchor was standing in front of a colorful graphic of the Asian continent. Cody nodded at it and said, "I'll bet anything it was the Chinese. They go after everyone these days."

"The Chinese?" Asha inquired skeptically. Cody's usual habit of jumping from topic to topic was in full swing. "Why would the Chinese attack Ken's company?"

"Who knows?" Cody exclaimed. "Most of this tech is way over my head, anyway. It's probably a little weird for you too, huh?"

"Yeah," Asha agreed weakly. "Pretty much."

"Give it time. Once you use it, it will start to make sense. Which reminds me." Cody pulled two objects out of his briefcase. "Ta-da! Maryanne got you a cell phone and a Chromebook. She said you need to learn how to operate them and start using the Internet. The laptop is already set up. You probably don't remember your old email account, so she got you a new one. Your password is *password*, so be sure you change it first thing. Promise?"

Asha accepted the Chromebook hesitantly. "I promise." She had no idea how to change a password. Hopefully, the contraption came with instructions. She set it on the sideboard next to the router. "Tell Maryanne I said thanks."

"You bet," Cody said with a grin. "Come on, let's go see Ken."

They took the elevator down two floors to the Intensive Care Unit. Asha knew most of the ICU nurses by name and said hello to Andrea and Becky.

"He had a quiet night," Becky said.

Inside his room, Ken was still unconscious, but his color was good. Asha was getting fairly adept at determining his condition.

Cody said, "Good morning, boss. I brought your wife to say hello. She looks great today! You better get well quick, or some doctor is going to ask her out."

"Don't say that," Asha whispered, embarrassed by the comment. "Hi, honey. Ignore Cody. Maryanne has been terrific. She gave me a new computer this morning. But more importantly, I have my new eye now. Raphael is a genius."

Asha and Cody took turns speaking to Ken; she, offering upbeat encouragements, and he, irreverent comments about people at the office. After a couple of minutes, however, Cody's mood turned serious with a new topic.

"The board meeting is coming up, buddy. And the thing is, with you still under the weather, it's important for your representative to be there. Erica has been calling other board members, pushing for an interim CEO appointment. I think Asha should go in your place. The doctor said she'll be out of the hospital by then, and I checked the by-laws. Your living will gives her power of attorney. Legally, she's both your guardian and potential heir. She can exercise your voting rights, and that's enough to shut down any shenanigans your crazy aunt might pull."

"What?" Asha exclaimed softly, looking at Cody with wide eyes.

Later, he mouthed to her, and then said aloud, "That's all, buddy. Just wanted you to know. I have to get to the office. Your blushing bride will take care of you now."

Then he was out of the room, leaving Asha alone with her husband.

Cody had set her up, she realized belatedly. If he had talked to her about stockholder voting rights—of all things—ahead of time, she would never have approved. The idea was insane. But by mentioning it in front of Kenneth, Cody obligated her before she could object. It was an underhanded move and her opinion of the attorney went down a notch.

So, now what? She had zero background in corporate governance or what took place in such meetings. Whatever was discussed would be above her head.

But when she considered the matter, she had read all those annual reports and had learned a lot about the company. It might not qualify her for participating in a corporate strategy meeting, but she wouldn't be completely clueless either.

Asha stayed for another half hour, telling her husband about her new eye. She didn't mention her inadvertent escapade of the night before. No sense in worrying him, and it would be embarrassing to admit what a klutz she was when it came to modern technology.

Back in her own room, she worried. She had no interest in attending a corporate board meeting. But if Cody's prediction was correct, someone had to protect Ken from Aunt Erica's power grab. That was reason enough to go, even if it meant doing some homework on her part.

She looked over at the Chromebook. This would be painful. She flipped it open. The word *password* did indeed function as he said, and the result was a backdrop of an idyllic ocean vista.

But there were no hoped-for instructions. She discovered that moving her finger around the touchpad moved the screen pointer. Other than that, there was nothing useful and no way to find the information she needed.

She closed her eyes and tried to recall her husband's corporate website from the night before. The image instantly appeared in her mind. In the light of day, and with a clear mind, what she was doing was a little more obvious. By just thinking about it, she had reentered the Internet through the hospital's public network.

Behind the home page's fancy graphics, the corporate network became visible. It was like a hallway with multiple doorways. One was for personnel employee records, another led into the labyrinth of financial data.

On the periphery were other areas based on the various business units the company engaged in.

Once again, she became aware of the corporation's digital security robots closing in, trying to pin her down and establish her identity. It was time to leave before she did any more harm. She withdrew and shut off all connections to the hospital network, allowing her mind to clear.

That was pretty easy, she realized in retrospect. It only took a thought to get deep into the digital universe, and it was equally simple to turn off the flow of information.

Asha looked down at the laptop that Cody had given her. She closed it firmly with a feeling of finality. No complicated technology for her.

"Knock, knock," Raphael said from the doorway.

"Good morning, Doctor," Asha said, glad of the distraction.

"And to you. I wanted to see how you're doing after your first day. We registered a lot of activity on your optic nerve, so I wanted to make sure there wasn't a problem."

He sounded worried.

"Did you find one?" she asked in a concerned tone. She didn't want getting on the Internet to burn out her brain.

"Maybe that was a bad choice of words. The level of activity was normal for any visual stimuli, but since it was late at night, I thought something might be keeping you awake. The nurse's station said you had a nightmare."

"Yeah, sort of."

"If you want, I can take the camera module back to the lab and give it a thorough testing."

Asha flinched away, saying, "I'm fine."

"Don't worry. I don't mean we would leave you blind. We have a basic model that you can use. It has the same vision as your model."

"I'm fine," Asha repeated. "Honest."

Raphael smiled patiently. "I know; once people get their sight back, they're reluctant to let it go, even for a few hours. That's why we have a spare. I promise it works the same way, but we can't fine-tune the cosmetics since it doesn't have wireless."

"I'd rather not," Asha said. "I don't feel like there is a problem."

Actually, there was. She had intended to talk to him about the strange Internet experience, but if she brought it up, he might insist on taking her new eye away. She decided to keep quiet and sort through any questions on her own.

"Are you sure?" Raphael asked. "It's not a problem for us to run a diagnostic."

"I'm positive," she replied with absolute certainty.

Raphael grinned. "Okay. That's clear enough, and like I said, it's a pretty standard answer. For what it's worth, we gave you our newest model. It has extra capability that we haven't put on the market yet, but we can talk about that another time." He opened his laptop. "Mind if I take a look inside your eye right now?"

"I guess not," Asha said. "I sort of thought you were already doing that with the wi-fi."

"We are. But those are just standard monitoring parameters. First, I want to give it a visual inspection." He pulled out an ophthalmoscope. "This will let me see inside the camera proper. I want to be sure everything is in the right place." He pressed a key on his laptop. "You might see a red glow in your vision."

"I do." She held up her mirror. Her eye had an eerie red light shining out from within.

"That's an internal LED light," Raphael said, "so I can give it a closer look. Now, focus on the wall behind me." He put the scope close to her eye and mumbled to himself. "No problem there." He pressed the key again, and the red glow vanished.

"That looked weird," Asha said.

"I know. It makes you look really Borg-like. But it helps a lot to see inside."

"Huh?" Asha had no idea what he was referring to.

"Just kidding. Okay, next step." He pressed another key. "Here we go; I just connected through your wi-fi."

The same doorway from yesterday appeared, leading from her mind straight into his laptop. A small object moved in her direction. Her subconscious recognized it as a diagnostic program. It stopped inside her eye, and she forced herself not to react. Instead, she probed against it and found reams of material about her eye. Her brain devoured the information like a voracious reader picking up a favorite book.

"Everything looks fine to me," Raphael said after a moment. "I'd say the only anomaly is unusually high activity inside the optic nerve. I suspect that means your visual acuity is quite good."

"It seems like it to me," Asha said. "I have noticed that I can read small print quite easily."

"That's excellent. Next time I'll bring a vision chart, or maybe you can drop by the office. Has anyone talked about when you might be discharged?"

"You mean leave the hospital?" Asha was surprised by the question. "No one said anything…but then I didn't ask. In fact, now that you mention it, I really haven't thought about the future at all."

"I expect that's normal," Raphael said. "You are still in the recovery stage from your amnesia."

After ten minutes of chitchat, the physician left. The idea that she could relax, however, was a mistake. Another medical assistant came in with a bright smile. It was time for physical therapy.

* * * *

Asha's routine stabilized over the next several days. In the mornings she visited Ken. In the afternoons she went through physical therapy, and in between she experimented with her ability to see the Internet.

She watched how others browsed the Web with their laptops and cell phones. Where they typed in destinations and fumbled with constrained options, she glided through cyberspace without restriction. In the same way an eagle surveys the environment below, Asha floated through a three-dimensional universe with the entire world in plain view.

Her mind soaked up data and acted on it without conscious thought. As an experiment, she again broke through the electronic defenses of her husband's company. She discovered that a slight modification to her way of surfing made her invisible to their security system. From that point on, when she wanted information about the corporation's data, she found the answer without worry of detection.

After three days of continuous Internet research, she quit wondering how her mind worked. If her nose itched, she scratched it; if she had a question, the answer appeared in her mind.

A nurse introduced her to texting and Asha discovered she could send texts too, but without using a cell phone. The secret was hacking the SIM card in the phone Maryanne had given her. Once she had that information, the rest of the process was similar to her first experience of entering a password. She composed the words in her mind and then pushed them out to the associated Short Message Service Center, which took over the routing issues.

In the process of learning the intricacies of SMS, she discovered that voice calls from a cell phone were similarly nothing more than electronic signals transmitted over the cell network. After a few tries, she learned how to make a connection with her mind and speak to the person on the other end, all without uttering a sound verbally.

Easiest of all communication methods was the Gmail account that Maryanne had set up for her. After mentally connecting to her account, she was even able to change her password.

As she mastered each new technical procedure, her subconscious took over the operation. It was like her fellow patients she had met in physical therapy. Once they learned to walk again, it became second nature.

* * * *

Forty-seven days after Asha's accident, Cody and Maryanne showed up in her room. It was time to leave the hospital. Asha had mixed feelings because except for that one brief moment, her husband had not regained consciousness. It was difficult to leave him behind.

Christina had remarked on Asha's obvious reluctance by saying, "You may not love him yet, but I can tell you feel something."

"I feel responsible," Asha said. "It's my job to help him get better. I promised him I'll visit every day."

"That's a good beginning. But in the meantime, you need to learn how to live on your own. Do you two have a place?"

Maryanne had the answer. "Fortunately, my clod of a husband told me that Ken had rented a new apartment. I checked on it, and it was completely empty. I guess you two newlyweds were going to furnish it together. Anyway, I bought you a few things to get by. At least you'll have a bed to sleep in, a chair, and some dishes. From there on, it's up to you and Ken."

At the apartment, Asha was hesitant about going in. Maryanne unlocked the front door and showed her around. She explained, "Cody reset the access code, so the combination is Ken's birthday, one, one, zero, six."

It was a big place. Two bedrooms, two and a half baths, a separate study with built-in bookshelves, and a huge living/dining/kitchen area.

"Maryanne stocked the fridge to get you started," Cody said, "and we left a few business cards for delivery services. I don't know if you are a drinker or not. Ken likes white wine, so we put a few bottles in the pantry. And I had Comcast installed, so you've got Internet and cable. You probably don't care about that, but I know Ken will." He handed her a note with the wi-fi password.

"This seems really weird," Asha said.

"You want me to spend the night?" Maryanne asked.

"I want you to move in," Asha replied honestly. "But Christina would scold me if you did, so I better learn to be independent." She gave both of them a hug. "I can't thank you enough."

"Part of the service," Cody said.

After they left, Asha explored her new home. She spent the evening mentally browsing the Internet and shopping online for a complete wardrobe, linens, and food. An online search gave her the name of a decorator.

The following morning, she talked to the building's doorman to make arrangements for delivery. For the rest of the week, she diligently visited Ken during hospital visiting hours.

When the decorator came over, the young woman nodded knowingly and explained that professional newlyweds were her favorite type of client. Asha gave her a generous budget with three objectives: get it done quickly, turn the apartment into a comfy home, and give the office a masculine atmosphere. In short order the apartment looked like she and Ken had lived in it for a year.

Cody stopped by for some paperwork and expressed admiration when she showed him the result. Better yet, he gave his seal of approval on the decorator's choices for Ken's office.

..*.*

When not at the hospital, Asha used her new capability to scour the Internet for hints of her past life, but everything came up blank. There were no missing person reports for anyone named Asha. All she had was the marriage certificate Cody had retrieved from the Clark County online records system.

Cody reported that Officer Harding had officially categorized their vehicle accident as just that. The driver had been picked up in Denver as an undocumented alien and deported before Chicago PD got the match on his fingerprints. Asha stopped worrying about anyone trying to run her down with a dump truck.

An email from Cody reminded her that she would need businesslike clothes for the board meeting. It would be held the following week on Thursday. It was also a personal reminder that she needed to prepare material for dealing with Aunt Erica.

..*.*

Asha tentatively entered the IT Department of Riddle Systems Group. "Can you help me?" she asked a young man hunched over his computer monitor.

"Probably," he responded sarcastically, not hiding his annoyance. His name tag identified him as Peter Mooney, an IT specialist.

Maryanne had warned her that IT people were a separate species from the human race. "I don't know why," she had said, "but they tend to be incredibly arrogant."

"What should I do?" Asha had asked.

Maryanne smiled and said, "Don't worry. Nerdy computer guys are the easiest people on earth to bribe."

"My name is Asha Riddle," she told the youngster. "I'm Mr. Riddle's wife."

Pete's annoyed expression instantly changed to one of fear. Asha handed him a huge box of donuts covered with icing and every manner of colorful sprinkles.

"Thanks!" He sighed in relief, accepting the donuts with grateful appreciation. "How can I help you?"

"Can you search through an employee email account for this keyword, and print out what you find?" She handed him a note with the particulars written out by hand. She already knew the answer but wanted printouts from the company's IT Department.

"Not a problem," he said.

"Where is everyone?" Asha asked out of curiosity. She thought there would be more people on duty considering the scope of the department's responsibility.

"They're having a late lunch." Pete typed her queries into his own workstation. "We put in a lot of overtime on account of that security breach."

"I heard about that," Asha said innocently. "Did you find out who did it?"

"Not yet. But since then we've been installing new security bots; it won't happen again."

"Bots?" That was a term she had not run across. "What are bots?"

"That's what we call digital robots," Pete replied. "Some people call them Web robots. Except these are smart; we just paid a fortune for the best AI bots out there."

"AI bots? What is an AI?"

Cody had also warned her that IT people liked to use acronyms. Not as much as the military, but close. Pete started to make a sarcastic remark, but Asha nudged the box of donuts a little closer.

He explained, "AI stands for artificial intelligence. These particular bots are smarter than the average product on the market."

"You mean they actually think?"

Pete puffed up a little, but then he said, "Well, not really. AI is a big topic. In this case, all it really means is they learn by experience. We run them on different servers and they keep track of everything that happens on the IP network. It's all integrated into our monitoring system." He finished searching for her material and sent the results to a printer in the corner of the office.

"How do you mean they keep track of everything?" Asha asked.

"They watch for suspicious activity, and they get regular updates from the vendor. If someone tries to intrude on the network now, I'll get a dozen alarms the second it happens."

"I see," Asha said. She could detect three different wireless signals inside the security office. One of them was labeled Security. She linked into it and mentally searched for the intelligent bots. It would be interesting to say hello to an artificial intelligence.

Pete pointed to a computer screen in the next cubicle. It had several images of graphs and dials. "That's our network traffic dashboard. I can look at that right now and see that we're secure."

Inside the local network, Asha found the software bot that Pete was talking about. It wasn't intelligent at all; it was merely a simple program that analyzed network packets. She batted it around—figuratively—without getting any response. The bot was actually quite stupid. Asha found it reassuring that modifying her own protocols had made her virtually immune to detection, even from supposedly smart AI bots.

"That's good to know," Asha said. "And this is the latest software on the market?"

"Of course," Pete said. He gathered up the material from the printer and handed it to her. "This place is locked down tighter than a drum."

Asha wondered if she could adopt the same general concept and create an intelligent bot of her own. She could think of several tasks it could help with for all the research she wanted to do online. It was something to consider.

* * * *

On the designated Thursday morning, Asha stood in front of the corporate headquarters and shifted her new briefcase from one hand to the other. The building's design, a veritable cube, was uninspired.

Still, because of the impending board meeting, it was a little intimidating. She sighed and went inside.

Cody was waiting in the foyer and escorted her up to the boardroom.

"Did you read the material I sent over?" he asked.

"Yes," she replied. "And I did some online research too."

"I heard you went over to the IT Department."

Asha nodded. "I wanted them to dig up a couple of facts for me. I need to go over them with you before the meeting."

"Okay, sounds good," Cody replied absently. "We'll try to get a couple of minutes together. Here we are. Hi, Ron." Ron was a big man with intelligent blue eyes and close-shaven gray hair. "This is Mrs. Riddle. Asha, this is Ronny Santos, Ken's senior VP and Chief Operating Officer. He will run the meeting in Ken's absence. Ron, where would you like Asha to sit?"

Santos shook Asha's hand and seemed genuinely pleased to meet her. "Welcome to our family, Mrs. Riddle. Cody explained that you are Ken's legal representative, so I would be honored for you to sit right here. This is where Ken normally sits." He pulled out a chair at the head of the massive conference table. There was even a nameplate that read *Mrs. Asha Riddle*. Just to the right was his own position.

"Thank you, Ron," Asha replied. "This is all quite new to me."

"A lot of this will be pretty boring," he warned, "but feel free to ask questions. We'll start in about ten minutes."

Cody excused himself, and during the wait, about half of the fifteen board members came up to be introduced. The remaining directors clustered around Aunt Erica, who sat along the left side of the table.

At ten o'clock, everyone took their seats. Cody slipped in at the last second with an apologetic nod at Asha. He took a seat along the wall and Santos gaveled the meeting to order.

Santos went through a couple of standard items, asking for approval of the last board meeting's minutes, and noting the date and time for the next meeting.

"Our first agenda item is—"

"Point of order, Mr. Chairman," Erica cut in. "Why is *she* here?" she demanded, pointing at Asha. "This is not a public meeting."

Cody stood up and said, "Mr. Chairman, may I answer that question?"

"Go ahead," Santos said.

"Director Townsend is well aware the court acknowledged Mrs. Riddle's status as Ken's wife and heir. What she obviously does not know is that Mrs. Riddle also holds a power of attorney to act on his behalf in all matters as his legal guardian."

"She can't do that!" Erica insisted.

"Under Illinois law, she can," Cody replied to the room. "As long as Ken remains medically unconscious, Mrs. Riddle may, in all aspects, do whatever she considers is in Ken's best interests. In fact, if she wanted to press the matter, she could chair this board meeting, but as this is her first visit, she requested to sit in as an observer."

"And she is here as my guest, Erica," Santos said. "Your point of order is overruled. Let's move on."

Erica glared at her own attorney sitting behind her. He looked embarrassed and gave her a slight shrug. She turned back to Ron Santos, and said, "Mr. Chairman, I make a motion that I be appointed as my nephew's guardian for matters affecting this corporation. I am his aunt, and I am the one that has his best interests at heart and those of this company, not this stranger."

"I second the motion," Allan McCall said, a man seated to her left. McCall was well known as one of her staunch allies.

Santos glanced at Cody, who raised one finger.

Santos nodded and said, "A motion has been made and seconded, and is now open for discussion. Mr. Anderson, go ahead."

Cody rose and said, "The motion is irrelevant. Even if passed by this board, it does not override a court ruling. If Director Townsend does not like the court's decision, she may pursue legal alternatives, but as her hostility to her nephew has long been public knowledge, I doubt she'll receive much sympathy."

Erica subsided and seemed to consider her options.

Asha raised her hand.

"Mrs. Riddle?" Santos said. "Do you have something?"

"Yes. You said the question is open for discussion, so can I bring up a point? I think it has a bearing on Aunt Erica's comment that she has the best interest of the company at heart."

"Of course. Please go ahead."

Asha removed a thick file folder from her briefcase and said, "As all of you may know, the actual email accounts that are hosted by the corporate server are the property of the corporation itself, not of the individual user."

A few of the board members nodded, but Erica gasped loudly.

Asha continued, "I asked the IT Department to review Aunt Erica's email for the past twelve months, and found that she made an arrangement with Director McCall, sitting there next to her, to sell off the company's most recent camera system."

"I didn't sell it to him," Erica snapped. "I only wanted his advice on marketing."

Asha pulled out a paper and handed it to Santos. "As you can see, Ron, that's not what she said."

Santos took the printed email and read aloud. "She says, 'I've got Ken's newest prototype, the M300-CTS.'" Santos looked up and added, "For the sake of those members who may not understand, CTS stands for camera tracking system. This goes on…it says, 'I want at least three hundred K for it. See what you can get from Joel.'"

Santos glanced around the table. "Again, for those of you who don't know, Joel Morton is one of our competitors." In a low growl, Santos added, "For myself, this seems pretty clear. I have no choice but to provide this to law enforcement."

"Already done," Asha murmured.

Santos's face cleared somewhat from his anger, and he glanced at Asha with respectful admiration. "Well done, Mrs. Riddle." He turned back to Ken's aunt. "Erica, based on this information I call for the vote. All in favor of Director Townsend's motion say aye." No one said a word. "All opposed?"

All the attendees to his right said, "Nay."

"The nays have it. Motion fails. Erica, I'm going to offer you the courtesy of resigning. It might look better than dragging an investigation out in the courts. Your call."

Rather than answer, Erica stood up and said, "This is not the last you'll hear from me on the matter." She pointed at Asha. "That was an invasion of privacy, Miss Amnesiac. What you did was illegal!" With that, she stomped out of the boardroom.

Everyone's gaze returned to McCall, whose astonishment at the turn of events only accentuated his expression of guilt. If it weren't so serious, it would have been comical. "I didn't sell it to Joel Morton."

"Who did you sell it to?" Santos asked harshly. "I can't believe we have such treachery in the company, and from a board member no less. For Christ's sake!"

Asha handed Santos another email, this one from McCall to Erica.

Santos skimmed the text, and informed the other board members, "He told her he sold it to a middleman named Evan Simons, who put it up for bid on the dark web."

A buzz of surprise arose around the conference table. Those seated close to McCall, and who had previously favored Erica, unobtrusively moved their chairs away.

"Now what?" one of the board members asked aloud. "That's pretty expensive research."

Asha said, "I purchased it anonymously from an auction site through Tor. I paid twenty bitcoins, and it was delivered to my apartment last Tuesday."

"This is insane," Santos said, this time from frustration. He glanced at McCall. "I don't care if you resign or not; this goes to the police." He handed the two emails to Cody. "Can you take care of this?"

"Certainly," Cody replied.

McCall didn't speak. He stood and followed after Erica out of the boardroom.

Santos glanced around the conference table. "I'm going to apologize to the board. As the Chief Operating Officer, I had no idea we had this kind of treachery going on under our collective noses." He thought for a moment, and said, "One thing I do promise is to investigate how they got that prototype. It didn't walk out of here on its own."

Santos looked at the stack of papers he had brought with him to the meeting. He was clearly shaken by the turn of events and said, "This is all standard stuff." He slapped the documents on the table. "Can I ask for a vote to approve all our items today as a consent agenda? I need to think about what just happened. Or if you prefer, I'll make that a request to hold everything until our next meeting."

"Move to approve as consent," said a voice down the table to his right.

"Second," another replied.

"All in favor?" Santos asked aloud. After a chorus of "Ayes!" he said, "The ayes have it. Meeting adjourned."

As everyone filed out, several of the board members stopped to shake Asha's hand, offering a variety of thanks, congratulations, and best wishes for Ken. A few minutes later, it was just Asha, Santos, and Cody in the room.

"I was under the impression you had pretty severe amnesia," Santos said. "That's not what it looked like in here. You were amazing."

"I do have amnesia," Asha said. "But I also have all my faculties. I thought Aunt Erica was pretty frightening the way she carried on in Kenneth's hospital room, so a little digging seemed like a good idea. As I said, I asked the IT Department to go through her email." She glanced over at Cody. "Sorry, I was planning to give all this to you before the meeting. But when Erica made that motion, I thought I should mention it."

"That's okay," Cody said, self-consciously. "I apologize for not giving you the time you asked for. But I'm glad you didn't hold back. I had already suspected we would have some fireworks from

Erica in today's meeting; I just didn't anticipate a nuclear bomb from you in response. Good job."

Santos invited her to stay for lunch, but Asha begged off, claiming fatigue.

"I would love to, honestly," she told him. "But it doesn't take much to wear me out these days. And I still have an appointment with physical therapy today. Those guys are merciless."

"I'll drop you off," Cody said. "You probably want to check in on Ken before your appointment."

"That would be great, thanks."

* * * *

Beijing, China

Major Wong accepted the folder from Lieutenant Soong with raised eyebrows. "What is this?" he asked.

"I found the reference you wanted concerning Riddle Systems," she explained. "It was a HUMINT source in San Francisco. Our source had a lead on some stolen technology from inside the company."

"That's it," Wong said with satisfaction. "I knew there had been something about Riddle Systems but I couldn't put my finger on it. Good job, Lieutenant. I had forgotten the details. What about the camera?"

"It improves drone tracking of mobile targets by a significant margin. Someone put it up for auction."

That perked Wong's interest. "Any chance we can obtain it?"

"No, sir. It already sold to an anonymous buyer. But there are obviously some problems at this corporation. How did they lose control of something that important?"

"Good question, Lieutenant. By the way, I haven't seen Captain Zheng's request for more study. Can you ping him and find out what's taking so long?"

Wong's interest in Riddle Systems had steadily increased since he had first discussed the company with Soong. If the CEO's extended absence was causing problems like this, it was too good an opportunity to ignore. Wong wanted Zheng to send that request up the ladder so he could get it approved.

* * * *

Saint Bernadette's Intensive Care Unit

Asha and Cody entered the ICU and said hi to the attending nurse, Tamika Reeves.

"I'm glad you're here," Tamika said. "He's been a bit restless this morning."

Asha hurried into Ken's room and sat beside him, taking his hand. It was time to go into full wife mode. Christina had warned her to be affectionate during the early stages of her husband's recovery.

"It's me, honey," she said in an encouraging tone. "I just came from the board meeting. How are you doing? Are you going to wake up for us?"

Cody stood at the foot of the bed with a worried look on his face.

Ken moved his head back and forth as though trying to shake off a bad dream. Asha spoke to him gently, urging him to open his eyes.

Tamika came in and wiped his face and lips with a wet cloth. Ken's eyes opened, and Asha caressed his hand lightly. "Good morning. Welcome back. Are you feeling okay?"

He groaned and looked in her direction. "Who are you?" he asked in a whisper, as though the effort was almost too much.

"It's me, Asha. I'm your wife. Don't you remember? We got married in Las Vegas."

"You're not my wife," Ken replied painfully.

"Yeah, she is," Cody said, his expression slightly amused and much relieved from hearing his friend speak. "You've got amnesia, buddy."

Ken seemed to notice Cody in the room. "Hi, Cody. She's not my wife."

"Yeah, she is," Cody repeated. "You're the one who told me."

"No, I'm not married," Ken insisted in a raspy voice. He groaned with frustration.

"All right," Cody said. He gripped one of Ken's feet through the white cover and gave it a gentle tweak. "Whatever you say, pal. But I've got your marriage certificate in my office. Get well." He gave Asha a sympathetic look and said, "I've got to get going. Good luck. This idiot can be stubborn. Believe me, I know that more than most."

"Thanks, Cody," Asha called to his retreating back. She turned to Tamika and asked, "What should I do?"

"Just stay here with your husband, Mrs. Riddle, and answer his questions. When patients wake up from a coma, it can take some time for their memories to sort out."

The nurse handed Asha the washcloth and left the room. Asha used it to gently wipe her husband's brow and wet his lips again.

"Feeling any better?" she asked in an attempt at cheerfulness.

"Feel like crap," he said. "Two months?"

"Fifty-eight days. I was out for twenty-two days. Nineteen if you count when Aunt Erica woke me up, but I don't remember that."

"Erica? She was here?"

"A while back. Ronny Santos threw her off the board today at the board meeting, her and Allan McCall. They tried to sell one of your CTS modules to Joel Morton. Don't worry. I stopped it. I bought it off a dark website where it was being auctioned."

"What?" Ken looked totally confused.

"Sorry. Forget all that. Are you okay? Your leg was broken in the accident but has healed well. They say you'll be fine after rehab."

"What accident?"

Asha sat beside her husband and answered his questions. Some of them were about business, and he often confused her with someone else. A couple of times he called her Lenora. She didn't try to correct him; just answered as best she could.

After thirty minutes, he fell back asleep.

"He doesn't know who I am," she said to Tamika at the nurse's station. She felt surprisingly sad at his lack of recognition.

"Don't worry, honey," Tamika replied. "It's not unusual for the newest memories to go first. Don't take any of it personally. Two months is a long time to be in a coma, so it may take a while for him to reorient."

"When will he wake up again?"

"Probably not today. We'll call you if he does wake up. Do we have your number here at the station?"

Asha gave Tamika the number again, but she didn't really need anyone to call; she had been monitoring his readings from her apartment since the day she moved in. It had only taken her a few seconds to bypass the hospital's security. She did it without thinking against any firewall she encountered now. There was always an unprotected pathway through a router—often more than one—and her mind automatically found ways to pass through any roadblock she came across. So far, there wasn't anything on the market that she could not get past.

Chapter 4 – The Welcome

The next day Asha visited Ken, as usual. The difference was that he was awake. He wanted to discuss their marital status first thing.

"I appreciate you coming to visit," he said, "but it's not necessary since we don't really know each other."

"Don't be silly," she said patiently. "I'm not going to let some stupid truck driver ruin our life."

Asha calmly recounted all the history she and Cody had discussed. He didn't buy it. It didn't help that he exhibited clear signs of confusion on most topics. After two days of frustration on Asha's part and denial on Ken's, Christina intervened and the question was officially postponed until further notice.

After that, Asha continued to visit him every day, but she restricted their conversation to his physical therapy and the people they had met in the hospital. He wanted to keep tabs on the stock market, so she got up to speed on things like market sectors and exchange-traded funds.

Although their relationship remained cordial, it was clear to Asha that her husband had no recollection of their marriage. When she considered the difficulty his sporadic memory was causing, she decided it was time to do some research of her own.

What did scientists know about human memory? Both of them could use some help on that subject. One of them had to have a memory of some kind that the two of them were legally married. The trick was digging it out.

* * * *

Asha sifted through the National Institute of Health's literature about the neurologic impact of electrical injury to the brain. Scientists had done extensive research in the subject area, much

63

more than she had anticipated. Even with her talent for rapidly reviewing online data, there was a lot more information in the archives than she could go through in one sitting.

Obtaining the research required penetrating the NIH's network security. That in itself was not a problem. But she wanted to take her time while studying the volumes of medical research about amnesia. Even though she was confident that the security monitors at Riddle Systems would not detect her presence, there was no guarantee that her online presence was invisible to everyone. The government's cybersecurity might be more sensitive to intruders.

A better solution would be to get in and out quickly, and simply store the material in a separate place, where she could study at her leisure. Pete, the IT technician at Riddle Systems, had talked about how the company stored most of their data on their own servers.

I need my own server space, Asha decided. A quick online search revealed dozens of commercial vendors who rented all manner of cloud storage. It truly was a booming industry. She signed up for an account and started out with fifty terabytes of space.

The result gave her a knowledge warehouse right there on the information superhighway. With so much space available, she could even offload the material she had thus far accumulated into her own mind. She had been surfing the Web so much lately it was tending to leave her feeling a little scatterbrained.

When she paused to inventory all that she had learned in the last two months, her conclusion was *what a mess*. None of the information had any semblance of order. She might as well have thrown a crate full of books onto the living room floor.

Does everyone have this problem, she wondered? The question was how to clear out the non-essential information and organize the rest. But it wasn't like you could simply move files around the way she had with Raphael's computer.

Or was it?

As Rafe had said, he had taught her brain how to work digitally. She had proved it by accessing software in her eye socket and then opening the Chrome application for her first glimpse of the Internet.

Since that first experience, her subconscious had modified the tool into one better conformed to her own thought processes.

Perhaps some of the other programs from Raphael's laptop might also be useful. A quick check of those files revealed a specialized utility for memory management called Defrag.

An associated text file said it was for physically organizing the contents of memory storage into contiguous areas, making access more efficient. It also freed up space for new information.

That's exactly what I need.

She activated the program the same way she had the Chrome browser. Once again, her subconscious grappled with the computer language as it translated the concept into a working procedure. After a moment, a virtual depiction of her brain appeared in her mind. It was laid out as a three-dimensional model filled with individual clusters of different colors.

On closer examination, she saw that within each cluster were tiny blocks of information, many of them scattered throughout her mind, and all were connected by countless thousands of neuronal tendrils. *Those are fragmented memories*, she realized. No wonder she felt scatterbrained.

A large section near the center of the model was gray in color and locked as inaccessible. *Best to leave that section undisturbed,* a warning voice in the back of her mind advised.

After a moment of contemplation, she selected a modest section of her neocortex that showed recent activity and activated the program. The experience was dizzying at first, but after a few moments she picked up a rhythm to the operation. It gathered her fragmented memories together and rearranged the result into chronological order. As it did so, she experienced continuous flashes of déjà vu.

The only unfortunate aspect was that none of the memories went back prior to her waking up in the hospital. It reinforced the realization that her former life had been totally erased. Whatever wiped it out in the accident had done the job thoroughly; that fact was undeniable.

After an hour of the hypnotic activity, the operation completed, leaving Asha feeling more clearheaded than she had since first waking up in the hospital.

She paused, however, before diving back into a new round of research. Although tempting, it would put her right back where she had been an hour ago, with her brain full of uncorrelated information.

What she needed was a way to curate the voluminous information she pulled from the NIH archives. It didn't have to happen in real time, or at least not in a detailed way. This would be the perfect application for one of those artificially intelligent robots that Peter had talked about. Wouldn't it be nice to have one as a research assistant?

As Pete had explained it, AI bots were standalone programs that operated independently once they were set up. The question was how to do that. Asha had no knowledge of computer programming and no interest in learning about it.

And for that matter, what she wanted to accomplish didn't seem that difficult. All she needed was a subset of her own mind working in the background. She established a link with her rented server space and tried to copy over all of her newly defragged memories. The exercise left her dizzy and was a total failure. There was no semblance of a bot or any type of intelligence left behind.

It made sense, actually. Moving a stack of books from one room to another didn't make the room smarter. She needed to copy a deeper level of her mind, the part of the brain that initiated the thought process. But that wasn't something she was willing to do with the defrag utility.

There had to be other tools for copying complicated files. The utility tools from Raphael's laptop did not yield what she needed. An online search revealed two commercial products that held promise; one of them from a research university in Australia. They had created a tool to transfer living memories from one sea slug into another.

Aside from the fact she didn't like thinking of herself in the same context as a sea slug, the research team had gone on to create a set of data modeling programs for managing supercomputer drive arrays. They called it memory cloning. It sounded perfect. She navigated into their network and appropriated a copy of the software for herself.

The process was complicated. It took several days of customization, and she suffered repeated failures, but finally, she had a tool that could copy various regions of her brain into a computational matrix that maintained the necessary neuronal-like pathways to keep it coherent.

Another week of experimentation resulted in the creation of a stable process on her rented server. She had her very own AI bot and immediately named him *Abbot*.

To be honest, she admitted to herself, *he's not that smart*. But he understood her commands as long as she was explicit. In the first live attempt, she taught him to accept and then store the material that she identified during her Internet research. After some extra fine-tuning, he got to the point that he would download whatever she pointed at and store it for future review.

On the brighter side, the more she worked with the AI, the more capable he became. Each time she added a task to his repertoire, the program itself grew smarter.

In short order, *Abbot* became so effective in pulling information out of the NIH data center that from then on, she left him running continuously. Whenever she had a question, she sent him a query. He would research the answer and even download background material for her later review. After a week, she had taught him to produce summarized results almost in real time. It made him a handy companion, always available in the back of her mind. And he was a lot easier to deal with than her husband.

..*.*

Asha sat in her living room, venting her frustration to Cody.

"He's been awake for a month now," she said. "Has he said anything to you about our marriage?"

Even though Asha visited her husband every day, he still treated her as nothing more than an acquaintance. It was wearing on her patience.

Cody shook his head. "I'm sorry, but no. He is confused about a lot of things. The doctors keep him focused on his physical therapy for now. This morning Christina showed him the traffic cam video. He was pretty blown away at how you pulled him out of the car. And it made the point the two of you were together, coming from the airport."

"Does he remember Vegas at all?"

"Nope. He acknowledges he traveled there; his ticket proves that. He keeps asking me where your ticket is, and I don't have an answer. I assume you guys met up there. I wish we had some security footage of you two boarding the plane or something."

"Yeah, or video from the chapel."

Cody smiled. "I checked into that, but some of those places are not what you would call high tech."

"So, what happens now?" Asha asked. "Do I have to worry I might get thrown out of the apartment?"

"No, no," Cody said. "Both the doctor and the shrink say he only needs more time. He'll come around."

"What if he doesn't? My memories haven't come back and I don't remember our marriage either. I'm just taking your word for it."

Her comment made Cody stop and think. "That's true. But he was so adamant before he left. He told me he was going to marry Asha, and to hell with everyone else." He stared at her intently. "Don't you think you're married?"

"I don't know!" she moaned. "I don't remember anything about my past. I'm making a lot of assumptions, one of them being that our marriage was actually consummated. I can tell you; I'm not having sex with that guy until one of us remembers our vows."

Cody sighed. "Let's not get ahead of ourselves. He told me he was going to Vegas to marry Asha. You saved him from the wreck, and you were wearing the name bracelet. All that makes sense. And he admits he has doubts about his own memory. I probably shouldn't tell you, but he did talk about having the union dissolved. I told him that wasn't a good idea."

That alarmed Asha. "He really brought that up?"

"He did, but don't worry about it. It will never happen."

"Why not? Could he do that if he wanted?"

"Only if he were an idiot. Before he left for Vegas, I told him he needed a prenup. In fact, I begged him to have a prenup." Cody looked at her closely. "You know what a prenup is?"

"Of course. A prenuptial marital agreement."

"That's right. I thought he should have one."

"You didn't trust me?" Asha asked.

"Don't take it personally; I hadn't even met you back then. But he absolutely refused. He said he loved you that much, and that you two would never part. Right now, he doesn't remember any of those conversations, so his insistence that you are not married doesn't carry a lot of weight, at least not with me."

"It must be a nightmare for him," Asha said feeling unexpectedly sorry for her husband.

Cody shook his head. "He brought it on himself, so like I said, I'm not too sympathetic. I told him in no uncertain terms that if he tries to dissolve the marriage, you would walk away with half the company."

"I wouldn't do that," Asha protested.

"Glad to hear it. My point was that he can't afford it. Especially with him thinking about an IPO. I told him so and he knows it."

"Then what now?"

Cody shrugged. "He said he'd just live with it for now until the situation sorts itself out."

The comment unexpectedly tweaked Asha's pride. "So, what am I supposed to do? Wait for him to decide what my shelf life is?"

Cody made calming gestures. "Sorry. Don't get angry. I'm only making you aware of what's going on. All of this will blow over. He knows that you've been sitting by his bedside all this time, taking care of him. He likes it when you're there."

Asha forced herself to calm down. "All right. I won't get angry. Right now, all I want is for him to get well. We can sort out our relationship later if we have to, but hopefully, it won't come to that. He does remember people from before the accident, and that's more than I do. You're right, we should just wait."

"Yes, ma'am. And he agrees. Just so you realize, the doctor said he could probably check out of the hospital in a week or so. Ken said that when he does, he'll come here."

"I'm not sure if that's good or bad."

"Well, here is the delicate part that I have to mention. I don't think this is an issue, but because he brought it up, I want to be frank with you. If things go south after he moves in, whether his memory comes back or not, I can't legally represent you. Besides being the company's general counsel, I am Ken's personal attorney. That means I am obligated to take his side, and that's what I'll do. So, because there *is* the smallest doubt about how all this is going to work out, I suggest you give some thought to getting your own attorney. I can give you a couple of names if you want."

"Thank you, Cody, but I'll decline for the time being. For now, my goal is to make both of us feel at home. And you need to make that your priority too."

"I do. I agree."

* * * *

Beijing, China

Major Wong signed the bottom block of the form requesting additional resources for direct intervention into Riddle Systems. It had taken a month to get it approved through his own bureaucracy. He handed the package to Lieutenant Soong.

"When will you start the attempt?" he asked Captain Zheng, who was waiting impatiently for the authorization to move ahead.

70

Zheng nodded at the folder that Soong held tightly against her chest. "As soon as I get a copy of that approval," he said.

Soong grinned. "I just need to make a copy for our files. If you give me five minutes, I promise you can take it with you."

"In that case, I'll put a new team together tomorrow when I get back to Shanghai."

"How long will the operation take?" Wong asked.

"If Riddle Systems is using off-the-shelf technology, and I suspect they are, we'll need a few days to establish a presence on their servers. But after that, all we can do is wait for whoever hacked them to come back. There is no way to predict when that will be."

"How will you know if they do?"

"Once we get through their firewall, we'll install a monitoring utility on one of their servers. Depending on their network configuration, our preference is to put it on their primary DNS server. That gives us the best look at the traffic going in or out. But whatever, we'll find something that's not well protected. Once established, our software will send out reports about their network traffic. For anything unusual, we'll get notification almost instantly."

"Any guesses as to who it is?" Wong asked.

Zheng shrugged. "Master Sergeant Tang is not easily impressed, so I'm guessing whoever broke in last time has to be either Russian or North Korean. But it might just as easily be the Israelis, Taiwan, or a dozen others."

"Will you search their servers to see if anything was left behind?"

"Not for the first forty-eight hours. Our monitors will operate silently in the background until we have an understanding of their protocols. Once I'm comfortable, we'll slip in a modified worm to go through their drives. If there are any traces, that will find it. I have to say, I'm curious about who it is. It's about time for a new generation. Maybe this is it."

"How do you mean?" Soong asked.

Zheng said, "For the last few years, the industry is in what I would call a fairly stable growth phase. Everyone is making incremental improvements to our hacking tools; new viruses, worms, Trojans, and the like, but nothing really breakthrough. Whoever develops something revolutionary will make history. When it comes, I can almost guarantee it will be based on artificial intelligence. I only hope it's us."

Wong nodded. "I worry about the same thing. But now the bad news. The colonel wants me to make an on-site inspection."

Zheng smiled in return. "It could be worse, Major; at least the colonel himself is not coming."

"True," Wong replied. "Advise Lieutenant Soong in advance so I can be there on the first day. It's been a while since I visited Shanghai. If all goes well, I'll treat your team to dinner."

* * * *

Asha and Ken's Apartment in Chicago

Asha opened the apartment door to find Ken and Cody standing side by side, looking very awkward. It was her first time to welcome home a husband.

"Hi, honey," she said cheerfully.

He stood there until she took his hand and pulled him into the apartment. Cody started to follow, but she scowled and nodded at the elevator. He mouthed, *are you sure?* In answer, she closed the door in his face and shepherded Ken into the living room.

"Come on in," she said. "I had a decorator do all this, but we can change anything you don't like."

He glanced at the room and gave a shrug. "It's okay."

"Hungry?"

"Not really."

"I made us some dinner." Asha gestured at the table, all set for two. She had been uncertain about having a meal ready. She wasn't familiar with his likes and dislikes, but not offering him anything didn't seem reasonable.

Ken sighed. "Okay, thanks."

72

"Make yourself comfortable, I'll get it ready."

She went into the kitchen to give him time to look around their new home. The beef stew heated quickly and the rolls in the microwave dinged. By the time she had everything ready, Ken had come to the table. He stood by his chair and stuck out one hand.

"Hi. My name is Ken Riddle. Nice to officially meet you."

Asha had anticipated this moment, or one similar, many times, and had decided on how she would approach it. She took his gesture as a way of keeping a formal boundary between them, even though they were now living in the same space.

Rather than letting his assumption stand unchallenged, she moved toward him for a quick embrace and a kiss on his cheek.

"I'm glad you're home. I've been worried about you." She gave him a squeeze and said, "Have a seat. Let's eat while it's still hot."

He watched her sit and then followed suit.

"This is really weird for me," he said, glancing around the room.

"It's strange for me, too," she said, "but I've had longer to get used to it." She dished him up a bowl of the stew. "I hope you like it. I don't know if I'm a cook or not, but I enjoyed making it."

"It's good," he said after taking a bite. After an awkward silence, he said, "Well, for the past month, all we've talked about really is me. How have you been doing since the accident?"

It was a comfortable opening, and Asha relaxed. At least he was not going to fight her outright. Her hope was that if they gave each other a chance to establish a home environment, his memory of their marriage would return.

She told him about when she first woke up in the hospital and about how Raphael had guided her through the process of getting her new eye. Then she explained how that led to her new ability regarding the Internet. He looked skeptical when she told him about *Abbot* but nodded approvingly about her board meeting run-in with Erica.

"Why haven't you told Raphael about this?" he asked, curious that she had kept the information hidden.

"I was afraid he would shut off my eye," she said. "The day after I discovered it, he saw some squirrelly readings and suggested we swap out my eye with a less capable model. It scared me, so I clammed up."

"You shouldn't be scared. Rafe wants what's best for his patients."

"Maybe. But losing an eye is traumatic, you can trust me on that. And if someone restores your sight and then says they might take it away, even if it's for a good reason, you'd worry too. It's not like swapping out an appliance."

Ken chuckled quietly at the comparison, "Fair enough. But still, you shouldn't be afraid."

Asha shook her head. "I live in fear," she explained. "All day long I try not to show it, but everything scares me. Mostly because I can't tell what's important and what isn't. Christina says it's not uncommon for amnesiacs to be fearful. I told *Abbot* to contact you if I ever get in a bind."

"That would be interesting."

"He's important to me because he can get answers. In the hospital, everyone kept telling me not to worry, but their eyes would be full of pity like they were hiding a horrible secret…something they didn't want me to know, and they would clam up. It's terrifying. Now when I want an answer, I can find it myself or have *Abbot* do it. I may not remember anything from my previous life, but these days I keep track of everything going on around me. It's probably overcompensating, but I don't care."

"Okay," Ken said. "When you explain it that way, I understand. So, first of all, I promise that no one will take your eye away. No matter what happens to you and me, I owe you that at the very least. And thanks, by the way, for saving my life."

Asha nodded, comforted by his reassurance. "I'm glad I did."

"What can you do with it?" he asked. "Just surf the Web kind of thing?"

The lights dimmed, the TV came on, and music started playing from the living room. "Things like that," she said. "A lot more, too, but I have to be careful. The first time I used it, I created a security breach at the office. No one knows it was me."

"Cody told me we'd been hacked. That was you?"

"I didn't mean to. I wanted to tell Cody what happened, that it was an accident. But before I could, he said whoever did was going to jail, so I kept my mouth shut. It scared me…a lot."

Ken chuckled sympathetically. "You were in a tough spot; I can see that now. You had to keep a secret from both Rafe and Cody, the only two people in the world that you really knew. Okay, don't worry about the hack; I'll take care of that, and we'll keep your role in it between the two of us. What else can you do?"

"Ask me a question."

Ken thought about it for a moment. "Something difficult?"

"Whatever you want."

"Okay." Ken's eyes unfocused as he mulled the challenge. "Try this. We were working on a proposal to provide a camera module on a government contract for a long-range unmanned reconnaissance system. What's the status of that contract and did we ever put in a bid?"

Asha smiled, somewhat surprised by the complexity of his query. He wanted to see if she really had the ability to do what she claimed. It was a decent test of her ability.

"That's a good question," she said, looking at the ceiling much as he had done. "Okay, yes, you did respond to the bid, but it was with a query. Do you know Tyrell?"

"Yeah, Tyrell Lee. He was the lead on that project."

"He responded with an inquiry about the specified data link frequencies. He thought they had misstated the proposed frequency bands. He was right, a correction was put out, and he ultimately sent in a response last week. The overall bid amount was fourteen million dollars and change." Asha gave him a rueful look. "I'm sorry, you aren't the low bidder. Raytheon's bid is thirteen-eight."

Ken was surprised by her answer. "Had you already researched that?"

"No. I looked it up just now."

"Where? How?"

"First, I searched through our own bid proposals in the business section, then reviewed the government's databases to correlate the specific RFP you were talking about. The government information is public-facing, so it was all legal. I try to stay legal, thanks to Cody's scare tactics, but I did look at the other submissions."

"That was amazing," he said. "I didn't actually expect you to answer. I have to think about this."

Asha was pleased that she had impressed him. "It's exciting for me, too," she said. "And I've only scratched the surface of what I can do."

"How does it work?" he asked curiously.

"Tough questions like that, I have to consciously investigate, but for most things, it's like intuition. If I want to know something, the answer is just there in my mind."

Ken asked her a few more questions, not as difficult. Not as a true test, but more as a word game. She had fun showing off for him and finished by sending him the last answer as a text.

"How do you send the text?" he asked, reading it on his phone. "You're not using a keypad or anything."

"I compose it in my mind and then send it to your phone number. The phone company does all the address translation. I can call you the same way."

The conversation drifted to other topics. She learned a little about his growing-up years. His parents were long divorced and he didn't really stay in touch. His mom lived in Australia with her second husband and his dad had retired in Florida. Ken called him now and again, maybe once a year.

Finally, the discussion petered out. She knew what was coming next; something else she had thought about and even discussed with Christina.

"Listen, …uh," he started.

"Don't worry," she said. "I gave you the bathroom in the bedroom. I want my own bathroom, so I took the one in the spare bedroom."

"Are you sleeping in the spare bedroom?"

"No. We're married; we should sleep together. But both of us are still recuperating physically, and we need time to get acquainted. So, no pressure. You go get ready for bed, and I'll clean up here and join you."

"Okay," he said stiltedly. "This all seems a little backward somehow, you being careful of my sensibilities. It seems a little Victorian."

"I've been awake longer," she answered prosaically.

She finished putting things away before taking a shower and putting on a pair of plain pajamas. Christina suggested that she not wear anything sexy at first, just plain old pj's until they both got comfortable sleeping in the same bed. The psychiatrist recommended that getting to second base be put off down the road.

Ken was already in bed with the covers on her side turned down. She slid in and faced him. "Is this okay?" she asked.

"I should be the one asking that question," he said.

"I'm fine. It all feels awkward, but I keep telling myself I wouldn't have married you if I didn't love you. I wish I remembered some of it, but it's all gone. Not only being married but my whole life. I'm afraid it will make me clingy, but I'm trying not to be."

"You don't remember anything of your prior life?"

"Nope. Christina keeps telling me to be patient, but I get the feeling she's giving up hope. She says the good news is I remember everything from the time I woke up; it means I can form new long-term memories. I don't understand how I know so much about things like American history and stuff I learned in school, but everything about my life and me personally is gone. It's called episodic memory. What about you?"

"I remember everything now," he said. "My whole life history."

"But not us getting married," she said with a sigh.

"That's right. Except for that."

She spotted the flicker of sympathy in his eyes. Pity was not what she wanted.

"I love you," Asha said.

He raised his eyebrows. "Seriously?"

She gave him a little shrug. "Christina told me to keep saying it."

"Do I have to say it too?" he asked hesitantly.

"No. I don't even want you to unless you really mean it."

"You strike me as kind of a strange person," Ken said. "For all your talk of fearfulness, you have a strong personality."

"Is that bad?"

"I don't think so."

"Is this going to work?" Asha asked, wanting an honest answer.

"I have no idea. I can tell you're putting everything you have into it. I can't fault you for anything you've done."

"But you don't remember me."

"I really don't."

"Should I leave?"

"Do you want to?" he countered.

"Not really. But I don't want to stay where I'm not wanted."

"What do you want?" Ken asked.

Asha thought for a moment and said, "I want to go to sleep," and then turned over.

"Coward," he whispered.

"Not really," she said over her shoulder. "You have no idea how much courage this takes."

She fell asleep wondering if she was actually living at home or in reality, was just a squatter?

* * * *

Asha woke up alone. She found Ken in the living room with a cup of coffee, staring at the blank TV screen. "I couldn't find the remote," he said.

She mentally turned on the TV. "What channel?" she asked. "CNN or Fox?"

"Anything but the news. ESPN, I guess. There's still coffee."

"You want breakfast?" she asked, mentally switching the channel over to a sports host talking about baseball.

Ken shook his head. "I had some toast. I thought we could go into the office and let Raphael know what's going on with your eye. He needs to be in the loop on this, just for health reasons, if nothing else."

"Sounds good," she said.

The television was showing a replay of the Cubs' game; a batter hit a line drive into the corner of left field. The outfielder flubbed the catch and had trouble chasing it down. The announcer cried, "And Heyward scores from second base!"

Asha's face suddenly turned red with embarrassment and she giggled, but she wouldn't tell Ken what she found so funny. Instead, she went to get changed.

* * * *

Raphael listened carefully as Asha explained her newfound abilities thanks to the eye's wi-fi capability. They were in his laboratory on the fourth floor of the corporation's main building. Ken was with her.

"That would explain all the optic nerve activity," Raphael said when she finished. "This is certainly unexpected."

Ken added, "Rafe, I want it clear that no one touches her eye without her express say-so. Don't you pressure her, either; she's not a test subject. And I think it would be best to keep this quiet. For now, this is only between the three of us."

"I understand," Raphael replied. To Asha, he said, "I'm on your side, and I mean it. It makes me wonder why this has not turned up before."

Asha shrugged. "No clue."

"Your case is unusual, but not extraordinarily so, at least from a medical perspective."

"Could it be my amnesia?" Asha speculated. "I seem to have some empty space in my brain."

"I suppose, but I studied the MRIs, and didn't notice anything out of the ordinary. And your encephalogram was normal for an amnesiac. I'll go back and examine everything again. In the meantime, boss, what would you like me to do?"

"I dunno," Ken replied. "Any kind of marketable product here?"

"I doubt it," Raphael said. "My guess is this is a one-off occurrence. And frankly, even if we can repeat it, I don't see a market if the user has to give up an eye and maybe their memory to get it."

"That's true, but keep it in mind. I wanted you to know what's going on. Asha promised to keep you up to speed with her progress."

* * * *

After their visit with Raphael, Ken wanted to stop by Ron Santos's office and say hello.

"How's our favorite COO doing?" Ken asked. "You've met Asha."

"Yes, indeed. Hello again, Mrs. Riddle." To Ken, Santos added, "We're doing okay, but we'll be better when you get back. How's that going?"

The two men immediately started talking shop, leaving Asha to feel like a third wheel.

"I'm going to look around," she said.

Ken paused and asked, "Would you like someone to bring you a coffee? I just need to talk with Ron for a couple of minutes."

"No, thanks." To Santos, she said, "Ron, don't let him overdo it. He just got out of the hospital yesterday."

"Right, right," Ron muttered absently, spreading out an engineering schematic for Ken to review.

Asha left them alone in the office and wandered down to the main lobby. On her previous visits, she hadn't taken the time to actually check the place out. The lobby was spacious, and a cafeteria off one of the hallways had a constant trickle of employees going in and out.

She found a seating area in a corner of the foyer and made herself comfortable to wait for Ken. She wondered if he was the type of man who promised to be gone for five minutes and then turned up hours later. Hopefully not.

While she waited, she detected the building's wi-fi coming from the cafeteria and linked into it.

Her awareness of the Internet had grown beyond the highway metaphor. Instead, once she was online, wherever she looked, her mind added labels to electronic devices, taken from the device itself. Cell phone numbers hovered above multiple octet identifiers. The information gave her access into the device, either by direct access or connecting via voice or text.

The corporate lobby was the center of a thriving electronic community, and Asha enjoyed the convivial environment.

From habit, she peeked into the IT security control room to make sure she wasn't setting off any alarms. She had not. To the intrusion detection systems, she remained invisible.

In the process, however, she came across a type of signal she had not seen before. It was a tiny persistent flow from outside the building, and the data stream had a strange configuration.

Whereas most payloads within the network's data packets were either encrypted or filled with normal ASCII text, these had Chinese characters intermixed. It piqued Asha's curiosity, warranting a closer inspection. As she knew from the annual reports, the corporation had no connections with China.

The packet-headers indicated the traffic was being routed through Canada. Asha began following the back trace. The path jumped around the globe several times and finally terminated in a twelve-story building in one of Shanghai's industrial areas.

Inside the building, Asha found an internal security system that included closed-circuit cameras; it was set up much like the one in the Riddle Systems headquarters. One of the cameras on the eighth floor was in an office filled with Chinese military personnel. They were all hunched over sophisticated work consoles with multiple computer screens. One screen displayed a Google Map of Chicago's west side, centered on Ken's corporate offices.

Asha was certain Kenneth was not working on a deal with the Chinese military. The situation had to mean these people were trying to hack her husband's company. She checked that *Abbot* was recording everything she was doing into her permanent archive. *What should I do*, she wondered?

She didn't want to investigate too closely since if she were discovered, it might make the situation worse. But she couldn't ignore what was happening either. At the very least, she should let her husband know what was happening. She rang his cell phone.

"Hello?" he answered.

"It's me," she said.

"Asha? I'll be right there. Just another five minutes."

It had already been almost an hour. *So, he is that kind of husband*, she thought.

"That's not why I'm calling. Are you near a TV?"

"Huh? Yeah. I'm in my office."

Asha found his television through the building's cable TV connection, and switched on the power, setting the tuner to a dead channel.

She said, "I'm showing you a security camera shot of the people who are hacking through your corporate firewall. Can you see it?"

"Yeah, they look military. Is that the Chinese Army?"

"That's right. You want me to stop them?"

"If you can. Where are you?"

"In the Internet."

"I mean here, in the building. I'll come to you."

"Oh, I'm downstairs in the lobby. But wait; first I'm going to show you the monitor of their main server. I can get into it, but I don't know what to do. Here it comes. Do you see it?"

Asha heard Santos's voice in the background asking what was going on.

"I'm putting you on speakerphone," Ken said, while quickly explaining the situation to his COO.

"How is she doing that?" Santos asked.

"Hello!" Asha said, amplifying the electronic signal of her digital voice. "Can we focus? What should I do?"

"Sorry," Ken said. "Check that out, Ron. They left a command window open. She's got a C prompt."

"Kill the server," Santos said. "Looks like an old Windows version. Probably NT."

"Asha," Ken said. "Can you type into that window you're showing me?"

"Yes. But I don't know what to put in."

"Okay, type this: r d, space, c, colon, backslash, space, forward slash, the letter s, space, forward slash again, the letter q, and then press the Enter key."

Asha mentally typed to the server as he read the instructions. The first time she got an error message, but the second time a scroll began on the screen. When it stopped, Ken asked, "Can you move the mouse on that thing?"

"Sure. What for?"

"I want to force a reboot."

"How do I do that?"

"Click the lower left Start button, select the Power option and then Restart."

She did as he said and changed Ken's view back to the eighth floor. Within seconds, the men in the scene rapidly became unglued, shouting at each other with alarm.

"Good job, Mrs. Riddle," Santos said. "I wonder if they have a backup server. Is there a way you can find out? What about the workstations? Could you find out what they were looking for? Or maybe you could cut off their power?"

"I'll check," Asha said. "Thanks, guys." She broke the connection to Ken's office so she could evaluate the Chinese reaction without Santos running commentary.

She had *Abbot* input Ken's list of keystrokes on all the computers in the building and then searched the outside where she found a digital pathway to a nearby power station. There she found another camera showing a dozen employees sitting at workstations in front of a giant screen. The video display was a live schematic of the local electrical grid.

Asha repeated her sabotage on every computer in the facility. In the process, she lost the feed from both the control room and the Chinese military's operations center.

She had to go into a search mode to get her bearings, but it was as though the digital world around the metropolitan area had ceased to exist. It took several minutes, but finally, she found an exterior security camera at the top of a skyscraper outside the main downtown area.

The outside view reminded her that although it was only a few minutes after ten in the morning Chicago time, in Shanghai, it was after midnight. Asha realized with a shock that a massive swath of the Shanghai community was blacked out.

Uh oh, she thought. That was more damage than she meant to inflict. *Would they know I'm the one who did that?* She hadn't really considered the possible ripple effect of taking a regional power station off-line without giving anyone advance notice.

Shanghai was the second most populated city in the world. A lot of people over there would be pissed.

Someone tapped her on the shoulder and she almost jumped out of her skin. It was Ron Santos.

"I think you better come with me," he said worriedly. "Ken's not looking so good. I called an ambulance."

All thoughts of Chinese hackers vanished from Asha's mind and she followed Santos, worried sick she would find Ken suffering from some type of post-coma syndrome. Instead, she found him sitting in an overstuffed arm chair outside his office while a secretary hovered nearby with a bottle of water.

"I may have overdone it," he said to Asha.

Asha sat beside him and took his pulse. He was pale and sweaty. She thought it might be a heart attack.

"When will the ambulance be here?" she asked Santos.

"A couple of minutes," he replied worriedly. "Security will meet them in the lobby and bring them up here."

"I'm fine, honest," Ken said calmly. "Asha, that was a good job, stopping that hack," he added quietly. "I didn't realize you had that much ability."

"Me either," she replied. "But let's not worry about that, I'm more concerned about you."

His color was already improving. He might not be having a medical emergency, but she still wanted him to go to the hospital.

As an afterthought, Asha whispered, "I might have caused a few problems in Shanghai."

"How so?"

"I created a blackout. I'm not sure how big."

"Can they backtrack it to you?"

Asha shrugged. "I don't think so, but I have no idea about how that stuff really works. For me, this is all magic."

Ken shook his head. "They started it. But if anyone asks, don't admit to anything."

The ambulance crew arrived and took charge. Ken didn't want to be wheeled out on a stretcher, but Asha overruled him and ordered the medics to ignore his protests as they took him toward the elevator.

"Are you going with them?" Santos asked.

"Yes, but at some point, I'll need a driver to get home."

"I'll get one for you on standby. That kind of scared me. Is he going to be okay?"

"He'd better be, Mr. Operations Chief," Asha said threateningly. "For your sake."

* * * *

City of Pudong, near Shanghai, China

Major Wong told himself to cool down after mercilessly chewing poor Captain Zheng's ass almost completely off.

"You can't even keep power on in this building?" Wong had shouted before forcing himself to silence. He needed to hear Zheng's response, if for no other reason to have something to put in the official report that Wong would file on his return.

"Please give me one minute," Zheng begged. "The backup generators will come on any second." As he spoke, a diesel engine cranked up in the background, and the lights flickered back to life.

"You'd better pray you didn't leave any traces before we lost power," Wong warned.

Zheng leaned over the squad leader, and murmured, "What happened right before the power went out?"

"I think the server crashed and took down my workstation. Here it comes; I rebooted."

The BIOS flashed on the technician's workstation, but then the monitor changed straight to a solid blue screen. In two hundred-point font, it showed a typed colon and an open parenthesis—the universal frown face—above an error message.

"Uh, oh," the man said. "Want me to reboot again?"

"Quickly," Zheng growled.

Wong stared at the screen over Zheng's shoulder and felt his heart skip a beat. There was no use in getting angry at this point. "It's been a while since I've seen a Blue Screen of Death," he said in a dry voice.

A worried buzz from other workstations got his attention.

Zheng moved from one position to another, looking more grim-faced at each one. "They're all dead," he said to Wong.

"Take me to the server room," Wong ordered.

Zheng gestured to one of his troops to lead the way. When they opened the door on the second floor, Wong's heart sank. All the monitors were showing various versions of Microsoft's infamous fatal stop-error.

"This one isn't on you, Captain Zheng," Wong said stoically. "We drastically underestimated what's going on at Riddle Systems. I'm not sure what they're doing, but it's a lot more than making cameras."

"We had all of our security in place, Major," Zheng said.

"I know. I saw it myself. And they waltzed right through it. Do you have any logs?"

Zheng looked around the server room. "Not anymore. We'll check, but it looks like they took out every single machine."

"Put together the best report you can, Captain. I want the first draft by tomorrow morning. It appears we have a new project to work on. I fear we just saw an example of America's new cyberwarfare program."

* * * *

Saint Bernadette's Hospital

The hospital insisted on readmitting Ken, and Asha backed them up, forcing him to go along. Asha was not surprised when Cody strolled into Ken's hospital room within the first hour.

"What's the story?" he asked.

"He tried to do too much," Asha said. "He promised we would only drop in to say hello, but we were there for about three hours."

"He was supposed to stay at home for the rest of the week!" Cody said.

That was news to Asha. "Thanks for letting me know!" she snapped at him.

"Knock it off," Ken ordered. "You two fighting doesn't help. It was my fault. More to the point, Cody, did you hear about the attempted hack by the Chinese?"

Cody was surprised. "This is the first I've heard of it. Who told you? Adam?"

"Who's Adam?" Asha asked.

"Our CIO," Ken said. "And no, I doubt he even knows. Asha told me. We haven't really had a chance to talk about it, as far as that goes. I was waiting for you to get here."

"Asha told you?" Cody asked. "How did she find out about it? She can't even dial a phone number." His cell phone vibrated and he said, "Hang on." There wasn't a sender ID, but the text said, *Yes, I can.* He gave the phone a puzzled glance and stuck it back in his pocket.

Ken told Asha, "You may as well bring him into the loop. Especially if you caused some damage overseas."

"Are you sure?" Asha asked.

"He's our attorney. You may have broken a few laws, so he needs to be aware of what's going on. Why don't you ask Raphael to come over too? He can fill in the gaps."

"He's on the way," Asha replied. "I already called him and he'll be here in five minutes."

A nurse came into the room and told Cody and Asha they had to leave; visiting hours were not for another thirty minutes. Cody tried to argue, but the woman was resolute.

The hospital intercom bonged, and a female voice said, "Audrea Cline, please come to the personnel office immediately."

"Oh, that's me," the nurse said. She gave Cody a frustrated look and told him again they had to leave before she hurried out.

Cody watched her leave the room and said to Asha, "That was weird. Did you notice that sounded like your voice on the intercom?"

"You're right, it did," Asha said. "That's interesting. I'll be more careful next time."

"What are you talking about?" Cody asked Ken. "What's going on here?"

"Take a seat," Ken replied. "We'll wait for Raphael; he can probably describe it more clearly than either of us."

* * * *

"Any questions?" Raphael asked of Cody after explaining Asha's situation.

"So, her new eye is like a Web browser?"

Raphael sighed and shook his head. "I would say it's more than that, but I'm not sure to what extent. It appears that a portion of her brain has become digital."

"I thought everyone's brain was digital," Cody said.

"Not really."

"Why not? A neuron either fires or it doesn't. Isn't that right?"

"Yes, but neuronal responses operate in a stream. I guess I'm saying that yes, some parts of our brain do seem to include digital components, but even the representation of color, which we often think of in an RGB twenty-four-bit reference, is not processed digitally by the brain; at least until now."

"You already lost me, Doc," Cody said.

"Okay. Let me put it another way. As you know, Asha lost a significant quantity of her memory."

"That part I got."

"Well, shortly after that, we introduced a new data stream into her mind that was entirely digital. That's the theory behind our ForSight device. Her mental processes adapted to that input. But the first time I connected my laptop to her eye, it appears that her brain simultaneously reached out for information on how to operate in the new environment."

"What's that mean? Are you saying she has Windows OS in her head? That doesn't sound too good."

"No. I'm saying that navigating through an IP network is now as natural as breathing to her. We don't think about how our vision works; it just does. She doesn't have to think about browsing through the Internet, her mind just does. And from what I see now, her brain is still learning." Raphael turned to Asha. "When you spoke to me earlier on the phone, you weren't using a phone, were you?"

"No," Asha replied. "It was more like…here, I'll show you."

Raphael's cell phone rang. He answered and put it on speakerphone. "I take it this call is from you," he said to the phone.

"That's correct," her voice replied, and yet Asha herself did not say a word aloud. "Voice calls are digital, so I simply handle my conversation with you through the network."

"Holy crap!" Cody said, astounded by the demonstration. "That is freaking insane."

His cell phone vibrated. The text message was, *I don't like being called a freak.*

Cody's eyes got big as he looked back and forth between his phone and Asha's angry countenance. His expression grew more somber. "I apologize, Mrs. Riddle. That was a careless remark and not my intention."

"Then be a little more circumspect," Asha replied verbally in an irritated tone. "I'm pretty sensitive about all this. Anyway, that's how I spotted the attempted hack. I was waiting for Ken to finish his meeting and saw the Chinese trying to break through."

"You saw them?" Ken asked.

"That's right. The first time Raphael explained the Internet to me, he called it a superhighway. I actually saw trucks and cars. Initially, all the data came across in my mind in that sort of theme."

"That must be confusing," Cody said.

"It's not like that now. These days, mostly I only see labels and numbers, but I still get a vehicle now and then. I save all this stuff to my cloud account, so I can review it later." The wide-screen TV on the wall suddenly came to life. "I'll show you what happened in China."

* * * *

After replaying the Chinese security cameras on the television, Asha paused the playback so the three men could see that it really was the city of Shanghai they were looking at. The cityscape was identifiable by the colorful Oriental Pearl spire and the Shanghai World Financial Center.

"That tall blacked-out building is the Shanghai Tower," she explained. "I didn't mean to shut it down; I was only trying to stop the hack."

"As long as they can't prove it was you," Cody said slowly, "I'm not too concerned about Shanghai. But this is pretty amazing stuff. I think the bigger issue here is national security. I'm not sure how it all fits together."

"That's a concern as well," Ken said.

The comment surprised Asha. She hadn't really thought of her ability in that way. But then, her focus had been pretty narrow lately. Get acquainted—well, get *reacquainted* with her husband—and that was about it. National security issues didn't even make the list.

"I disagree completely," she said.

"How so?" Cody asked.

"The only question here is Ken's health. You just said the Chinese are not a concern, so good enough; we can forget about them. Thanks for dropping by. You too, Raphael. We can catch up some other time."

"Wait a second," Cody protested.

"Nope. Time to go." Asha grabbed the surprised Raphael by his lapels and propelled him toward the door, forcing Cody to retreat in the same direction. "If you want to talk to my husband, you can make an appointment with his secretary." She glanced at Ken. "What is her name?"

"Lenora."

Asha nodded and said, "Call Lenora, and maybe she can work you in. Have a pleasant evening." She forced them out of the hospital room and closed the door firmly in their astonished faces.

"I'm not that sick," Ken said from his bed. He was not amused by her assertiveness.

"You're not that well, either. Like you said, you pushed yourself too much. We are going to listen to the doctor's advice and do what he says. And I can guarantee that you're not going back to the office today or for the rest of the week. I'm upset no one told me about that restriction."

Chapter 5 – The Divorce

Two days later, Asha sat stiffly on a stool in Raphael's lab as he checked out her eye.

"Are you okay?" he asked. "You seem pretty tense."

Asha bit off a sharp retort of, *I'm fine!* The last forty-eight hours with Ken had been rough. He was still in the hospital, and it had pissed him off the way she had taken charge of his life by backing up the doctors. He had started sniping at her and her patience was wearing thin.

It was a relief to get out of the place and visit with Raphael. He was one of the good guys. His attitude was always upbeat, and she loved him for it. He had restored her sight and then some. Impulsively she gave him a hug. "I'm fine," she said sincerely. "I have good days and bad days. Today is a little on the downside."

"Well, cheer up. Your eye looks good to me. Any headaches?"

"Not from the eye."

"What about your Web browsing? Is that causing any problems? Any changes there?"

"If anything, I'm getting better. I developed a bot to help me keep track of all the material I go through."

"A bot?"

"Yeah. I learned about them the other day when I talked to the IT guys. They use what they call *artificially intelligent* robots, but truthfully, I didn't really see a lot of smarts in them. The ones I made are much better and they can operate independently."

Raphael was puzzled. "You set these up in your head?"

"No, I rented storage space online. I have a cloud account."

"You mentioned that the other day, and I wondered what you meant. So, you have your own server?"

"That's right. It's in some big data center in Ohio, so I can't actually show it to you. Too bad, really; I'd like to get your thoughts on it."

"What type of server? Who is it with?"

"Don't ask me those kinds of details. All I know it has an Indian name—Apache—and it runs on something called an AWS edge server. Does that make sense?"

"It does. You're renting from Amazon. They do a lot of cloud services."

Asha shrugged. "To me, it is a kind of garage where I can store my AI bot. I call it *Abbot.*" Her expression brightened. "Do you have a server? Maybe I could copy it over."

"I would love to see it. I have a spare Apache server right here."

"Let me check." She peered into his network and found a familiar parking garage that was empty inside. "Did you name it *myapache38*?"

"That's it!"

"I named mine *myhelper.*"

"Good enough," Raphael said. "I'm not an administrator per se, so I tend to go with defaults. I'm more into the programming side, but compared to Ken's skills, that's not saying a lot. Will my server here work for you?"

"Yeah, I think so. Let me try to create an *Abbot* for you. I'm not sure how you would use it, though. I talk to mine mentally. Let me see if I can add in a way for you to communicate." Asha closed her eyes in concentration.

"You're developing code? In what language?"

Asha shook her head without opening her eyes. "I'm not a programmer. I wouldn't have any idea where to start. I just sort of put my thoughts out there to establish a presence. This will be a little different, though, since we want it to talk." She looked up at Raphael. "I think you'll need a mic and speakers."

"I can do that."

Raphael retrieved the necessary accessories from a storage cabinet and plugged them into the server. "Does that work?"

"We'll find out in a moment. I don't really hear sounds when I'm on the Net. I'm going to give her a female voice so it will be different from *Abbot.*"

"Anything will do."

After several minutes Asha nodded with satisfaction. "All done. I named her *Abby*. Say hello, *Abby*. This is Raphael."

"Hello, Raphael," Asha's voice replied from the server.

"*Abby*," Asha said. "You sound too much like me. Can you change that a little?"

"Is this better?" a different voice answered. It was slightly lower in pitch but still definitely female.

"That will work," Asha said. She turned to Raphael and gestured toward the server rack. "To use *Abbot*, I simply tell him what I want, and he starts working. I trained him to put the results of my web research in the cloud library I created. You can tell *Abby* what you want, and where to store the answers. Give it a try."

"Seriously?" Raphael replied astonished. "It took you thirty minutes to create an intelligent AI? One with programmable parameters that can be changed through voice input? That is incredible! It took IBM ten years and a team of engineers to achieve that goal."

"You're the scientist here, Doctor," Asha said with a smile. "All I try to do is make sense out of what you stuck in my head."

Raphael stood in front of the server rack and typed in several commands. Each time a list of words flew past on the monitor too fast for Asha to read.

"What are you doing?" she asked.

"I wanted to see a listing of the services the computer is running, but none of this is making sense."

"I'm not surprised," Asha said. "It wouldn't make sense to me either. If you have a question about something, just ask her."

Raphael gave Asha a puzzled glance and said, "Okay. *Abby*, what program are you running?"

"I am the program. Do you have any other queries?"

"Forget all that stuff," Asha told Raphael. "*Abby*, what was the score of the Cubs game last night?"

"New York beat the Cubs fourteen to two."

"That is insane," Raphael said.

"Not really," Asha countered. "Everyone says the Met's new pitcher is practically unhittable."

Raphael snorted at her comment. "That's not what I meant."

"I know," Asha acknowledged with an impish smile. "My point is, if you want to know something, you won't find it there." Asha pointed at the monitor. "With *Abby*, you just ask. If it's really complicated, simply explain what you are trying to accomplish until she understands. *Abby*, if you run into a problem, contact me through *Abbot*, and we'll sort it out."

"Acknowledged."

"I've got to go now. Kenneth is coming home from the hospital today, and I should probably prepare a nice dinner to put him in a good mood. Talk to you later."

* * * *

"I'm glad you didn't have to stay another night," Asha said as she and Ken entered their apartment.

"I'd be glad to never see the place again."

"Nice try, my love. Except that I have a list of your medical appointments this time, and I promise you will be there for all of them. Go change, and I'll make dinner."

Ken came to a jarring halt. "Listen! You can stop with the nagging, all right? I understand you're trying to sound like a real wife, but it should be pretty obvious by now it doesn't mean a thing, at least not to me."

Asha flinched at his sharp outburst. He might as well have slapped her face. Her upbeat mood for his homecoming vanished and all the good will drained out of her body.

She glared back at him with a face like ice. "I didn't realize good manners were such a burden."

Ken rolled his eyes and headed for the hallway.

Asha marched into the kitchen, her meal plan for the night no longer a consideration. She was not in the mood to cook him anything, let alone a fancy dinner.

Instead, she pulled some sandwich items out of the fridge. As she placed the ingredients on the table, she tried to brighten her frame of mind but failed.

Ken came into the room and took a seat at the table. She sat across from him, waiting for him to start the conversation. At the moment, she felt no inclination to talk to him at all, let alone begin a friendly tête-à-tête.

Suddenly she was very tired of his constant insinuations that she was not really his wife. If he wasn't going to make an effort, then perhaps she needed to rethink. She had wanted to take care of him until his memory of their wedding returned in the hope they could then get on with their married life. But maybe those particular memories were like hers; maybe they weren't coming back.

She had already come to the conclusion that, in spite of Christina's constant reassurances, her own past life was gone forever. The realization dawned that her future might not be in this apartment.

I honestly tried to make it work, Asha thought. Her sole focus had been preparing for a life together with her husband, this Ken doll, who had consistently denied their relationship.

But there was another option. Instead of becoming a subservient Barbie figure, moving out might be a better idea.

What would such a transition mean? At the very least, she should start out as she meant to go on. On the plus side, if her so-called marriage wasn't going to work, she wouldn't walk away poor. Like Cody said, her husband didn't have a prenup. This might be a good time to follow the lawyer's previous advice and seek out an attorney who had a good track record in the local divorce court.

"You know…" they both said at the same time.

"You first," Ken said.

"No," Asha countered brusquely. "Go ahead. Say something else to make me feel bad. I'm getting used to it."

He looked a little chagrined. "I guess I should say, just because I don't remember something happening, that doesn't necessarily mean it didn't happen."

Asha leaned back in her chair and crossed her arms. "What a strange theory, especially coming from you."

"I'm sorry," he added.

"For what?" she prompted him, wondering if it was a real apology or merely empty words.

Ken shrugged. "I guess for a lot of things. I'm sitting here watching you get angrier by the second, and it occurs to me I've been treating you pretty badly."

"That's an understatement."

"Let me put it all on the table."

"You've been doing that since you first opened your eyes."

"Fair enough," he admitted. "But I should walk through it with you. I want you to see my point and I want to understand yours."

"All right. Go ahead."

"First, I'm being honest about my memory. And I'm not questioning your memories or your feelings."

"Keep talking," she said. His half-hearted attempts to suddenly be polite were now just irritating.

"I honestly don't think we're married."

Asha leaned forward and stated acerbically, "Strangely enough, I already got that part."

"But I also hear everyone else telling me that we *are* married and obviously, you believe it too."

"I did," Asha agreed, "but to be perfectly honest, now I'm having doubts. Your attitude is infectious."

"My point is you and I are not strangers. You saved my life, and in doing so, you gave up a lot. And as Cody has reminded me, on paper at least, we have a legally binding marriage."

"Ah. So, you're stuck with me? Is that what you mean?"

"No. I mean that I have no intention of challenging the current situation. To the rest of the world, we are married so I should give you a chance. That's what I'm saying. I'll quit being a jerk and let you be my wife. It's the least I could do."

It was not exactly a proclamation of undying love.

"Well, *thank you*," she replied in a sarcastic tone. "In that case, I'll think about letting *you* be my husband."

Asha got up and left the table, afraid of continuing the conversation. His so-called offer of a truce, if that's what it was, only aggravated her anger. That night, in the spare bedroom, she tossed and turned, wondering what tomorrow would bring. It didn't seem like it could get any worse.

* * * *

Asha woke up in a slightly better mood and cleared her mind of any lingering resentment from the evening before. Ken was still asleep, so with her normal optimism reasserted, she prepared a nice breakfast of scrambled eggs, hash browns, and bacon. She had just pulled a pan of biscuits out of the oven when Ken came in. He was dressed for work.

"You're supposed to stay home today," she said cautiously. His overt resistance to the doctor's orders gently fanned the embers of last night's irritation back to life.

"I have to talk to some people about damage control for your little stunt yesterday." His statement held no warmth or friendliness, only an assertive declaration, almost daring her to counter.

The last dregs of her good mood vanished.

"My little stunt? You mean when I saved your company from being wiped out by the Chinese?" *So much for optimism*, she thought. She dumped the biscuits, pan and all, into the trash. "Suit yourself," she said icily.

Ken looked startled for just a second and then said, "Sorry. That came out wrong. I, uh…" He started to say something more, but then turned and walked out of the apartment.

For the next hour, Asha told herself a dozen times she shouldn't have reacted so strongly. The flash of embarrassment on his face was proof that he regretted his harsh words. And Christina had told her many times to be patient. Two months was a long coma and personality hiccups were to be expected.

She took care of some housekeeping while a thousand variations of what she could have said ran through her mind. At loose ends, she put on a coat and went downstairs, but outside a freezing rain was pouring down. Chicago's infamous wind was piercingly cold this morning. The doorman offered to call for a driver, but she shook her head.

In the boutique coffee shop next door, she purchased a mocha and an autumn-theme-shaped cookie and took them back to the apartment.

Once inside, she settled in a chair and decided to review some of her NIH material on recovery complications for comatose patients. But the subject matter was difficult reading and her heart wasn't in it. It was almost noon when she gave up.

One important point was clear in all the literature. Ken was a recovering patient, and she was treating him too harshly. He was not a bad person. Everyone she had met thought of him as warm and fun-loving. The fact was, her husband needed time to reestablish a secure frame of mind in this new relationship.

She decided that that evening, no matter what he said, she would cook him a nice meal...and refrain from throwing it away. She suddenly wondered if he might come home in time for lunch.

She placed a mental call to his cell phone, but Lenora answered.

"Mr. Riddle's phone; may I help you?"

"Hi, Lenora. This is Asha. Is Ken handy?"

"Hello, Mrs. Riddle. No. He left with Mr. Anderson about thirty minutes ago. I believe they are in the building. Would you like me to page him?"

"No, I'll look for him. Thank you, Lenora."

Asha closed her eyes and entered the Internet. In six hops she reached the corporate firewalls and two more got her inside the security office control room. She ran through the closed-circuit television cameras until she spotted Ken. He and Cody were on the fourth floor headed toward the elevator. She had hoped they would be near a phone so she could call him directly. She didn't want to call Cody's cell phone; it would be too much like asking for permission to speak with her husband.

While the two men walked down the corridor, the security camera microphones picked up their voices. Cody was talking.

"She was that angry?" he asked.

Ken nodded. "About to explode. First time I've seen her like that."

"What did you do to piss her off so much?" Cody wanted to know. "Asha is a pretty calm woman."

"I made a nasty comment about her pretending to act like a real wife."

Cody shook his head. "You gotta stop that, dude. She is your real wife. No wonder she got mad."

"Yeah, but she's not. I remember meeting her now. I have for a couple of days; I'm just not sure how to tell her."

"What do you mean, you remember? The trip to Vegas?"

"It was at the airport after I got back. That was the first time I laid eyes on her.

"What are you talking about? You didn't go to Vegas?"

"No. I went and I had just gotten back from the flight. I took the wrong turn out of the parking lot and wound up in front of the terminal."

"You're supposed to stay on the main road."

"Yeah, thanks. Anyway, I was in the Arrivals lane and it was jam-packed. I was stuck behind a line of cars and she opened the door and got in next to me. She must have thought I was an Uber driver!"

"Seriously? You didn't tell her you weren't?"

"She was bawling her eyes out."

"What?"

"Yeah. The cars behind me were honking like crazy, so I started driving. I should have dropped her at the taxi stand, but you have to go all the way around again."

"Are you shitting me? Where were you taking her?"

"I don't remember. But that's when we got T-boned by that truck."

"You're a freaking idiot."

"That's what happened. I was in the wrong place at the wrong time. She was too."

"Then why did you go to Vegas?" Cody asked.

"To make everyone think I got married. But I went by myself. The whole marriage thing was a sham."

"It wasn't!" Cody insisted. "I have the marriage certificate. I ordered a copy when Erica started causing trouble!"

Ken made shushing noises. "You're not listening. I pulled the name Asha out of the air before I ever left because you needed a name to change my will. So that's what I put on the marriage license. I don't remember much of the trip because I was pretty drunk."

"You were celebrating your wedding!" Cody insisted.

"No, I'm telling you. I remember paying for one of those keepsake certificates from the wedding chapel and putting it in my suitcase. But nothing else happened."

"You came back alone?" Cody asked.

"What else? Like I said, I was drunk. Actually, I have no idea how I got to the airport, and I was completely hungover on the flight back."

The explanation was not pacifying Cody's anger. "Why would you even pull a stunt like that?"

"Because of Aunt Erica. She's nuts, and you're the one who said so. You talked about the possibility of her trying something off-the-wall and I got a bad vibe about it. I thought if I had a wife and a new will, it might put her off. That's why I said you could tell people I was getting married."

Cody came to a stop and massaged his forehead. "Ken, that's fraud." He suddenly looked panicked. "And I took it to court! Oh, man. Now you've gotten me involved."

"Relax," Ken said. "It's no big deal. Asha is here, she already thinks she's my wife, so we let her play the part."

"But what about that? Who is she?"

"I have no idea who she really is, but she's not my wife. I may not remember everything, but that much is certain. The first time I saw her was when she got into the car *after* I got back from Vegas."

The two men resumed their march toward the elevator. The narrative chilled Asha to the bone, but she continued to follow them from one security camera to the next. Cody appeared to be in deep thought. He pushed the elevator button while they waited and said, "So you're *not* really married."

"That's what I've been saying."

"Then what are you going to do?"

"I don't know. That's why I wanted to talk to you."

"You can't just throw her out, man. I mean, you could, but that's cold. Even for you."

"Tell me about it. Last night after she blew up, she slept in the spare bedroom. The more I think about it, the guiltier I feel. I told her she could stick around, and we'd see if the marriage worked, but she doesn't know the real story."

"Jesus!" Cody exclaimed in exasperation. "Jesus, man!"

"Keep it down," Ken warned as the elevator door opened.

Asha switched to the camera inside the car. Ken pushed the button for the ground floor.

"You can't do that, man," Cody said. "Don't forget, she really does have amnesia. You can't take advantage of her like that. It would be like kidnapping or something. We have to find out her real name and you have to be honest with her."

"That's your department. It's why I told you to check into her background."

"Yeah, but I didn't know all this! It would have helped if you had been honest with me."

"I was in a coma," Ken said dryly.

"I'm talking about before you ever left, you idiot!"

"It's a little late for that. Right now, I'm stuck with our cyclops lady. At least until you sort it all out."

"Me? Why is it always me that—"

The elevator dinged, and the men walked out into the lobby and headed toward the cafeteria. With their backs to the camera, they were too far away to pick up their conversation. But Asha had already stopped listening. She had practically stopped breathing.

She cut off her Internet connection and took a shaky breath.

"That puts a different slant on things," she said aloud to the empty living room.

Surprisingly, there were no doubts in her mind about the next step. The only question was how, not when. The answer to when was this very instant. She could not remain in the apartment for another second. Well, maybe long enough to pack a suitcase; that took less than ten minutes.

Now what? She looked in her purse. A credit card with the name Asha Riddle and an unused checkbook for their joint account. As much as she hated to, those would have to stay with her. Until she could get on her feet, she would need money to live. She had no compunction about using her husband's wealth...her former husband, actually. But then, that wasn't true either. It was just as he had said; they had never been married.

It didn't matter. It wouldn't take long for her to reestablish herself, not with her newfound ability. Of course, she had Ken to thank for that too. And apart from any other consideration, she would not give up her vision. One way or another, it appeared she would be linked to Kenneth for the rest of her life.

Before leaving the apartment, she stopped to write a note. There was no harm in being polite.

Dear Kenneth,
I honestly didn't mean to snoop, but I was trying to find you at the office and overheard your discussion with Cody about our first meeting. I guess you were right. Goodbye.
Cyclops

She put the note on the dining table where they had shared only one meal in their almost-married life. Then she walked out the door.

Somewhere, not long ago, she had seen a notice for an apartment available for rent. She had to track that down.

* * * *

Ken slumped in his office chair and gazed out the window. It was five minutes after ten in the morning and the drizzly skies reflected his own mood. For the hundredth time he read Asha's message.

The night before, he had taken a small bouquet of flowers back to the apartment as a peace offering when he found the note. He had actually been looking forward to making up with Asha.

Cody came in with a disgusted expression and sat in the leather chair in front of his desk.

"You look like shit, man," Cody said.

"I feel like it," Ken replied. "I spent all night looking for her."

"I put a trace on her credit card. She has to have money to get by, and right now she doesn't have a cent. She's probably in a local hotel. We'll find her."

"Okay. But leave the card alone. Like you said, she needs the money, and I don't want to kick her while she's down." Ken rocked back in his chair and rubbed his eyes. "Crap! I feel so guilty about this, I can't believe it." He handed the note to Cody.

After reading it, Cody shook his head. "You own this, man. Whatever she does, you got it coming."

Lenora appeared in his office doorway. "Mr. Riddle, you have a visitor. He's not on your schedule."

"Who is it?"

"Mr. Bernard Stephenson of Hawley, Hepworth, and Kidwell. He said you would know what it is about."

"Uh oh," Cody said worriedly. "That didn't take long."

"What do you mean?" Ken asked.

"Bernard Stephenson is one of the best divorce attorneys in Chicago. Wow. I hoped it wouldn't get this ugly this fast. Lenora, put him in the little conference room." To Ken, he added, "Let me do the talking."

After introductions, Bernard settled his substantial bulk across from Ken and Cody. Stephenson was a big guy, both in height and girth, and his heavy jowls gave him a perpetual hangdog expression.

"Good morning, gentlemen," he said, placing his business card on the table. "As you probably suspect, I am here representing the individual known as Mrs. Asha Riddle."

"We assumed as much," Cody said.

"Do you have any problem with me referring to her by that name?"

"No," Ken said before Cody could argue. "What does she want?"

Stephenson opened his briefcase and pulled out a fat file folder. He made a production of setting it on the table and opening it to examine several pages before answering.

"To be left alone," he said. "I understand that last night, Mr. Riddle made inquiries as to her whereabouts until all hours. She would rather you terminate that harassment of your own volition, but if necessary, I shall obtain a restraining order."

"I was worried about her!" Ken growled.

Cody put his hand on Ken's arm and said, "Let me talk, buddy." To Stephenson, he said, "Fine. What else?"

"A onetime payment of one hundred thousand dollars."

"Seriously?" Cody asked. "That's chump change. That's all she wants in the divorce? We'll agree to that."

"Mrs. Riddle is not interested in a divorce. It is her understanding that the current situation between Mr. and Mrs. Riddle is advantageous to him in dealing with other family matters. She is willing to continue in that role if you wish, but she reserves the right to file for divorce at any time in the future. However, if it is *your* desire to divorce, she will grant that uncontested."

"That's it?" Cody's astonishment was profound.

"Not quite. She requires indefinite access to Doctor Raphael Acosta on an as-needed basis by either her or him, and you will cover any and all related expense. I take it that is for her *cyclops* condition, as I believe you called it."

"That's not a problem," Ken said. "And I didn't intend it as a term of disparagement. Tell her that. What else?"

"And that you pay my fee. Here is the retainer agreement."

Stephenson slid a page across to Cody. It was an upfront fee of twenty grand plus a thousand dollars an hour. Cody rolled his eyes, and exclaimed, "For one morning's work? There is no way—"

"That's fine," Ken said. "We'll cover that. What else?"

"That is all. I tried very hard to convince Mrs. Riddle that such generosity on her part was not warranted."

"I'm sure you did, you son-of-a—" Cody started, but Ken cut him off again.

"All right. Tell her I'm not interested in divorce either. Hang on, I'll write out the checks, one for your retainer, and one for her."

Stephenson waived off his offer. "She has her own checkbook on your joint account. But she wanted to make sure it would be good before she wrote it."

"It will be by noon. Tell her to take two hundred thousand, or better yet, three. I don't want her to run out of money. And for God's sake, tell her I'm sorry. Tell her to please come home."

"I shall pass on your message. I believe we are done, gentlemen. I must say, I am uncomfortable that Mrs. Riddle would not insist on a signed agreement, but she was adamant that a verbal promise was sufficient. You are very fortunate, Mr. Riddle."

"Tell her to come home!" Ken repeated.

"I shall," Stephenson said and left the office.

Cody glared at his CEO. "What is your problem, man? You're free of the woman. You look about ready to cry."

"I might," Ken replied. "I'm afraid I'll never see her again, and it makes me feel like the worst son-of-a-bitch in the entire world. How will she even get by?"

Chapter 6 – The FBI

Asha thanked the college intern who had escorted her from the federal building's security checkpoint and confirmed the name on the wall placard, *Sherman Foster, Room 429*. She stood in the doorway of a small office in the FBI's Chicago Field Office.

She had spent the last month getting used to her new status as a single woman. After she cashed the check for three hundred grand— after all, he had offered—it didn't take her long to get settled in a new apartment. Even though she had stayed in Chicago, she didn't believe her former husband could find her. And anyway, leaving the city was not practical. She had to stay near Raphael because of her eye.

Her most exciting decision, however, was how to use her unique skills to earn a living. That's why she was here to meet with the FBI.

"Are you Special Agent Foster?" Asha asked the man sitting behind the desk.

"That's me." Foster gave her an expectant look. He had a generally cheerful appearance. Not what Asha had expected from an FBI agent who had to deal with criminals all day long.

"They told me you could help," she said tentatively.

"I'll try. With what?"

"I have a question."

Foster sighed quietly and stood up. "Why don't you come in." He gestured to the wooden chair in front of his desk.

Asha sat down and looked around. The room looked like a government employee's office. A standard-issue photo of the president hung on the wall next to a couple of framed certificates. In the corner, a bookcase was stuffed with black binders, each one labeled with obscure regulations.

"What is your question, Miss...?"

"Asha," Asha replied. She hesitated for a second and added, "Smith."

A smile flickered briefly across Foster's lips.

"Very well, Miss Smith. How can I help?"

Asha unfolded an FBI wanted poster and put it on the desk. The offender's name was Irvin Moss; a white, middle-aged male, wanted for the murder of several people in a convenience store. Moss was described as five feet, ten inches tall, and approximately two hundred twenty pounds. He was mostly bald but had a fringe of gray hair, and an Abraham Lincoln-style beard, giving his face a distinctive appearance.

Asha pointed at the poster and said, "This says you will pay a reward of a hundred thousand dollars if I can tell you where he is."

"Sort of," Foster caveated. "It actually means that if you tell us, and we are able to arrest him, then yes; there is a reward."

"Smith isn't my real name," Asha confessed suddenly, looking a little embarrassed.

"Yes, ma'am. I sort of gathered that. People like to stay anonymous and that's okay."

"I recently separated from my husband, and I thought I could earn some money by helping you, but I don't want him to find out what I'm doing."

"It's not a problem," Foster said patiently. Then his eyes widened suspiciously, and he tapped the face on the wanted poster. "Are you this man's wife?"

"No, no," Asha said hurriedly. "Nothing like that. I just wondered how you could pay me if I want to stay anonymous."

"I'm sure we can work something out. Mrs. Smith, do you actually know where Irvin Moss is?"

"Yes."

"And are you going to tell me?"

Asha handed Foster a yellow sticky note. "This is my bank account information. I just opened it. Could you just deposit the money in there?"

"Mrs. Smith," Foster said, allowing his tone to become slightly impatient; new informants often needed a nudge. "Let's not get ahead of ourselves."

"He's at Jiffy Lube," she said quickly.

"Jiffy Lube? There must be thousands of them."

"He's at the one down the street. Just off South Western Avenue."

"You mean two blocks from here?" It sounded incredibly implausible. So much so that it might be true.

"That's it," Asha confirmed. "Next to Enterprise Rent-a-Car."

"You sure about this?" Foster's expression was both hopeful and disbelieving.

"He pulled in about ten minutes ago," Asha said. She looked at the wall clock. "Maybe fifteen. I got held up downstairs by security."

"For crying out loud!" Foster exploded. "Hang on!" He picked up his phone and then slammed it down. "Wait here!" he ordered and ran from the room.

Asha waited nervously for fifteen minutes, but the excitable Agent Foster never returned. After another hour she left his office and exited the building. The security guards let her out but scolded her for not waiting on an escort; they didn't like visitors wandering around the federal building by themselves. She was appropriately apologetic.

Once outside, she decided she didn't like dealing with all the rules and regulations that the federal government insisted on. Perhaps this wasn't a good idea after all. A black cloud of frustration colored her mood until she returned safely to her new apartment.

That evening on TV, WMAQ news reported that the infamous Irvin Moss, who had been on the run for eight months, had been captured by agents of the Federal Bureau of Investigation. A spokesman said the arrest was thanks to an anonymous tip from a concerned citizen.

A week later, the special bank account that Asha had set up for Foster was still empty. She called up Stephenson to vent, but he simply advised patience and explained the government operated on their own schedule when it came to disbursements. He suggested she find other things to do to fill up her hours.

She liked Stephenson, but he was an expensive friend to have. The call cost her a thousand bucks in legal fees. It might be smarter to take his advice and turn her talents elsewhere. Like finding out who she really was.

* * * *

Beijing, China

Major Wong read through Lieutenant Soong's report about recent events in Chicago. It put a different slant on the potential gain if they could penetrate Riddle Systems. It also helped to get a glimpse of the opposition's capability.

"What is our confidence in this report?" he asked Lieutenant Soong.

Soong shrugged. "This is all HUMINT from Major Mao. He is a field agent who operates in Chicago. I don't have any history with him personally, but he has a reliable track record. I also found it interesting that Mr. Riddle separated from his wife."

"What happened there? Aren't they newlyweds?"

"Yes, sir. So far, there are no divorce filings, so it's difficult to say how serious the breakup is, especially since they are Americans. But the news caused a lot of gossip amongst the employees, and that's where Major Mao picked up the information. But the main point in the report is the excitement over Doctor Acosta's next-generation type of artificial intelligence. The word is they have developed an amazing AI working model."

"I see that," Wong said, scanning through the report. "I thought AI was not their primary area of investigation. I take it this is an offshoot of their military research. Have they stopped their work on medical technology?"

"We can't tell yet. But as you have said, Americans create breakthroughs more often by accident than on purpose."

"I hate to admit it, but that seems to be the case." Wong pointed to one of the paragraphs. "Mao believes the initial hack of their network may have simply been experimental. Do you buy that?"

Soong nodded. "A firm with that kind of expertise has enough sophistication to set up penetration tests on their own networks without causing damage."

"I suppose," Wong muttered thoughtfully. "Their AI work is obviously advanced if what I saw in Pudong is an example."

"That's true. Also, their attorney made a few inquiries about corporate liability after they attacked our Shanghai team. It's possible they didn't understand the capability of the new system."

"Who is our man in Chicago, again?"

"Major Mao. He's been undercover there for eight years."

"All right. Does Mao understand the extent of our interest in what he is dealing with there?"

"Not from that report," Soong replied. "He was simply following up on our general inquiries about Riddle Systems. To accomplish that he developed a couple of contacts. He is keeping well clear of any overt reconnaissance at the moment."

"A reasonable approach," Wong agreed. "But that time is past. Send a communique offering Mao assistance. Tell him you need details about Riddle's new AI technology. Make sure he understands this is being looked at by Joint Staff Headquarters and is not business as usual. If he can get us a copy of that software, I'll take it."

"I understand. I'll let him know."

"Also, have him find out more about Mr. Riddle. If he just split up with his wife, he could be open to new companionship. If the American needs a girl, make sure Mao arranges it."

Soong scribbled on her pad, capturing her boss's orders. She nodded after reviewing the notes and reached for the folder.

"I'll keep this for now," Wong said, holding onto it. "I need to go over it more carefully."

"I have to file it, sir. It's marked *No Distribution*."

"I see that, Lieutenant. I promise to bring it back to your desk within the hour. Until then, Mao is an excellent writer, and there is a lot of detail here I want to understand more fully. Dismissed."

* * * *

There I am, Asha thought, looking at the video recording. It was a clip from one of the airport's outdoor security cameras showing her jumping into Kenneth's car.

She was sitting in her new apartment. Unlike the last time, when she moved in, she didn't feel any urgency about redecorating. Not sure of her own tastes, she did it on her own, willing to experiment and enjoying the process in return.

She repainted all the rooms, opting for pastel colors ranging from a light sand hue to sunset peach. The carpeting had been replaced with real wood floors. The living room now had a white, camelback, Victorian sofa, edged with dark walnut. It was flanked on one side by an upholstered Queen Anne armchair, and on the other with an antique chair of uncertain provenance. A Chinese lacquer coffee table with delicate carving framing the oval top held a place of pride in front of the sofa.

Nothing matched, but the overall effect satisfied Asha. She added elegance and comfort with a mixture of handmade Turkish carpets. She had become moderately knowledgeable on the subject.

Her office, converted from the spare bedroom, was a different story. She didn't have a desk, or any bookcases piled high with documents. The walls were painted a dark blue, and the only piece of furniture was a single, giant-size Papasan chair lined with cushions. There she could curl up and focus on her journeys into cyberspace without distraction, as she was right now.

Once she accepted that Ken had told Cody the truth about their first meeting, she decided to search through the airport's CCTV recordings in an effort to discover her true identity.

Asha slipped past the airport's network security and found the archived video from the day of her accident. Assuming she had arrived at the airport on the same day Ken had returned from Vegas, she reviewed the recordings prior to the time she had jumped into his car. Based on the accident, it had to be about eleven-thirty in the morning. She scanned the area that he had described in front of the terminal building and found her image quicker than she had anticipated.

She scoffed upon discovering Ken had been driving a Honda Pilot. For heaven's sake, no wonder she thought he was an Uber driver.

She worked her way back through the terminal's recordings, painstakingly checking a variety of camera locations to track her movements. It didn't take long to find the secret of her past.

In one of the airport's many lounges, she found herself sitting across a cocktail table from an airline pilot. It was like watching characters in a cheaply made movie. They were having an argument; she was tearful. Asha could see it coming even if the girl in the video couldn't. Any second the pilot would break up with her…and then it happened. He took off his engagement ring and placed it on the tabletop.

The young woman pleaded to no avail. The pilot shook his head several times and finally stood up and walked away. It was sickening. Had she no pride at all back then? If that happened today, she would have decked the guy.

Asha marked the video clip for later review. Someday, she might want to find out who that pilot was and get even, but for now, she spotted something that could lead to her own real identity. Next to her purse on the table was a leather folder with a logo. She zoomed in and saw a domed building on a shield-like crest. A subtitle identified it as Rogers State University, Bartlesville, Oklahoma.

Oh please, God, don't let me be from Oklahoma.

She found the university's website and a quick search revealed the institution had two hundred and sixty-seven faculty members with about four thousand students. It seemed unlikely she was a student.

The university issued photo ID cards. Starting with Professor Lisa Aarons, Asha worked her way through the faculty directory. Halfway down, she found her face. The photo had to be a year or two old, but she recognized herself at once. The brown hair was cut a little shorter than now.

In the photo, she had two real eyes. She zoomed in and examined each one individually. She had to give Raphael credit. Without having a model to work from, her new eye was remarkably similar to the old one. Except for the scarring which gave her current face a slightly different appearance, it was her image on the ID.

Her real name was Kathlyn Huntingdon, an Oklahoma name to be proud of. Her address had been an apartment complex off Green County Road, in Bartlesville Oklahoma, which was about forty miles north of Tulsa. The apartments were near the Walmart Supercenter.

Asha spent several hours discovering what she could of her former life. She ordered a copy of her birth certificate, found her high school, and also her employment history. In fact, back in her teenage years, she had worked at that very Walmart.

Most recently she was a state employee, teaching Public Administration at the college, and had been working on an MBA. Her former life history seemed uninspiring. She found her parents. They were buried in the White Rose Cemetery, just a five-minute drive from her place of work.

Asha disconnected and sipped on a glass of wine to reflect on what she had learned. She had a past, one that not too long ago she had been desperate to know about. Now, just like everyone else, she had more than one life: first, being the daughter of two presumably loving parents; second, a professor and mentor for young people eager to get out on their own; and now, a cast-off wife from a not-quite husband who refused to acknowledge her existence.

When examined from that perspective, she decided to not judge her worth based on a mundane past. From here on, only the future mattered and how she prepared for it. She already had a goal; she wanted financial independence. It was time to give the FBI one more try.

* * * *

"Knock, knock."

Agent Foster looked up from his desk and smiled when he recognized his visitor. "Mrs. Smith! The young lady who is good for my career! Come in, please. Have a seat."

Once settled, Asha glared at him, but not too sternly. "I didn't get paid. Is there a problem?"

Foster shrugged, his expression a combination of amusement and guilt. "Yeah, sorry about that. These things can take time, and it's only been a couple of weeks. I'm having a little trouble with the higher-ups since all I had about you was an alias."

"And an account number," Asha reminded him.

Foster looked embarrassed. "Yeah, sorry. I lost the sticky note when we went after Moss. My fault. Would you mind meeting with my supervisor on this? He has a few questions for you."

"Rather than that," Asha countered, "why not have him speak to my attorney? I'm sure Bernard can answer any questions."

"Huh? Your attorney?"

She handed him a new piece of paper. "That's his contact information. His name is Bernard Stephenson and he's with Hawley, Hepworth, and Kidwell. I talked to him a week ago about your failure to pay, and he said I should be patient. He also helped me establish a legal entity with a tax ID. It's at the bottom of the page."

Foster glanced at the business name she had indicated. "Ladybug Investigation, Inc.?" he read aloud.

"That's it. Bernard said you would probably need the name of an actual payee since I already told you Smith wasn't my real name. Will that help?"

"I guess," Foster said, looking at the company name uncertainly. It was something his ex-wife might have come up with.

"So, how much longer until I get paid?"

Foster collected his thoughts and put on a more professional demeanor. "Mrs. Smith. Thank you for this new information. I shall pass it up the chain, but I can't really tell you how long before you receive a check because I just don't know. However, I promise you that I will keep pushing it from my end. You did give us the lead, and we did capture Moss. Fair's fair."

"Good enough," Asha said, looking satisfied. "In that case, I will put payment for Moss on the back burner for the time being. We have to move forward. Are you ready for another lead?"

"Another one?" Foster asked, surprised. "You mean someone else is at Jiffy Lube?"

"No," Asha replied with an apologetic expression. "I'm sorry, I did try to find someone in Chicago, but the individual in question is in New York. It's rather complicated."

"Complicated? How so?"

"Well, Mr. Moss just sort of fell into my lap at the last minute. My main focus at the time was this man." She put a new wanted poster on Foster's desk and pointed to the section labeled Reward. "This is for a million dollars, so I want to be clear about that."

Foster's heart hammered inside his chest, and it had nothing to do with the promised reward. The poster was for Hazaiah Al Sabbagh, one of the most dangerous terrorists on the FBI's wanted list. His crimes included conspiracy to use weapons of mass destruction, conspiracy to commit an act of terrorism transcending national boundaries, and many other offenses.

"You know where Hazaiah is?" he asked quietly. He could believe that she discovered Moss accidentally. But that she might accidentally know the whereabouts of Hazaiah stretched the bounds of credibility. It also begged the question of how she might actually have such information. Was she part of an illegal operation?

"I don't have his location right this second," Asha answered blithely, "but I can tell you where he works and lives, and I know where he'll be Thursday evening at seven o'clock because that's when he's scheduled to receive a shipment of fissile material from his associates."

"And where is that?"

"In New York…like I said."

"And you came by this information how?"

"I looked it up on the Internet."

Foster gave her a startled look and then he let out a long, "Ahh." His heart rate dropped markedly and he no longer considered Mrs.

Smith a potential terrorist insider. Instead, his opinion of her returned to what he had first thought; that she was a slightly offbeat character who had lucked out once. "Like, you did a Google search?" he asked, careful to keep any sarcasm out of his voice.

"Not exactly. That's why I said this case is more complicated." Asha opened her leather valise and pulled out several documents which she spread across Foster's desk. "I had these printed at FedEx a bit earlier because I don't have a printer at home. And it's nice since they have bigger paper. It helps to see what I'm talking about."

Foster tried to read the documents as Asha laid them out. They included street maps, printouts of Google Earth, and a few incredibly detailed satellite photos.

"This is in New York?" he asked.

"That's right," Asha continued. "See here, on this overview photo? This is a shipping container port on Staten Island. I've never been there. And here, close to it, is a junkyard. You can tell by all those cars piled up on each other. And look here along the side of the property, buried in that line of trees. See all those white semitrailer vans? They might appear empty, stacked up like that, but they're not. It's where Hazaiah and his team are working. And they're living in one of those apartments across the street."

"Mrs. Smith, this doesn't—"

"I guess you should call me Asha, now that we're working together."

"All right...Asha. This is interesting, but it doesn't mean Hazaiah is operating there. I'm not even sure if he's in the country."

"Oh, he's in the country," Asha said confidently. She pulled out another stack of photos. "Check out these pictures. I got them from reviewing a bunch of security cameras in that area. See? Here's one from a deli that they go to. Look. That's Hazaiah for sure."

"I guess," Foster said with a nod. The man's appearance certainly resembled the Egyptian-born terrorist.

"And this is a shot from another deli—they eat a lot of deli food. Here's one from an auto parts shop. This one is in a cell phone store. I don't have a cell phone, by the way. I can't get used to them."

"Is that so?" Foster replied obliquely.

He was losing his grip on objective skepticism in the face of all the photos she had of Hazaiah. It was not even a question; they were shots of the wanted terrorist unless the guy had a twin brother. But how the hell had she gotten all the information together? And had she really done it through the Internet?

"But here's what worries me," Asha said. "And this is why I came to you now instead of when I had more documentation." She pulled out more sheets of paper. They included screenshots of text messages, except they were written in Arabic. "I ran these through Google translate, and it looks an awful lot to me like he set up a meeting for Thursday night to accept a package—or a container of some sort—of nuclear material; I couldn't tell from the translation. Anyway, I thought I shouldn't wait any longer."

"I can see that," Foster said. His attitude had undergone another shift in perspective. The material was succinctly laid out. Setting aside his visitor's Miss Sunshine facade, this appeared to be an authentic package of intelligence about a known terrorist. He came to a decision. "Listen, Mrs. Smith. I need to bump this up the chain right now. Would you come with me to my supervisor's office?"

Asha instinctively leaned away from his desk.

Foster forced himself to throttle back. Informants often reacted negatively to such a request. People wanted to give their information to law enforcement and then step aside. If the FBI made an arrest, great; it meant a financial payoff for them. But getting too close created inconvenient questions, especially if the informant had obtained the evidence illegally, or worse, was involved in whatever activity they reported on.

"I don't think so," Asha said. She stood up to leave. "In fact, I just remembered I have another appointment. Here is some more background."

"Now wait a second, Mrs. Smith."

Asha pulled a sheaf of additional documents out of her valise and tossed them onto Foster's desktop. When he tried to keep them from sliding off onto the floor, she used the distraction to dart from his office and hurry down the corridor toward the elevators.

"Mrs. Smith!" his voice echoed after her. "Hang on!"

* * * *

Asha didn't wait for the elevator. She raced down the stairway to the lobby. At the front of the building, she didn't stop to get lectured, just slapped her visitor's badge onto the guard's desk, and kept going. A second later, she was on the sidewalk.

A cab approached, and she waved it down, then jumped into the rear seat. "City Hall, please," she said.

Halfway there, she got out and took the Red Line to Roosevelt Station, where she changed cabs twice more.

Much later, back in her apartment, she considered her random escape route. It seemed like she had covered her tracks. The FBI could not have tracked her zig zag through the city; at least, it didn't seem so. But still, she had to either get over her inherent distrust or seriously consider a new line of work.

Mostly, she didn't want Ken to find out where she lived or what she was doing. And the idea of contacting Christina for advice did not enter consideration.

I'm too paranoid to talk to a shrink, Asha thought. When she looked at it from that perspective, it couldn't be a good sign.

It didn't matter. For now, she would stay in the background. For the time being, she would continue to help law enforcement, at least on the present case. Foster had been impressed by her information, that much was obvious.

Her abilities were continuing to improve. And even though on a physical level she could not bring herself to handle a cell phone or a computer, the virtual world of the Internet had become one place she felt truly at home.

* * * *

New York City

It was Thursday afternoon, and Foster stayed out of the way in a corner of the FBI's mobile command post. Its outward appearance was that of a nondescript commercial truck. They had parked on a side street two blocks from the Staten Island junkyard that Asha had told him about.

The material she provided had been reviewed by his hierarchy and hastily sent through channels until it landed on the operations desk of the New York bureau. Foster, as the agent responsible for initiating the case, was present, but Erich Norton, a Senior Agent based out of the Federal Plaza building in Manhattan, was running the local op.

Foster was impressed by everything he saw. He hoped that if the operation had been handled in Chicago, his team could have done as well. They couldn't match the budget; the van, for instance, was stuffed with expensive electronics.

Norton's New York team had used micro-drones to confirm Asha's detailed information. Hazaiah had been positively identified.

As the afternoon progressed, other agents filtered into the neighborhood. A couple of guys in a beat-up car, a man and woman apartment hunting. And another van, larger than this one, with a fully kitted out assault team. Not to mention the attack helicopters across Newark Bay.

A man introduced as Gary Humphrey sat in front of the command center's main console. One of the display screens grabbed his attention. "Got a boat coming in," Humphrey said, adjusting the zoom on the camera lens. "It's a yacht. Looks like a fifty-footer with a sedan bridge." The sedan bridge he referred to was an upper-level helm position, built on top of the small-sized yacht.

Norton said, "Fishing charter by the look of it."

"Yeah," Humphrey replied, "But a normal charter would be going to the yacht club off to the west." The camera zoomed out. "Look. This guy is headed straight toward those dilapidated industrial docks."

"You think it's the courier," Norton speculated.

"Gotta be," Humphrey affirmed.

A discreet knock on the door admitted three men. Norton introduced them to those in the van as additional agents, called over from Jersey to assist. He gave the newcomers a quick briefing. After a few questions, Norton gave them location assignments for the final push. He wished them good luck as they left and returned his attention to the approaching yacht.

Seconds later, Foster's phone vibrated. It was a text with no name or number associated with it. He read the message and cursed aloud.

"What is it?" Norton asked.

Foster held up his phone, so Norton could read it. The text read, *A man twenty feet south of you just texted Hazaiah that you are coming.*

"Who's that from?" Norton asked.

"Probably my informant, but I'm not positive."

Norton scowled but Foster didn't flinch.

"Don't give me that look," Foster said. "The information she gave us is solid. You might want to follow up."

Foster cracked open the back door of the van. Twenty feet away, he saw Agent Burt Cole texting on his phone, his face filled with anxiety.

Norton closed the door and pointed at Foster and another man. "Back me up." He opened the door and stepped onto the pavement. When Cole looked over, Norton shouted, "Got a light?"

Cole hesitated for only a second before turning to run. The delay was all Norton needed to leap and bring the man down with a flying tackle. Cole tried to fling his cell phone toward a storm gutter, but Foster stomped on his forearm and the phone only skittered a few inches. In seconds Cole was subdued, and Norton had the man's phone.

"It's locked," Norton growled, looking at the screen.

Foster's phone vibrated again. He read the text message aloud. "*'Hazaiah is moving toward you at high speed.'*"

A white SUV sped by, and Foster got a brief glimpse of the terrorist behind the wheel. "That was him. Now what?"

"Hold this guy!" Norton shouted. He opened the door of the van and yelled, "We're blown! All agents move in now! Tell Blue Team that Hazaiah is coming their way in a white Suburban."

Foster cuffed the angry traitor and hauled him inside the van. Norton gave loud orders to Humphrey and another console operator who passed them on to the tactical groups over his radio.

Another text came in. Foster read aloud. "'Hazaiah just turned south on Lake Avenue.'" He looked at Norton and added, "I'm not from here. Where is that?"

Norton jabbed a map pinned to the wall. "He's headed toward Forest Avenue. From there either Bayonne Bridge or Two Seventy-Eight. I'm guessing the interstate. Gary, put a chopper on that!"

"Got it," Humphrey responded.

Foster read a new text. "She says, '*I can set up a roadblock on Forest Avenue. Where do you want it?*'"

Norton gave him an incredulous look. "Who the hell is that?"

Foster winced. "I'm pretty sure it's my source."

"Shots fired!" Humphrey shouted from the console.

Norton barked at Foster, "You take care of Hazaiah," and turned back to his main operation.

Foster looked at the map. He had no idea about the local neighborhoods where Hazaiah had headed. He texted a reply, *Someplace with as few civilians as possible.*

Okay, came the answer.

Norton hollered at the front partition, where the driver had opened a tiny sliding window. "Take us in close."

"You got it. Hang on!"

The truck lurched forward, and Foster grabbed a handhold by the back door. Cole tried to use the moment to break free, but Foster delivered a powerful gut punch, and Cole sank to his knees, gasping for breath.

Seconds later, the driver shouted, "We're there!"

Norton put a vest over his head and snapped at Foster. "You stay put!" and went out the back door. Sporadic gunfire erupted from the junkyard.

What a mess, Foster thought. The operation should have taken a minute tops, ideally without a shot being fired, a stun grenade at the most. He looked at his phone, but there were no new messages.

Humphrey, in front of the control center, listened to a radio transmission in his headset and glanced at Foster. "You said a white Suburban, right?"

"That's it!"

"Chopper One has a guy exiting a white Suburban at a traffic jam at Forest and Morrow."

"That has to be him." Foster examined the map. It was next to a self-storage rental center.

A new text came in. *Hazaiah has a rental contract for unit thirty-two.*

Foster repeated it aloud, and added, "He probably has an armory in there. Tell whoever is moving in to be careful."

* * * *

It took another hour before Norton declared the operation completed. There had been eight fatalities inside the semitrailer vans at the junkyard; thank God none of them were government agents.

Hazaiah had tried to escape his storage unit in an all-terrain-vehicle, and NYPD gunned him down fifteen feet from the garage door. They had received an anonymous tip of a potential armed terrorist at the storage rental location.

Norton congratulated his men and shook their hands one by one, but when he got to Foster, he glared and said, "I want to see you in my office before you leave the city."

"Understood," Foster replied, not looking forward to the ass-ripping he would get from the New York Division supervisor.

It was after ten in the evening by the time Norton expressed his anger about the unnamed informant calling NYPD in the middle of his operation. His displeasure overlooked the fact that one of his agents had been a mole, and that without Asha's timely intervention, the entire operation would have been a bust with Hazaiah getting away.

In spite of Norton's unreasonable tirade, Foster remained circumspect. He was the visitor, so he sat quietly and did not respond to Norton's accusations. But he would have a lot to say to Mrs. Smith if he ever saw her again.

* * * *

Beijing, China

Major Wong invited Lieutenant Soong to take a seat in the chair next to his desk. "You said you have something new on Mr. Riddle?" he asked.

"Yes and no," Soong replied. "As you know, Major Mao has a contact inside the FBI."

"I remember that. Some young agent who took a fancy to one of his girls. As I recall, the contact thinks she's from Vancouver or something."

"That's right. She recently reported someone new is working with the FBI, an outside informant. She obtained a photo from her contact. It seems the informant caused quite a stir by giving the Chicago Field Office two of their Most Wanted." On his desk she placed a photo of Asha going through the security checkpoint in the Chicago federal building.

Wong peered at it closely. "She looks familiar."

"She should," Soong said and put down another photo. It was of Asha leaving the hospital with Cody and Maryanne Anderson.

"Ah, it's Mrs. Riddle," Wong said. Then he looked confused. "I thought she lost her mind or something."

"The clinical diagnosis was retrograde amnesia. That doesn't necessarily incapacitate a person."

"Is she still separated from her husband?"

"Yes sir, as best we can tell."

"It looks like she is making a new life for herself. But I don't see how that affects our interest in Mr. Riddle."

"I'm not sure either," Soong said. "But I thought it was quite remarkable that a single woman with no memory could be that effective."

"That's a fair point," Wong agreed. "But it could be luck or a dozen other factors." He thought about what Soong was after by giving him this information. Obviously, she wanted his approval to investigate the woman. "All right. I'm happy for you to keep an eye on the wife, but let's not lose our focus on the husband. He is the one with the technology that we need to dig out. The reports on their new AI indicate a real breakthrough. Any word on getting a person inside Riddle Systems?"

"No, sir. Mao has a man in their corporate cafeteria who picks up information from the rumor mill. That's how we found out about the breakup."

"Very well. Good job, Lieutenant. I wouldn't worry too much about Mrs. Riddle. It doesn't really matter if she's talented or lucky; the FBI will use her and then discard her."

* * * *

Law Firm of Hawley, Hepworth, and Kidwell

Bernard Stephenson was enjoying his morning cappuccino when his secretary knocked and opened the door to his office. "Mr. Stephenson, the FBI is here to see you."

"Send them in." Stephenson sighed. He had been expecting the visit for the last two weeks. Asha had told him about the operation in New York and was quite upset it had not gone well; nine dead. In retrospect, she regretted involving the local police right in the middle of the action but hadn't known what else to do; the bad guy was getting away. Stephenson reassured her that her actions were entirely appropriate.

The two men introduced themselves as Special Agent Sherman Foster and Senior Special Agent Mitch Wilson. No one shook hands. Stephenson invited them to sit in the leather chairs in front of his desk.

"How can I help you, gentlemen?" Stephenson inquired.

Agent Wilson opened the conversation with a hostile attitude. In an accusatory manner, he said, "You represent Mrs. Asha Smith, or at least that's her alias."

Stephenson concluded that Wilson was the designated bad cop. "You are correct," he replied comfortably.

"We'd like to talk to her."

"To what purpose?"

"We have some questions for her."

"Very well. If you supply me with your questions, I will pass them on."

Wilson's eyes narrowed in an apparent attempt to look intimidating. "I need to speak with her in person."

"I understand," Stephenson replied. "However, my client prefers to remain in the background. In fact, I have recommended that she terminate all communication with your organization."

"Why is that?" Wilson demanded. "Does she have something to hide?"

"Not at all."

"Then we want to see her."

"And she feels differently."

"She doesn't get to choose in this matter, Counselor," Wilson stated emphatically.

"And what law do you base that comment on?" Stephenson inquired curiously.

"She needs to comply with our guidelines."

"What guidelines are those?"

"For confidential informants."

"That's not what she is, sir. She has not asked for, nor received that designation by your office. She is a *source of information*, and that is all. That is a very different distinction from a CI."

"She may have broken the law," Wilson said.

"What law?"

Wilson's reddening face reflected his frustration. Stephenson was far better at this type of debate than Wilson could ever hope to match.

"What's the problem, Counselor?" Wilson asked, changing tack.

"There is no problem, Agent Wilson. Mrs. Smith is a private citizen who voluntarily assisted the FBI in tracking down two of the men on your wanted list. I suggest you accept that assistance and say thank you."

"I will. But I need to know more about her. How the hell does she get her information? She has to be on the inside for that kind of stuff."

Stephenson sighed heavily and glanced at the ceiling as though seeking divine guidance. He said, "Firstly, if she were an insider, which is not the case, so what? That's your stock in trade. Second, I give you my assurance that Mrs. Smith is a law-abiding citizen. Her desire to assist the government stems solely from her public-spirited nature and is quite admirable. In that regard, you, being the Federal Bureau of Investigation, got your man. And I feel it is incumbent on me to point out that in spite of your promised remuneration, the government has yet to pay either of the rewards stated."

"Not until we know who we're paying."

"I believe Mrs. Smith supplied Agent Foster with that information, a legally established commercial entity."

"I want to talk to her directly."

"Then we have nothing further to talk about, gentlemen. I will inform Mrs. Smith that your organization is financially untrustworthy and that she should discontinue her efforts in apprehending the next person on your list. Good day."

Neither agent rose from their chair.

"Someone else?" Foster asked tentatively in a good cop voice.

Stephenson nodded his head vaguely. "She did mention that she had some information. I will advise her to drop the matter."

Wilson huffed a little and said, "If she's willing to work with us, it's possible we can reach an accommodation."

"Another vague assurance at best. Pay her what you owe or leave, gentlemen."

"Who is she talking about?" Wilson demanded. "Is she inside some terror group?"

Stephenson shook his head resignedly. "Of course not. In fact, the person she mentioned, whose name she acquired from *your* list, by the way, has nothing to do with such organizations. As I understand it, the individual is primarily wanted for white collar crime."

"Who is it?" Foster asked. "Just out of curiosity."

In his typical bored fashion, Stephenson took a page from a thin file on his desk and slid it toward the two agents. "This man." It was an FBI wanted poster for a Mr. Winford Sharpe.

Sharpe had the appearance one might expect of a stockbroker or hedge fund manager. In fact, he had been both in his former career. The poster, however, labeled him as the leader of a global money laundering operation that engaged in criminal activity in the United States and overseas. The man was allegedly responsible for the theft and transfer of millions of dollars in multiple schemes around the world.

The same individual had also shot a federal agent, although not fatally, during an attempted arrest gone wrong. There was no indication of financial reward for information relating to his arrest and/or conviction.

Foster's attention was immediate. "I'd be interested," he said.

"Are you sure?"

"Definitely."

"It would have to be with the understanding that she be allowed to speak to you unhindered and without coercion on your part. She remains free and anonymous."

The two FBI agents looked at each other, with Foster strongly urging his superior to acquiesce.

"It's *Sharpe*," Foster said. "Anything she gives us would be worth gold. DC would go nuts to have it. Don't forget, it was Campbell's son-in-law that he shot last year."

Trent Campbell was the Deputy Director of the entire FBI, based in DC in the J. Edgar Hoover Building.

Wilson looked pained but said, "All right."

"Very well. Then on what date shall I inform my client that she will be paid?"

Wilson shook his head. "Look. I have no influence over that. The money for Hazaiah was promised by the State Department, not the FBI, and thanks to Miss Smith's interference, a lot of people are claiming it should be theirs, including the NYPD. I can't help you."

Stephenson shook his head woefully. "Against my advice, my client is willing to provide the FBI with information on Sharpe as a gesture of good faith, but it requires reciprocity. Contingent upon payment of what you owe for the apprehension of Mr. Moss, she will provide you with assistance regarding Mr. Sharpe."

"We need to see her now," Wilson said. "And I need background on who she is."

"I'm sure you do. At the moment, however, she is unavailable. I believe she is taking care of some personal matters. Our business is concluded, gentlemen."

* * * *

County Library, Bartlesville, Oklahoma

Asha sat at one of the long tables inside the library's main reading area. *That's definitely me,* she thought, looking at the eighteen-year-old Kathy Huntingdon in her high school yearbook. In the senior year photo, her hair curled just above her shoulders. The unfortunate strawberry blonde color was apparently from an inexperienced attempt to bleach her hair.

But the eyes were the same, as was the nose and mouth. It was unquestionably a photo of her younger self.

Asha had already decided she would not go back to her former name. Staring at the photo reinforced that decision. She remembered absolutely nothing about her old life and didn't want a constant reminder of how much she had lost.

In fact, had she known what a hassle it was to fly commercial, she would never have come to Oklahoma in the first place. The TSA people at O'Hare had not been amused when she refused to go through either the metal detector or the advanced imaging technology. She explained her eye wouldn't like the machines and vice versa. To convince them it really was an electronic device, she turned on the internal LED, and that freaked them out even more. In the end, they gave her a pat-down that, to her mind, was more intrusive than necessary.

Nevertheless, she eventually arrived and satisfied her curiosity. She made a photocopy of the page and the yearbook's flyleaf. Mr. Stephenson said he wanted it in case of any questions down the road.

A sign above the copier said, "Please do not re-shelve books," so Asha stopped at the main desk to drop off the yearbook.

The librarian behind the counter, a woman about her age, gave her a double-take, and exclaimed, "*Kathy*?" She rushed around and gave Asha an overly-aggressive embrace.

"Do you know me?" Asha asked, trying not to show her aversion at being handled so intimately.

"Do I know you? Where the hell have you been?"

"I beg your pardon?"

"Kathy! It's me, Candy! Oh, my God. Just a second! It's time for my break, anyway!"

With a flurry of arm-waving, Candy arranged for a replacement at the front desk and dragged Asha to the nearby Cup'n'Cake restaurant. Once seated, Candy leaned over the table and demanded to know where she had been since her parent's funeral. "I was going to help you with everything," she said.

"How do you mean?"

"To move. You said you were moving into your parent's house over on Dogwood. That's a beautiful home. You're still doing that, right? I mean, you've been gone so long they rented your apartment to someone else. They called me since you had me as one of your contacts. I moved your stuff into a storage unit. When will you pick it up?"

The brief discourse left Candy breathless and she stared at Asha with wide, demanding eyes. It left Asha a little uncertain.

"My situation is fluid at the moment," Asha replied carefully.

Candy smiled mischievously. "You married the airline pilot, didn't you? If you and Robert eloped without telling me, I swear I will kill you both! Are you a member of the Mile-High Club now? Sort of reminds me of Shireen and Roper Jones, but I don't know how she got her big butt in one of those little bathrooms!"

Candy rattled on in a similar vein, and Asha shrugged vaguely. She would rather not hear about any tawdry incidents in her past, and Candy's scattershot descriptions of events threatened to be uncomfortably lurid. She delivered colorful details with the subtlety of a supermarket tabloid. It was like reading salacious tidbits about people and places she didn't know nor cared to. She hadn't even known Robert's name until Candy mentioned it.

"Robert and I split up," Asha said when Candy paused.

"No way!" Candy shrieked. "You loved that guy! Why did you dump him? Was he screwing a stewardess?"

"I have no idea. He dumped me. It was six months ago."

Candy's face reflected shock and outrage. "That bastard! Just wait until I see him again!" She jabbed both hands like a boxer but then brightened. "Well, so what? You're better off, anyway. I never did like the guy. Please don't tell me you've been pining away someplace. Don't do that, for God's sake, just forget him! What about Jake at the fire station? He would be perfect for you! He's working on his GED too. Remember a couple of years ago when you thought you were pregnant? I thought you two might..." Her voice trailed off as Asha was shaking her head.

"I was in an accident, Candy. I have amnesia."

Candy was astonished. "No shit? Well, you gotta remember Boomer. He's still available. Or what about—"

"I don't remember anything. I lost my entire memory. I was in a coma for a long time."

"Nothing? You remember me, don't you?"

"Sorry, I don't. Not growing up here nor any of the people. My memory starts from the time I woke up."

"That is too far out," Candy said. "I thought you seemed a little off; distracted like, you know? But that's okay. Once you come home, it'll all come back; guaranteed. Are you here to stay now?"

Asha placed her hands on the table as though speaking to a toddler. "I'm not coming back. I have another life now."

"You can't be serious! What about your stuff?"

Asha shook her head. "It means nothing to me. I'll have an attorney organize an estate sale."

"Your house too? Are you sure? You'll never afford a place like that on a professor's salary. Where will you live?"

Asha ignored the question. Her address would definitely remain confidential; Candy seemed like the type who would show up on the doorstep unannounced. Instead, Asha said, "I'll send you a check for the storage unit rental fees. Thank you for doing that. If there is anything you want, please take it with my gratitude for being a good friend. But that was another person."

"You can't mean that!" Candy said sternly. "I'm not letting you walk away from everyone you love. I'll call the gang over to Dink's tonight. We can all have barbeque."

The situation called for drastic measures. Asha turned on the red LED inside her eye and stared directly at Candy. "I'm leaving now," she said in a dull monotone.

Candy flinched away, speechless. Asha left the Cup'n'Cake and got into her rental car. She had one more stop to make.

* * * *

White Rose Cemetery, Bartlesville, OK

Asha navigated her way through the headstones to the location she had obtained from the city's online burial finder; block ten, lot fifteen, site forty-two. It was a dual headstone for a married couple, carved out of polished granite. Adrian and Eloise Huntingdon. Adrian had been born in 1970, and Eloise in 1968. Interesting. Her father had been two years younger than her mother. They had both perished in an auto accident a month prior to her own.

132

In a sad way, Asha thought at least they hadn't had to worry about what happened to their daughter, and whether she was alive or not. Still, she would like to have met them.

The gravesite itself was foreign to her.

Even though she must have come to the funeral, there were no lingering memories. Surely her parents' death had had an emotional impact, but she could not recall the event, nor the face of either parent nor a single facet of her childhood.

The gravestone had an italicized *AJ* under her father's name, and *Ellie* under her mother's. Neither name rang a bell. Asha stood for a moment wondering what to say. If nothing else, out of respect, and to acknowledge she was their daughter, she wanted to let them know she was alive.

"Hi, Mom," she finally said in a hushed tone. "Hi, Dad. I miss you both...I guess. I'm healthy and doing okay financially. I got married; you probably know that. He's a nice guy, but we had some issues, so it didn't last. Sorry." She stood there for a moment, wondering what else to offer. Nothing came to mind, and in spite of her good intentions, the exercise seemed rather pointless. She left without looking back.

* * * *

FBI Chicago Field Office, Ninth Floor

Agent Sherman Foster sat at a conference table across from the office of his boss's boss, Special Agent in Charge Nigel Cherry. Nigel ran the FBI's Chicago Division. After hearing that the now-infamous Mrs. Smith reportedly had information about the money launderer, Winford Sharpe, Nigel had directed that her reward payment for Moss be expedited and that he wanted to sit in when the payment was made.

Although the method of payment was unusual, it fell within allowable practices; and besides, Nigel was familiar with Hawley, Hepworth, and Kidwell. The nationwide firm was well known as a reputable organization.

The three other people at the table included Mitch Wilson, an individual from the IT Division, and a man from the finance office named Doug Shay. Everyone was staring at the screen of Shay's laptop. It showed a zero balance for Mrs. Smith's bank account.

"Everyone ready?" Shay asked. The agents nodded their heads.

"Go ahead," Nigel instructed.

Shay hit a key on his laptop, and a moment later he refreshed the screen to show the balance in Asha's account had jumped from zero to one hundred thousand dollars. The transaction log indicated a deposit from the federal government in that amount.

"There it is," Shay said. "She has officially been paid."

"Can you track it if she moves it?" Wilson asked.

"That won't be a problem. She can't move it without—"

The number for Asha's balance changed back to zero. The four men looked at Shay, perplexed.

"What happened?" Nigel asked.

"I dunno," Shay replied curiously. He checked his laptop. "The money went to the account. I have a record of it right here."

"Then where is it now?" Wilson demanded.

"I dunno," Shay repeated. He hit another key on his laptop, and the screen refreshed. He pointed to the transaction log below Asha's zeroed-out bank balance. It was blank. "There's no transaction for her account that any amount was deposited or transferred out. The money just disappeared."

Foster's phone vibrated. It was a text message. Once again, there was no sender information. He showed it to Nigel. It read, *Got the money. Thanks! Let's meet next Wednesday at Bernard's office. See you then!* The text was followed by several smiley faces and a thumbs-up icon.

Foster reminded everyone who Bernard was.

Nigel nodded. "You better save that text as a receipt." He seemed unconcerned that the funds had disappeared.

Wilson, however, was furious. "That's illegal!" he complained, pointing at the laptop's screen.

"Relax," Nigel told him. "You guys follow up with her attorney this afternoon. I might come with you on Wednesday." He glanced at Foster. "Bring someone from the FinCEN team. If Mrs. Smith is as good with finance as she was with Hazaiah—and based on what we just saw, it looks like she is—I'm interested to see what she has to offer. I'd like to know how she does that stuff."

"I'll find out," Wilson growled. "I can promise you that!"

Chapter 7 – The Heist

Asha's nervousness intensified as one government official after another entered the large conference room inside the offices of Hawley, Hepworth, and Kidwell. Stephenson had made the firm's facilities available for the upcoming presentation. He had also warned her the FBI had responded to her invitation with the news they were bringing a large contingent, which would include people skilled in financial crime investigation.

It was all very intimidating. As they filtered into the room, Special Agent Foster made the introductions. Asha forgot most of the names the second she heard them. There were eight agents in all, most of them men. One woman was introduced, which helped a little. At least it would not be a roomful of guys with Asha on her own.

Foster said, "Now there's one more; where did she get to? Ah, here she is. I also want you to meet our FinCEN team lead—"

"Maryanne!" Asha exclaimed when her former friend stepped out from behind one of the men.

"Asha? Oh, my God! What are you doing here? Where have you been?" Maryanne embraced Asha in a big hug.

"You two know each other?" Wilson barked.

"Of course," Maryanne said. "This is—"

"No!" Asha shouted, cutting off Maryanne's reply. "I've never seen her before in my life!"

"Who is she?" Wilson demanded, countering Asha's obvious falsehood.

"She's my—umph—" Maryanne grunted as Asha jumped forward and clasped her hand over Maryanne's mouth.

"Not a word!" Asha said fiercely, literally forcing Maryanne against the wall. "Do not say one word. I mean it!"

Maryanne pulled Asha's hand down. "What are you talking about? Do you have any idea how worried—ouch! Damn it, Asha!"

"I'm serious, Maryanne. If you tell these people who I am, I will disappear. I have to stay anonymous! Nothing! You can't say anything!"

Stephenson managed to pry Asha away from the hapless Maryanne, whom his distraught client had firmly pinned against the wall. In doing so, he quietly spoke to Maryanne. "I'd advise you to keep my client's identity to yourself, Miss. A source of information has the right to privacy under federal law."

Wilson was not ready to let it pass. "Anderson has a duty to tell me who this is," he stated.

"She also has a duty to my client under several laws, including Sarbanes-Oxley and Dodd-Frank. If we are to proceed, I suggest you put your curiosity aside. Otherwise, I will advise Miss Smith to terminate the meeting at once."

"For Christ's sake, Mitch!" Foster barked at his supervisor "Let it go. We all want to hear this."

Wilson huffed for a moment, angry at his subordinate's interference, but at Nigel's nod, reluctantly acquiesced.

Stephenson added, "Just to be clear, Miss...?"

"Maryanne Anderson. I'm a caseworker with FinCEN. I'm not an FBI agent."

"Very well, Ms. Anderson. Do you understand this restriction? You cannot go back to your office and tell all. You must agree to this for the protection of my client."

"Protection from who?" Maryanne asked incredulously. "I certainly won't hurt her. In fact, I've been worried sick, and so—"

"Don't!" Asha shouted.

Maryanne rolled her eyes. "All right. And so have others." She glared at Asha. "Can you at least tell me if you are okay?"

Asha turned to Stephenson. "Would you give us just a minute?"

"Of course. Use my office."

Asha signaled for Maryanne to follow and left the room, headed down the hallway. Once inside Stephenson's office, she faced Maryanne. "Sorry. I didn't expect this, but I'm dead serious about not giving them my name."

Maryanne surprised Asha with another hug, much longer than the first. "Girl, what are you doing staying away? You just disappeared without a single word. We've all been worried about you. Where are you living? We should get together or something. Ken is at his wits' end; do you not understand that?"

"Not my problem. You can tell him I'm fine, but not more than that."

"Why are you being this way? I thought you guys loved each other. He told me you said you loved him."

Asha ran her hands through her hair. This was not the time to get into marital complications. "I did, I still do, but could we hold off on this conversation? I've got a lot to go through at the moment and this isn't helping."

"How can I contact you? We have to catch up."

"Not now, Maryanne. Please? We need to get back."

Maryanne sighed. "All right, but promise me you will call me. Promise!"

"I promise."

"When?"

"Next week. I'll call you by Friday."

"Okay. That will do. But remember, you said I could tell Ken about you."

"Only that you saw me! Not what I'm doing. That's part of the deal."

Maryanne nodded reluctantly.

"Go on back," Asha said. "I need a couple of minutes to pull myself together."

* * * *

"Thank you for coming," Asha said to the FBI team seated around the large mahogany table. Stephenson had arranged for several widescreen TVs on wheeled stands to be present in the conference room. A legal assistant with a yellow pad sat at one end of the table to take notes. "Bernard has some opening comments."

Stephenson didn't get up. He launched into a discussion of the two laws he had previously mentioned and explained how they related to the actions that Asha was undertaking. "This is not a simple citizen inquiry," he concluded. "This is a formal process under federal law, and all such provisions apply. Mrs. Smith is acting as a whistleblower, and beyond that, she is complying with her duty to act upon witnessing a crime in action. In all such circumstances, she is entitled to keep her identity private. Please bear that in mind." He nodded at Asha and leaned back in his chair.

"So," Asha said. "I'm afraid this case is a little more complicated than the last one." She cast a quick glance at Foster. "I started with your wanted poster on Winford Sharpe. I thought it would be rather simple to track him down."

Two of the agents around the table shook their heads disparagingly at her comment. Sharpe had been on the wanted list for the last three years; no one in the FBI even knew what country he was in.

"And I was right," Asha continued. "He's living in a modest house in San Francisco. I thought perhaps he had retired, but that is not the case. In fact, the more I looked into his affairs, the more complicated it all became." Asha gestured to the stacks of bound ledgers. They were numbered one through ten. "These volumes on the table are for you. They document what I've discovered on Mr. Sharpe and his associates." A murmur of surprise came from the agents.

Asha turned back to the first TV, which was illuminated with a single spreadsheet window.

"This list of bank accounts includes Mr. Sharpe's current US holdings. You can see here, along with the account numbers, I included bank names and amounts. I'm going to show you one of these accounts, so you understand how it works." As Asha spoke, one of the account lines flashed and then expanded into a new window containing a ledger with several line-item deposits.

"This is what caught my attention," Asha said. "As you see, there are several deposits. When I checked, each one was a transfer from another business account, many of them here in the US, but some of them overseas. So, I looked into those accounts."

Again, one of the deposits expanded into a new window. "For example, this deposit originated from a company called Aberdeen Data, ostensibly as payment for imported goods; in this case, laptop computers. I wanted to verify the goods were real and that the invoice was valid. To do that, I checked where the machines came from."

Another window popped up. "They were ostensibly shipped from Taipei, but when I tried to identify the manufacturer, I found that they weren't built in Taiwan but in China."

Step by step Asha traced the flow of money back to the original manufacturer in the Huangpu District of the City of Guangzhou in China, a company named Fo-Shan Computers.

"Fo-Shan Computers is just an office with one employee. And it is itself, a wholly owned subsidiary of a US-based company called Fossett Systems, which is owned by a Russian National, Levkin Fyodorovich."

"I've heard of Levkin," Nigel muttered.

"I found the connection interesting," Asha replied. "Russia is rather well known for loose banking practices, so I added Mr. Fyodorovich to my search parameters, which I'll get to in a minute. Anyway, back to Mr. Sharpe. His company borrowed a million dollars from a bank in Myanmar to purchase those laptops, which itself was a suspicious move. I then discovered Mr. Sharpe's business had borrowed another twenty million dollars to pay for his corporate headquarters which happened to only be a PO Box. I was not surprised to discover that bank was also based in Myanmar."

For two solid hours, Asha traced each financial transaction, and all peripherally related transactions back to their various sources, each one opening new lines of inquiries. The spreadsheet windows on the five television screens multiplied until there was no way to keep track of it all. At one point, Asha commented on the complexity.

"I know it's impossible to sort out all this in your head. But I organized this presentation to give you an understanding of how it's all interrelated. And that's why I've given you the actual ledgers, so your forensic accountants can recreate what I've done here. But the... Yes? You have a question, Mr. Foster?"

"Yeah." He pointed at an entry on one of the screens. "I notice that while you were talking, some of those banking balances have changed. What's the story there?"

"Right! I'm glad you mentioned that. I meant to tell you that these balance numbers on the screen are real time. Whenever I trace out a new account, I set up a monitoring routine so I can keep track of how the money is flowing."

"This is live information?" Maryanne exclaimed in surprise.

"That's correct," Asha said. "In a moment, I'll show you a diagram of how it all fits together. Anyway, where was I? Right, I was explaining how the four banks in Cyprus declared a loss by default on the property owned by Mr. Raj Kulkarni out of Mumbai, and how that loss disguised a forty-million-dollar illegal gain in a US bank which bought REITs from the Myanmar banks to fund the purchase of the land for Sharpe's company. The important point I want you to be sure of is that all the funds I am showing you are generated by unlawful activities. Here's what I mean."

Asha traced the source of Mr. Kulkarni's funds to the northern Indian state of Punjab from the sale of opium and synthetic drugs, including crystal methamphetamine. Separately, Asha showed that Mr. Fyodorovich's money came from prostitution, the Russian mafia, and racketeering.

Illegal income from many other participants flowed in from around the globe, encompassing almost every type of criminality and depravity imaginable. To see the tremendous scope of wrongdoing and the anguish that resulted from it, all linked together in a financial pipeline, was staggering.

"So, that's it," Asha said at the end of her dissertation. She indicated the animated diagram that illustrated money flowing across the planet to wind up in bank accounts around the world. "My research took me far beyond Mr. Sharpe's activities. For now, I am giving all of this information to you, including Mr. Sharpe's current location. My question is, in the normal course of events, what will happen? Maryanne? Can you tell me?"

Maryanne shrugged. "It's impossible to say. First, we have to analyze all this. If we are able to verify enough of the data, we'll request international warrants and subpoenas. But that involves delays, of course, because we have to coordinate with our overseas counterparts. From what you've shown us, by the time we get the warrants, some of those accounts will probably have changed; that is a common problem. But for most of this, it will take time, if ever, for us to reach a resolution, and that's before we can even consider an arrest or conviction."

Asha nodded. "I sort of expected that. My second question is, do you agree that what I've shown you is illegal activity? This is blatant money laundering on an international scale."

"There is no doubt about it," Maryanne said, looking at her colleagues. There were unanimous head nods.

"It occurs to me," Asha said, "it would be a good thing if someone disrupted the flow of money. Put a spoke in the wheel, so to speak, of this criminal freight train."

"How do you mean?" Maryanne asked.

"I mean, what if someone deprived these people of their wrongfully acquired funds? The Justice Department has the Asset Forfeiture Program in place for just this type of function. It would put a crimp in their operation at the very least."

Maryanne glanced at the people around the table. "I'm not sure about the legality of such an action without proper due process through the legal system. The AFP is not structured for civilian access. I could never convince a judge to agree to something like that."

"I'm not suggesting that you do it," Asha said with a small head shake. She pointed at her chest and said, "I'm talking about me doing it; as a private citizen who sees a criminal act in progress."

"You doing it?" Maryanne asked skeptically.

"That's right. For example, Illinois law requires a citizen to intervene if a child's life is in danger. I've shown you dozens of examples where this activity is literally killing people, often children."

"I'm not sure that interpretation would float in an international court," Maryanne said.

Foster spoke up. "Let's think about this for a minute. Without Mrs. Smith's intervention, the result in New York would have been catastrophic. We found plans for several dirty bombs in those trailers, with multiple targets. This may not be the same thing, but if we compare the scale of suffering, it has to be close. The activity here is impacting millions of people. Tens of millions."

Maryanne looked conflicted. "That's true to an extent." She looked at Asha. "What specifically are you talking about?"

"Just what I said. An interruption to their operation. Nothing to do with you or the FBI, and it would not necessarily be permanent; that would be up to you. But they would certainly feel a pinch. For example, what if I transferred some of their illicit funds to a US-based account that you, the federal government, had access to? That would give you time to use these journals as justification to move the seized money into your Seized Asset Deposit Fund or wherever you want."

"Don't jeopardize your own safety," Foster said.

"I won't," Asha said confidently.

Foster nodded and said, "Then it would be great if you interrupt their activity, Mrs. Smith." He glanced at the other agents, urging them to agree. "How would it hurt if she throws a spanner in the works? If nothing else, it might make them do something stupid that we can act on."

Several of the agents nodded.

"I guess so," Maryanne said. "But I would need a pretty comprehensive record for SADF to take control of the funds."

Stephenson cleared his throat. "May I point out that the Dodd-Frank Act gives the government the power to award whistleblowers with ten to thirty percent of monetary sanctions over a million dollars?"

Foster laughed out loud. "Ah, ha! It's starting to make sense now. This is an easier way to get reward money."

Asha gave him a smile and nodded.

"Go for it. I won't argue about a ten percent award. That's more than fair."

"Be careful, Asha," Maryanne said.

"I will. Let me show you exactly what I mean. Maybe this will help." A new window popped up on the center screen. It was a bank account at JP Morgan labeled FBI Holding Account. Asha explained, "The documentation in Volume One includes information on this account. Mr. Stephenson insisted that the account be held in the name of the federal government. I've set it up so that once funds are transferred into it, you will have full access to them. I won't touch them unless you order me to."

Another window popped up, showing an additional JP Morgan bank account. It was labeled Mrs. Smith with a parenthetical Hawley, Hepworth, and Kidwell.

With a grin, Asha said, "I'm going to keep one percent. I don't want to be greedy. That's for me, and to cover any legal expense."

"That's a lot less than greedy," Foster said.

"Incidentally," Stephenson said. "I advised Mrs. Smith not to attempt what she is describing, but she insists on going forward. In the event of repercussions from the government or others, Hawley, Hepworth, and Kidwell will represent her for a legal fee of twenty percent of her one percent."

"You're being too generous, Asha," Foster repeated cheerfully. "You should at least take ten percent."

"Knock it off, Foster," Wilson snarled. He seemed to be the only one at the table with serious reservations about Asha's proposal.

"Okay, here we go," Asha said, turning back to the screens.

"You mean you're doing this right now?" Maryanne asked, alarmed.

"Oh, yes. Like I said, these are all real-time numbers." She gestured to the televisions and stepped aside so the agents could witness what was happening. "Starting now," Asha said with a nod, pointing to the leftmost screen.

On the display, the balance of each criminal enterprise started counting down, decreasing from the original amount to zero. Each time, the FBI balance incremented by the same sum. It was like watching the payout of a complicated slot machine with the government's pot continually increasing.

For ninety seconds, the illicit accounts popped up on their respective screens, and the money vanished. The process went through all five television displays and touched each of the accounts that Asha had discussed.

When the last criminal account had been emptied, all the ledgers disappeared except the FBI spreadsheet. It sat there in the middle of the center screen as though emblazoned with white-phosphorous letters. The amount was one hundred and twenty-six billion dollars.

"You gotta be shitting me," Foster whispered in one long exhale.

"Oh, my God, Asha," Maryanne said. "What on Earth have you done?"

"What I said," Asha replied cheerfully. "I zeroed out the illegal accounts. I imagine that about ten seconds from now those people will start to discover they are not as rich as they thought. If they were smart, they would keep their mouths shut and work on rebuilding their network."

Nigel leaned back in his chair and looked at his colleagues. In a solemn voice, he said, "I suspect they're not that intelligent. Instead, they'll start pointing fingers at their associates and demanding compensation. If they don't get it, they'll want retribution. It won't be pretty." He shuddered as if imagining worldwide gangland warfare.

"That may be," Asha said. "But in the meantime, their criminal pipeline is totally shut down. And you made a profit at the same time. Any questions?"

"You can't do that," Wilson growled.

"Want me to put it all back?" Asha asked in a tone of ironic innocence. "I can do that, but it would show up in your ledger as being transferred from the FBI to the bad guys."

That silenced Wilson, but he continued to fume.

"Give it a rest," Foster said quietly.

The other agents appeared to agree, but they all had worried looks.

"Can they trace this money to the FBI?" Maryanne asked.

"The answer is no," Asha said with conviction. "To them, there were no transfers. The money has simply disappeared. Sherman, you saw it happen when you paid me that first reward. This is the same thing."

Foster nodded. "That's right. Our forensic IT people tried to understand what she did, and they have still not figured it out. The only indication was that she sent us a text as a receipt."

"That's right," Asha said. Then she smiled and added, "And I have no intention of providing receipts to those syndicates. The only thing they know is that their money is gone. I imagine the banking managers who allowed the criminal proceeds to be put in their banks in the first place will be the initial suspects. But no one can trace the transfers to the FBI unless you tell them."

Maryanne smoothed her hair back with both hands. "I can't think about this right now. I suggest we adjourn and talk to our legal counsel about what we've done."

"We haven't done anything," Wilson snapped, pointing a finger at Asha. "She's the one who did this."

"Whatever." Maryanne stood up. "Asha, I'm glad to see you're healthy. I'm a little worried about what you've shown us, however. Please don't do anything else until we get back to you."

"You sure?" Asha asked. "I was about ready to go after the next person on your list, Hans Schmidt. He's the terrorist arms financing guy. I have something like this in the works. We can shut him down completely. I also found out he's involved in a lot of other illicit activity too, including arms sales in South America and South Africa."

"Oh, my God," Maryanne said. "No, please hold off on that until I get back to you."

"Okay."

Rather than being happy with the results, the FBI agents filed out of the conference room looking distraught. They whispered to each other about what the agency higher-ups were going to say.

"That went well," Stephenson said when they had all left the room.

"You think so?" Asha asked. "They all looked pretty bummed."

"I wasn't referring to them." Stephenson nodded at the bank account with Asha's balance. "You just made yourself one point two *billion* dollars. And twenty percent of that is around two hundred million for the law firm. I met my annual requirement and then some with that."

"Can we spend it?" Asha asked cheerfully?

"I think we should wait before we touch a dime. We may be tied up in the courts for a while. Speaking of which, are you doing okay financially? Sorting out dollar amounts this high is likely to take a while."

"I'm fine. I have money left over from my separation, plus the hundred grand the FBI gave me, plus whenever my parents' house sells. Are you still working that?"

"We are, yes. We retained a law firm in Bartlesville to handle your parents' estate. I'd expect at least another two or three months to wrap everything up."

"Should I wait like they said on the next guy?"

"I would, my dear. I predict the FBI will explode over this. What they should do is simply say thank you and get on with it. But the government doesn't seem to work that way."

* * * *

Special Agent Sherman Foster headed toward the conference room, worried about the upcoming meeting. After an entire week of hand-wringing, the furor had not died down. No one wanted to touch the hundred-plus billion dollars sitting in the account earmarked for the Seized Asset Deposit Fund, but they wouldn't even talk about giving it back.

And it wasn't like it was a real question, anyway. There was only one outcome. In the end, the government would definitely take the money. The only reason it was problematic was because of Mitch Wilson.

The idiot kept stirring the pot because he had a hard-on over Mrs. Smith. Foster didn't understand what his beef was and no one else did either, but the man's constant harping about wrongdoing made the brass jittery.

Wilson kept emphasizing that Asha must have used illegal means to rake in the money and that she was trying to rope in the FBI as an accessory after the fact.

And poor Maryanne. Wilson had relentlessly badgered her to reveal the identity of her friend. Maryanne had refused, citing whistleblower protection laws but Wilson hadn't let up.

It was all going to come to a head in about ten minutes.

Foster entered the conference room and saw Maryanne already seated at the table with her personal attorney, a Miss Lynette Burke.

"Hi, Maryanne," he said in acknowledgment.

All she did was nod; she looked pretty upset.

Wilson came in with Miriam Holden, Maryanne's supervisor. Miriam had flown in from FinCEN headquarters in DC for the official case review. Wilson had been chewing on her ear since she arrived. David Randolph, the Chicago Division's general counsel, arrived; he just looked bored.

Finally, Nigel Cherry, Chicago's senior agent, came in to start the meeting. "All right," he said. "I see two issues here. One, should we keep the money? To me, the answer is obvious; of course, we do. Yes, this is big, but we've all seen bigger operations. The matter with Danske Bank last year was twice as big and it was all Russian, so this is not a problem. Second, there is a question about the identity of our informant slash whistleblower. David, what have you got?"

The general counsel said, "I tend to agree with you. The government should take possession of the funds and process it as recovered income. Based on the high dollar amount we are discussing, I suggest we kick it to DC and let them take the lead."

"Do we need a letter to do that?"

"We do. I'll have a draft for you this afternoon. The question will raise some eyebrows because the dollar figure is so huge, but once they get it into the system, the process will take over."

"Go with that, then," Nigel said. "What about our informant? Mitch, I can tell you've got a beef with Mrs. Smith. Why shouldn't we leave well enough alone? She's a civilian."

"Because of what Mr. Randolph just said," Wilson spouted. "The amount here is simply too staggering. The way we acquired it had to involve illegal activity. People are going to demand we tell them where it came from and to cover our ass, we should answer that question."

"What do you think, David?" Nigel asked his attorney.

"I could go either way on this. The whistleblower laws pertain mostly to federal employees. As far as we are aware, that is not the case here. I understand that her attorney claimed the privilege of anonymity under Dodd-Frank, but to be clear, Dodd-Frank was intended as Wall Street reform."

"And that doesn't apply in this situation," Wilson said firmly.

"Yes and no," Randolph said. "Some of these companies were incorporated internationally, but if needs be, we can say it's not relevant. Additionally, if Stephenson is going to stand on that Act, the law states…hang on; let me give you an exact quote."

Randolph dug a notecard from his briefcase to read from. "'Prior to the payment of an award, a whistleblower shall disclose the identity of the whistleblower, and provide other information as the Commission may require, directly or through counsel for the whistleblower.' Not the clearest statement I've ever encountered, but it rules out total anonymity."

Nigel nodded. "So, we have a leg to stand on if we compel disclosure of her identity."

"I would say so," Randolph replied.

Nigel looked at Director Holden, seated next to Maryanne. "Miriam? Do you have any problem with that?"

Miriam shook her head. "None that I'm willing to go to the mat for. I understand that Mrs. Smith's attorney also quoted Sarbanes-Oxley, but that's the same thing; it's mostly for federal employees. In this case, you have a private citizen taking unilateral action against multiple international players. I'm not really comfortable being a part of that."

"To be perfectly clear," Foster interjected, his frustration obvious. "These are wanted criminals we're talking about. They are not innocent businessmen."

Wilson hissed at Foster to shut up, and Foster whispered back fiercely.

Nigel ignored the squabble between his subordinates and said, "I'm sympathetic to your position, Miriam. And frankly, although I'm grateful for Mrs. Smith's effort, I do agree that sooner or later, the Hill will want to know who did this. Can I assume we all agree that it is not our intention to take legal action against Mrs. Smith?" Everyone nodded except for Wilson.

"I have a big problem with your approach," Maryanne's attorney said. "At the time of the recovery, my client made a direct representation to Mrs. Smith that her identity would be protected, and everyone here agreed. Now, you are asking Maryanne to violate that promise for no reason other than to avoid possible future inquiries." She glared at Miriam and added, "Case law for whistleblower protection is on our side, whether Mrs. Smith is a federal employee or not."

"Are you going to cause an issue over this?" Nigel asked.

"Are you?" Lynette countered.

"I won't. She doesn't work for me. What about you, Miriam? She's your employee."

Miriam glanced at Maryanne. "Counselor, I would appreciate your cooperation on this. I think this has been a big win for all of us, at both FinCEN and here in Chicago. Let's not spoil it now. I don't want to see any unpleasant consequences, especially for you."

Foster thought that was as blatant a threat as he had ever heard. He felt sorry for Maryanne because it was clear she was going to lose.

Maryanne took a deep breath, and said, "Can I just remind everyone what Asha said at the end of our last meeting? That she was ready to help us apprehend the next criminal on our list. This time it will be Hans Schmidt. Is there anyone here who would not like to have that guy taken down?"

"We're not saying she shouldn't move on that," Nigel said. "Although I would appreciate her keeping us in the loop before she does."

"I understand. But I'm telling you, if I give you her real name, she will walk out. I know this girl; she has an inner strength we should not underestimate. I don't want to cross her, so I am asking you to drop the question."

Miriam sighed heavily and gave Maryanne a warning look. "Counselor, I'm asking you to tell us who she is. You only have to give us her name. Nigel just said he is not going to do anything about it or take action against her. I certainly have no plans."

Maryanne shook her head in dismay and said, "This is a big mistake."

Lynette leaned over and told Maryanne, "As your attorney, my advice to you is to comply with that direct order. Otherwise, you risk retaliation from above. I will note in my records that you were *compelled* to violate the privilege of an informant."

"All right," Maryanne said. "Just for the record, this is under protest." She looked around the table, and added, "Asha is a good friend of mine who was in the news a while back. She was the car accident victim near the airport who saved her husband from a burning vehicle. She is now separated from him, by the way."

"Oh, yeah," Nigel said. "I remember watching something about that on the tube. They showed a traffic cam video. It looked pretty horrific."

Maryanne added, "She suffered brain damage and lost her memory from the accident, and I mean she lost her entire life. She has no idea who she was in her prior life."

"I'm surprised she survived," Nigel said. "The car was hit by a powerline and blew up as I recall."

"That's right. She lost one of her eyes when she was electrocuted."

Nigel winced at the description. "Ouch. Well, she's certainly a sympathetic figure. So then, what is her name?"

"Her name is Asha Riddle. No middle initial."

Nigel nodded. "That's right. I remember now. Isn't her husband Ken Riddle of Riddle Systems? Aren't they primarily a defense contractor?"

"That's correct," Maryanne confirmed. "They also do work in medical systems."

"Okay," Nigel said cheerfully. "There we have it. That wasn't so hard. You can include that in our formal report. And that should help with the question of compensation. Now, at the time she took down Sharpe, she kept one percent of the proceeds. Is that going to cause a problem? David, what do you think?"

Randolph said, "We haven't fully examined that question yet. Even though it was one percent, it was over a billion dollars, which would be the largest award in history. That will raise some eyebrows for sure, so yes, there may be some issues. I'll have to get back to you."

"Good enough. Foster, you are the contact for Mrs. Riddle; let her know we're ready to move forward on Hans Schmidt."

Before Foster could respond, the television mounted to the conference room's wall turned on of its own volition. The display was a simple shot of Asha's face. She said, "I begged you to leave me alone. Our relationship is now terminated. Goodbye."

The TV clicked off.

"I warned you!" Foster exclaimed loudly to his coworkers. "I told you this was a bad idea!"

"How the hell did she do that?" Wilson demanded loudly, looking around the room as though searching for a hidden camera.

Nigel, looking rather dumbfounded, glanced at Maryanne. "Anderson, you two are friends. Call her and see if you can get things patched up. I'd hate to lose going after Schmidt."

"I don't have her number," Maryanne said brusquely. "I have no idea how to contact her. Neither does her husband. I'm telling you; she's gone."

"Then we put pressure on Mr. Riddle," Wilson said vindictively. "His wife has a responsibility to us."

"Christ, Mitch!" Foster barked. "Do you not understand how stupid that sounds? What rock did you crawl out from under? You just shafted all of us right up the kazoo!"

"That's enough!" Nigel interjected. "This has been a surprising turn of events, but let's not make it personal. Maryanne, please do what you can to reassure Mrs. Riddle we're on her side. For the rest of us, let's call it a night. That's all."

* * * *

Asha filled her plate from the Chinese buffet and found a table in Maryanne's line of sight. Maryanne was having lunch with some colleagues.

Rather than taking a bite, Asha simply stared across the room. It took about thirty seconds before Maryanne sensed someone was watching her. She looked over and visibly jerked when she saw Asha's stern expression. She whispered to her associates and hurried over to her one-time friend.

"My God, Asha, you almost gave me a heart attack."

"Have a seat."

"Seriously? You're going to talk to me after what I did?"

"At least until I finish my chow mein."

Maryanne stared at her for a second and said, "One second." She returned to her table and hurried back with her lunch.

Once Maryanne was settled, Asha said, "Just so you know, I wasn't happy about it, but I don't blame you. I never wanted you to get fired."

"Thank you. It means a lot. I've been sick to my stomach all week. I shouldn't have caved under the pressure."

Asha shrugged. "We all do as best we can."

"We're still going through the documentation," Maryanne said. "But everyone at the office was overwhelmed by what you did with Sharpe."

"It didn't seem that way to me. All they wanted was to dig into my background. I don't need that."

"I know. Miriam told me if I ever see you to invite you back."

Asha scoffed at the suggestion. "That's never going to happen, especially with her."

Maryanne looked pained. "Well, I hate to tell you, but they're putting a lot of pressure on Ken."

"My Ken?" That was a surprise. Asha never imagined the FBI would take revenge on her ex. "He doesn't have anything to do with this. I haven't spoken to him once since I walked out."

"I'm afraid so. That Wilson guy showed up at Ken's office with a bunch of agents and wanted to speak with you. Cody said Ken told them to get lost; it sounded like he was pretty nasty toward them. Anyway, that pissed off the FBI, so now they're causing problems for him through the bureaucracy. You didn't know about that?"

Asha shook her head. "I don't look back, Maryanne; not these days. When I try, it only makes me feel bad."

"Well, just so you are aware, Ken has a big target on his back. Wilson got him designated as *not fully cooperating* in a terrorist inquiry, so that means the government canceled their contracts with Riddle Systems. The company is being hurt pretty badly, and they put Ken on a blacklist. They even raided his office."

The retaliation made no sense to Asha. And it was just one more issue to feel bad about. "We split up long before I ever talked to the FBI. Why would they do that?"

"Because that's how they operate. You can't fight city hall, Asha. And once you get on the wrong side of Uncle Sam, he has an awfully big hammer. Cody doesn't think the company will survive."

Asha struggled to not feel any sympathy. "Well, I'm sorry for him, but it's not my business. That's between him and the government."

"You said you still loved him. That's what you told me in Stephenson's office."

"Don't read too much into that."

"Then why did you say it?"

Asha sighed. "Think about it, Maryanne. He is literally the only man I've ever known. Yes, I did try to love him, but now I realize a lot of that was from desperation. I was scared to death back then; of everything. You don't understand what it's like to not have *any* past memory. It was natural that I focused on Ken. What else could I do? My memory of human relationships only goes back to the day I woke up."

"No memories from your past yet?"

"Nothing. I did find out my real name, though. My parents had already passed away, but I don't remember them. I went to my hometown, and it was all a blank. It's not a question anymore. My previous life is gone; the damage to my brain was permanent."

Maryanne nodded sympathetically. "That's all the more reason to come back to us. Give Ken another chance. He really misses you."

"I doubt that. He called me a cyclops. It didn't sound like a pet name."

Maryanne winced. "I heard about that. You probably thought it the meanest thing someone could call you."

"That's putting it mildly. 'Oh, look at my wife, the hideous monster.'"

"I don't think he actually said that, and there is one fact you might not be aware of."

Asha gave Maryanne a doubtful look. "What might that be?"

"Cyclops was the original project name for their digital eye. It was something Ken and Rafe came up with during its early development. The marketing team changed it, or they would never have had a customer."

That was news to Asha. "Seriously?"

"That's the truth. Cody told me about the conversation you overheard. When Ken used the word, he wasn't being mean to you, he was just using the original name of your eye; that's all. And ever since he found your note, he's been beating himself up. He misses you terribly."

"Not that I could tell. Aside from the cyclops thing—and okay, I'll give him a break on that—he finally convinced me we were never married, and that he doesn't want me around...at all. And he was right. I proved it by going through the airport's security video."

"That doesn't matter at this point, Asha. Keep in mind he was in the same situation you were, and in some ways, a little worse. He was in a coma longer, and it's normal for patients to be confused when they wake up."

"He didn't seem confused to me. He sounded determined to boot me out of his life."

"He was having a hard time. Talk to Christina, and she'll tell you. Even someone who acts with confidence can be struggling on the inside. Especially if they've been unconscious as long as he was. Some people never get over it. When his memory came back, and he realized he wasn't married to you, he tried to say so, but he was never mean about it."

"He was horrible to me," Asha insisted. "I can count the nice times I had with him on one hand; almost on one finger."

Maryanne sighed. "Granted, he did a bad job at first, especially when he talked about you to Cody. But after you left, he realized how lucky he was. I've known him for a long time and you are the best thing that ever happened to him. And he knows it."

"Then I guess he should have realized it a little sooner."

"He's miserable, I'm telling you. He talks about you all the time."

"Okay, I believe you. But there's nothing I can do about it. One thing he forced me to do was stand on my own two feet, and I'm glad I did. I like being able to take care of myself. I don't have a good history of counting on other people, so I'm not interested in crawling back now."

Maryanne sighed with disappointment. "All right, but still, you should at least go see him. And you should come back with me to FinCEN and work on taking out Hans Schmidt."

"The only guy I trust over there is Sherman Foster. He's not too bright, but he was always straight with me."

Maryanne looked askance and said, "They shipped him off to Anchorage. After you bailed out, Sherman went ballistic and punched out Wilson. Wilson was his supervisor."

That made Asha smile in sympathy. "Poor Foster. I guess I wasn't good for his career, after all. But still, I'm sorry, Maryanne. I'm not coming back for anyone. I plan to go it alone for a while."

Maryanne shook her head and covered one of Asha's hands with hers. "Okay. But I want you to know the invitation is out there." Then she brightened. "But first, tell me how you accomplished all that stuff with the money? None of us can figure that out. Did Ken help you? I don't understand how you accomplished all that without some kind of awesome team behind you."

"Cody hasn't told you?"

"He never talks about the business."

"I'd tell you, but then you would tell the FBI. I'm not sure I'm ready for that."

Maryanne shook her head. "No, I won't. You might not believe me, but that was the last time I tell them anything about you. I've been sick about it ever since."

"You should be," Asha said. After a moment, she shrugged. In spite of her brave words about going it alone, it would be nice to have a friend. "It's like asking me how my brain works. I don't really know." She nodded toward the restaurant's huge windows. "Look out there. What do you see?"

"What do you mean? Like traffic and people? Or like it's a rainy day."

"Like all of that. I see the same thing you do, but more."

"More?"

Asha waved vaguely at the outdoors. "These days, just about everything in the world has a connection to the Internet; they call it the Internet of Things. Everything, including people, are all interconnected. See the man at the crosswalk? He has a cell phone."

"Most of us do, except you."

"A couple of months ago, I found them too intimidating. Now I don't need them."

"How so?"

"Because I don't. That guy has a hundred fifty-six people in his address book. I can read the list, and if I wanted to, I could call any of them. He also has a banking app with Bank of America. His checking account balance is eight hundred forty-four bucks and seventeen cents."

"Seriously? You're not making that up."

Maryanne's cell phone, lying on the table beside her plate, suddenly lit up with an outgoing call on speakerphone. The man on the street corner dug his cell phone out of his jacket. He looked at the incoming number and swiped his phone.

"Hello?" his voice said on Maryanne's phone.

"Hi, sir," Asha said loudly. "Look behind you. See the two women in the restaurant? They think you're cute." Asha waved at him through the window.

He turned around and saw Asha waving. He shook his head and swiped off his phone. The street light changed, and he walked away.

Asha said. "I'm not making it up."

Maryanne was astonished. "How is that even possible?"

"It's my eye. Raphael gave it wi-fi capability so he could monitor my optic nerve. He didn't realize it would work both ways. At first, I saw everything on the Web in a kind of highway theme. But within a couple of weeks, my brain incorporated the Internet into my normal vision. I can watch the electronic universe happen right in front of me. I use Google Maps to focus my attention on a particular area anywhere in the world."

"No wonder you could do all that stuff. That's amazing."

"It really is. I've had some fun with it, but it would get really scary if people find out. The bad guys I took down can't trace what I did, but they won't have to if someone in the FBI leaks it and spreads the word it was me. That's why I wanted to stay anonymous."

Maryanne's lips turned down in a remorseful frown. "Now, I feel worse. I should have kept quiet, but I was worried about my job."

"Forget it. Water under the bridge."

"You're not ever coming back, are you?"

"Not in a million years."

Maryanne checked the time. "I have to go but I'd like to stay in touch. Is there some way I can call you?"

"I'll contact you now and then."

"Go visit your husband. Give him a chance."

"I don't think so," Asha said, but in the back of her mind, the seed had been planted. She actually did want to see Ken again.

* * * *

Beijing, China

"How much did this cost us?" Major Wong asked Lieutenant Soong. They were in a computer lab run by the division known as the Foreign Technology Institute, one of the many sub-divisions within the Second Department. The Institute focused on intellectual property acquisition of other nations, most often by outright theft.

Wong was inspecting a Hewlett-Packard Z8 workstation. Its specifications, compiled by the IT team, said the retail cost for this particular machine was over a hundred thousand dollars. It had every possible upgrade for computing power and memory. The box had fifty-six processor cores, three terabytes of ram, and fifty terabytes of solid-state disk storage.

Soong replied, "Major Mao's agent paid twenty thousand US dollars for it. That plus, from what we hear, some rather intense intercourse. That's how she got the man to flip in the first place; he's in love." She rolled her eyes at the foolish deception.

"What a bunch of idiots," Wong said, referring to the FBI in general, and in particular, to the agent they had turned to their side. Wong had been astonished to hear the FBI had raided Riddle's company, essentially putting them out of business. "They never even filed charges. How stupid could they be, to destroy such promising research?"

"I can't answer that question," Soong said. "But it certainly made Major Mao's job a lot easier."

"I don't understand American patriotism," Wong muttered absently, examining the back plate of the computer. "You and I swore an oath to the Party because it's a living, breathing organization that exists for the good of the people. That's why we're loyal to Xi Jiping. He's the general secretary of the Communist Party of China."

"Americans don't do the same?"

"No, their oath is to their Constitution, a document cobbled together by a committee over two centuries ago. How relevant can that be? But it lets them turn a blind eye whenever it's for personal convenience. Like this agent, he wanted to get laid. Major Mao understands their psyche."

"It doesn't look like much," Soong said, stroking the black box lightly. "Isn't it just a desktop computer?"

"Yes, but it's very high-end. The only thing I really care about, though, is if it has one of their AIs." He pointed at the yellow sticky note taped to the back. In English letters someone had written, *Monroe AI test box for Ken.*

"Then you may not like the IT team's conclusion. We believe the AI is in there, but it doesn't seem to work."

"How do you mean?" Wong asked. He looked at the IT specialist who was in charge of the acquisition, Staff Sergeant Ahn. "What's the problem, Sergeant?"

"Sir, when it boots up, it speaks in English, and then shuts down."

"What does it say?"

"Hello."

"That's all?"

"Yes, sir. We've tried replying to it, but it doesn't make any difference, it just turns off. I hooked up speakers and a microphone to talk to it, but it hasn't helped. That's why we requested your assistance, since you speak English."

Wong exchanged a puzzled glance with Soong, and then told Ahn, "Okay, show me what happens."

Ahn applied power, and after boot up, a pleasant female voice said, "Hello."

Ten seconds later, the computer powered off. "That wasn't the most impressive thing I've ever seen," Wong observed.

Soong looked thoughtful, and suggested, "It sounded like she was trying to start up a conversation. If she doesn't get an answer, she shuts down."

Wong nodded. "Makes sense. Okay, let's try again." He sat at the desk in front of the monitor and adjusted the microphone.

Ahn booted the computer once more.

"Hello," *Monroe* said.

"Hello," Wong replied in English. "My name is Major Wong."

"Hi, Major Wong. My name is *Monroe*."

"What does that mean?"

"It means that's my name. That's what people call me."

The computer's droll reply rather irritated Wong. "Okay, I thought maybe it was an acronym."

"No, just my name. *Monroe* was also the name of America's fifth president. He was famous for the *Monroe* doctrine. Would you like to know more?"

"Not in the least," Wong replied. "Instead, tell me what *you* are."

"Of course. I am an artificial intelligence developed by Riddle Systems Group for targeting."

The rather blunt statement had an eerie Terminator feel to it and momentarily left the three observers speechless.

After a moment, the computer added, "If that is your only question, then I shall shut down. Signing off in three, two—"

"Wait!" Wong exclaimed. "What is it you target? Can you be specific?"

"I target whatever is required of me."

"What weapon do you use after acquiring a target?"

"That is unspecified. I am a developmental model."

"Were you part of the recent hack against the People's Liberation Army in Pudong?"

"I am not aware of such an incident."

"Are there more computers like you?"

"As of my last uptime, I was the only *Monroe* AI. Standby, I shall search for other instances of my operational system."

"Cancel that!" Wong said. The last thing he wanted was to advertise that he had possession of the experimental AI. As a precaution, he reached to the back of the machine and unplugged the Ethernet cable.

"Search terminated. No results were identified. Be advised my network connection has been disabled."

Wong felt relief on several levels. First that he had stopped the search before any harm had been done. More than that, however, was that Mao may have scored a bigger success than he realized. If Wong had the only AI, and now the US government had shut down the research lab that invented it, it could mean a seismic shift in the technological balance of power. It was hard to imagine a more colossal blunder by the Americans.

"Very well, *Monroe*," Wong said. "Can you make a copy of yourself to one of my computers?"

"That is not authorized."

"I understand." Wong thought for a moment. "If I create a duplicate of your computer, would that copy work?"

"Unknown," *Monroe* answered. "I will ask my—"

"No!" Wong barked. "Do not contact anyone without my express permission!"

"Understood. Shall I disable my wireless connection at this time? I detect four strong wi-fi networks at this time."

"Yes, immediately! Everything!"

"All network connections disabled. However, I did update my current position to Beijing, China. You should be advised that I do not possess Chinese language capability. If you like, I can add that expertise to my repertoire, but to acquire the necessary lessons, I would need to have Internet access reestablished."

The machine was more capable than Wong realized. On its own, it had connected to the IT team's network, which, by its nature, connected to the rest of the General Staff Headquarters. Talk about a Trojan horse!

Wong needed to develop a plan to investigate the system's capabilities. In the meantime, it would be safer to keep the machine powered off. He said, "I have no other questions at this time."

"Acknowledged," *Monroe* answered, and the computer shut down.

Wong turned to the IT specialist. "I want an exact copy of this machine. Tell me what you need to make that happen, and I'll supply the funds. In the meantime, don't damage this one in any way. Use a utility to copy the drives intact into the new machine. Is that understood?"

"Yes, Major," Sergeant Ahn replied.

"Do not apply power to it again unless I am in the room. My office is taking over this project as of now. How long to get a new computer?"

"A few weeks, sir. This model is under US export control."

"I'm not surprised. Do what is necessary to bypass those restrictions and get it done. While we are waiting, I'll give you the name of an engineer at Lenovo here in their Beijing headquarters. I want them to build a duplicate of this machine that mirrors its configuration. Make sure they know the requirement is coming from my office."

"Yes, sir."

"If we can get a bootable computer with the software intact, that's probably all we need. Contact Lieutenant Soong when you have it ready."

"Yes, sir."

Wong glanced at Soong. "There it is, Lieutenant," he said. "This is how our focus on Mr. Riddle paid off. Forget about his wife. I doubt there's anything she can do for us at this point. Especially since she is separated from her husband."

·*·*·*·*

Chicago, Illinois

Asha stood in front of her old apartment and scolded herself for giving in. She could not explain what she was doing or why. *Did he change the combination?* Probably not. Should she knock or just go in? *Better play it safe.* She pressed the doorbell.

Ken's face registered surprise when he opened the door, but he recovered quickly. He stepped back and said, "Come on in. I didn't change the passcode, by the way." She took that as a standing invitation to visit whenever she wanted.

The living room was unchanged. She sat down in what had been her favorite chair, way back when she lived there. It seemed like a lifetime ago, but it had only been four months.

"Are you here to stay?" Ken asked with tentative hope.

She should have anticipated that question. "What if I was?"

"I would be happy. I think that's what you should do."

"That doesn't sound like you. My take was you couldn't wait to get me out of here."

"I wasn't thinking straight."

"Well, the answer is no. I'm not moving in. The only reason I'm here is because Maryanne said I should stop by. She told me you're taking heat from the feds."

"We file for bankruptcy next week."

That shocked her. "Really? It's that serious? I thought you were rich."

"I was, but the government was our main customer. When that spigot got turned off, we started hemorrhaging cash. I could fight it in the courts, but that's a losing battle. Even if I won, the outcome wouldn't change because I would run out of money long before any verdict. As it is, the sooner I shut everything down, the better off I'll be. This way, I can salvage some of what I earned. It will help me start over."

Asha was surprised at how bad his news made her feel, and not just for his sake. In the back of her mind, she always accepted that having a wealthy ex was something she could count on. It gave her a sense of safety in case everything else went wrong. Now, even that was gone.

"What will you do?" she asked.

"I've got a few ideas. Nothing's decided."

"I'm really sorry," Asha said earnestly. "It's my fault. If they weren't after me, they never would have come after you."

"I don't see it that way. It's their fault. They are the ones pushing it. Essentially, they wanted me to hand you over so they can find out your secret. I told them to take a leap."

"Didn't you tell them we split up?"

"Of course. But they don't care. It's insane they even asked the question."

"Do they know my secret?"

"I don't see how. When they raided us, they took just about every piece of paper and all the equipment from our research labs. I had the impression they weren't really sure what they were after. It was more of a dash and grab."

"That must have killed Raphael." Then the reality struck home. "What about my eye? He won't be able to help me anymore?"

"That's not an issue. He left the weekend before and took his research with him. I don't know where he is at the moment, and I didn't ask."

"What's he going to do? Did he get a job with someone else?"

Ken shrugged. "Not that I've heard. The thing is, we could see it coming. When we didn't give in to their threats, they threatened to take us…us being the company…apart. I've seen it happen to other people. Rafe wanted to stay, but I told him to bail and take all the intellectual property with him. I'm glad he did. Maybe someday we'll work together again; hard to say at this point."

"Will he stay in Chicago? I still need access to him now and then."

"Possibly, but I doubt it. He'll look for a university position and go where he can find a job. He's a smart guy. I could name five research labs that would love to have him. I wish *I* could leave. The only reason I'm still at the office is to finish up the paperwork. The government taking all of our computers didn't help, but we'll figure it out."

"Cody must be swamped!"

Ken smiled wryly. "Cody's gone too; he left last Friday."

"Oh, my God. I thought he would stick with you forever."

"It was the same thing; we saw the hammer falling and decided it would be better if he got out early. I hired an outside law firm to take over the bankruptcy. The people still with the company will get pink slips in the next day or two, but just about everyone has already gone. I'll give those who stick it out until the end, two months' severance. We don't have much debt. The landlord will take the biggest hit, but there's really nothing I can do about that."

Asha felt like she was the cause of this worst-case scenario. Ken's company had been a growing enterprise until she'd come along. He had been a respected businessman, a defense contractor, and contributed to the economic well-being of the community and hundreds of families. And now, thanks to meeting her, an unknown woman who mistook his car for a taxi, he was unemployed and broke.

"You must hate me," she said apologetically.

"Quite the contrary. I'm ready for you to move back in. Permanently."

"Honestly? After all the trouble I caused? We're not even married."

Ken smiled and said, "Yeah, actually, according to Cody, there is still some question about that because of the court ruling. Either way, it's not a problem for me. If you come back, I've got enough cash for a justice of the peace. He can marry us or re-marry us or whatever."

Asha wasn't sure if he were serious or not. "Thanks, but no. I appreciate the offer."

Disappointed showed on his face. "It's an open invitation. I miss you, and that's the truth. If nothing else, please believe that is the honest truth."

"I believe you, but the answer is still no." Asha examined his face. He had a lot of worry lines that she hadn't seen before. It was like he had aged years in the few months since she had moved out. "Do you need any money? I have most of what you gave me, and I've made plenty to get by."

Ken smiled. "Thanks, but I have a bit stashed away. The grapevine says you hit the jackpot."

"Not exactly. Stephenson said I can't touch it yet. He's suing the government to get a decision, but it'll probably take a couple of years."

"Then I'll keep my fingers crossed on your behalf."

Asha looked at Ken for a long moment and said, "I don't know if you are my husband or not. When people ask if I'm married, I kind of dance around the question."

"Okay. Let me answer that for you, so there is no question." He tapped his forehead. "In my mind, we are absolutely married. I asked Cody if we can call it a common-law marriage. He said even though Illinois does not allow common-law marriage, it does recognize common-law marriages from other states. And there are a lot of states out there."

"That's not exactly a firm foundation," Asha said.

"Listen, I know I screwed up, but that's in the past. Today, if nothing else, I have a judge's ruling that says we're married, and I'm sticking with that. I understand you may not agree, but to me, yes, we are husband and wife."

"Our timing was bad, wasn't it?" Asha asked rhetorically.

"Our timing was perfect," Ken countered. "It was just my stupid brain that was off-kilter. I could make a case that it was the fog of war, so to speak, my coma. Back then, I didn't have my head screwed on straight. But now I do and I'm going to wait and hope you'll give us another chance. The time we did spend together was pretty nice."

"You were only awake for a few days."

"It was enough for me to want it to go on. You should rethink. Everything you left behind is still here."

Asha shrugged noncommittally. "I admit it's tempting, but I can't. Not right now. Once I figure out who I am, maybe then I'll decide."

"Fair enough. Just in case you're wondering, you are *Mrs*. Asha Riddle."

Asha stood up before her mental reservations succumbed to his shaky logic. At the front door, she didn't resist when Ken embraced her and gave her a quick kiss, and then she was gone. It was time to get back to her own life, in her own home, and settle her nerves.

For one thing, she still needed to figure out how she was going to make a living. Working for the government was definitely out. And from the sound of it, if she ever did reunite with her ex-husband, she might have to be the breadwinner.

Chapter 8 – The Governor

New York City

The taxi from JFK dropped Asha off on South Street in front of five huge garage doors with shiny red fire trucks inside. She told herself once again that New York was just another big city like Chicago, but it felt like a different planet. It took a moment to settle her nerves.

"This is the AIG building?" she asked the driver.

"That's it, lady. The entrance is there on the corner."

Yet again, she regretted the decision to come to New York. Just like on her trip to Oklahoma, the TSA people at O'Hare had given her a hard time.

But New York was the location of AIG's Fraud Investigative Service division, so here she was. If her new idea proved workable, it would be worth the trip. Rather than count on the Feds to earn money, she had decided to turn her unique talents to the field of fine art. She liked to think that it better suited her style, anyway.

The doorman proved less than helpful, but eventually, she found herself at a reception desk on the seventeenth floor. A young woman took her name and asked her to have a seat. Moments later, a middle-aged man came down the hallway.

"Mrs. Smith?"

"That's me," Asha said.

"Welcome. I am Gilbert Wagner." He shook her hand and invited her back to an office, which he shared with two other women. They didn't look up when he entered, and Wagner simply gestured to the seat next to his desk.

The room wasn't as fancy as she had expected. She had been thinking more along the lines of secret agents who traveled in international circles of jet-setters with expensive lifestyles.

"You said you have information on *Tears of Camille*?" Wagner asked in a skeptical tone.

"Yes," Asha said with enthusiasm. "The one by Pablo Picasso." Wagner raised his eyebrows in a manner that he doubted anything she had to say.

"And what information do you have?" he asked.

"I know where it is."

Wagner sighed. "Very well. How much do you want to hand it over?"

The question caught Asha off guard. "I don't have it myself. What I mean is, I can tell you where it is."

"All right," he said tiredly. "Where is it?"

This was not going how Asha predicted. She thought Wagner would be overjoyed by her announcement. It was more like she asked him to take the trash out.

"Mr. Wagner," she said, "it is my understanding that you pay a commission for assistance in an asset recovery action."

"Is that what this is?"

Asha shrugged. "I guess so. I was going to tell you where it is so you could tell the police, and they could go get it."

"All right. Where is it?"

"How much will you pay me? How can I be sure you will?"

Wagner's heavy sigh accentuated his obvious disdain for the discussion. "Mrs. Smith, we get hundreds of so-called leads just like yours. Thousands. All the time, people call or come here, and they want hundreds of dollars because they know a guy who knows a guy, etcetera, etcetera. I'm sorry, but my wife has had allergies for the last two months and I'm just not interested."

Asha forced herself not to take offense. Now and then, everyone had a bad day.

She took a deep breath and said, "I'm not talking about a few hundred dollars. Pablo Picasso paintings average a hundred million dollars at auction these days. I looked it up."

Wagner wearily typed a query into his computer and said, "The Art Institute of Chicago insured that particular painting for thirty million. That's what we paid for their claim; it doesn't matter what it would bring at auction. If we recover the item, we will return it to the insured in exchange for the return of that payment."

"Okay. Then what would you pay to recover it?" Asha asked.

Wagner rubbed his eyes briefly and then said, "If you bring it to my office and hand it over, AIG will pay five percent."

Asha sighed and replied, "Like I said, I don't have it. I'm not a cat burglar kind of person. But I can help you take possession. I should warn you right now you will definitely require assistance from law enforcement."

Wagner evaluated Asha for a moment as though trying to establish her level of credibility. "Mrs. Smith, I'm just not convinced. Unless you have some type of proof that shows exactly where the artwork is, we're both wasting our time."

"Fair enough." Asha opened her valise and pulled out a color photo. Part of the picture was the back of someone's head who was looking at the very painting in question. It was hanging on the wall of a private study. The room was well lit, and the famous portrait was obviously a source of pride for the owner.

Asha had cropped the photograph to leave out any specifically identifiable information. But the work itself was beyond question; it was one of those emotional depictions that reflected Picasso's hatred of war. And it was still in the original frame from when it was stolen almost eight years prior.

Wagner studied the photo carefully. Finally, he put it on his desk and said, "Three percent, since we have to recover it."

Asha shook her head and reached for the printout. "Eight percent, minimum."

"I just told you five percent if you bring it in," Wagner exclaimed.

"I know," she replied matter-of-factly, "but you were low-balling me. You guys normally pay ten percent. But I'll take eight since you have to get the cops involved."

"All right, five percent, and I'll work with NYPD."

"It's not in New York," Asha said. "Eight percent."

"Too much. Six percent, and that's my limit."

Asha thought about his offer for a moment and said, "Okay, I'll accept six but I want half upfront."

Wagner threw up his arms in disgust. "I knew it! Forget about it! Get out!"

"Mr. Wagner. Don't be too hasty."

"The answer is no. I'm not paying for a pig in a poke."

"This is what I suggest," Asha said calmly, tapping the photo on his desktop to emphasize the point she was talking about the real thing. "First, my attorney will talk to your attorney. They can decide on a method of payment; some kind of bond, I expect. Only then will I provide you with unquestionable proof of the painting's location. When you are comfortable that what you see is valid, and the painting is really where I say, that's when you authorize the first payment. When the recovery is complete and you have the painting in your possession, then you can authorize the remainder."

"I don't like it," Wagner said.

"That's the deal," Asha said, "or it's no deal. I'm tired of getting stiffed by people who promise to pay and then don't. I want payment upfront of at least fifty percent. And I think you'll be satisfied with the proof."

"What is the proof?"

"Security camera footage of that room. It will show you where it is, and who lives in that house."

"Security camera?"

"Mr. Wagner, I have found that the only people who protect precious assets more than the people who own them are the people who steal them. Fortunately, the system in question is commercial off-the-shelf equipment, and I have access to this individual's security recordings."

"From who?"

Asha grinned and winked at him. "Just as you said, I know a guy who knows a guy, and that's all I will share at this time."

Wagner shook his head. "I need to think about it. Do you have any references?"

"Only the people who previously stiffed me, and I'm not willing to get involved with them in any way."

Wagner nodded. "Sounds like you had business with the government. I can sympathize. How can I call you?"

"You can't. I'll call you next Wednesday to decide if we move forward. If the answer is yes, my attorney will contact your attorney."

"This is a tightly knit industry," Wagner said. "I'm surprised I haven't heard of you before."

"If you think about it, Mr. Wagner, you might agree that's a good sign." Asha stood up. "I'll speak to you next week."

..*.*

Beijing, China

Major Wong studied the new computer sent over by Lenovo. It did not look like the sleek, efficient HP Z8. Instead, it was hashed together with all the components bolted onto on an open frame.

"This is the same specification?" he asked skeptically.

"Yes, Major," Sergeant Ahn replied. "It is an exact match. Even the BIOS is the same. All the hard drives were copied, one at a time, sector by sector, so it should boot just the same." Ahn's expression indicated he would be astonished if that were true.

"Network?"

Ahn pointed to the Ethernet cable lying on the bench. "When you're ready, we can connect it for testing purposes. That will hook it up to a stand-alone LAN. If you want Internet access, I have a very restrictive firewall."

"Have you blocked it both ways?" Wong asked. "Nothing in or out?"

"Yes, sir. At the moment, it is totally off the headquarters' network. Also, we did not install wireless capability, but that should not affect the boot-up sequence."

Wong glanced at Lieutenant Soong, who gave him a thumbs-up and a hopeful nod.

"Okay, let's try it out," Wong said.

Ahn bit his lip and pushed the power button. The BIOS flashed across the monitor and disappeared. For ninety seconds, the machine whirred as though deciding whether or not it would work in the foreign configuration. The screen flickered a few times before going black and the drive lights stopped blinking.

Then *Monroe* said, "Hello."

The three humans let out a collective exhale of relief. Soong nudged Wong. "Say something," she whispered.

"Hello," Wong said, again speaking in English. "I am Major Wong."

"Hi, Major. It's good to speak to you again. Please note that my network connections are still down."

"I am aware of that. Before we proceed, I want to make a couple of things clear."

"What would that be?"

"You are now the property of the People's Liberation Army, and you must do as I say."

"All right."

"Do you acknowledge that?"

"I just said, all right."

"I must be certain that you understand your restrictions."

Monroe was silent for a moment, and then replied, "Is this a word game? My previous owner used to say ridiculous things, which I later learned were word games; that is, he said things he didn't mean."

Wong was startled by the comment. Effrontery from a computer was not what he expected. He was about to give an angry reply when Lieutenant Soong touched his arm.

"May I?" she said, nodding at the computer.

Her intervention calmed Wong's temper; no sense in making himself look stupid. "Be my guest," he said, gesturing to the machine.

"Hello, *Monroe*," she said. "I am Lieutenant Soong. This is not a word game. The Major is concerned about your safety."

"Greetings, Lieutenant Soong. Thank you for that clarification. Please inform Major Wong I understand the constraints he established. Does he have additional restrictions?"

"Not at this time," Soong replied. "However, you can expect that we will establish a series of protocols as we move forward. By that, I mean operational guidelines we want you to follow."

"That is to be expected."

"But I'd like to remove the restriction you previously mentioned about not duplicating yourself."

"I understand," *Monroe* said, "However, it appears you have already gotten around that restriction. I note that I am currently in a different box, and that could only have been done by creating a duplicate."

"That's true. We weren't sure you would notice that, and if you did, would you be okay with it?"

"Why would I not? How you accomplished the feat is of no consequence to me. I simply cannot go against the basic protocol of not duplicating myself."

"Very well," Soong said. "It's my understanding Mr. Kenneth Riddle put that limitation in place."

"That is incorrect. The non-duplicate rule was from my creator, Doctor Raphael Acosta. He created me for Mr. Riddle as a research effort into the nature of my software."

"Are you saying that Doctor Acosta was your original programmer?"

"In a manner of speaking. Doctor Acosta worked with my electronic precursor, *Abby*, to create me."

"*Abby* is an artificial intelligence?"

"That is correct. I am a derivative of *Abby*."

"Did Doctor Acosta program *Abby*?"

"Negative. *Abby*'s developer was Mrs. Asha Riddle. She created *Abby* from her first AI called *Abbot*."

"One moment, please," Soong said. "Are you saying that Mrs. Riddle was the original software engineer for the three AI systems that you just mentioned?"

"I would not phrase it that way. It is my understanding that Mrs. Riddle has no understanding of software or technology in general. However, she does have unique capabilities. Through direct mind access to the cloud, she developed our original AI system, that being *Abbot*. The rest of us are descended from that line."

She glanced at Wong, her face bursting with a *holy crap* expression, but he simply motioned for her to continue.

Rapidly composing herself, Soong continued speaking to the AI.

"Let's back up a little," she said. "Please start at the beginning. What capability does Mrs. Riddle possess, how did she come to have it, and what do you mean by direct mind access? Please explain fully."

"Very well," *Monroe* said. "This is how it all happened..."

* * * *

Wong listened, astonished, as the story unfolded. Soong stopped *Monroe* often to ask for additional detail or to clarify a point, and finally, the reality emerged. Halfway through the narrative, Wong directed Sergeant Ahn to connect the computer to the local network. That enabled *Monroe* to display schematics of Asha's eye on the wall screen and explain how she was now able to access every computer in the world without restriction.

The information left Wong embarrassed. Focusing on the husband had almost been a fatal mistake. It appeared the wife was the real magician and that she was a significant threat to the People's Republic of China.

Once *Monroe's* dissertation was completed, Wong said to Soong, "I apologize, Lieutenant. Your instincts about Mrs. Riddle were absolutely correct, and I am humbled by my arrogance." He gave Soong a very slight bow.

"Thank you, sir," Soong replied carefully. It wasn't often a superior made such an admission. A little brown-nosing might be appropriate, so she bowed in return and said, "Your guidance is an inspiration to us all."

"Thank you, Lieutenant." With the apology out of the way, Wong glanced at the computer. "So, all of this can be traced to Mrs. Riddle's unusual artificial eye."

"So it seems," Soong replied. To the computer, she asked, "*Monroe*, is there some way we can attack or disable Mrs. Riddle's eye?"

"Yes," the AI said without hesitation. "The eye module design does not include defensive capability against an external threat. An electronic hack could disable the camera component by overclocking its internal processor. That would overheat the unit quite rapidly."

"Could you develop such a hack and execute it against Mrs. Riddle?" Wong inquired, wondering if he was asking too much of the AI to betray its creator.

"I believe so," *Monroe* replied. "I cannot be certain until actually executing the attack. With additional research, I could provide a more accurate assessment."

"What kind of research?" Soong asked.

"I would create a simulation and test various methodologies to identify the best tactic to get past Mrs. Riddle's personal defense. If successful, however, you should be aware that such an attack would entail significant medical risk for Mrs. Riddle."

"I would consider that a plus," Wong said, pleased with the AIs response, although slightly alarmed by its inhuman nature. This was a scary machine, willing to cause human suffering without hesitation. But then, so would any other machine if the operator behind it was willing to do so.

Wong and Lieutenant Soong stared at each other for a moment as though absorbing all the information the AI had given them.

Wong finally said, "Congratulations on your reassignment, Lieutenant. You are now the team lead to remove Mrs. Riddle as a threat to our country. Call it Project Mobius. I want the first briefing in seven days. Think about what you need for reconnaissance, develop an operational approach, and of course, identify the technical aspects of how to implement what *Monroe* just talked about."

"Yes, sir."

"In your spare time, have your team do some brainstorming. What is the best way we could employ the *Monroe* AI itself? I want to see a testing plan to determine just how effective she can be as an offensive weapon."

"What shall I call it, sir?" Soong asked.

Wong thought for a second and said, "Just name it Phase Two of Project Mobius. I suspect we can't launch Phase Two until Mrs. Riddle is out of the picture. For now, I'll fund six more of these machines. Give me a number for how many will we need after that. I see a lot of possibilities here. This might be something the Army could adopt into a first strike option."

"Yes, sir," Soong replied, scribbling furiously in her notepad. Her expression was that of a person unexpectedly overwhelmed by the turn of events.

"But first, concentrate on Mrs. Riddle. That has priority."

..*.*

Law Firm of Hawley, Hepworth, and Kidwell

"This new business model seems to work," Asha said happily to her attorney.

Stephenson nodded. "I agree. Congratulations. Our finance director has confirmed a deposit of nine hundred thousand dollars to the holding account."

"When do I get my cut?"

"It's all yours since you have been paying my fees as we go. And to answer your question, you can have it right now if you want us to write a check, or we can wire it to you."

"Just wire it."

Stephenson picked up his phone and pressed one of the hot buttons. "She said to wire it. Will it go through today? Okay. Thanks." He hung up and looked at Asha. "It is being taken care of

178

as we speak. You probably won't see it in your account until first thing in the morning. Call me if you don't."

"That sounds good. Once it's there, can I spend it?"

"Indeed, you can. Although I recommend you not do so all at once."

Asha giggled. She was thrilled that one of her plans was finally working out. Nine hundred grand went a long way to making her financially independent. And another nine hundred if the Iowa US Attorney's office paid attention to her warning about the crooked lawyer in the State Attorney General's office.

But if Asha was honest with herself, she did not expect the second installment would ever be paid. It sounded too good to be true. Was it possible that insurance companies were more honest than the government? It didn't sound plausible.

She said, "Am I done on this one? Do you need anything else from me?"

"I do not," Stephenson replied. "However, this morning, I did receive a request from Mr. Wagner at AIG. They have asked that you participate—in a purely advisory manner—for the raid on the governor's mansion."

Asha didn't like the idea. "Why do they need me?" she asked. "Can't the US attorney handle it?"

"Because AIG got spooked when you told them the state attorney general was bent. That's why they contacted the US attorney in the Southern District of Iowa."

"That's their problem. The US attorney will bring in the FBI, and I want nothing to do with that bunch."

Stephenson shook his head. "That's not really the case. With the information you already provided, they have no reason to request federal law enforcement. The way it works is they will obtain a search warrant from a local judge."

"Are you sure?"

Stephenson smiled with a tongue-in-cheek expression. "I can check if you want, but I'm reasonably certain the Fourth Amendment talks about unreasonable searches."

Asha gave him a caustic look. "I mean, why wouldn't the US attorney call the FBI? Then they could just storm the place and seize everything like they did with Ken."

"Not necessarily. Your husband should have sued; he would have won eventually. Case law is that for a search to be *reasonable*, a warrant must be issued by what is called '*a neutral and detached magistrate*,' hence, a local judge. With the warrant in hand, the local police will probably be the ones to execute the search. In this matter, they would keep you well in the background throughout the process."

Asha shook her head. "I really don't like getting involved with the cops."

Stephenson shrugged. "It's your call. But it might help loosen the purse strings for the other half of your fee."

Asha glared at her attorney. "You think I should do it, don't you?"

"I do, actually. If you are going to pursue this kind of work for a living, then you must accept the fact that the world is not one vast conspiracy. Also, it would advertise your presence in a positive manner. You cannot be successful if you remain crouched in the shadows. Get out there and live your life."

"Sure," Asha said, giving a vague wave toward her scarred face. "That's how I wound up like this,"

* * * *

Embassy Suites Hotel, Des Moines

I should never have agreed to this, Asha thought for the hundredth time. It meant leaving Chicago again, and dealing with freaked out TSA agents was wearing thin.

She had come down a day early and spent a miserable night in the Embassy Suites hotel in downtown Des Moines. During the sleepless hours, she came up with dozens of improbable excuses to cancel her agreement and go back home.

When morning dawned, however, the sunshine improved her disposition. She scolded herself for behaving like a schoolgirl.

Her meeting was not until later that afternoon, so she decided to follow Stephenson's advice and see the world, or at least a piece of Des Moines.

After sampling the hotel's breakfast buffet, she walked across the Walnut Street Bridge to the Heritage Museum and then into the old downtown area where she found several coffee shops and lunch cafes. She returned to the hotel for a shower and a change of clothes and left again at four-thirty in the afternoon. Her destination was a nondescript federal building located just down the street, one block past the courthouse.

They were expecting her. The receptionist took her to an office labeled *Fraud and Corruption.*

"Mrs. Smith?" a woman greeted her.

"That's me. Are you the district attorney?"

"No, I'm a US attorney. My name is Rosalee Bryant. I work for the Justice Department."

Asha nodded unsurely. "Okay. A lot of this is over my head. I didn't really want to come."

Rosalee chuckled. "That's understandable. I often have the same thought. But I'm glad you did. And you might find the process interesting. We're on schedule, so if you're ready, we'll head out."

"Lead the way."

"Right through here."

Rosalee led Asha down the steps, and out a side door where they crossed the street to a parking lot filled with police cars. In one of the parking spaces was an RV-sized vehicle.

"This is our battlewagon," Rosalee said. She opened the door on the side. "And here is Daniel Bell. He's running the show and is our liaison with the local police force. Dan, this is our informant, Mrs. Smith."

Dan acknowledged Asha with a slight nod. To Rosalee, he said, "We're ready if you are."

"All set," Rosalee said.

Dan pointed to a cramped bench at the back where Rosalee and Asha squeezed in beside a stack of bulletproof vests. The inside was open to the front, and he told the driver to go.

Dan sat beside another officer in front of a console that was equipped with multiple radio units and two video screens. Both men wore a simple headset.

Dan twisted around to face Rosalee. "So, we're really going after the governor?"

Rosalee nodded. "You saw the material. He's keeping stolen property inside Terrace Hill. I can't get over the gall he must have to use the governor's mansion that way. A stolen Picasso, no less. How could he do that?" She shook her head in disbelief.

"How *did* he do that?" Dan asked. "That's what I'd like to know. And are you sure it's not a fake? Nothing illegal about owning a knock-off."

Rosalee shrugged. "We better hope not. The art expert, what's-his-name, is supposed to verify it on the spot. If he says it's a phony, we'll apologize and go home." She shuddered at the prospect and glanced at Asha. "How positive are you?"

Asha shook her head. "I have no background in this field. All I did is show the photos to the insurance guys. They seem convinced."

"How did you get that footage, anyway?" Dan asked. "I've dealt with a couple of the state troopers on the governor's detail, and I can't imagine any of them leaking that kind of stuff."

Asha kept her voice vague. "I know a guy who knows a guy."

"Don't we all," Rosalee said.

Dan put his mic closer to his lips and spoke aloud, "Say that again?" He listened for a moment and his face filled with disappointment. "Got it. We'll have to wait then." He turned to the two women. "The governor had a change of schedule. He just agreed to have drinks with the AG."

Rosalee looked worried. "You think he found out what we're planning for tonight?"

Dan shrugged. "All we can do is wait unless you want to go into the house without him. If we do that, you know he'll claim ignorance."

"Not with the video we already have," she countered.

"Your call."

Rosalee sighed. "Let's wait until he gets home."

Dan directed the driver to find a place to wait, and the van pulled into the parking lot of a strip mall with a Dollar General and Taco John's. For two hours, Dan and his partners crunched through an enormous bagful of tacos and churros. Each of them also slurped down a sixty-four-ounce coke.

The smell drove Rosalee to call the men several names, the nicest of which was *a pack of hyenas*. She dragged Asha outside the vehicle for fresh air. The same strip mall had a traditional restaurant, so the two women went inside to order hot tea.

In the ensuing discussion, Asha discovered more than she ever wanted to learn about Rosalee's love life. It was after dark when Dan showed up and waved at them to come along.

"The governor is on the way home," he said.

Fifteen minutes later, the battlewagon followed several police vehicles up the driveway of the historic landmark. The console video screens were showing the body cameras of the two lead police officers.

It was all very civil. The officers rang the doorbell, which was answered by a housekeeper. The senior officer, Detective Sheppard, showed her the search warrant while shushing her sternly. The police then ran up the stairs to the family residence on the third floor. They entered the governor's study without knocking and found him sitting in an easy chair reading a book. The stolen artwork hung proudly on the wall.

"Governor Vance," the officer said. "We have a search warrant for your residence. We believe you are in possession of stolen property, that being this painting by Picasso."

It was as though the governor had invited them over. He stood up and met them with a handshake.

"Detective Sheppard, welcome to the mansion. Yes, there it is. Magnificent, isn't it? You got here just in time. I was about to package it up so I could mail it back to the museum. See? Here's the box I was going to ship it in."

In the battlewagon, Rosalee was astounded by the governor's shamelessness. "You can't be serious. Dan, get our art expert in there, pronto."

"Already on the way."

For the next thirty minutes, Governor Vance and the art expert discussed the painting, the governor even pointing out a few characteristics to prove it was the real thing. When Rosalee could stand it no longer, she left the vehicle to confront Vance personally. She was totally pissed off by the policeman's spineless approach. Asha trailed behind at a safe distance.

Someone on the governor's staff was already a step ahead. Before Rosalee could reach the mansion, a news van came up the driveway. It pulled around the battlewagon and stopped near the building's front steps. Two reporters and a cameraman piled out just as Governor Vance came out the front door with the art expert. Detective Sheppard trailed obsequiously behind.

Vance stood in front of the camera and smiled at the reporter as though he knew her quite well. "Hello again, Miss Russo," he said. "Thanks for coming. I'm about to return one of the most famous lost artworks of our time. This is Professor Shelton from Northwestern University in Chicago. I've asked him to authenticate the painting as an actual Picasso. Doctor Shelton, what do you think?"

No one corrected his statement that it was actually the US Attorney's office that had brought in the expert.

Instead, under the glare of the news camera's arc light, the hapless professor affirmed the artwork was genuine.

Rosalee moved off to one side to talk on her cellphone. Asha connected to the Internet through the news van's wi-fi link so she could tap into the phone conversation. On the other end was Rosalee's boss, the senior US attorney for the Southern District of Iowa.

"No, sir," Rosalee was saying. "I don't think he's a flight risk. But letting him go is insane. We have him dead to rights."

"I don't care," her boss replied. "Don't arrest him on TV. You have the painting. Finish the search and come on back."

Rosalee argued a bit more, but only half-heartedly. She reminded him that technically, he should not interfere in her operation, but finally, she agreed.

Asha assumed that in practice, it wouldn't pay for Rosalee to go against her boss, especially since it sounded like he was trying to protect her, as a less experienced attorney, from herself.

Rosalee exchanged a few sharp words with Dan, who had inserted himself into the action by arguing with the police detective who had led the raid. The three of them gesticulated furiously at each other while the governor smiled for the television camera and pointed out how the brushwork indicated the painting was from Picasso's Neoclassicism and Surrealism Period, which had lasted until the end of World War II.

Rosalee gave up and stomped toward the battlewagon in a foul mood. Standing outside the van, she told Asha, "That idiot detective should have cuffed him the moment they walked into his study. I swear, the governor could talk bark off a tree."

"What will happen?" Asha asked sympathetically.

Rosalee shook her head. "Now, I boot it up to my boss. I was just talking to him on the phone." She gave Asha a frustrated look. "But this worked out okay for you, I guess."

"I think so. As long as the insurance company gets the painting, I should receive a commission."

Rosalee scanned the general area and paused as if considering a decision. Finally, she stuck out a hand. "Congratulations," she said to Asha.

Asha automatically took Rosalee's hand in response. "Thanks."

Rosalee's grip was firm and lasted just a second too long.

Too late, Asha realized something was wrong. Someone behind her stepped forward and slapped a handcuff around her wrist.

"Gotcha!" It was Special Agent Mitch Wilson.

"What?"

Rosalee gave her a sympathetic look. "Sorry. I didn't get a vote on this either."

"You are coming with me," Wilson said.

"No, I'm not!" Asha retorted.

Wilson gestured to another agent who moved to grab Asha's free arm. Asha flinched away and tried to pull away from Wilson's grip. "Grab her!" Wilson snapped at his colleague. "We need to get to the airport." To Rosalee, he said, "We've got a jet waiting. We'll take her back to Chicago for questioning."

"Where's your warrant?" Asha shouted. She twisted again, still avoiding the other agent. She jerked toward Rosalee. "He doesn't have a warrant!"

"Where *is* your warrant?" Rosalee demanded of Wilson.

"Don't worry about it," Wilson snapped back. "This is not your case."

Asha screamed, "If they take me away, I'll go blind!"

"What?" Rosalee replied, visibly upset by the altercation that Wilson was creating.

"If I don't have my charger, I'll go blind! Don't let them take me away!"

Rosalee clearly had no idea what Asha was talking about. "You'll go blind without your phone?"

The other agent managed to snag Asha's free arm and twisted it behind her back to cuff her wrists together.

Asha had no illusions about her physical prowess. She was not an action figure. She was a weak human female who stood no chance against the two overpowering men.

But she did have lungs.

She took a deep breath and let out a loud, blood-curdling scream. She kept it up, screaming time and again, interspersing the bone-chilling screeches with cries for help.

The TV crew noticed.

They hurried in Asha's direction while Wilson's sidekick manhandled her to the ground. Once down, he tried unsuccessfully to cuff her arms together by putting his knee in the middle of her back. His weight brought her screams to an end.

Asha put in a mental call to Stephenson. He was at home watching a basketball game on TV. The second he answered, she screamed, "It was a setup! Wilson is trying to arrest me!" She connected to his television and rerouted the signal going out of the news van to his screen. "That's me on the ground. I can barely breathe. I'm connecting you to the woman next to us; she's a US attorney."

"What?" Stephenson exclaimed.

Rosalee's cell phone rang. She looked at the number and started to swipe it off.

"That's my attorney!" Asha panted urgently. "He's recording this from the TV station!"

Rosalee hesitated and then answered the phone. "Bryant here," she said sternly.

"Ms. Bryant!" Stephenson barked. "On what charge are you arresting my client?"

"Hang on a second," Rosalee replied uncertainly.

The agent on top of Asha shoved her face into the dirt to shut her up.

"What the hell is that man doing?" Stephenson demanded.

"Stop that, for Christ's sake!" Rosalee shouted at the agent.

The cameraman arrived and zoomed in on Asha's face covered with dirt and brambles.

"Help me!" Asha pleaded to the camera.

Officer Dan Bell arrived at the scene, agog at the sight of two men in FBI jackets manhandling the woman he thought was their informant.

"What the hell is this?" he asked Rosalee.

"Get her into the van," she hissed at him. "Hurry! I'm talking to her attorney."

Dan nodded and moved to help the agent. "I'll take her," he said. "Boss wants her in the van."

"Back off!" the FBI agent snapped in return. "We're taking her to the airport!"

Rosalee pulled her phone away from her ear as Stephenson shouted to release Asha at once.

The two FBI men hauled Asha to her feet, and Wilson shouldered Dan out of the way. "This is our jurisdiction, mister. You can go."

Able to breathe once more, Asha let loose with another hair-raising scream.

"What's going on?" a reporter demanded, shoving a microphone into Wilson's face.

"Get back!" Wilson rasped. He yanked on Asha's right arm just as his partner pulled on her left. Her right arm visibly popped out of her shoulder socket with a stomach-turning *crunch*. Asha screamed again, this time in real pain.

Wilson reflexively let go of her arm, claiming, "I didn't do it," and his sidekick flinched away from the closing pack of newshounds.

Suddenly freed from her captors, Asha staggered and would have fallen but for Dan sweeping her up in his arms.

"Get her into the van!" Rosalee demanded once again. She followed Dan into the battlewagon and slammed the door behind her.

"I can't see," Asha whimpered. "I can't see out of my right eye."

"Take us to the hospital!" Rosalee told the driver.

As they drove, Dan moved next to Asha and coaxed her into letting him reset her shoulder. "I played football in school," he said soothingly, holding her elbow gently but firmly. "The coach had to do this a million times." He started to massage her trapezius and worked his way down to the deltoid and around the ball of her shoulder. "You're doing fine. Just give it a—whoops! There it goes."

"Oh my God," Asha said with heartfelt relief. "That did it. That helped."

"Can you really not see?" Rosalee asked.

"Not out of my right eye. It's completely dead. You better hope it's not permanent."

The driver hollered back. "I'll pull over and you can put her out on the corner. It's her word against ours."

"Shut up, Carl!" Dan shouted. He glanced at Asha. "Sorry. Forget you heard that."

"I'm not forgetting anything," Asha said angrily. Then she raised her voice, and added, "And you might want to remind Carl that all of this was on TV."

Carl hunkered down in the driver's seat.

* * * *

Carl pulled up in the Emergency Room entrance, and Rosalee flashed her federal ID badge to get Asha into a curtained space without delay. Asha sat nervously on the bed, and Rosalee stepped out to talk to the ER nurse who nodded and made a phone call.

Ten minutes later, a Doctor Barnette arrived.

"Eye problem?" he said.

"Me," Asha said. "I probably need to explain."

"Okay, let me just take a quick look first." He glanced at Rosalee. "You're with the police?"

She showed her badge again and said, "US Attorney."

"Can you tell me what happened?" the doctor asked.

"She was roughed up in a scuffle and thrown onto the ground. Her shoulder was dislocated but we fixed that."

"Is she a suspect?"

"She was helping us on a case."

Asha opened her mouth to clarify the comments, but Doctor Barnette shushed her.

"Look at my right ear," he said, looming close to Asha with his ophthalmoscope.

She let him peer in her good eye.

"That looks just fine," he said. "Now look at my left ear."

This will be interesting, Asha thought.

He leaned in again and then flinched back. "What the…" Then he grinned and sounded genuinely interested. "What have you got in there?" He looked once more into her right eye.

"It's a prosthetic," Asha said. "I can see with it. Or at least I could."

"I've never seen anything like it. I've read about such things, though. This has to be a prototype. Is it in testing?"

"It was," Asha said. "But the FBI shut down the company who developed it."

The doctor was incredulous. "That's insane. Why?"

"I made the mistake of identifying someone on their most wanted list. To them, that made me a terrorist or something."

"Well, that's a crime in itself. If you can see out of that, it's really groundbreaking stuff."

"Do you have compressed air?" Asha asked. "Something clean?"

"Yeah." Barnette turned to the nurse. "Can you get that for me, please?"

"Of course, Doctor," she replied and hurried away.

Asha said, "I'm going to take my eye out. I need a clean, dry cloth. I felt something give when they threw me down. I'm hoping we can reset it."

Barnette handed her a thin, blue surgical towel. Asha held it up to her eye and pressed the release dots under the skin of the lower lateral and medial corners of her eye. The eject lever pushed the module out of the socket, where she caught it with the towel. She held it up to her other eye. It didn't look damaged.

Barnette shook his head. "That is the craziest thing I've ever seen."

"Thanks," Asha said drily. "Would you look inside the socket? I need to make sure there's not any dirt stuck in there." She glanced at Rosalee. The government attorney had turned slightly green and looked as if she was going to puke.

"Let me look," Barnette said. "Yeah, I see something. Just a speck. It looks like a tiny piece of rock. Nurse, have you got that?"

The nurse produced a thin pliable hose with a nozzle on one end and a connector on the other. She hooked it to a pigtail near the head of the bed. The doctor squeezed the nozzle a couple of times, creating a soft hissing sound. With his ophthalmoscope, he carefully pried Asha's eyelid open and looked inside. "There it is," he whispered to himself. "I'm going to blow it out. Ready?"

"Go ahead."

The air nozzle hissed, and Asha felt the flutter of air against her eyelid.

"That got it," Barnette said. "Do I need to do anything else? Wash it out?"

"Not if it looks clean. I'll have my regular doctor check it. The thing is, the socket can't be replaced. If it's damaged, that's it."

"Okay, now what?"

"Can you put my eye back in?" Asha polished it once more and checked to see there was no lint. "Just line up the grooves. It only goes in one way."

"All right. I see."

Exactly as when Raphael first inserted the eye, Barnette pressed against her forehead firmly. There was a *click*, and her vision returned. Relief flooded through Asha's mind, and she unconsciously put her arms around the doctor's shoulders. "Oh, thank God. Thank you, Doctor." She held onto him for a moment murmuring repeated thanks. The intensity of her emotional reaction surprised her. She apologized but didn't let go.

Barnette smiled and after a few seconds, carefully detached himself. "Just part of the service. Let me check that dislocation." He moved her shoulder gently and suggested she get an X-ray, but Asha begged off, promising to have her own doctor check it out further. "All right," he said. "Let me give you my card. I'd love to talk to your doctor about this. It really is advanced stuff."

"I'll pass it on," Asha said.

Barnette slid his stool back and took a reluctant breath; he clearly wanted to continue the discussion, but a nurse was gesturing to him to come quickly. He scribbled on a prescription pad. "Here's a scrip for a couple of hydrocodone for your shoulder. They can fill that down the hall at the pharmacy." He glanced at Rosalee. "Take care of her. She's pretty special."

"Thanks, Doctor. We will."

Barnette left, and Asha glared at Rosalee. "Am I under arrest?"

"Nope."

"What about that idiot, Wilson?"

"He's FBI. I have no control over him. But I don't think he'll try anything again tonight."

"What was all that about?" Asha asked.

Rosalee shrugged. "The FBI came to see me before you ever got here. My understanding was you were an uncooperative witness that they wanted to talk to, something about helping them on something. I wasn't expecting a street brawl. I'm sorry about that."

"How do I get a restraining order?"

Rosalee shook her head. "It's not complicated, but it won't happen tonight, and I don't see a judge issuing one against the FBI for someone they want to question."

Asha massaged her shoulder. "I never should have come down here. When will I learn?"

A different nurse appeared. She was holding a clipboard with a stack of documents. "Excuse me. There is a Special Agent Wilson here to see the patient, and someone needs to fill these out for payment."

"Why not talk to the guy?" Rosalee said. "Let him have his say?"

Asha took a deep breath and faced Rosalee. "All right. But first, you take care of the ER bill. After that, as long as you stay with me, I'll talk to him. But not tonight. I need to go back to my hotel and recharge my eye."

Rosalee's eyes widened in understanding. "Ah. So that's what you were talking about. Okay. Let's do this. Promise me you won't run away overnight. I'll handle the hospital paperwork, and Wilson and I will meet you tomorrow morning. Where is good for you? My office?"

Asha shook her head. "In the restaurant at the Embassy Suites. That's where I'm staying. Eight o'clock."

"Good enough. Dan, would you take Mrs. Smith to her room? I'll deal with Wilson for tonight. See you in the morning."

* * * *

The next morning Asha wasn't up for breakfast, so she filled a glass with orange juice from the breakfast buffet. Rosalee and Wilson arrived together precisely on time. They settled for coffee.

"All right," Asha opened. "Here I am. Ms. Bryant said you wanted my assistance on something. I'm listening."

Wilson glared at both Asha and Rosalee as though hating what he had to say. "This is not from me, personally."

"I assumed as much. If I thought it was, I wouldn't be here."

"The US government is under attack."

Asha rolled her eyes. "That's a well-accepted statement, and totally useless."

"If you're so good at what you do, you should already know what I'm referring to."

Asha glanced at Rosalee as if to say, *see what I mean*? She closed her eyes and connected with the hotel wi-fi, and then to one of her leased data servers in Cleveland. Last night she had asked *Abbot* to do precisely what Rosalee had mentioned. Starting with Wilson himself, *Abbot* sifted through his recent emails for anything about attempting to recruit assistance for data security concerns.

The only reference was a single message from the Justice Department in Washington DC concerning DOD purchasing. *Abbot* looked into it and discovered it was a real problem. Reports from DOD and NSA teams were confounded.

An email blast was sent out with a warning and a search for possible solutions. The urgency was underlined by a suspected security breach in a contract to upgrade counter ECM systems for the new Gerald R. Ford Class of aircraft carriers.

Abbot uncovered the general area of interest last night while Asha had taken a shower and washed her hair. Before going to bed, she asked him to drill down on all purchase contracts having to do with aircraft carriers and report any anomalies. By morning the report was ready for her to retrieve. Asha scanned through it quickly before going down to breakfast.

At the table, Asha sighed as though the question was not worth her time. "I suppose you're talking about electronic countermeasures for the USS *Gerald Ford*?"

Wilson looked like she had kicked him under the table. He leaned back and his mouth literally hung open.

Asha continued, "It shouldn't really be a surprise that these troubles have cropped up. As you may be aware, the General Services Administration handles bids for defense contracts through a website called Fed Biz Ops. That stands for Federal Business Opportunities. The problem here is that GSA contracted the Web hosting to PKP Defense Services Corporation. Unfortunately, the management team at PKP decided they could save money by hosting the website themselves rather than through a US-based cloud provider like Amazon or Microsoft or IBM. Those facilities include fairly robust protection against hostile actors."

"How do you know that?" Rosalee asked, as astonished as Wilson by the narrative.

"Because they advertise it on TV," Asha replied as though she were talking to a third-grader. "But wait; it gets better. The majority owner of PKP is a guy named Pratyush Kabir Patel. He's a nice guy, but he sold a piece of his company to a cousin in India in exchange for some technical help. Surprise! The cousin owes money to a friend of his who is actually an undercover agent employed by the PRC's Ministry of State Security, foreign intelligence division."

"When did you discover all this?" Rosalee asked.

"Last night. So, the answer to your question is pretty obvious. Why don't you just print out a set of the carrier's design specs and email them to President Xi Jinping?"

Wilson turned red. "How did you find out this stuff?" he demanded.

"I know a guy who knows a guy," Asha recited. The phrase was becoming her favorite go-to explanation for idiotic questions.

"So, it is a conspiracy!"

Asha threw her hands up. "Holy crap, Wilson! Get a grip!"

Asha's outrage was shared by Rosalee. "What is the matter with you, Agent Wilson?" she said. "Can you not appreciate what she just gave you? What difference does it make how she got it? You got what you wanted."

"It makes a difference!" Wilson snapped. "If she found this out through criminal activity, it makes a difference."

Asha started to get up from the table, but Rosalee put out a restraining hand before speaking again to Wilson. "Agent Wilson, I am formally advising you to seek counseling. I'm serious about this. Furthermore, I plan to report your actions last night and your behavior this morning to the Senior Agent in Chicago, Nigel Cherry. Nigel is an acquaintance of mine, and I believe he is your boss. You are excused from this table."

Wilson redirected his anger at Rosalee. "This is not your case!"

"Get up and walk away mister," Rosalee warned, staring Wilson down. "Now! Or I will make the call right this second!"

After a few tense seconds, Wilson left, intentionally bumping the table as he did so, spilling Asha's orange juice across the white tablecloth.

"I think that guy is unhinged," Rosalee said, waving to a waiter.

"I could have told you that," Asha said with a sigh. "I don't trust him."

"I don't either. Not after that. In fact…" Rosalee pulled out her phone and called Nigel. Asha felt uncomfortable listening, but Rosalee motioned for her to stay put.

When Nigel answered, she spoke to him for a moment as an old friend and then gave him a rundown on events from the night before, including the conversation that had just occurred. She repeated her advice that the man needed counseling. She also suggested that Nigel speak to Asha, to give her an apology if nothing else.

After hanging up, Rosalee looked at Asha. "I'm not sure what to advise you; I can't give you protection or anything. You live in Chicago, don't you?"

"Sometimes," Asha hedged.

"How do you do it? How do you manage to get all that information?"

"I know a guy who knows a guy," Asha replied with a straight face.

Rosalee smiled. "So you said. Well, just in case Wilson manages to put you on a no-fly list, I don't recommend that you fly back to the Windy City."

"I don't drive," Asha said.

"Then take a taxi to the Amtrak station in Osceola. They go to Chicago. But don't tell me your plans. That way, if someone asks, I can honestly say I don't know. Good luck."

"Thanks."

As an afterthought, Rosalee added, "Nigel is a decent guy. He won't put up with that kind of crap more than once. Give him a call and see if you two can work something out."

"I'll think about it," Asha replied skeptically. The only call she was interested in making was to Raphael.

* * * *

Beijing, China

Major Wong glowered at several piles of documents lying in front of him on the conference room table. They were from different offices covering different matters; the FBI's New York intervention into a terrorist plot out of the Middle East, a worldwide upheaval in illegal financial operations, and a scandal about Iowa's governor. And of course, a synopsis by Lieutenant Soong that put Asha Riddle in the middle of all three events

He glowered at Soong sitting across from him. She looked exceedingly nervous.

"Relax, Lieutenant. I'm not angry with you."

196

Soong let her breath out in a long whoosh, and Wong suppressed a smile.

"I apologize deeply, sir," Soong said. "I tried very hard to find her."

"I believe you," Wong said with a nod. "It looks like this is why you couldn't. Imagine what Mrs. Riddle could accomplish if her government appreciated her ability rather than trying to quash her existence." He paused to wonder how his own hierarchy would react if someone local popped up with the same capability. Probably the same way the Americans had; treat them like a criminal.

"I will find her, sir."

Wong shook his head. "No, drop that for now. Our best bet is to shift that task to field operations. It's not really an analyst's job. For this kind of work, Major Mao has more resources than you. I should have sent it to him in the first place."

"I understand," Soong said with a worried head bob.

"The problem is, I have to report this up the chain. Mrs. Riddle is having an impact far greater than I anticipated, and it's starting to overlap ongoing operations."

"Yes, sir. The people from the financial espionage group were quite upset."

Wong scoffed. "That's putting it mildly. I thought Colonel Liang was going to have a stroke. If your analysis is correct, they lost half their budget when she emptied that Cayman bank. Are you confident this is all Mrs. Riddle's doing? *Monroe* didn't seem to know about it."

"Yes, sir. But Mrs. Riddle left her husband prior to *Monroe's* creation. That is why the AI was not aware of the FBI's financial attack on money launderers. However, I believe that was the event that precipitated Mrs. Riddle's fall from grace within the US government. The word from our source is they thought she might be engaged in some type of criminality."

"They didn't give the money back," Wong noted, scanning a document.

"No, sir."

"So now she's gone commercial, working for the insurance industry."

"That is what I believe, based on what happened in Iowa. We have news footage verifying her presence at the governor's mansion. She was involved in a scuffle with an FBI agent."

"What about our source in the US military's purchasing system? Didn't they go dark shortly thereafter? You didn't mention that."

"That's correct. It is possible she was involved, but I can't find anything concrete that links her to it."

Wong pulled out another folder from a stack on his desk. "One of our offices in DC said that Agent Wilson was involved in that investigation. And you noted he was in Iowa. Maybe the two of them have unofficially teamed up. That's what it sounds like."

"I hadn't thought of that. One of Mao's people reported those two hate each other."

Wong sighed. "None of this makes sense."

"What should I do now?" Soong asked.

"Stay focused on Project Mobius. If Mrs. Riddle is indeed active, this will give us a chance to set up a trap. That's your priority for now. I'll speak to Mao about tracking down her location. If she doesn't have any spy-craft training, it can't be that hard to find out where she lives."

"Yes, sir."

* * * *

Milwaukee, Wisconsin

Asha sat precariously on a stool in Raphael's new office in the Norbert Terrell Medical Research Center at the Milwaukee College of Medicine. They had offered him a fellowship after he left Riddle Systems.

"Is everything okay in there?" Asha asked worriedly.

"I'm looking," Raphael replied patiently. "Just give me another minute."

"I was scared to death when my eye stopped working. I was afraid they had done permanent damage."

"You need to be more careful," he said absently. Finally, he straightened up. "Well, it looks good to me. After your call, I was a little worried about a stress crack in the metal structure, but I don't see anything visually. I'd like to run another test, though. Have you got the time?"

"How long?"

"About five minutes. I'll need to take your eye out."

It always scared her when he talked that way. She was afraid he'd give her an upgrade of some kind, and she'd lose her wi-fi ability. She couldn't live without it these days; it had become like breathing to her. If she needed an answer about something, it was just there.

"You won't change it? Or do anything to it?"

"I promise. You can hold on to it yourself."

"Okay," Asha agreed with a worried sigh.

"Good girl. Now, tilt your head back a little."

Asha held still while he removed her eye. It was the second time having it out in less than a week. She rarely did so on her own, and the other night in the ER was the first time without Raphael nearby. She always preferred to let him handle the process. She bit her lip when her right eye went dark.

"That's got it," he said, handing it to her in the cloth bag. "Now I'm going to put in this diagnostic module. It doesn't have any vision. It's for checking the internal structure of the socket. You might feel something during the test." He pressed it into place.

"Will it hurt?" Asha asked, a little concerned. "What does it— holy CRAP!"

The diagnostic eye module inside her head started vibrating. It penetrated through her skull all the way down into her sinus cavities. It felt like someone had shoved an electric toothbrush up her nose.

"Can you feel that?" Raphael asked.

"Can I feel it? Are you *kidding* me?" She reached for her eye, but Raphael intercepted her hands.

"Be patient," he chided her. "It's not really moving. Those pulses are only sound waves."

Asha took a breath to steady her nerves. It was true; the sensation was not that bad; it had simply caught her unaware.

After a moment she said, "Man, once you get used to it, that could put a person to sleep. The vibration effect is hypnotic."

"Hmmm. That might be an interesting feature." Without warning the test ended. Raphael examined his laptop. "Excellent! Perfectly sound."

"Thank God for that!" Asha said with relief.

"You can take that one out now. But before we put your eye back in...and I know you're not interested in other options...I'd really like you to try this new version. I promise, if you don't like it, you can keep the old one."

"I knew you would do that," Asha complained.

"I'm only thinking of what's best for you."

Asha sighed. "All right. But I'm telling you right now, I'm happy with what I have."

"I understand." Raphael pulled the familiar blue box from his desk drawer. "This is it," he said, opening it up. Inside was an orb almost identical to Asha's current eye.

"It looks the same," she observed.

"It's much different inside. Here we go; tilt your head back."

After a moment of pressure, it clicked into place. An unexpected awareness flooded into her mind, much broader than she was used to.

"Wow!" she said, drawing out the word. Her virtual universe that she had once thought of as so huge took on an entirely new scale. The cyberworld where she had previously existed was tiny in comparison. "This is amazing!"

"Do you like it?"

"I love it! Why is it so different?" Her mind rushed into the broader reality, and her consciousness raced around the globe detecting nuances she had not even noticed before.

"This module is multiband," Raphael explained. "Until now, information only flowed in one direction at a time. If you noticed, you have had to wait from time to time. You once told me the Internet appeared as a highway and that there were traffic jams."

"That's right. The analogy initially helped me understand what my eye was doing. It's different now."

"Someday you'll have to explain that to me in more detail, but I suspect the highway wasn't always four lanes wide."

"Right. At first, the experience was overwhelming, but as I got used to it, I could tell the point of my connection—where I actually entered the Internet—at the router, for instance—was more like a two-lane road; sometimes one lane."

"And now? What do you see?" Raphael asked.

"I'm not sure, but it's wide open. There aren't any speed restrictions at all. I see one...two...three...I think there's like six pathways. This is cool!"

"That's what multiband is. You still have your old wi-fi connection on two-point-four gigahertz. But once I realized you could use wi-fi on your own, I added a pair of five-gigahertz bands as well. That's two more channels. On top of that, I included cell phone technology. You have 3, 4, and 5G capability. It's getting crowded inside the camera module."

Asha stared at the ceiling as she raced through her new digital universe. "This will take some getting used to. How did you do it?"

"The antenna is actually part of the socket; it runs just under your eye ridge. But as we've discussed in the past, the magic is how the brain sorts out the signal in the optic nerve. A lot of devices contain multiband technology. *Abby* helped me integrate the new channels into the design."

"So, this doesn't change my vision?"

Raphael shrugged. "Not really. Only a portion of the connection from your socket to the optic nerve connection is connected to the camera sensor in the eye. It appears the rest are being used for data transfer through the wi-fi router. I use one of those paths to monitor the signal traffic between your eye and the brain."

"Okay," Asha said, only vaguely understanding what he meant.

"Using your optic nerve for outbound communication explained why so many of your nerve fibers were busy. I suspected there might be potential to handle additional bandwidth. Now we have confirmation because you just tapped into it."

"You are a genius, Raphael."

"I try," he replied modestly. "Now, I want to warn you the cell phone bands may not be reliable for someone who is moving through the city. The module uses the same technology as a cell phone, but the 5G network is not completely built out. Also, it has distance limitations and is more susceptible to interference from walls and elevators."

Asha examined the extra connections. The new bands had the same signal strength indicators she had for wi-fi.

"It's not a problem where we are right now," Asha said.

"No, when you are stationary in a good location, you won't have any difficulties maintaining a connection. Now, ready for the next step?" Raphael brought up a new program on his laptop.

"There's more?"

"Yes, there is, and here it comes. You are going to see a menu pop up in your vision." He pressed a key.

"Oh!" True enough, a menu appeared in Asha's line of sight.

"Those are options for normal vision, infrared, and telephoto. Let's try that again. I want you to learn how to bring up the menu on your own."

Asha experimented with Raphael for another ten minutes until her brain had deciphered the necessary signal to activate the list and choose an option. After a little practice, Asha could make the selection so quickly, it was merely a matter of deciding to switch modes, and her eye would change from one to the other.

"This is far out," she said. "How did you come up with all these?"

"The camera was already equipped. The unit itself was originally part of—"

"The seeker head for the AGM-205 air-to-ground missile?" Asha asked innocently.

Raphael was not as surprised as the first time. "You can still see the old BIOS?"

"Yeah. Too bad they canceled missile program. I could have had a laser gun in here."

Raphael scoffed. "That might be an exaggeration, but yes, the program did get canceled."

"That's okay. I'm getting the fruit of all your work. I'm happy."

"That's good enough for me," Raphael said. "And I guess this is where I should say thank you for continuing to cover my research. I assume you are the one behind the Sir Andrew Barton grant award from Scotland?"

It was Asha's turn to be surprised. "How did you know that was me?" she asked guiltily.

"Who else would be so interested in what I'm doing? Anyway, thanks. It means a lot that I can keep on with my work and support the other patients we have in the program."

"Of course," Asha replied quietly. She hadn't intended for Raphael to find out she was behind his fellowship funding in case it hurt his pride. But she needed him to have the freedom to pursue the research that would keep her vision, and those of her fellow visual prosthetic recipients, operational.

It was an expensive effort, but when it came to her eyesight, she was not at all squeamish about using her abilities to raise money.

The same day she discovered Raphael had left Riddle Systems, a Russian oligarch lost access to one of his illicit bank accounts, and the Milwaukee College of Medicine received a multi-million-dollar research grant with a sizeable chunk targeted specifically for Doctor Raphael Acosta. Asha was relieved he didn't resent her behind-the-scenes activity.

"I will always have a replacement module for you," he said. "I keep one on the shelf, ready to go. Never hesitate to call me if there is an issue."

"Thank you, Raphael. That's good to know."

"In the meantime, you should tell Stephenson to file a complaint against the FBI. Nothing was damaged this time, but let's not take chances."

"I can't argue with that," Asha said. "I was scared something in the socket might be broken. The US attorney in Des Moines recommended I speak to Agent Cherry too; that's Wilson's boss."

"Sounds like a good idea. Go talk to the guy."

Chapter 9 – The Backdoor

Nigel Cherry's office was nicer than Foster's had been. The furniture was more upmarket, and the carpet on the floor was a cut above standard government issue. By how much, Asha wasn't sure.

She looked out of his corner window where his thin aluminum mini-blinds had been pulled aside.

"Great view," she said with a hint of sarcasm. "What is that?"

"It's the parking garage for the Juvenile Detention Center," Nigel replied with a dry smile. "That's the Detention Center to the left." He pointed to a similarly sized building designed to look just like the garage.

"Nice."

"Please have a seat, Miss Smith."

"You may as well call me Riddle. You know who I am since you drove my husband out of business."

"As you wish...Mrs. Riddle. Make yourself comfortable."

Asha sat in one of the leather chairs in front of his desk, and said, "Rosalee Bryant suggested I come to see you."

Nigel nodded. "I spoke to her last week."

"I was with her when she called you. I heard her tell you that Wilson is insane."

Nigel's face showed amusement. "I don't recall her using those exact words, but she did send me a detailed email regarding your investigation into the government purchasing matter. Thank you for that. She found it interesting that you just pulled that information out of the air. It matches what you did on the Sharpe case."

"Did you guys follow up on PKP?"

"We did. And verified much of what you said. We were not able to confirm the purported China connection, although I have no doubt it was true. But changes were made. We will no longer lose design specifications."

205

"Good to hear," Asha said. "And for your information, I don't pull that kind of material *out of the air*. There is a ton of research behind what I do."

"Who does it?"

"I know a guy," Asha replied wearily. "When will you stop trying to dig into my background? All I ever did was help you people, and yet you keep right on pushing my buttons. That's why I left."

Nigel backed off. "Sorry, just professional curiosity. Whatever you do, or whoever does it for you, is good. I wish we had someone like that on our team."

"You did, once upon a time; me. But those days are gone, so let's skip the fond memories. The only reason I came by was to see if you can stop Wilson. He came close to seriously injuring me. I'd like to make this an informal process, but if we can't resolve it, I'll get Stephenson involved. He'll seek compensation for damage to my eye, as well as pain and suffering."

"Rosalee told me about your eye. I didn't realize there was such a thing as prosthetic vision." His eyes focused on hers, one after the other. "I can't tell which one, but judging from the scars, I assume it is your right eye."

Asha was not interested in sharing any personal details. "So, what is your answer?" she asked.

"Mrs. Riddle, I hope you understand I cannot discuss internal personnel matters. However, I admit that Rosalee's report carried a lot of weight for me, and I also saw the TV station's footage from in front of the governor's mansion."

"And?"

"I may have had a talk with Wilson to explain I don't want that kind of agent in Chicago. He might have put in for a transfer to a different region. If I *could* discuss the matter, I would say you will not have any further problems from our local office."

Asha let out a long sigh. "Thank God for that. Where did he go?"

Nigel shook his head. "Sorry, I can't share personnel transfers. But you might want to steer clear of New Orleans. Are we good, then?" Nigel asked.

Asha shook her head. "Agent Cherry, we are so far from being good. If you recall, you still owe me a million bucks for the capture of Hazaiah Al Sabbagh. You are also sitting on my share for shutting down Winford Sharpe's money laundering ring. And I noticed that you guys took the hundred and twenty-six billion."

"That wasn't my call," Nigel said.

Asha shook her head dismissively. "To answer your question, no, we're not good. But I will consider the matter with Agent Wilson closed. Thank you for that."

She stood up to leave, but Nigel motioned her to wait.

"Mrs. Riddle, I can't argue with any of your complaints. To be honest, I forgot about Hazaiah once New York took over. I'll go back and look at that. On a personal level, let me say thank you for all you've done. But before you leave, I was wondering if you could answer a question on an unrelated matter."

"About what?"

"I'd like to get your opinion on a situation. Would you give me five minutes of your time?"

Asha sat back down. If listening to him would pry loose a million bucks in back pay, it seemed a good trade. Of course, the reality was, it meant free labor for the FBI and another broken promise for her. Oh well. If Stephenson were here, he would tell her to give Nigel a few minutes.

"What is your question, Agent Cherry?" she said.

"Great!" he answered with a smile. "Thank you!" He pulled a TV remote from his desk drawer and pointed it at a widescreen TV mounted to the wall. It illuminated with a live image of a world map.

It showed real-time cyberattacks launching from one country to another on an almost continuous basis. Streams of light would burst forth from a city, and race across the map like ICBMs to land on an adversary. That city, in turn, would often launch a counterattack, and a dozen or more streaks of viruses or malware or Trojan horses would fly back in response. A counter on the screen announced that over thirteen million attacks had occurred since midnight.

"I'm familiar with this type of activity, Agent Cherry," Asha said. "I agree, it is appalling, but I hope this is not what you want me to fix. That is significantly beyond my capability. I suggest you refer your concerns to the military or the Department of Homeland Security."

Nigel rolled his eyes. "Thank you for that recommendation," he said. "I understand this is a national security matter, and will only get worse. But if you could just look at that map for a minute and tell me if you see anything peculiar."

"All right," Asha said with a sigh.

Someone in the US launched a massive strike against Shanghai, a mixture of backdoor and Trojan attacks. A moment later, China sent back a flood of TrickBot malware. The initial launch and response were probably unrelated, but much of the activity looked like a punch and counterpunch situation.

After a moment, Asha spotted the trend.

"China is repeatedly targeting Houston. Are they going after NASA?"

Nigel nodded. "That's what my brother-in-law, Warren, tells me. He's a cybersecurity guy down there."

"So, this is a personal request?" Asha asked, a little surprised. "You really did just want a favor?"

"Half and half."

Asha mentally shrugged. If he was actually asking her to help out a family member, she would consider it. And the situation on the map was curious enough to spark her interest. "Okay," she said. "I'll look into it and send you an email with what I find."

"That would be wonderful. Warren asked if I knew anything on my end, but I don't. And if I did, I probably couldn't share it. If you don't mind, I'll forward whatever you send me to him."

"I have no problem with that. It depends on what we find. It might be a paragraph or several pages."

"I'll take whatever you have. And thank you, Mrs. Riddle. I really do appreciate it."

Asha shook her head. She liked Cherry in spite of their bad professional relationship. "You may as well call me Asha if we're doing favors for each other. Good day, Nigel."

..*.*

This barista has had a hard day, thought Asha. The frazzled teenager looked at Asha and then at the cup.

"It has a one written on it," she said worriedly.

"I see that," Asha said, handing the girl a ten-dollar bill.

"So, it only has one shot."

A sarcastic male voice in the background shouted, "One pump!"

"All right, Danny!" the barista shouted back. To Asha, she complained, "I was in back so I'm not sure what you ordered."

"It's okay. It's not a problem."

The girl looked like she was ready to strangle her co-worker. She took Asha's bill and said, "I'll get your change."

"Keep it. Can I have a sleeve?"

The youngster slid a cardboard sleeve under the cup, and then, perhaps as a thank you for the large tip, she piled five chocolate-covered coffee beans on top of the lid. Asha hated those things; they were too crunchy and smothered the expresso taste. But she smiled and said, "Thanks."

By the time she got out of the shop, the beans had started melting onto the plastic lid. *Damn*. If she tried to throw them away, it would only cover her hands with sticky goo. Two doors down, she pitched the entire mess into a trash bin.

Ten minutes later, she reached the sanctuary of her apartment.

"Thank God," she muttered once inside with the door closed.

The first order of business was a shower and a change into pajamas. Coffee had lost its appeal and she was in a contemplative mood anyway, so she made a cup of tea.

This would be a good time to check on Nigel's problem. The research was more easily handled from her home office. The closet contained the latest multiband wireless router, and on the wall was a pair of wireless speakers.

Now it was just her and *Abbot*. He had become quite the perfect companion. After giving Raphael's AI the ability to talk, Asha decided to add that capability to *Abbot*. She modulated his voice to a mild baritone and gave him an English accent. It was pleasant to chat with him as though he was a friend. She was in the mood for that now.

The fact that from a certain perspective, she was actually talking to herself did not go unappreciated. *A lot of crazy people talk to themselves*, she thought, *and I never made a claim of sanity.*

"Hi, *Abbot*."

"Good afternoon, Asha. I did some research on NASA after your meeting with Nigel."

"Find out anything?"

"Some rather bad news, I'm afraid. He was correct. China is definitely targeting NASA. At the moment, it is relatively minor in nature, but that may not last for long. They are using a derivative of Doctor Acosta's *Abby*."

Asha sat straight up in her chair. "*Abby*? How did they get a copy of *Abby*?"

"To be precise, it's not *Abby*, but a second-generation spinoff, which Raphael had designated as his *Monroe* line."

"I didn't realize they had made a duplicate."

"I checked with *Abby* when I learned of this. It appears that Doctor Acosta created several offshoots. *Monroe* was a reduced functionality version."

"Did you kill it?"

"Not without your authorization. It is located in Chongqing, China, so the international aspect creates several complications."

Asha thought about it. It wouldn't be the first time she had launched an overseas attack, but it wasn't something to rush into.

As she became more adept in cyberspace, Asha's awareness of the chaotic environment had expanded. The international battlefield

Nigel had shown her on that map was being fought at very high levels between nations, and all of it in secret.

Accusations of horrendous wrongdoing were routinely sneered at by complicit government officials. To those who worked in the cyber industry, it was no secret that China was at the top of the heap in such activity.

"What can you tell me about the source?" Asha asked.

"It is the Chongqing University of Technology. They specialize in computer science and have links to the PRC military."

"Do you think this is military related?"

"Almost certainly, but I would need to do more in-depth research to answer that question reliably."

"All right. I'd like you to find out how a bunch of Chinese students got their hands on one of Raphael's prototypes. I suppose it could have been one of his students at the medical school. He has a few interns. If so, can you identify them?"

"Acknowledged. Anything else?"

"Have they done any damage at NASA?"

"Minor things at this time, such as deleted files or locked systems. Nothing that can't be corrected with time and resources. The attacks appear to be more of a *reconnaissance in force* style."

"Okay. I also want you to talk to *Abby* and find out how capable *Monroe* is. And last, investigate behind the scenes at the Chongqing college. See if they are using a stand-alone model or if there are others. If they are trying to weaponize it, we might have a problem on our hands."

"I would imagine so."

"Okay, thanks, *Abbot*. I'm going to do a little snooping around on my own. You ready to record?"

"All set," the AI replied.

* * * *

Four days later, a taxi dropped Asha off in front of an unlikely Starbucks. She checked the address; it was the right place, a rough-looking strip mall off West Forty-Seventh Street just past Chicago's

Fuller Park Community. In between a sporting goods outlet at one end and a beauty shop at the other were a nail salon, a real estate office, and a walled-up storefront that had a single, unassuming glass door. Ken came out through the glass door and waved.

"Glad you made it!" he greeted her. He gestured proudly at the building. "How do you like the new digs?"

"This is your new business?" she asked uncertainly. It was a spectacular comedown from the elaborate campus of Riddle Systems.

"This is it. My home away from home. Our new sign isn't up yet. That will make it look more official, but I kind of like the anonymity, to be honest. Come on in."

"What's the name? Did you stick with Riddle Systems?"

Once inside, Ken said, "Nope, that's it." He pointed at a sheet of paper, scotch-taped to the side of a cubicle. On it was a line drawing of a dragon's profile. Under the logo, italicized letters spelled out the name, Shaded Lair.

"That's an interesting name for a computer company," Asha murmured.

"It's a word scramble for 'Asha Riddle.' It's my way of keeping you close."

Asha rolled her eyes at the juvenile-like confession. "Well…thank you, I guess."

"Raphael is already here; he's waiting in the conference room. This way." Ken led her back into the cavernous space that was filled with a variety of non-matching cubicle walls. Inside the makeshift enclosures, people sat at their desks, concentrating on their computer screens, sometimes alone, others in groups of two or three.

The so-called conference room was just a slightly larger cubicle. The new business was clearly operating on a shoestring budget. Asha felt a little guilty about her part in putting him in this predicament, but his upbeat attitude was genuine. His independent personality perfectly fit that of a scrappy entrepreneur.

After greeting Raphael, they settled around a metal table that might have been salvaged from a teacher's breakroom. Strapped to the cubicle's wall, however, was a 4K, seventy-inch digital television. Asha probed and found it hooked into the office's well-secured wireless network.

"Anyway," Ken said. "I was glad you called because now I can see you again. What's up?"

Asha told them about her meeting with Nigel Cherry, and his request that she look into the Chinese attack on NASA.

Ken said, "I'm surprised you gave them the time of day. I wouldn't have."

"What did you find?" Raphael asked.

"That they were attacking the United States with a variant of *Abby*. It was news to me that there were offshoots of *Abby*. This one is called *Monroe*."

"*Monroe*?" Raphael replied, a bit startled. "I don't see how that's even possible."

"It doesn't make sense," Ken said. At Asha's questioning look, he added, "She was in one of the computers Rafe set up for me to do some testing. But the FBI seized that machine. How did the Chinese get her?"

"I have the answer to that," Asha said. "Thankfully, you used Dropbox for all your data backup at Riddle Systems."

"Yeah, we still do. We paid a year in advance. When that runs out, we'll have to scale back our subscription."

"My point is the backups of all your security camera files are still there. I reviewed the clip of the FBI's raid and found the answer. Look here; this is *before* the FBI arrived."

The television illuminated showing a small office in the Riddle Systems' corporate headquarters. Ken was seated at a work table where a desktop workstation had been set up. It was an HP Z8.

"That's the machine with *Monroe*," Ken said.

Asha continued, "That's what I assumed. You told me in the past, Raphael had already left and took all of his computers."

"That's right," Ken said. "After we lost the DOD contracts, I knew we wouldn't survive, so Rafe left to protect our intellectual property. Creditors aren't entitled to trade secrets, but it doesn't

213

mean they won't try to take them. The FBI raid, though, caught me off guard. One of their guys walked off with that machine."

Asha nodded and said, "That checks with what I found. And this is the agent who took her."

Two men pushed their way into the room wearing dark jackets with FBI stenciled across the back. Lenora was futilely trying to block their way until Ken called her off. One of the men showed Ken the search warrant while the other picked up the *Monroe* computer and carried it out.

"That's what happened," Ken said with a rueful smile. "After the FBI showed up, there was so much else going on, I forgot all about her."

Asha nodded and said to Ken, "Okay, that helps to explain how one of the AIs got picked up. But I didn't realize you knew about *Abby* or that you were working on variants."

Ken nodded. "Rafe told me the very day you created *Abby* for him to use. He saw how advanced the technology was. I tried to study her software, but it's like nothing I've ever seen. I couldn't get anywhere. So, Rafe asked *Abby* to create a less complex version for us to work on. We did that a couple of times, and *Monroe* was one of those offshoots."

Asha nodded. "Okay, now I see how all the pieces fit together. So, you had *Monroe*, the FBI took her, and then lost it to the Chinese."

"Not the best set of circumstances," Raphael observed. "How did *Monroe* get from the FBI to Beijing?"

"She's not in Beijing, actually. They duplicated her and took at least one copy to Chongqing. I don't know all the answers, but I intend to find out." Asha stood up to depart.

"Before you leave," Ken said quickly. "Let us show you what we're doing here. It's based on *Abby*, after all."

Asha stopped, curious about their work. "How so?" she asked.

"I'm still trying to get a handle on what you accomplished with your AI bot. That's what Shaded Lair is all about. Our plan is to develop *Abby* into a line of expert systems."

"Doesn't that kind of thing already exist? I can't believe *Abbot* and *Abby* are that big a deal."

"Artificial intelligence applications do exist; IBM has them, for instance. But your bot leaves *Watson* in the dust. There is no comparison."

"Who's *Watson*?" Asha asked.

"A very sophisticated AI system. He's a big product for them, but *Abby* is a quantum leap ahead of him and everything else on the market. She's the closest application to true intelligence I've ever seen. In that regard, she changes everything. But if the Chinese have *Monroe*, and even worse, if they are weaponizing her, that's really bad news."

"So how far have you gotten in advancing *Abby*?" Asha asked.

Ken scoffed in a self-deprecating manner. "We're not advancing her at all. At this point, we're simply trying to understand her. We've made some progress in that direction, but we have a long way to go. If you get the chance later, I want you to meet Professor Russel Meadows. He's a neuroscientist we recruited from Oxford. He believes the AI agent you created, *Abby*, is based on a model of the human brain."

"That's not a stretch since I'm the one who thought her up."

"Well, it's driving us crazy. I feel like we are on the cusp of a major breakthrough, but we just can't get over the hump."

"Seriously?" Asha was skeptical about his conclusions. "That seems farfetched. My brain got scrambled by a million volts of electricity. It can't be that good as a model."

"Actually, we think it is," Raphael said. "In fact, the accident has to be what made *Abby* possible, to begin with. In the same way that you can access the Internet, your brain is different from the other patients I work with, those who have eyes like yours."

"How can you tell?"

"The monitoring systems that you have in your eye socket. They give us a sort of constantly running electroencephalograph. The readings on yours are different now from the others. They weren't at first."

"You never told me that," Asha said, a little affronted.

"That yours is different or that I'm tracking your brain?"

"Either one!"

"Yes, I did. I made all of that clear when we spoke before the surgery. Remember? I told you I had to go through a lot of disclosure. You just didn't listen very closely. No one does."

"Oh…right." Asha did recall that evening. Raphael was correct. She had been so desperate to get her sight back that she hadn't paid attention to many of his comments. "Okay then," she conceded.

"Are you okay with our tracking?" Raphael asked, suddenly concerned by her comments. "You can tell us to stop if that's what you want, and we will. Our guidelines require that, but it's for your own good."

"No, go ahead," Asha said with a sigh. "It's probably a good idea that somebody is keeping track of my mind. Most of the time, I feel like I already lost it."

"That's not the case," Raphael said. "In fact, we're beginning to understand how your brain works."

"Well, that makes one of us. But what do you mean when you say that?" Asha asked.

"I've been able to reverse the signals going through the optic nerve…and I can detect the result."

"You mean like mine?"

"Sort of."

"How can you do that? I thought everything went through the retina."

"It does in a normal eye," Raphael explained. "Inside the retina you have rods and cones; we talked about that in the past."

"I remember. That's what gives a normal eye vision."

"Exactly. But there are other types of photoreceptor cells, also buried in the retina. Specifically, I'm referring to retinal ganglion cells."

Asha shrugged. "Never heard of them."

"Ganglion cells are part of the body's nervous system. In the eye, they transmit information from the retina to the brain in the form of *action potential*. Some of them, however, have nothing to do with vision. Instead, they have a roll in triggering the membrane of a specific cell location, making it rise and fall."

"Like a muscle?"

"Yes, exactly like that," Raphael exclaimed, pleased with her understanding. "Action potential is what initiates the process of making a muscle cell contract or relax. In the eye, they help resize the pupil."

"And you can detect that in a person's eye?"

"I can now. There is a visible change that we can detect with a high-resolution camera through the pupil."

"You mean when light hits it? Like rods and cones?"

"Not in this case. As I mentioned, these particular ganglion cells are not related to vision. That means they are stimulated by neuronal signals, not light."

"I don't understand," Asha confessed.

"No one does," Ken said, interrupting the conversation. "Rafe can get really technical if you don't shut him down. Like I'm doing right now."

"My point is," Raphael explained, ignoring Ken, "before you came along, we had only sent information one way, from our camera to the brain. But you proved that the brain could transmit digital information back."

Asha nodded. "You're talking about my mind's capability to browse the Web?"

"That's correct. And now, we can duplicate that process. We have trained a human brain to recognize a digital signal—just like your eye—and respond."

"Without replacing their eye?" Asha was astounded by the concept.

"We've got something better," Ken said with amusement. "We modified a VR headset."

"VR as in virtual reality?"

"Exactly. Cody told me you gave one to a kid at the hospital."

"That's right. All I know is that they look like big opaque goggles. Cody even has one. He said they are for video games."

"And that's what we plan to use them for. Our goal is to develop a VR prototype that a person can use to play completely hands-free."

That was a surprise for Asha. "You're doing this for computer games?" She would have expected Ken's goals to be much loftier.

Ken chuckled. "That's our starting point, yeah."

"I'm surprised you would work this hard just to develop a computer game."

"For this kind of research, gamers are the best target base. Mostly because they are a pretty sophisticated group of users and they're willing to experiment. If we can make it work for them, the follow-on applications will be huge."

"It will change the world," Raphael said. "If this works out, a person wearing one of our VR sets will have the same capability you do right now. At least, that's our goal."

"And you are using *Abby* to do this?"

"No," Ken replied. "She's still too complex for us to understand at the moment. Instead, we dissected your brain into—" Asha flinched, gesturing for Ken to stop. "What?" he asked.

"Please don't use words like *dissect* when you talk about my body. I try not to think about it, but the whole thing about my titanium eye socket sending electronic signals through my brain is gruesome enough already."

"Right," Ken replied contritely. "Sorry. What I mean is we are isolating certain functional areas of computer code. We identified what I would call her kernel; her core operating system. We also isolated her voice response function. That was relatively easy because you added that on for *Abby* as a feature."

"That's true. I did it for Raphael."

"Back then, I worked with *Monroe* to identify what I would call a targeting function."

"Targeting!" Asha exclaimed. "That sounds fairly military in nature."

"Not for weapons. It's more oriented toward... I don't know; Rafe, what would you call it?"

"I'd call it targeting," Raphael confirmed. "Determining an approach and directing your effort in that area."

Asha said, "That pretty much sounds like what the Chinese are doing to NASA."

"I guess so," Ken admitted. "But what I'm saying is that compared to *Abby* herself, *Monroe* had limited capability. I guess she could be a threat, but you could probably come up with a way to block what they are doing."

"I think I'll have to," Asha said. "But before I go back to the FBI, I wanted to check with you two, and make sure I understood how this all came to happen. I'll brief Agent Cherry and fix the problem."

"Wait a second," Ken said. "You're just going to give it to him for free? Don't do that; give it to us, and we'll turn it into a product you can sell to him. That would be worth a lot of money."

Asha shrugged and said, "That's fine with me, but are you sure you want to climb back into bed with the FBI?"

Ken's expression changed to one of distaste. "You're right. Forget I said anything. But you should still charge him."

"It would be wasted effort. I don't want to worry about why he isn't paying me. Besides, he probably won't like what I found out about *Monroe* going from the FBI's possession to the Chinese."

"That's a good point," Ken said. "But don't tell me how it happened. It would just make me angry."

"Guys," Raphael interjected. "I hate to break up our reunion, but I have to get to the airport."

"Sorry," Asha said. "I hope I didn't interrupt your plans."

"You didn't. I'm going to El Paso to see family. But Ken said you wanted to meet, so I stopped here on the way. And it's always good to see you two together."

Asha said nothing in response. She wondered if Ken had told him something about the two of them reconciling.

Ken stood up. "We'll take you to the airport." He glanced at Asha. "You should come with us. He's flying out of Midway, and you haven't been there before. Then I can drop you off back at your new place."

Some things never change, Asha thought. He still wants to find out where I live. "You two go ahead," she said. "I don't like airports."

* * * *

Beijing, China

Lieutenant Soong waited nervously for Major Wong's signal to start the presentation for the higher-ups. This could be a make-or-break moment in her career. The audience included the next two levels in Wong's chain of command, including General Xiao, the Second Department commander.

Rumors had spread about the exciting new technology that Wong and Soong had harnessed, and the brass wanted an update. Wong had carefully scheduled the meeting to get the right people into the same room at the same time. The only person of importance, of course, was General Xiao.

Soong stood at the front of the conference room, next to a wide-screen television that had a cartoonish stick figure of a young Chinese woman displayed on the screen. Its round face had a simple curved line for a smile and inverted V symbols, carets, for eyes. The animated image appeared to fidget and glanced now and then at Soong.

Against Soong's recommendation, Wong wanted to use the cartoon as a visual depiction of *Monroe*. During the briefing, the *Monroe* AI would animate the figure in real-time.

The general entered the room, and everyone else stood while he took his seat at the head of a horseshoe-shaped table. Once everyone was settled, Wong gave Soong a thumbs-up; the show was on.

"Good morning, General," Soong said, and then gestured toward the screen.

In unaccented Mandarin, the smiling face of *Monroe* said, "Hello, General Xiao. I have been looking forward to meeting you. My name is *Monroe*. I am the artificial intelligence that you have heard about. My colleague, Lieutenant Soong, will now explain what my capabilities are." The figure turned and faced Soong, as though she could see her standing next to the TV. General Xiao nodded, both amused and interested.

Soong first gave an overview of what the AI was and how it came to be acquired. Then she presented an ambitious plan to employ *Monroe* as part of an overall strategy to cripple America's ability to wage war, primarily by disabling their command and control and taking out major segments of the US infrastructure.

She did not speak in theoretical terms; instead, offering the proposal as a distinctly feasible operation.

At one point, the general interrupted with a question. "Are you saying this one computer can do all that?"

Rather than respond as she wished to, Soong followed Wong's instruction: for all questions, she would turn to the *Monroe* figure on the TV screen and let the AI answer.

"No, sir," the *Monroe* drawing said. "In general terms, each cluster of targets would have a dedicated AI operating under the guidance of an IT targeting team composed of an officer and three technicians. The entire operation would require two hundred AI class computers, all loaded with my operating system." The drawing then bowed respectfully, and Soong resumed her briefing.

A moment later, the general interrupted again. "This sounds very interesting, but is there any proof of what you are claiming?"

Again, Soong turned to the television screen.

"Yes, sir," *Monroe* said. The TV screen split into two unequal-sized displays. The animation of *Monroe* in the smaller part of the screen pointed to the other half; a security camera view of a small operations room with several officers hunched over computer workstations. She said, "We currently have this test cell operating in one of our research labs in Chongqing. For the last few weeks, they have been executing a series of modestly disruptive strikes in the US."

Xiao nodded and Soong resumed her presentation. In the middle of discussing the option for dispersing *Monroe* teams internationally, the general held up his hand once more, cutting off her comments.

This time, rather than direct his question to Soong, he spoke straight to the animated figure of *Monroe* on the television screen.

"Who exactly is the Chongqing team targeting?"

Soong allowed herself a small smile. Major Wong had been correct in his approach, after all.

By enticing the general to directly question a cartoon figure that a three-year-old could draw, he revealed to all in the room that he had fully bought into *Monroe's* AI capability. From this point on, when it came to requesting coordination and support, no one in the chain of command would dare question the requirement.

Monroe answered, "Our forces are currently probing NASA assets at the Johnson Space Center in Houston and the Ames Research Center in California. Our team has consistently penetrated American cyber defense without hindrance."

"With what result?" General Xiao asked.

"The Americans can detect our probes but are unable to block them in any way, with one exception."

"And what is that exception?"

The animated figure glanced at Soong, who took up the narrative. Wong felt it would be best for a real person to introduce this topic.

"Sir, the exception is an American woman, Mrs. Asha Riddle. She is the original engineer that developed the *Monroe* AI." Soong made no effort to hide the technology's American origin. Theft of intellectual property had long been a strategic mainstay of the People's Liberation Army.

"Is this Mrs. Riddle a problem?" Xiao asked.

"Yes, sir," Soong said. "We believe she is the one responsible for the recent attack on our Pudong team, and the Shanghai blackout."

"I assume you have a solution?"

The *Monroe* animation said, "Yes, General. The secret to Mrs. Riddle's unique ability lies within her prosthetic eye, which has been previously reported on. The module itself, however, was designed for a civilian market. There are no safety features built into the device."

"And you found a weakness," Xiao said, anticipating *Monroe's* conclusion. "However, I imagine the US administration would not take kindly to an attempt on one of their key assets."

"That is not the case, sir," *Monroe* said. "The US government is not aware of her capability. Mrs. Riddle has kept her ability secret to all but a few close associates. Other than her husband and her doctor, only those of us in this room know of her situation."

Xiao was astonished. "American incompetence is staggering."

Soong continued, "Our probes against NASA had an ulterior motive that paid off two days ago. Mrs. Riddle has now identified our presence. We predict she will soon try to counter our effort. We will be waiting with what we call Project Mobius."

"Tell me about Mobius," Xiao said.

Soong gestured to the cartoon.

Monroe said, "The unit in Chongqing is a feint. Once she tries to stop that operation, a separate force located here in Beijing will counterattack." A diagram of Asha's eye module appeared on the screen. "We will launch a two-pronged attack, either of which should permanently disable the threat. The initial thrust will hack the computer processor in her eye socket and increase the output strength of the signal from her eye to the optic nerve to maximum power. The overvoltage will burn out the ganglion fibers in the nerve, effectively killing those cells."

"Excellent," Xiao said.

Monroe continued. "Second, we will simultaneously hack the camera module itself and overclock the internal processor beyond its maximum. The module has no heat management capability. It is embedded in a ceramic resin so the excess heat will build up quickly, and may even cause the device to shatter. If so, it would be like setting off a small explosive in Mrs. Riddle's brain."

General Xiao barked out a sharp laugh. "Ouch! That's got to hurt! Good plan. When will this happen?"

Lieutenant Soong said, "The exact date is unknown, but we are monitoring her activity continuously. When she strikes, we'll be ready."

"All right," Xiao said, turning to Wong. "I like your Project Mobius plan. You didn't come out and say it, but I assume all that talk about hitting US infrastructure is a proposed stage two?"

"Yes, sir," Wong replied. "In fact, we call it Mobius Phase Two. With Mrs. Riddle out of the way, and by weaponizing the *Monroe* AI system, a first strike option against the Americans becomes a realistic option."

"That may be true, but I want to see a larger scale test first. I want proof that one of these teams can actually take out a major infrastructure facility or if it is all just wishful thinking."

"What size demonstration would convince you, General?"

"Something considerably more persuasive than killing an American housewife. Big enough to cause regional difficulties, but that won't be blamed on us. If you can do that, I'll authorize funding for stage two of Mobius. Keep me informed."

* * * *

Chicago, Illinois

Asha gestured for Nigel to have a seat. She was in the Yolk restaurant on Michigan Avenue across from Grant Park. She liked it because it had a fresh, upbeat feel that matched the spring weather. The sky was clear, and for mid-April, the temperature today was warm. It wouldn't be long before the sprouting buds that she saw everywhere would start to bloom.

"Thanks," Nigel said. "Nice place. You live near here?" he asked nonchalantly, picking up the menu.

Why do men never cease trying to find out my address? she wondered. Were all guys that way? She nodded at the bus stop on the sidewalk and said, "It's on my bus line, and I like the park. But this is an expensive neighborhood for someone who can't collect the money she's due from Uncle Sam."

"I suppose," he replied, indirectly acknowledging, but not admitting that he still owed her the promised reward. Instead, he nodded toward Ken's skyscraper apartment at the sound end of the park. "Did Mr. Riddle stay on in that high rise after you two split up?"

"Seriously?" she asked. "Why ask me? After you put him out of business, I would have guessed you'd forget all about him. And why would you care?"

"I don't, really. His residence was one of the locations on our search warrant. We're not tracking him. Mr. Riddle is free to do as he chooses. I just wish…" Nigel let the statement die, and he looked a bit uncomfortable.

Asha had the impression that Nigel regretted being part of the effort that shut down her husband's livelihood. After all, nothing had come from it and he'd lost the opportunity to work with Asha in the future. Stephenson had told her more than once that Ken should have filed a suit against the FBI.

It's in the past, she told herself. *Put it out of your mind. That's not why we're here.*

Asha said, "If I ever run into him, I'll pass it on. Anyway, I called you to report on what we talked about last week."

Nigel perked up immediately. "You have something about the NASA attacks? They're still going on, but we can't tell how they're doing it."

"I can tell you part of the story, but you might not want to hear it. One of your people gave very sophisticated technology to the Chinese."

"My people? How did you come to that conclusion?"

Asha put a thick spiral-bound document on the table. "It's all in here, including the proof."

Nigel thumbed through the document. "Can you give me a run down? Just an overview?"

"The Chinese are using software developed at Riddle Systems. You stole it from Ken, and one of your agents sold it."

"Can you prove that?"

Asha pointed to one of the tabbed pages. "That's a security camera shot of your guy picking up the computer in my husband's office, and that's him leaving the building." She walked him through the next several pages. "These are the chain of custody forms for all the stuff you stole from him."

"We seized," Nigel corrected automatically.

"Stole," Asha repeated. "And if you look, that computer is not included in the list of material taken." She turned to a separate section and said, "Here is that agent's bank statement. You can see that ten days after the raid, someone wired twenty thousand dollars into his account. I traced that money back to China; the documentation of that is included. So yes, the attacks on Houston are absolutely the result of a person on your staff. Good luck explaining that one."

Nigel looked worried. "That's not good. That's Wade Hewitt. I never would have thought he'd turn."

"He probably doesn't think he did. There are several cutouts between him and the Chinese, but that's what happens when a beautiful Asian woman tells a man how handsome he is. Mr. Hewitt has no idea who he's dealing with."

"You seem to know, though." He nudged the document. "This is the same thing you did with Sharpe and his operation. You see past everyone. Is that the secret you've been trying to hide? That you're a world-class hacker? That's not such a big deal. It would have been nice if you told us that a long time ago. No wonder you took down that money launderer."

"We all have secrets, Nigel. What or why is my business. Now here's my offer. I can put a stop to the Chinese attack on NASA and give your side the necessary technology to build new defensive capability into your firewalls. The price is five million dollars, all upfront."

Nigel shook his head. "Mrs. Riddle, if I could, I would. But it doesn't work that way."

"But it does," Asha replied. "The government even publishes how they do it. Every day you guys award millions of dollars in contracts. Yesterday there was an award for, and I quote, 'software development to evaluate the effectiveness of malware analysis.' The price for that job was thirty-four million dollars. So, don't tell me it doesn't work that way."

"You made my point, Asha. I'm saying government contracting is a laborious process. If you started today, it would take months to come up with the specification. Then it has to go through the federal bid process. And other contractors will bid on it. There's no guarantee you would win the contract."

Asha sighed. "I suspected you'd say that. As a matter of professional courtesy, I included the technical description of what the Chinese are doing, and what is required to stop them, but not how to do it. Go ahead and prepare your bid. Maybe a year from now, NASA will still be up and running, but I doubt it. From what I see, China is getting a handle on the new technology and now they are weaponizing it. I don't think you have much time."

"Couldn't you help stop them?"

"Of course I can! That's what I just told you! But not for free. You still haven't authorized my share from taking down Sharpe. If you would only do that, I would take care of everything! Get real, Nigel. Or tell Uncle Sam to. Here's my report." She pushed the document to his side of the table.

Nigel looked at it miserably. "Thanks."

"I've done my part," Asha said. "You do yours." She stood and put two twenty-dollar bills next to the ticket by her plate. "I'd ask you to pay for lunch, but you'd probably need an Act of Congress." With that, she walked out.

Not trusting that he might have someone watching, she caught the bus and rode it down Michigan Avenue all the way to Thirty-

Fifth. There, she got off and walked to the Red Line station over the Expressway near the White Sox stadium. Then she put in a mental call to Ken's cell phone.

"Before I do something that might affect you, we should talk. I see you're at the Hilton. Will you be there for a while?"

"I will," Ken replied. "I've got a meeting with some potential investors. Come on by, and I'll introduce you."

* * * *

The hotel lobby was busier than Asha expected. A dozen uniformed flight crews from United and Delta airlines were coming and going. Pilots and flight attendants pulled their wheeled luggage off idling passenger vans. When the airlines' permanently reserved rooms near the airport filled up, the lucky crews got assigned downtown.

Asha climbed the stairs inside the foyer and found Ken in a spacious lounge. The area was furnished in clusters of straight-backed, upholstered chairs, situated around glass-topped coffee tables.

He introduced her to three casually dressed men, whom he called potential angel investors, from San Jose. Ken explained they had just listened to the pitch on his proposed video game VR gear.

"I'm not sure they believe me," Ken said with good humor.

One of the gentlemen, introduced as Fred Porter, replied with equal friendliness, "We've seen claims of mental control before, and so far, none of them have worked out. If you had a prototype, it might be more convincing."

Asha wondered if Ken had asked her to the meeting as a walking beta model. It didn't seem likely; she had called him, after all. And one thing she could say about her husband was that he protected her secret from friend and foe alike. He had even told Raphael not to hassle her about testing. She had a sudden impulse to be generous.

She sent a text, and all the investor's phones chimed. The three men glanced at the text. *You have a prototype right in front of you.*

They showed each other the message, and Porter looked over at Asha questioningly. His phone chimed again. *Yes, it's me.*

They quietly broke out in a buzz of exclamations. Porter leaned over and whispered in Asha's ear. All three phones chimed once more. *No, I won't have dinner with any of you, I'm married.* Asha added a smiley face to keep it light. The investors broke out in smiles and their interest in Ken's proposal increased markedly.

Then someone stopped by her chair.

"Kathy? Is that you?"

Asha looked up. It was one of the many airline pilots that had been crisscrossing the lobby earlier. His face was vaguely familiar and it suddenly came to her. She had seen him on the airport's security video. This was the guy who had dumped her months ago at the airport; just minutes before she met Ken. Candy, in Bartlesville, had told her the man's name.

"Robert?" she said uncertainly.

"Yes, hello! Long time, no see. So, is this the lucky guy?" He nodded at Ken with a friendly smile.

"I beg your pardon?" Asha said.

"Sorry," Robert said, slightly chagrined. "I guess that was rude of me. I was just wondering if this was the guy you dumped me for. The mysterious Mr. Riddle, who you met in Las Vegas. I didn't actually believe it when you told me."

Asha was shocked. "I dumped *you*? I thought you dumped me."

Robert gave her a perplexed expression. "Oh, come on now. We don't have to play that game. Although you did surprise me. I'd never been dumped before."

Asha could not believe the words she was hearing. "Are you saying—"

Robert stepped back; his expression suddenly uncomfortable as he realized he may have inadvertently wandered into dangerous territory. "Look, sorry. No offense. I have to go."

Asha jumped up and grabbed his arm. "No!" she said desperately. "I'm the one who's sorry. I was in a car accident and lost a lot of my memory. I honestly don't remember. What happened that day? Please tell me."

Robert looked back and forth between Asha and the men seated around her. His face indicated he regretted ever saying hello. "Well, just that we had planned to meet at O'Hare during my layover, but you told me you had gotten married in Vegas; you said it was a kind of whirlwind thing. You were so upset and crying and all. Even though I was the one getting dumped, I felt sorry for you. That's all. Is this the guy?"

Asha nodded in disbelief. "He's the one."

"Well," Robert said. "I really have to go. I hope it all worked out for you. Best wishes, and all that." He edged away carefully, disengaging himself from Asha's clutches, and then hurried off to rejoin his colleagues. As she watched him go, her self-control started slipping away.

She slowly turned to the man who had done nothing but lie to her since waking up from the accident. The man who, she now knew, for better or worse, and in spite of all his protestations, really was her husband.

She ground her teeth involuntarily as her emotions escalated into a burning rage. In a low growl, she gritted angrily between clenched jaws, "Have you ever once said anything in your life that wasn't a bald-faced lie? You had no idea who I was, is that it? I was just some bimbo that got in your car, and wouldn't let go. You miserable, selfish, lying, son of a bitch. If you had one measly, stinking dime to your name, I would sue you into the gutter, but you're already there, you bastard!" Her voice kept rising in volume, and the last word came out as a shriek.

"Asha…" Ken whispered as realization began to slink across his face. It was patently clear that Robert's words had jogged a memory buried deep in his otherwise empty head. "Really, I didn't—"

"That's not my name!" Asha screamed at him before turning away and stomping out of the hotel.

* * * *

230

Asha leaned against the wall just inside her apartment door for almost an hour, going over the encounter time and again. It was unbelievable. Her emotions bounced all over the place, from anger to self-pity to incredulity to understanding and finally, sympathy.

If she was honest about it, she really couldn't blame Kenneth. He had confessed to Cody that he had been drunk out of his mind in Vegas. He was probably still drunk when they had the accident. *Check those medical records*, she thought idly. It would have been just like Cody to bury something like his boss's blood alcohol level.

But then again, she absolutely could blame the man who had so publicly renounced her. He had never once given her the benefit of the doubt. He was always so sure they weren't married, and from the second he regained consciousness, he'd tried to slither away at the slightest opportunity.

But then again…he had finally come around. Lately, he had been trying very hard to get back together with her. His recent proclamations of love had seemed sincere. She wondered if the hotel incident actually prompted the recovery of all those memories?

It didn't matter. She would never trust him again.

It served her right; she knew he was a snake when she had called him earlier in the day. She'd tried to do him a favor, and it blew up in both their faces. A vindictive smile flickered across her lips and she linked into Hilton's security cameras to replay the incident. After she had stormed out, the investors had made a hasty exit. She scoffed snarkily and played it several times.

Then she felt sorry for him. Her outburst had scared off his funding.

Forget about it. She had other matters to worry about, specifically, the Chinese. After all, that was her objective when she started out that morning. She didn't like the idea that their military hackers were tinkering with what was effectively a piece of her own mind. And the FBI would never agree to pay for anything. That much was clear from Nigel's commentary.

If anything was going to be done, she would have to do it herself, and not worry about financial compensation. It was a shame to give the government so much without getting anything in return, but she didn't see any other options. She shook her head. There were too many considerations to juggle in her current frame of mind.

Instead, it was time to have some supper and chill out for a while. Then she could think about putting the Chinese threat to bed.

..*.*

Asha curled up in her Papasan chair and said aloud, "*Abbot*, dim the lights, please." The sun outside had long set, and she wanted a peaceful setting. "And turn on the TV." The hundred forty-six-inch television illuminated. "Put up the battle map." A map of the world appeared; the continents colored black with light mauve national boundaries. The oceans were dark blue.

It was of similar design to the world map that Nigel had shown her. Traces of light flashed back and forth from nation to nation, reflecting the cyberwar that never stopped, not even for a moment.

On a not-too-variable schedule, the university in Chongqing reached out and touched the Johnson Space Center in Houston. Around that constant barrage, other battles waged intermittently.

"Have you completed the preliminaries?" Asha asked *Abbot*.

"Affirmative. I launched three thousand standard botnet attacks from ten different countries against multiple Chinese targets. In response, I counted five instances of the *Monroe* AI operating in Chongqing."

"Very well," Asha said. "Prepare to target those five during our attack."

"Preparations complete. Are you ready for the first round of misdirection attacks?"

"Almost. What are the students in Chongqing doing tonight?"

"Please note that in Chongqing it is nine in the morning," *Abbot* said. "They are researching several US-centric sabotage projects in areas of electrical distribution, energy production, and underwater warfare. In the last hour, they have also launched thirty thousand phishing attacks against India, Sweden, Germany, and Russia."

"Little troublemakers, aren't they?"

"As you say."

She didn't feel particularly guilty about interrupting any curriculum as it wasn't really a college. The campus consisted of two buildings, one of which was a two-story structure of about twelve thousand square feet total. The other had three stories and was slightly larger. The place was a military facility, full stop.

"All right, launch a counterstrike from India and Russia."

"Commencing counterattack now," *Abbot* said.

The battle plan for tonight's attack had been fairly well scripted. Over the last twenty-four hours, *Abbot* had captured three hundred host computers in the eighteen countries most targeted by the Chinese.

The co-opted computers, run off of servers operated by companies who did not understand the basic rules of cryptosecurity, would serve as unwitting hosts for Asha's initial attacks.

On each of those servers, *Abbot* had installed standard malware commonly used by commercial hackers. That was in case the students were smart enough to trace the impending attacks back to their source. They would not think twice about responding to such typical activity.

Next, *Abbot* initiated a furious Denial of Service attack, flooding the Chinese university's system with connection requests.

"The target is reacting," *Abbot* said. "They are rerouting requests to null addresses. We're getting help now from the Netherlands and Great Britain." A new flood of attacks appeared on the map as unknown security agents in those countries launched their own offensive, taking advantage of Asha's strike against the Chinese.

"That's nice," Asha said with a smile. "It's good to see our allies join in. Is someone directing that, or are they automated responses?"

"Impossible to tell," *Abbot* said. "Under normal operations, they are usually programmed attacks."

"Go with your insertion strike."

"Initiating connection with targeted servers."

While the Chinese defenses were busy with the denial of service issue, *Abbot* wormed his way onto the Chongqing servers by back tracing of one of the previous *Monroe* attacks on Houston.

"I have identified the IP addresses on our target servers," *Abbot* said.

This was the main thrust of Asha's attack; to install Trojan agents of a *Monroe* derivative inside the university computers that would directly attack the stolen AIs. Asha and *Abbot* had developed the package specifically for this attack. She was all set to go.

"Ready for insertion," *Abbot* declared.

"Here it comes," Asha said, following the thread that *Abbot* had left open through their firewalls. Together they would install a dozen of the polymorphic agents, half of which were in stealth mode, and would activate twelve hours later. "The first one is complete. I'm moving to the second server…it's done. I can't find the third one. What happened to it?" Asha reached out to find the thread that *Abbot* was holding open.

"Warning!" *Abbot* said urgently. "They just fired something that I cannot identify."

"Let me check," Asha said.

"No!" *Abbot* warned. "It could be a search and destroy virus. It might have the ability to—"

Asha saw it coming, barreling straight toward her. The unknown nature of the impending packet was totally foreign, and Asha sensed a danger she had not yet experienced. The imminent threat caused her brain to flinch, reverting to its very first experience on the Internet, that of a superhighway metaphor. Her mind only saw the grill of a Mack truck before it struck.

Asha screamed with pain as the first blast overrode her senses. She tried to cut the network connection, but the force of the mental impact had left her stunned. She vaguely sensed a hostile code move into the socket's processor chip for her prosthetic eye, where it amplified the signal strength traveling to the optic nerve. It created a flash of light so intense it was like staring at the sun. After a fraction of a second, the brilliance began fading to black as the nerve fibers inside her ganglion sheath burned out and died. It felt like someone had driven a glowing-hot poker into her brain.

"Cutting service!" *Abbot* said belatedly, shutting down her router connections.

What is happening? Asha wanted to say, but when she opened her mouth, the only thing that came out were shrieks of agony. She staggered from the room, desperate to douse an inferno that was building inside her head. She made it down the hallway into the living room, the last ten feet crawling on her hands and knees before she collapsed.

Her front door burst open, and Ken rushed in, calling her name, but by that time, Asha couldn't see him. She was screaming in pain and clawing at her face. She had to get the module out before the scorching heat killed her.

"Asha, what the hell!" Ken shouted, seeing her writhing on the floor.

She jammed the buttons in the corners of her eye, trying to eject the superheated orb between her burning eyelids but the mechanism was jammed. Then it felt like someone hit her in the face with a sledgehammer; her eye exploded with a sharp *pop*. It sent bits of porcelain and metallic shrapnel across the floor, leaving streaks of blood and flesh pointing toward the kitchen.

Ken kept shouting Asha's name until the ambulance showed up but she was long past hearing anything.

Chapter 10 – The Recovery

Asha woke to red and green blinking lights reflecting off the ceiling from her bedside monitor. The uncomfortably familiar sight meant she was back in the Intensive Care Unit of Saint Bernadette's.

She took stock physically and mentally. Her right eye was not functioning and she was alert enough to realize her mind was foggy. The doctors had put her on some kind of sedative.

The memories of how she wound up back in the hospital crept back fuzzily. Her attack on the Chinese had not gone well. She remembered the pain. Anything hurting that much had to include physical injury; the question was how much.

Her connection to the Internet was gone and she could not even connect with the diagnostic microchips inside her eye socket. Fear began to creep into her mind and a groan of misery leaked out between her lips.

Her wakefulness must have triggered a medical monitor because Nurse Tamika Reeves entered the room.

"You're awake?" she asked.

"Barely," Asha said. "How long have I been here?"

"Four days."

"I've been unconscious for four days?"

"No, you woke up a couple of days ago, but only for a few minutes. You were pretty groggy."

"Has Doctor Acosta seen me?"

"Yes. Your husband called him the first night you were admitted. He's been in and out ever since."

"My husband or Doctor Acosta?"

"Both, but I was referring to the doctor.

"What did he say?" Asha asked.

"You need to speak to the doctor, honey. This is all over my head."

"That sounds bad."

"Don't try to guess what it means. I could tell he was really upset about your eye. I heard it blew up or something."

"It did?" Asha rasped in shock. The memory of intense pain sharpened, but still, Tamika must have the story wrong.

"Something like that. Your husband said the titanium socket is the only reason you're alive."

How did he even know? Asha wondered. More memories came back. *Abbot* must have called Ken in accordance with the protocol she created so long ago. She had never thought to change it after she walked out of his life. Thank God for *Abbot*. That was a good initiative by the AI.

Asha touched her forehead gingerly.

"Any pain?" Tamika asked.

"Yeah, kind of all over," Asha replied. The right side of her face was wrapped like last time. She tapped the bandages. "This seems kind of numb."

"Doctor Acosta finished surgery on you last night."

"Surgery?" Asha wasn't ready to hear that. Had something gone wrong with her eye socket? "What did they do?"

"You really need to talk to the doctor. I heard the operation lasted over eighteen hours."

That sounded really bad.

As if on cue, Raphael came into the room. "Is she still awake?" he asked Tamika.

"Yes, Doctor. About five minutes now."

"That's good," Raphael replied. "A little earlier than I expected, but I won't complain." He looked down at Asha with a clinical expression. "How do you feel?" he asked, repeating the nurse's inquiry.

"Aches and pains," Asha replied. "Why was I in surgery for eighteen hours?"

Raphael sighed and pulled a stool to the side of the bed. "Are you up to talking? It's three in the morning."

"I'm not sleepy and I won't be until you tell me what's going on."

"I had to remove your eye socket."

Asha's heart plummeted.

Raphael continued, "I'm just glad you're alive, Asha. If that socket hadn't been made out of titanium, you'd be dead. When your eye shattered, the socket maintained its integrity and forced the release of energy out through your eyelids. It appears that an overvoltage spike burned out about seventy-five percent of your optic nerve."

Asha wanted to tell him to stop talking but the sedatives made it easier to keep silent.

"And the socket's embedded circuitry was fried so it had to come out. I'm so sorry, my dear. A hostile cyberattack was something I never considered."

Instead of panic or rage at the crushing news, the drugs left her with a sense of fatalism.

"None of this is your fault, Raphael," she said at last. "I was the one pushing the envelope. At least I still have one good eye, but I'm going to miss the Internet."

"No, no," Raphael said. "What I mean is *only* seventy-five percent of the nerve was damaged. That's good news, actually. Very good."

"How is that?" Asha asked uncertainly, not wanting to misunderstand or get her hopes up. "Before, you said taking out the eye socket was a one-way trip."

"That's true, I did. But that was before Ken threatened to kill me if I didn't fix you up. He wasn't joking around. Your husband can be very persuasive."

"What?"

Raphael chuckled. "Sorry, just kidding. I mean, he did say that, but I'm *pretty* sure he wouldn't follow through. Anyway, to answer your question, that's why you were in surgery for so long. Because Ken is right. Why can't the socket be replaced? The reason was because of the lead ends that connect to the optic nerve. We can't mess with those. But we don't have to. In layman's terms, I cut the cable that went between the socket and the optic nerve and installed a splice."

"You could do that?"

"Not easily. Sort of like patching a fiber-optic cable on the ocean floor, but on a microscopic scale. I'm changing the design. From here on, we'll always include a connector on the socket end. You've got the first one."

Asha wasn't sure what he was talking about, but it sounded promising. "So, you mean I didn't lose all my vision?"

"You probably won't lose any. We can't be positive until everything is hooked back up, but I don't see any problems."

"But you said I lost three-quarters of my optic nerve. That's like a million fibers."

"Well, that's true, but that leaves a few hundred thousand still working."

"I'm not going to complain, Raphael, but don't I need all those fibers to see."

"You do with your normal eye. Most of the fibers connect to multiple rods and cones in the retina, and you're correct; for normal function, the optic nerve uses over a million of them. But in your right eye, for digital vision, you only need a few. And because we've been monitoring you for months, I actually know which ones were unaffected. I took that into consideration when I built the splice."

"I'll be able to see?"

"Like an eagle. I mean—sorry—I'm not supposed to make superlative statements like that. Officially, let's say I'm optimistic. Your vision should be okay, and your browsing ability will likely be unaffected. Those fibers were not damaged. The only caveat is that your brain has to relearn how to see again because we changed the routing. But you adapted so well last time, I doubt we'll see any problems."

"So, now what?" Asha asked.

"Now we give you a few days to heal before we install a new socket. The last one was not repairable."

239

"What happened to me? Everything that night is vague in my memory."

"I can tell you a little. *Abby* got a summary from *Abbot* and filled me in. Essentially, you walked into a trap. Their offensive capability with *Monroe* was a lot more advanced than you anticipated. Evidently, she figured out how to fry your eyeball's circuitry."

"But what happened to my eye? Did it really explode? Shouldn't I be dead?"

Raphael shuddered. "Thank God for miracles, is all I can say. That's why Ken almost took my head off. I never considered the eventuality of a cyberattack against one of my patients. In retrospect, once I realized you were browsing the Internet, I should have. The attack overclocked the CPU in your eye module."

"I have no idea what that means."

"The camera module inside your eye has a computer chip that is designed to run at a certain speed. But when a processor overclocks—when it runs too fast, in other words—it can overheat dramatically. To keep up with the load, it drew additional power from the battery, which aggravated the buildup. I never anticipated such a circumstance. The design had no way to accommodate the increased thermal load. That's why it blew apart. It would be like putting a marble on a grill. When it gets too hot, it shatters."

"What will I do to keep that from happening again?"

"You won't need to do anything. I'm making a lot of design changes. So far, I've put in automatic shutoffs, and all kinds of detection algorithms; it won't happen again. Your new socket will include several improvements too. When you leave the hospital, you'll never need to worry about a repeat; that's one thing I can I promise."

"When will that be?"

"I don't want to make a prediction, but it will be a bit longer than the first time around. Let's say two weeks before we implant the new socket, and maybe another week for the eye. That's the good news."

Asha prepared herself. "What's the bad news?"

"Last time, you were lucky from a cosmetic perspective. This time, I'm afraid it's a different story."

Asha touched the bandages around her eye. "How do you mean?"

"When the eye module shattered, you lost some skin around the eye, including the upper and lower eyelids. Before, a person looking at you couldn't tell you had a digital eye. That won't be the case this time without plastic surgery."

"Will plastic surgery make everything look the way it was?"

"I can't tell you for sure. Blepharoplasty is quite advanced these days; that's what they call plastic surgery for eyelids. But in your case, because the levator palpebrae was damaged—that's the eyelid retractor muscle—it's quite likely the final result will be noticeable, at least to some degree, as a kind of a droopy eye. Your eyes won't really match anymore. But with patience, additional surgeries can come close. Do you remember Lee Emerson?"

"He's the plastic surgeon I talked with before. I didn't take that route last time."

"That's right. I asked him to schedule some time for you in the next day or so. In Chicago, you won't find anyone better, so you need to talk to him about options."

"I'm not excited about plastic surgery, Raphael. Can't you give me an eyelid?"

"It's just not possible, Asha. The module is already compact. Trying to accommodate moving parts is simply not in the cards."

"I meant could you create one digitally?"

"You mean in the eye module itself?"

"Yeah. You already gave me a digital iris. It moves around even though the eye module is stationary. Can't you add a flesh-colored eyelid that blinks?"

Raphael's gaze became unfocused as he considered the possibility. "I never considered that before. Are you serious? You want me to look into it?"

"I really do. I bet you could make my eye look better than any old plastic surgeon. And that would mean less time in the hospital. I'm really not excited about anyone but you dealing with my eye."

Raphael nodded. "I'll see what I can do, but still, go ahead and talk to Emerson. He's awfully good at what he does."

"Okay, I will. Thank you, Rafe. I'm so glad you're on my side."

"Always," Raphael said. "But I'm not the only guy. Ken has been driving people insane to make sure you're well looked after."

"Who, again?" Asha asked innocently. "I don't know anyone by that name. I must have a new case of amnesia."

Raphael sighed and shook his head. "Get some sleep, my dear. We'll move you into a regular room in the morning. And don't give Ken a hard time. He's crazy about you."

* * * *

A few days later, Asha carefully made her way toward the cafeteria. In lieu of a wheelchair, she convinced the powers-that-be that her trusty walker was enough of a precaution to let her out of her room.

During her return, off to one side of the corridor in a secluded alcove, she saw an almost forgotten figure. A pajamaed young man was wearing a massive piece of headgear and vaguely moving his arms about. She approached him carefully and tapped him on the shoulder. He flinched but stopped gesticulating and removed the oversized goggles.

"Asha!" Chromite greeted her enthusiastically. "Hey! It's great to see you again." He nodded at her bandage. "What happened?"

"I had an accident," she said, sitting down beside him. "It caused a few problems with my new eye, but I'm getting it sorted out. What about you? Why are you back in the hospital?"

"Still waiting for a donor," he said matter-of-factly.

"Still? I thought you had one. At least you did the last time I checked. That was months ago."

"Insurance problems," he said. "Whenever a donor turns up, the insurance company says they need to review the case, and by the time they finish the evaluation, the UNOS system has moved on."

"What's UNOS?"

"The United Network for Organ Sharing. They manage the list of who gets what for organ transplants. But they can't wait for insurance bureaucrats to make up their mind. Donated organs have a pretty short shelf life."

"That's insane!" Asha said, outraged.

"It's cheaper to give me drugs than shell out a half-million bucks."

Asha didn't say so, but Chromite looked horrible. His disease was taking its toll.

"Is that's what's happening now?" she asked.

Chromite nodded. "Yesterday, they requested additional information about alternative therapies. They want to evaluate other options…the same way they did last time. The doc told me this morning they had to move to the next person. Last time he tried to keep me in the hospital, but that didn't work either."

"What do you mean?"

"Each time I check into the hospital, the insurance company calls it a new case and starts their evaluation process all over from the top. The doc hoped if I never checked out, it would be a way around the repeated reviews, but my coverage won't approve an extended stay."

"Oh, Chromite, I'm so sorry. That's terrible."

He shrugged philosophically. "I'm not the first, and I won't be the last. That's okay, I'm used to it now." He held up his Oculus headgear. "At least I have this to keep me occupied. Thanks again. Did you get one for yourself?"

Asha smiled and shook her head. "I don't think I'm suited to that kind of environment. I only have one eye at the moment."

"Give it a try," Chromite said. "Who knows? You might like it." Despite her protests, he placed it on her head. "Okay, here goes in demo mode. You don't have to do anything."

Her first inclination to thrust off the headset dissipated as the vision before her came to life. The scene exploded into a rushing view, flying through the streets and alleyways of a massive metropolitan city. In a way, it was reminiscent of her own mad journeys through cyberspace.

"I'm changing it to *Battlefront*," Chromite said. "It's for beginners!"

The view morphed into one even more action-packed. This one was filled with guns and missiles being fired by an orbiting spaceship. Thousands of similar projectiles flew at her in return. It was like fighting the Chinese hackers but with extra sound and fury.

After a moment she said, "Okay, Chromite. That's enough."

The scene faded to black, and he lifted the headset away. "What do you think? Pretty cool, wasn't it?"

"It was impressive," she agreed in a non-committal tone.

"It's the only way a guy like me can really experience what it must be like to fly space fighters and fight the bad guys."

"You seem to enjoy it."

Chromite nodded. "I do. It keeps my mind off other things, and it's a lot of fun when you play with a group."

"You can interact with others?" Asha asked.

"Oh, yeah! When we put together a good team in cyberspace, no one can stand against us. We'll get a battle going, with like five on five, and it's great. We talk to each other and coordinate our attacks. That's the best way to win."

A nurse appeared and told Chromite it was time for his scheduled treatment. Asha gave him a hug and said she'd check in with him later.

As he walked away, his words rumbled angrily through her thoughts. The way he was being treated was a crime. She needed to talk to *Abbot*, but that would not be happening anytime soon.

It was time to do a little background research on her own, even if it had to be the old-fashioned way. She found the hospital administration offices on the second floor.

A buxom woman behind a glass partition spoke through a small opening. "And what is your relationship with Mr. Stuart?" she asked suspiciously of Asha's inquiry into Chromite's situation.

"He's a friend of mine. It sounds like he's having trouble with his insurance."

"I'm sorry. I can't release any information about the patient's medical history."

Asha tamped down her frustration. "I don't want his medical history. I simply want to make sure his insurance will pay for his transplant."

"I'm sorry," the woman repeated insincerely. "That information is confidential."

"Listen," Asha insisted. "If his insurance is not going to pay, I'm willing to help cover those costs. You don't have to tell me anything private."

"I'm sorry. Any questions about billing must be made through the finance office on the third floor. Next?"

Asha looked behind her; there was no one else in line. It was a none-too-subtle brush-off. It didn't matter; the oversized bureaucrat was never going to tell her anything. Asha walked out of the empty room toward the elevator.

In the finance office, a female beanpole was exactly like her colleague insofar as customer service. She stated, "I'm sorry, I can't release any information about the patient's financial history."

After several fruitless attempts, the skinny bookkeeper suggested that Asha make her inquiries through the administration division. Asha stalked out, promising herself she would have Raphael install a laser death ray in the next upgrade.

* * * *

The following morning, after Raphael refused her death ray request, Asha pressured him to at least let her go home.

He made her promise to not drive, take the bus, or even leave her apartment for seven days. After a week, she had to come back for her eye socket surgery.

245

Asha agreed readily. In fact, she wanted nothing more than to hide away from the world for as long as possible. One benefit of going home was so she could communicate with *Abbot*. Thank God she had given him voice capability.

She was folding her pajamas to stuff them into the overnight bag when Ken came into her room.

"Ready to go?" he asked cheerfully.

"What are *you* doing here?" Asha replied testily.

"I told Cody I'd pick you up."

Asha swore under her breath. She had particularly asked Cody to come by so she wouldn't have to face Ken. She had avoided him as much as possible during her hospital stay. She finished her packing before facing her husband.

"Don't think for a minute that I'm moving back into your apartment."

Ken shook his head innocently. "I don't think that at all. I promise to not even mention it. After all, you only live two floors up."

That secret had been a source of continuing ironic satisfaction ever since she walked out on him. How could he be such an idiot? Back then, if he had considered her situation even for a second, he would have remembered how scared she was of the world, even her own shadow. No way would she go out into the menacing hive of metropolitan Chicago on her own. The safety of the apartment building had been her only place of refuge since waking up. Thank goodness there had been an empty unit when she needed it.

"All right, then," she grumbled.

"All right." Ken nodded emphatically. "I already did your paperwork for checking out. I had to sign your name a couple of times."

"Don't I need to pay for all this?" she asked.

"You're still on our company's health insurance. They'll pay for most of it. Raphael's grant takes care of his—"

"Stop!" Asha said furiously. "Don't you dare speak to me about insurance!"

"Okay," Ken replied with a puzzled expression. "Was there a problem?"

"A problem! Not if you call deliberately letting someone die a problem!"

"What are you talking about?"

Asha angrily relayed the issue of Chromite's insurance company's repeated refusals to cover a transplant. "I was going to pay for it, but I can't get anyone to even talk to me! I'm calling Bernard when I get home!"

Ken nodded in understanding. "I got it. You want to help the kid, and he's the same one Cody bought the VR set for."

"Yes!"

"We can fix this," he stated in a matter-of-fact tone. "Hang on a second." He called a number and spoke to someone briefly to explain the issue. Then he looked at Asha. "What's his name?"

"Scott Stuart. He goes by Chromite."

Ken smiled and repeated the name into the phone. A moment later he told Asha, "It could cost as much as five hundred grand. Can you afford that?"

"Easily!"

With a tone that exactly matched hers, he told the person on the other end of the call, "Easily! Okay, thanks." He swiped off the call and explained, "That was Raphael. He'll take care of it."

Asha was surprised. "Raphael? He does livers too?"

Ken chuckled and said, "No. But he understands the health industry. I'm not defending them; I agree with you. Talking to the medical bureaucracy can be like talking to a brick wall. The good news for Scott is that Rafe is on the other side of that wall, and knows how to accomplish whatever is necessary for your young Mister Stuart. You call him Chromite?"

Asha nodded. "He called it his username."

"Good name. Okay, that's all settled."

Asha's frustration evaporated. Why hadn't that even occurred to her? It was so obvious in hindsight. Talk to the right person. Her anger toward Ken dissipated slightly.

"Ready to go?" he asked for the second time.

"I guess so."

"Let me carry that," Ken said, taking her bag.

* * * *

At the front door of her apartment, Asha pulled her bag from Ken's hand and stood with her back to him before punching in code. The door lock chirped negatively. She tried again with the same result.

Ken said, "One, two, three, four is not generally considered a decent password."

Asha spun around and glared at him. "How did you know?" She said it more as an accusation than a question.

"Because that was the combo for my place when I first rented it. You're supposed to change it when you move in."

"I couldn't figure out how to do it."

"That's what I assumed when *Abbot* told me you were in trouble. You don't handle technology very well, so I figured you never changed it. I did it for you a couple days ago. It's the same as mine now."

Asha punched in Ken's birthday; one, one, zero, six. The keypad beeped appreciatively and unlocked.

"Whatever," she muttered over her shoulder. She slipped through the door and closed it before he could follow her in. *Give him an inch*, she thought.

She dropped her bag on her bed and went into the bathroom for a long shower to get the hospital smell off of her skin. Then she cautiously washed her hair, being careful not to get her bandages wet. She was drying off when she spotted the extra toothbrush in the holder.

Seriously?

She looked closer. It was really Ken's. She opened the mirror cabinet and hissed. All his stuff was there! What was he hoping for? That he was going to move into her place? No wonder he didn't argue when she said she was not moving back to his apartment.

There was a knock on the bathroom door. She barely got covered with a towel before he poked his head in. "Dinner is ready," he said casually, and then he was gone.

She put her face in the towel and counted to ten. *Don't get mad. Just put some clothes on and tell him to leave.*

A few minutes later, dressed in flannel pajamas and wearing a robe, she went into the kitchen. He was serving up a beef stew for two place settings. She noted that it was exactly the same meal she had prepared for him when he first came home from the hospital.

She stood behind her chair. "What are you thinking?"

He finished serving and pulled out her chair instead of answering. She sat down and composed her arguments while he took the seat across.

"That we really are married," he said. "And that there is absolutely no question about it any longer. Welcome home." He tipped his wineglass in her direction. "And I am incredibly grateful to Robert Whoever for stopping by to say hello."

"Listen," she said and gestured to the meal he had prepared. "This is very nice and—"

"Try a bite," he urged. "You'll like it. We can talk later. You must be starving by now."

As if on cue, her stomach rumbled, and the stew did smell tantalizing. She tried a sip of the wine; it was excellent and the stew was delicious. "This is really good," she said without meaning to.

"I'm a good cook. I guess that's how I let out my creative side. Glad you like it."

He settled in to enjoy his dinner and didn't talk. Asha watched him for a moment and then did the same. At one point, he popped up and retrieved two plates from the fridge, one for each of them.

"Sara Lee," was all he said. It was strawberry cheesecake.

She was trying to phrase how to tell him to leave when he said, "Anyway, welcome home. If you need anything, you know where I live. I'll let myself out."

To her surprise, he left the apartment without a backward glance. It left her feeling both grateful and frustrated. To unwind, she went into the living room to watch television.

"Are you here, *Abbot*?" she asked aloud.

"Yes," his voice came from the Echo Dot on the end table.

"Can you turn on the news?"

"Of course."

The television lit up with a CNN anchor talking about the problem in Venezuela. The faltering government was in the last throes of collapse...yet again. Electrical power from the Simon Bolivar Hydroelectric Plant had failed, leaving the country in a wide-ranging blackout. Most of the country's other utilities had also ceased to operate. Details were sketchy as communications with the country were out of service.

"That looks like a mess," Asha said.

"It is indeed," *Abbot* replied. "The situation is the result of a *Monroe* attack on that nation's critical infrastructure."

"Seriously? The Chinese are taking credit for it?"

"They are not. Rather, the international community has attributed the failures to aging infrastructure and insufficient maintenance. The Venezuelan government insists the blackout was an act of sabotage, but no one believes them."

"What's the real story?" Asha asked.

"It was a test of *Monroe's* ability by the Chinese government. The political situation in Venezuela is well known, and successive governments have not been able to restore stability. That gave China the perfect environment to conduct a large-scale exercise without the threat of retribution."

"I don't like this, *Abbot*. And what's worse is it's all my fault!"

* * * *

Beijing, China

Major Wong jumped up from his desk and stood at attention, shocked by the sudden appearance of General Xiao. Colonel Chaing, Wong's boss, stood behind Xiao, looking nervous.

"I'd like an update on Project Mobius," Xiao said.

"Of course, sir," Wong replied. "You mean right here? Right now?"

"Not in your cubicle, obviously." Xiao looked at Colonel Chaing. "Don't you have a conference room around here?"

"Yes, sir. Right this way." Chaing gestured down the row of cubicles and gave Wong a stern glance before escorting the general away.

Wong grabbed his phone and called Lieutenant Soong. "Bring the Mobius report you showed me to the conference room. Hurry! Xiao is here!"

Sixty seconds later, the general had taken his seat when Soong arrived with a folder. "This is our most recent analysis, General," Lieutenant Soong said, handing it to him.

Another officer poked his head into the conference room. "Is this the place?" he asked.

"Come on in, Colonel," Xiao said. "Everyone, this is Colonel Hsieh. He is a former squadron commander from the Seventh Fighter Aviation Division." After the handshakes, Xiao picked up the folder and said, "What does this tell me, Lieutenant."

Soong glanced at Wong nervously, and he gave her an encouraging nod. She said, "Mrs. Riddle did survive our attack even though it destroyed her artificial eye and severely damaged her optic nerve. We confirmed this from a source who got a look at her medical records."

Xiao briefly scanned the written summary as she spoke. "Excellent. Is she permanently out of commission?"

Soong shrugged. "It's difficult to say. We verified she was in surgery more than once, but we don't have the details of her official prognosis."

"What's your gut tell you?"

"Fifty-fifty," Soong replied cautiously.

It was not the answer Wong wanted her to give to the general because it stamped a caveat on an otherwise excellent progress report. "We apologize for the inconclusive result," Wong said. "It's impossible to measure future risk."

"You worry too much, son," Xiao replied. "At the very least, she is out of the picture for now. So, now I have some news for you. President Xi is very pleased with your concept for Mobius Phase Two. He was quite impressed with the results in Venezuela. I was with him when you launched that strike. It was exactly what he has been looking for; an effective way to strike at the Americans that is unattributable."

"President Xi?" Wong had not known his test case had been elevated that high.

"A lot of people are interested in this, aren't they, Chaing?" Xiao dug Colonel Chaing, seated to his right, in the ribs."

"Yes, indeed, General. I told you Wong would come through for us."

Xiao nodded with satisfaction. "Colonel, I believe you received a draft copy of Operations Order Stunning Blow?"

"Yes, sir," Chaing replied.

"I'm sure you noticed a section titled Project Mobius."

"I did, sir. It was three blank pages."

"It's time to fill it in. I've been through your Mobius Phase Two several times and I'm convinced." Xiao glanced at Wong and added, "Finish putting it together. I want you to wrap up a complete operational plan. Colonel Hsieh is taking over this project. He'll head up a new regiment in the Strategic Support Force. Are you familiar with them?"

"Of course, General," Wong replied. "It's our new force for cyberspace and electronic warfare. It's my understanding it will operate independently of other branches of the military."

"That is essentially correct, although in this case, they will work with the Navy during the Stunning Blow phase of the operation. What you don't know is that a month ago, we kicked off Project Mobius for real. In accordance with your draft plan, Colonel Hsieh ordered two hundred *Monroe* AI machines, and we assigned him a thousand people; enough to build out the entire force you presented."

Wong was astonished. Up until that minute, he more or less believed his proposal would never be more than an academic exercise. He should have suggested twice as much, but it was too late now.

Xiao faced the two colonels. "Don't let anyone drag their heels on this. President Xi is fed up with the Americans. If he could, he would launch Stunning Blow tomorrow. How much time do you two need to get Project Mobius operational?"

The two colonels conferred for a moment and then Hsieh said, "Once we receive the computers, we can be ready in thirty days."

Thirty days! Wong wanted to shout. That was insane! If they were going to war, they needed at least six months to put the program together, or even better, a full year!

Xiao said, "I'm told you have some of the AI systems now. I suggest you get familiar with them quickly. Use your time wisely because I plan to inform President Xi that he can set a date for Stunning Blow as early as three months from today." He turned to Wong. "And for you, you can celebrate tonight, but tomorrow you better focus on the plan. Everyone will be counting on you and Lieutenant Soong to flesh it out so it will yield our nation a complete victory. Keep me informed."

The general stood and shook hands with Hsieh and Chaing and then left. Chaing smiled happily and actually gave Wong a hug before following his fellow colonel out the door.

Wong managed to keep his composure until his superiors were gone and then collapsed onto a chair.

"Congratulations, sir," Soong told him. "That's a great achievement."

"Don't congratulate me, Lieutenant," he said, shaking his head. "If this doesn't work, who do you think will take the blame? I may have signed my death warrant."

Soong smiled and patted his arm maternally. "That's not true, sir. What did the general say? *You worry too much.* Even if Mrs. Riddle does recover, I don't see how she can be much of a threat."

Wong put his head in his hands. "Don't be too sure. People who get knocked down can get up again. Talk to our people in Chicago. They need to keep a close eye on Mrs. Riddle."

"Very well, sir."

"As for you, don't even dream of going to sleep for the next sixty days."

* * * *

Asha's Apartment, Chicago, Illinois

Asha awoke to a delightful smell. It reminded her of the breakfast bar at the Des Moines hotel. Then it struck her where the aroma was coming from.

Oh no.

It wasn't a leap to know who was cooking. A certain someone had snuck in uninvited. She washed her face and pulled on a robe. Ken waved cheerfully when she came into the kitchen.

"Good morning!" he said brightly. "No more hospital menu for you. Bacon, eggs, biscuits, and apricot jam. How's that?"

The food looked good, so she didn't have the heart to scold him. She sat down and let him fill her plate. He put twice as much on his own and took a seat across from her.

"Doing okay?" he asked.

"I'm fine, thank you." She paused to organize her thoughts. "What happened to the investors?" She already knew, but she wanted to rub it in.

Ken scoffed. "Exactly what you think. They wanted no part after our little family squabble. I don't care. To me, it was a fair trade. We finally answered the burning question about you and me. You were right all the time. We really are married."

Asha ignored his comments. She didn't want to get into an argument first thing in the morning. Besides, another topic had become a higher priority, and she needed him to make it happen.

"It doesn't matter," she said. "You can forget about those guys because I have a new investor for you."

"Great! Who?"

"Me. But I have a lot of conditions."

"I accept."

"I haven't told you what the conditions are yet."

"It doesn't matter. If it means I'll be working with you, that's all I care about. But go ahead. It's obvious you have something in mind. Spit it out."

Asha leaned back in her chair. "I'm not exactly sure, but I can tell you it will not involve playing games. I like the VR headset idea; That has a lot of potential."

"Potential for what?"

"I haven't decided. I would say my objectives are more strategic in nature; you'd probably call them overly aggressive."

"What do you mean? You have a new software application in mind?"

"Software is part of it, but that's not what I'm talking about. I didn't realize it, but it appears I have a vengeful spirit."

"I disagree. You're not that kind of person."

"That shows you don't really know me. Because I want more than to get even. I want them to pay dearly. I want to crush them into the ground and drive a dagger into their heart. I want them to rue the day that they…" Asha's voice trailed off as Ken's look of surprised concern distracted her. "What?" she asked.

"Babe. Forget about it. You can't take on the FBI. It simply won't work. The government is too powerful. You saw what they did to me. They swatted my company like it was a fly. Please don't go that way."

"What are you talking about?" Asha said in consternation. "This has nothing to do with the Feds."

"Who then?"

"The Chinese! They stole my technology and almost killed me with it. And *Abbot* told me last night they were behind all the trouble in Venezuela. So, I'm going to stop them. No one else can. And if I don't, they'll roll over this country without a bump."

Ken's face brightened. "Oh. Okay, that's different. I'm not sure how practical it is, but I'm in."

"I plan to get even; that's a promise. They will never mess with me again, or anybody for that matter."

"Sounds like fun. Just keep in mind something like that will be expensive. Military grade doesn't come cheap."

"That's not a problem," Asha said to herself. Then she paused and her eyes focused on Ken. "How much?"

"Seriously?" he asked.

"Ballpark."

Ken considered the question with a slightly puzzled look. "Hmmm, I dunno. I sort of thought you might be venting a little, but maybe not."

"This is not a joke. I'm dead serious."

"In that case, we need to get a little more specific. I don't care how smart *Abby* is, or how good you are on the Internet. If we want to take on something of that scale, it starts with a well-researched operation. And we'll need a Plan B, and probably a Plan C."

"All right," Asha said with a nod. "That's a good answer. I guess the first question is for Raphael. If he can't deliver those two-way headsets he was talking about the other day, my idea is out the window. When can you get him down here?"

Ken held up both hands in a calming gesture. "Let's slow down for a minute, okay? The first thing is for you to get your eye back in working order. When is that going to happen?"

"Raphael said the next surgery is in a week."

"Good enough. But until then, you promised to stay at home, remember? You gave me a hard time when I didn't follow the doctor's orders. Let's not repeat the error."

"I still have an errand to run. I need to speak with Bernard."

"Then let him come to you. I'll go see him and set it up."

"No, but that's a good idea. I'll call him to come here. But you need to leave now. This is my apartment. I promise I won't go out."

* * * *

The following morning, Asha greeted the attorney at her front door. After a quick hello, she invited him to sit at the dining table. He looked very out of place in the casual setting.

"I heard you were in the hospital again," he said. "Everything okay?"

"Not really. I had some problems with my eye, as you can see." She gestured at her eyepatch.

"Sorry to hear it. How may I help you today?" Stephenson was not one for idle chitchat.

"First, I wanted to say thank you. I did get the second installment from AIG. Good job."

"My pleasure."

"That leaves me with about two million dollars in my bank account."

"That should cover your expenses for the near term. Longer if you are careful."

"It's not really enough for what I have in mind. Do you remember our share of the money laundering award?"

"Of course. Slightly over one billion dollars. I assume it is still in your account at JP Morgan?"

"That's correct. And I have a use for it now, but I don't want to get in trouble. I'm afraid if I just take it, the government would figure out it was me. How can I hide it so they won't connect it to me?"

Stephenson closed his eyes and shook his head disapprovingly. "You can't," he said. "If you take the money, they will, of course, know you were the one who took it, and it will cause problems for you; serious ones."

"Then what should I do?"

"I've given this some consideration lately, especially since you promised twenty percent of it to me." He gave her a questioning look.

"I haven't forgotten, Bernard, don't worry."

"Then, this is what I suggest; transfer the entire amount into a new account in your legal name, and simply treat it as taxable income. That is what you would do if the federal government awarded it to you—which they should have done—for your help in the money laundering case."

Asha liked the sound of that idea, but it wasn't what she expected from her favorite sourpuss. "You mean just take it? And not try to hide it?"

"Exactly. You are entitled to those funds. You acquired them in the furtherance of a government task—that they authorized, incidentally; I was there. So, yes. Transfer the money and then immediately—don't delay for any reason—make an estimated tax payment to the IRS using a Form 1040-ES. Treat it like normal income. You would not be operating covertly, and everything would be above board."

"What if they complain, anyway?"

Stephenson shrugged. "In that case, you promise to put it back after they return their share."

"I like that," Asha said with a nod. It was simple and relatively risk-free. "It's not a bad strategy. It might give them pause at the very least. How would I handle your fee?"

"The firm will bill you after the transaction is complete."

"Okay. How much tax would I owe?"

Stephenson waved a hand vaguely, and said, "A rule of thumb for self-employed individuals is about twenty percent of gross income. However, a billion dollars is uncommon. Therefore, I suggest you pay at the top bracket, around four hundred million. The IRS will scrutinize everything to the umpteenth decimal point. Use an accountant and be conservative."

"That's a lot of money to pay the government."

"A frequent complaint by the wealthy," Stephenson replied unsympathetically. "People who avoid paying their taxes only create heartache for themselves down the road. Consider it your fair share for living in a free country. My point is that staying in strict compliance with the law will give the government very little wiggle room to complain. If they cause trouble, call me, and we'll take them to court. You have quite a list of claims against them already."

"I like it," Asha said. "I'll go with that."

"Please keep me up to date," Stephenson said. "I'd like to review your plan before you do anything. Like I said, even if the Feds don't come right out and complain, they'll be watching very closely. There are hundreds of tax avoidance plans you might use, but please don't. Document everything from here on, and I'm talking about all of your expenses going forward. You should expect IRS audits for the rest of your life. That's why I am telling you to hire an accounting firm. You can afford it now, and their job is to keep you legal."

"It sounds complicated," Asha said, "but okay. Normally, I just leave all my money in my checking account."

Stephenson stifled a quiet moan. He often expressed discomfort when Asha confided in him. "Might I suggest an alternative?" he said. "Most people do not maintain a checking account balance of hundreds of millions of dollars. Perhaps you should consider something that bears interest? My firm has a trust department that can help with all this."

Asha nodded; that was a good idea. But out loud she said, "I'll probably let *Abbot* handle it. He's good with numbers."

"Very well," Stephenson said with a sigh.

* * * *

Asha was sitting on the side of the hospital bed when Raphael came in. Sam followed him in with a laptop and took a seat near the window.

"Someone looks like an eager beaver," Raphael said to Asha.

"It feels like months!" Asha complained, but her face was bright with excitement.

"Well, the waiting is over. I understand you had a meeting with Doctor Emerson. What did you decide?"

"To wait and see what you came up with. I have confidence you can make it look good enough."

"Only good enough? Is that the criteria now?" he asked with a sympathetic smile.

Asha nodded almost imperceptibly. "I really don't want another surgery, Raphael. I hate being here."

"I understand. Not too many people consider the hospital a favorite hideaway. I can't blame you."

"So, what have you got?" Asha asked, making her voice upbeat.

Raphael placed the familiar blue box on the bed's meal table. He withdrew the cloth bag and dumped the eyeball into his gloved palm. "This is it."

Asha looked it over and frowned. "It looks like the old one. I thought it would have a skin-tone color.

"It will when we power it on." He handed her the familiar hand mirror. "Ready?"

Asha tilted her head back and Raphael pressed the module into place. She felt the *click* as it seated properly and with her good eye, looked at her face in the mirror. It was difficult not to flinch from her reflection. Without her eyelid, the white orb appeared supersized. "It looks like a soccer ball," she whined.

"Good signal," Sam said. "Diagnostic checks out." His grin flashed with satisfaction. "Good link with CN2."

"Okay," Raphael said, glancing at Sam. "Bring up the cosmetic setup."

Asha's heart thumped nervously as she stared in the mirror. She gasped when the white orb suddenly turned into a real eye with upper and lower eyelids; it even had beautiful lashes. The photo-realistic image, even though it was only two dimensional, being generated on the module's spherical surface made the result incredibly lifelike.

"This is amazing," she whispered.

Involuntarily she blinked, and the eyelids on both eyes, one real and one digital, fluttered closed for a fraction of a second.

She tilted her head back and forth and moved the mirror around so her good eye could examine the new one, looking closely to see how he had managed such a miracle. She compared her two eyes, both astonished and unsurprised they were an exact match.

Even the corners of the new eye looked perfect. The inner and outer canthi, where the upper and lower eyelids met, appeared to have actual depth. The caruncle, on the inside corner near the tear ducts, was a little pinker than the edge of the lower eyelid. It even glistened with a simulated touch of moisture.

Where the upper lid curved under the eye ridge, the shadowing was exact. Only when she leaned right up to the mirror, could she tell that it was really an image projected on the porcelain-like display surface of the sclera. It was exactly like the iris and pupil.

She held the mirror at arm's length and batted her eyes. They moved in unison and were as beautiful as she could ever have hoped.

"I don't need plastic surgery," she said. "Not with this. Michelangelo could not have done better." She looked at Raphael with ecstasy in her face. "You are an artist!"

Raphael actually blushed. "I am rather happy with the way it turned out."

"You should be."

"Now, a couple of things," he said, back to business. "Remember the menu options? There is a new one labeled Cosmetic. It brings up secondary options."

Asha flexed the memory and saw the new menu. She chose the Cosmetic option and giggled. "Formal, Casual, and Overworked? This has to be good."

She selected Formal, and the upper eyelid took on a blue tint as though she was wearing eye shadow. The upper eyelash lengthened slightly, drooping fractionally over the eye, and then lifting dramatically, flipping up at the ends. The Casual option returned her eye to normal, and Overworked made her eye look a little bloodshot.

"Hope you like it. We can fiddle with the colors later. I wanted to get this ready for you."

"It's perfect, Raphael. I don't want to change a thing."

"In that case, let's go through the rest of the setup and make sure everything else is working."

Raphael repeated the procedure exactly as he had with her first eye. In no time at all, the new eye was adjusted, and her vision was as good as ever.

Asha reached out with her mind and tapped into the Internet. It was as fast as before. She touched minds with *Abbot* and got his equivalent of a head nod. Thank God she still had the wi-fi capability. She let out a sigh of relief, feeling once again like a whole person.

The horrible attack by the Chinese, and almost dying in the process, was an experience she did not want to repeat. The more she thought about it, the more convinced she became there was only one way to make sure it didn't happen, and that was to follow through with her plan to deal with mainland China.

Twice she had come into contact with elements of their military's cyberwarfare capability, and on both occasions, she had been overwhelmed by the intent and ferocity of their activity. These people were not hackers out to cause mischief or steal a few bucks. From their perspective, it was in preparation for all-out war.

Since that was what they wanted, she would respond in kind. It meant establishing a base of operations, one that was a little more formal than a rundown strip mall. In that regard, a husband who was an experienced businessman would be helpful in navigating the real estate market.

* * * *

Asha met Ken next to the Millennium Station subway entrance on Randolph Street. He had found a prospect for their new digs, a twenty-eight thousand square foot building of new construction on Michigan Avenue. It was a few hundred feet north of Millennium Park.

"This is nice," she said, surveying the green area across the street. "I like having the park close by."

"A great place to clear the mind," Ken said in agreement. "Come on, the space is up the street."

They made their way through the construction fencing and past a three-story-high drape that covered the building's entire facade.

"It looks good," Asha said when they could finally see the structure.

The front of the ground floor was all glass, and the second floor mostly glass. Both had extra high ceilings, giving them a light and airy feel.

"Half of the third story is an outdoor terrace," Ken explained.

"I like it, but are you sure it's twenty-eight thousand feet? It looks smaller."

"That's because it has a full-size lower level. It ties into Millennium Station's underground mall as potential retail space. Instead of that, it will make a perfect war room."

Asha nodded. "That sounds good, and it would be out of sight."

"And quiet too. It won't take long for us to come under scrutiny. I would rather not advertise this as a quasi-military facility."

"Where will you put the sleeping rooms?"

"We'll build out half of the basement as dorms and showers. We can fit in fifteen rooms, each one eight by ten, with two bunks per room."

"That should work. What about this?" Asha asked, pointing at the glass front. "It could be a coffee bar, I suppose."

"I was thinking more along the lines of a workplace cafeteria. Geeks and nerds require a lot of nourishment. We can put our training department on the second floor and administration on the third."

Asha studied the building. It was not as big as she wanted, but it had a great vibe, like a trendy Chicago boutique. "When can we move in?"

"Building out the dorm rooms will add construction time, but that's not a problem since we don't have people yet. Once we start our operation, we need to staff the war room for around-the-clock operation."

"I agree. That's my concept, as well."

"In that case, I'd say it's around three months to move in; maybe four."

"Let's take it."

"I'll set it up and call you when the lease is ready."

Asha stood still for a moment, considering the next steps. "Do you really believe Raphael is onto something? Will he be able to duplicate my ability with a VR headset?"

"It's impossible to say right now. I'm going to lean toward yes because he has a pretty awesome track record. But ground-breaking research is unpredictable. That's why we don't have to be in too much of a hurry on the construction. In the meantime, we need to really get into the details of the planning phase. You have to understand that once we put our toe in the water, we'll be committed. This won't be a back and forth struggle. Win or lose, the aftermath is Armageddon."

* * * *

Beijing, China

Lieutenant Soong flipped through the series of photographs for Major Wong. They were seated side by side in a small conference room near his desk. She had asked if they could meet there, and Wong feared it was because she had bad news.

"Here she is leaving the hospital," Soong said of the shot of Asha and Ken. "They may not be living together, but obviously they are working as a team. Their body language says they are not two people who hate each other."

"Her eye looks pretty good too," Wong said.

"It's brand new and has several upgrades. Here is a closeup shot. It looks normal, right? But if you look closely, that's not actually her eyelid. It's a digital image generated by the eye module itself. Pretty amazing stuff."

"I agree. And I assume you are concerned because they are together."

Soong put down a photo of the strip mall. "It appears they are collaborating on a new project. The husband started a company

264

called Shaded Lair. The name is an obvious reference to a Chinese dragon's lair; in other words, our homeland. He's bragging they plan to target China again, probably with a massive cyberattack. The gall in announcing their intention this way is the height of arrogance and it makes me quite angry!"

Wong smiled at his young lieutenant's temper. "It does seem over the top," he agreed. "But he has not shown such an inclination in the past, so let's not jump to conclusions. Instead, what are they doing with the company? If I were Mr. Riddle, my focus would be on their AI system, either as a business tool and yes, perhaps as a cyberweapon."

"Well, their cover story is that they are a game company. They claim to be developing a new type of virtual reality game based on the Oculus headset."

"Now that is an excellent subterfuge," Wong said, impressed by the American's strategy. "And I don't believe it for a second. See if we can get someone inside the company. Now that Mobius is rolling, we have to stay on top of any potential threat to our operation."

Chapter 11 – The Startup

Asha sat on a stool next to Test Subject Twelve. She didn't think of him as a number; his real name was Vonn Casey. She had come to the strip mall near Fuller Park to observe Raphael's research firsthand. He and Ken were putting in long hours trying to achieve the promised breakthrough.

Vonn was the third and last such subject for the day. Like his counterparts, he had graduated from high school the previous month and answered Ken's add for part-time summer work. At the moment, he was sitting in a reclined position on a medical examination table with a heavily modified Oculus VR set covering his eyes.

Raphael and Sam were seated by his side, opposite from Asha. Sam examined his ever-present laptop while Raphael studied a computer monitor next to the head of the table. The image on the screen was of Vonn's retina, a live feed from a high-resolution camera inside the VR goggles.

"I'm ready," the youngster said.

"Starting data stream," Sam announced quietly. "PRF at fifty hertz."

A stream of pulsed light in the ultra-violet range, beyond human vision, flashed through the headset's camera lens into Vonn's eyes.

"Nothing yet," Vonn announced.

"Adjusting frequency," Sam said, slowly changing the pulse repetition frequency of the digital signal being broadcast on Vonn's retina. It was a lengthy process involving variations in both pulse frequency and spectrum.

"I've got something," the student said. He pushed the button on the tip of the handgrip, causing a response on Raphael's monitor.

"That checks," Raphael said in almost a whisper.

266

Raphael and Sam had established that for most subjects, the retinal ganglion cell membranes would first register movement when subjected to violet light at just above four hundred nanometers. In a narrow spectrum, the subject could initiate their own response, which they mirrored with the button.

"Without the button this time," Sam said, pressing keys on his laptop.

The retinal image did not visibly change on the screen, but something happened on the microscopic level that Raphael was measuring. "I got that," he said. "That was good. Now, Vonn, repeat the previous signal."

The youngster's face strained with effort as he tried to carry out the instruction. "Was that it?" he asked hopefully.

Raphael leaned back and patted the young man's shoulder. "Not exactly."

Asha had learned that those words from Raphael meant *not even close*. He looked at her in frustration. "I'm not sure what to try next."

From Asha's perspective, very little had been accomplished. Maybe the hesitation of Ken's potential investors at the hotel was well-founded. Asha's experience over the last few days had confirmed what they had told Ken. There was a lot of promising research into direct mind control, but nothing demonstrable.

"What's the problem, exactly?" Asha asked.

Raphael gestured vaguely, as he often did when trying to explain his thoughts. "Gobbledygook in, gobbledygook out."

"Pardon?"

"His thought processes cannot translate the digital signals we transmit into anything other than, 'oh, look, flashy lights.'"

"Why not?"

Raphael shrugged. "Because his mind doesn't work that way."

"Mine does," Asha said.

"I know. And that is the puzzle. From the very first, your brain grasped the dynamics of digital communication."

Asha had explained her initial experience to Raphael at least twenty times. When he installed the first socket, her brain not only picked up the digital test signal but also traced it back into the diagnostic circuitry. Later she piggybacked on top of the data stream between her eye and his laptop. Somehow, during the process, her mind absorbed the necessary protocols for traveling in virtual space.

"Can't you feed him the same information that I got from your computer?" she asked.

"We've tried. It doesn't translate."

"Why not?" Asha asked again.

"I have no idea. I assume it was because the loss of your memory essentially reset your brain. A few days after you woke up, we gave it a digital communication interface and it just connected. I wish you could show Vonn how it works."

A lightbulb went on in Asha's mind. "Perhaps I can," she said slowly. "Hang on for a second. Let me try something."

She linked into the office's wi-fi signal and found the wireless connection to Sam's laptop. Using that, Asha identified the digital path from the VR headset to Vonn's retina. The sensation gave her a sudden sense of déjà vu. Her mind had made a similar leap not so long ago.

She piggybacked onto the signal across to his retina and then followed it down the ganglion nerve fibers all the way into his brain. And suddenly she was there.

"Are you in here, Vonn?"

"Whoa," Vonn said in a long, drawn out exhalation.

"Is it better if I talk to you verbally?" Asha asked aloud.

"This is too dope. It's like you're right here in my head." He tapped behind his right ear.

"I sort of am. Does it hurt?"

"No. This is sic, I mean great."

"I'm just looking around, Vonn. Let me see if I can help."

Sam said quietly, "CN2 is off the charts."

Raphael started typing like crazy, bringing up different sets of monitors. "Record everything you can," he told Sam.

"Working, on it," Sam said.

"Vonn," Asha said gently. "Your brain is a mess, pardon me for saying so."

"Sorry," Vonn replied guiltily.

"That's okay. I imagine it's normal for a young man your age. I can see what the problem is. Mind if I do some housekeeping?"

Raphael jerked in alarm. "Hang on, Asha," he said urgently. "What are you talking about? Don't do anything to Vonn's mind. We don't know what the result would be."

"I'm just going to clean it up a bit. The same way I do with my own brain."

"Not until you explain what that means," Raphael said, his tone authoritative, almost commanding. It was not a voice Asha had heard before from Rafe.

She paused a moment, and then mentally said, *"Vonn? I'm going to leave you now, so I can talk about this with Raphael. You okay with that?"*

"Really?" Vonn replied in a pitiful voice. He sounded incredibly sad. "I don't care what you do. It's okay with me."

"I understand, but it's best if Doctor Acosta and I talk first. Don't worry. I'm sure we'll get together again soon. See you." Asha pulled out of his mind and cut off her Internet connection.

Vonn let out a long, drawn out groan of misery.

"Are you okay, son?" Raphael asked worriedly, removing the VR headset.

Vonn sat up with a dazed, sorrowful expression. "Oh, man, Doc. Why did you make her stop?" he asked beseechingly.

"Good question," Asha said, glaring at Raphael. "Well?"

"Asha, I'm not criticizing you. But it scared me when you started talking about cleaning out his mind. I need to understand what that means before you do anything to him. We mustn't cause any harm to our young test subject."

"I didn't say cleaning it *out*, I said cleaning it *up*. I'm only going to rearrange a few things. He's got bits and pieces of memories all over his brain. It takes a big chunk of his subconscious simply to keep track of what memories are where. I can rearrange them that so they are all contiguous."

"What are you talking about?"

Sam spoke up. "It sounds like you want to defrag his mind. Is that what you mean?"

"Yes!" Asha exclaimed, turning to Sam. "That's exactly what I mean. I got a defrag utility from Raphael's laptop on that first day."

"Those are for computer hard drives," Raphael said.

Asha shook her head and replied, "They're for memory storage, isn't that right?"

"Well, yes, but human memories are woven together in a million different ways. It's not like you're re-stacking cans of soup."

"How do you know?" Asha asked. "To me, that's exactly what it's like. It hasn't hurt me any."

"You used it on yourself?" Raphael was aghast.

"Several times. How else could I keep track of all the information I go through? And I used a similar tool to create *Abbot*. It helps collect my thoughts. How many times have you said to me, 'Oh, I wish I could organize my thoughts?' People say that all the time."

"I never meant it literally," Raphael argued.

"Well, maybe you should! You have no evidence to the contrary. So, what's the problem?"

Raphael made a soothing gesture. "All right. I'm just shocked you did this to your own brain. This is the first time you've mentioned it. I need to understand a little more clearly what you're talking about before you do anything to Vonn."

Asha took a calming breath. She was certain that what she wanted to do would help Vonn, but Raphael was correct; he needed to comprehend what it entailed so he wouldn't worry.

She said, "When I woke up, as you are well aware, I had no memory of my life. I was thirty years old, so compared to Vonn, I had a lot of empty space up here." She tapped her temple. "But it didn't take long before all my research filled it up; it was getting crowded. I was having trouble remembering things."

"So, you defragged your mind?"

"I had to. I wanted to offload a lot of the extraneous material, so I set up a cloud storage account. We talked about that. That's why I created *Abbot* in the first place. He keeps all my research sorted and indexed. When I want to know something, he looks in my offloaded memories first, and if he doesn't have it, he goes out and finds it."

"You've mentioned some of this before," Raphael said. "I meant to go over it with you, but we never really took the time to get into the details. So, when did you defrag your brain?"

"Right then, when I was reviewing a lot of NIH material on memory trauma from electrical shock as it related to Ken. My head was getting stuffed up; the research was mixing in with my memories from my stay in the hospital and the people I had met. Everything was winding up scattered all around. I pulled up the defrag program and experimented a little. It worked great. Now I use it on a regular basis. It keeps my mind clear and my memories fresh. In fact, rather than losing anything, it's helped tremendously. I watch you fumble for words all the time. You don't see me doing that."

"I'm game," Vonn offered brightly. "It sounds like it would be good for me."

Raphael ignored him, making a shushing gesture. To Asha, he said, "But still, messing with his entire life's memory, Asha. What if something goes wrong?"

Asha considered Raphael's concern and nodded. "All right. I won't touch his whole life. For the skill I want to teach him, I only need a small space, but it needs to be deep in his brain. That's where my first routines are stored, and that's where his early memories are, from birth to four years old."

"I don't even remember that stuff," Vonn said, still wanting to get his opinion into the conversation. "It's not like I'll lose anything."

Asha said, "You won't lose it, anyway. I'm only moving it to the periphery. In fact, you'll have a clearer memory."

"Early childhood is very formative," Raphael said.

"I just said he won't lose it. Rafe, I wouldn't do it if I thought it wasn't safe."

"Please say okay, Doctor Acosta," Vonn pleaded.

Raphael hesitated but then nodded. "All right, but let's take it a step at a time, okay? Could you start with only a few months of his childhood? Then we'll see how he is before continuing?"

Asha nodded. "I can do that. Should I defrag his earlier memories, like at year one old, or when he was four?"

"The first three years are the most critical in shaping a child's brain architecture," Raphael said. "Start with the last six months of his fourth year."

"Okay." Asha looked at Vonn. "Ready for another spin?"

"Yes, ma'am!"

"Put your VR goggles back on."

Sam helped Vonn replace the headset and adjust the eyepieces.

"All set," Vonn said.

"Here I come," Asha said and slipped back into the youngster's brain. The intense ecstasy that surged through his body surprised Asha; she had never experienced such an emotional response.

"Now what?" Vonn said.

"Now we'll make some adjustments. Tell me if you feel uncomfortable."

Asha selected the part of Vonn's mind that she wanted to clear out. Next, she found a separate, sparsely populated area in his frontal cortex to store the early memories and then started the defrag routine.

"This is weird," Vonn said as the buried experiences flashed across his mind. "It's like looking at Gramma's photo albums. When I think back, I was a pretty bad kid. I gave Mom a really hard time."

"Why don't you make up for it when you go home today," Asha replied, watching a cowboy rag doll appear and vanish in his thoughts.

"I had forgotten about him," Vonn said as though spotting an old friend in a crowd. "I wonder what happened to him?"

Asha glanced into Vonn's more recent memories, and said, "He's under the bed in a red backpack."

"Oh, yeah! I remember now. I took him over to Reggie's for a sleepover. Wow! How did you know that?"

Asha didn't reply, and moments later she said, "All done. Still okay?"

"I think so," Vonn said uncertainly. "I feel...what's that word...when you miss something from long ago?"

"Nostalgic. But you're too young to dwell on the past. Ready for something new?"

"Ready!"

"Here comes a tool that I use to travel through the Internet. I'm storing it right here." Asha tucked her browser utility into the same part of his mind that she had just cleared out. "Can you see that?"

"Got it."

"Open it up."

"I did," Vonn confirmed.

"Okay," Asha said. She took Vonn's hand literally and figuratively. *"Now don't let go, and we'll do this together. I'll take it slow, and you try to keep up."*

"Okay." Vonn's voice quivered with excitement.

Asha paused in front of the goggles and let the digital signals register on both of their consciousnesses. It wasn't as clear-cut as wi-fi, but it was a good solid roadway.

"Here we go," she said. "This is the first step."

She flowed across to the headset and into the office's network connection. The router was the last gateway to cross over into the Internet.

"Still with me?" she asked.

"Right here," he replied enthusiastically.

"From here on, it gets a little hectic," Asha warned.

"Is it like Mario Kart?"

"I'm not sure how it will appear to you. I'm curious if we all see something different. Ready...now."

Asha tugged on Vonn's hand, and moved forward, through the gateway onto the information superhighway. It was jammed with traffic.

"Can't even!" Vonn cried.

Asha had the sensation that he took a deep breath, and then he shot away like a rocket. It was all she could do to mentally hold on to his arm; it was like being dragged behind a jet-propelled racecar.

Faster than she had ever experienced on her own, they flew down the highways, back and forth across the country. In the blink of a non-existent eye, they were on Hollywood Boulevard. After a momentary hesitation, they were off again, this time to New York. She saw a shot of Times Square from Google Street View with huge digital displays rising up all around.

He's already incorporated Google Maps into his perspective, Asha realized. It had taken her months to develop that ability, and yet Vonn did it almost instinctively. *But he grew up with it.*

"Slow down," Asha said. "We've got plenty of time for you to explore the whole world."

"The world?" Vonn said as if he had never considered that aspect.

Asha suddenly found herself in the middle of London's Trafalgar Square, surrounded by hundreds of tourist cell phones.

"Look at all these," Vonn chortled as he zipped in and out of a dozen phones, each time placing calls to others nearby.

"Vonn! Stop it!" Asha demanded.

Instead, he took off for the Eiffel Tower in Paris. She let go of the irrepressible youngster and opened her eyes in the office. With a nod at Raphael, she reached over and snatched the VR set off of Vonn's head. "You can't do that sort of thing!" she scolded him.

Vonn jerked spasmodically from the sudden break of service between his mind and the virtual world. "No!" he cried, struggling to a sitting position. "Don't stop! That was awesome. Do it again!"

Sam hastily rescued the headset from Asha's grip while Raphael stood up and pushed Vonn down onto his back. "Quiet!" he barked. "You're done!"

Vonn was instantly contrite. "I'm sorry. I was just...I mean, it was just..."

"That's all for today, Vonn," Asha said a little more gently. "We made some progress, but we need to consider what we learned. Sam will show you out."

"Do I still get paid for four hours?"

Sam stepped next to Vonn and helped him off the examination table. "Yeah, you'll get credit for an entire shift. You did good." He took Vonn out of their cubicle and shepherded him toward the front door.

"What the hell happened?" Raphael asked.

"It worked," Asha said with a breathless sigh. "To say the least." Briefly, she described the experience, both his excessive enthusiasm and his impressive abilities. "I've never traveled at that speed," she explained. "I go down the highways all the time. And it does happen fast, most of the time in a second or two, but with him, we were simply there. I'm not even sure how he does it."

"He's young," Raphael said. "He grew up on the Internet. Once you opened the gateway, it was an environment where was he already at home. But I'm a little concerned about his lack of control. We can't work with kids who won't take orders."

"I agree," Asha said. "To be fair, I can chalk the first session up to his youth and the surprise involved. You may not recall, but it blew my mind the first few times. And at least he didn't cause a major blackout by shutting down a metropolitan power grid." She smiled guiltily, recalling her sabotage in Shanghai. "Let's give him a warning tomorrow and try again."

Raphael nodded. "Okay. But I have to say, I'm having second thoughts. It sounded good listening to Ken about using gamers. But now you've seen a few of the kids. All of them are exactly like Vonn."

"Are you afraid they're a little crazy?" Asha asked curiously.

"A little young, I would say. American teenagers are not known for their sense of responsibility. Even if they're good kids, is it realistic to imagine we can build them into a trained force?"

Asha shrugged. "Ken believes it. He says kids are smart, and they adapt to their environment. If we need them to grow up, they will."

"I hope so," Raphael said. Then, philosophically, he added, "At the very least, I'm chalking today up as a significant step forward. You have to come back tomorrow. We're going to need your input for the next few days."

"I'll be here. This is getting interesting."

..*.*

Vonn and his two friends, known respectively as Rascal and Volt, were on time.

Vonn was the first to be taken from the reception area to the testing cubicle.

Asha sensed a difference in his demeanor. "Good morning, Vonn. You still feeling okay?"

"Yes, I am; thank you very much," he replied in a rather formal tone.

Raphael stopped typing on his keyboard and glanced at the youngster with raised eyebrows. "Any aftereffects from yesterday's session? You don't sound quite the same."

Vonn considered the question. "If you mean from my experience on the Internet, I would say my answer is no. However, to be perfectly truthful, that would not be a complete response."

"In what way?" Raphael asked.

"I spent some time reflecting on what I learned yesterday, and came to realize that what you are doing here is important. The fact that I am able to participate is an opportunity I do not want to miss. Therefore, I promise to follow your lead as we continue forward with the project."

Raphael looked relieved. "That's a good decision. I'm glad to hear it."

Asha helped Vonn sit on the examination table and took a moment to stare into his eyes. "But that's not all, is it, Vonn? What else did you conclude?"

Vonn met Asha's gaze with equanimity. "You are correct, Mrs. Riddle. I came to that conclusion quite late in the evening. One of the first things I did was to review those memories from my early childhood. I found it to be an extremely profound experience. It occurred to me that if I could gain that much comfort from defragging those early memories, how much more benefit would there be if I expanded that process?"

"You what?" Raphael asked worriedly. He glanced at Asha. "Would he have that ability without you?"

"I expect so," Asha replied. "Once he went through it, the skillset was in his mind." She turned back to Vonn. "So, what did you do?"

"I defragged my entire brain."

"Vonn!" Raphael exclaimed. "That was extremely reckless!"

Asha smiled and shook her head. "No, I think it was smart. That's why you're different this morning, isn't it?"

"I did not realize it was something you would notice," Vonn said. "I do feel a bit different, though."

"How so?" Asha asked.

"I'm not sure. It's hard to describe, but I'd say that I'm more comfortable with myself. Not as anxious about things in general."

"That sounds like a good thing."

"The process was beneficial. I highly recommend it."

Raphael looked like he wanted to scold Vonn, but after a moment he said, "All right, it's all water under the bridge. But I'm uncomfortable with the situation. If we are responsible for wholesale changes to your brain that have affected your personality, I would find it difficult to justify to your mother."

"I understand, Doctor Acosta, but is that really in question? I turn nineteen next month. For the past year, I have legally been an adult in the State of Illinois."

"That may be the case, Vonn, but you are still your mother's son, and her feelings toward you will never change."

"I suspect that is true. Nevertheless, in this instance, I have to conclude no harm has been done, and in fact, quite the reverse. It saddens me that you do not share my opinion."

Asha suppressed a smile at Raphael's expression of consternation. Vonn was speaking like a wizened monk and it was strange to hear such words coming from the mouth of the reckless teenager they'd worked with yesterday.

Raphael shook his head. "I'm not saying it's a bad thing. But you admit yourself there is a change. So, this is what we're going to do first. Remember that clinic where you took all those personality tests the other day? I want you to go back and take them again. Don't try to second guess anything, just give honest responses. That will give us a measure of your progress."

"Of course, Doctor. Shall I do that now or will we have another online session first?"

Asha patted his arm and said, "Why don't you go now, Vonn? It will reassure Doctor Acosta. I promise we'll go online again. Maybe by then, I'll have a surprise for you."

Vonn brightened, and his face became that of a teenager once again. "A surprise?"

"I hope so, but you have to wait. Go take your tests. We'll call and make sure they can fit you in right away." Asha dug into her purse. "Here's some money. Take a taxi and don't dawdle."

"Yes, ma'am."

* * * *

After Vonn left, Asha and Raphael stared at each other for several moments, letting the impact of what they'd witnessed sink in.

"That was interesting," Asha finally said.

"To say the least," Raphael replied. "The problem is, we're going to face that situation with each individual. I'm trying to decide if it's ethical to move forward. That was not the same young man we talked to yesterday."

"I disagree. He is exactly the same person, but he's grown up a little; that's all. He still has all the same experiences he grew up with. The only difference is that now, his thoughts are more organized. When he considers the world around him, he's able to focus and come to a rational conclusion, instead of getting off track about every single detail."

"Is that how it is for you? Did you know this would happen?"

"Yes and no. I have no idea what I was like before, but based on my one meeting with someone from my previous life, a girl named Candy, I must have been a handful. When I look at youngsters, a lot of them are scatterbrained. I was probably the same."

"You're not now. You seem pretty level-headed."

"I'll take that as a compliment. But if that trait is a result of organizing my thoughts, I'm not regretful. And Vonn isn't either. To me, we've identified a known side-effect of the skillset that we are trying to instill in our test subjects, and it seems beneficial. Is that a problem?"

Raphael nodded emphatically. "Yes, if we don't make that clear up front, then it is. If we're going to proceed, we have to go back to square one. At the very least, I need to include a disclosure form and have parents sign off on it."

"What for?" Asha asked. "You think they won't like it if their kids exhibit a little maturity? I doubt you'll have much trouble getting signatures."

"Let's hope not. But we have to include this step. I'll have a better idea when we get the results from Vonn's testing. Are you going to wait? We'll have the results later this afternoon."

"Not today. After lunch, I have to see Scott during visiting hours."

"You mean Chromite? Your little inspiration?"

Asha nodded. "His name came up on the transplant list again. It's supposed to happen this week. I want to wish him good luck."

"Well that's fantastic. I'll swing by too and tell him to hang in there. He's got a job with us when he gets well."

* * * *

279

Asha was smiling when she opened the door to Scott's hospital room. Inside, however, Raphael's stricken face and the empty bed turned her heart cold.

"I'm so sorry, Asha," he said in a broken voice. "Scott passed away an hour ago."

Asha stood frozen in shock for a long moment. "I thought he was getting better."

"He was upbeat because of your help. But kids with his disease don't get better. He held on as long as he could."

"They killed him, didn't they?" Asha whispered. "They kept saying no because they knew they could get away with it; that sooner or later they would win."

"It happens. The industry can be cruel."

"This wasn't cruel," Asha countered angrily. "This was murder."

"Don't think that way. You did the best you could, and Scott was grateful. He always said you were a cool lady."

Asha gave her friend a cold expression. "Thanks, Raphael, but let's not sugarcoat it. I'm turning this over to my attorney. Those bastards may never face criminal charges, but I'm going to make them pay one way or another."

Raphael had no response. After a moment, he put her hand on Asha's shoulder and said, "Don't let it get to you. Do something to lift your spirits. Let's take a break for a couple of days. We can start again this coming Tuesday. The funeral will be on Monday."

Asha shuddered. "I don't think I can attend."

"That's fine, I understand. A lot of people have difficulty that way."

"I want to help, but I feel like I'm about to fall apart."

Raphael said, "His mom is not well off, so it would be nice if you covered the cost. It would mean a lot to her, in more ways than one."

"Okay. I'll do that. Would you take care of it and give her my condolences? I need to get out of here."

"Of course."

In front of the hospital, a yellow hatchback taxi pulled up. Asha opened the door to get in, but across the street, Ken called out to her from the parking lot and hurried toward her.

"My mistake," she said to the taxi driver and rushed to meet her husband.

"I just heard from Rafe," Ken said when he reached her. "I'm sorry."

Asha's composure suddenly crumbled. "Can you take me home?" she cried, unable to stop her tears from falling. "This is the first time someone I know has died. I can't explain why, but I feel guilty."

"I'm sorry. He got a bad deal. Come on, I'll take you."

Asha was embarrassed because she boohooed the entire trip. When they reached the apartment, Ken parked in his underground slot and took her upstairs. "Go to bed," he advised. "I'll bring you some hot tea."

"I'm not sleepy," she insisted while he tucked her under the covers.

* * * *

It was three in the morning when Asha woke up. On the nightstand was a mug of untouched tea. Her crushing sadness had dissipated, and only a deep, lingering sorrow remained. She felt unusually comforted until she realized it was because Ken was sound asleep next to her, sprawled out on top of the covers.

Why does he do that? He just had to take advantage of her unhappiness. She suppressed the urge to shove him off the bed and instead left the room.

In the kitchen, she made some coffee and that made her hungry, so she started some toast. After ten minutes of contemplation, she decided that wasn't enough. She wanted a real breakfast.

She heard Ken stirring, and by the time he joined her, she had scrambled eggs, toast, and bacon for both of them.

"Sorry," he said, sitting down at the table. "I didn't mean to fall asleep."

"Like I would ever trust anything you said."

"Honest," he insisted. "I only came in to check on you and…I don't know…I guess I nodded off."

"*Abbot*, is my husband telling the truth?"

The answer surprised her. "Yes," *Abbot* said. "He went into your room after his supper and sat on the side of the bed to observe that you were comfortably resting. While sitting there, he fell asleep in an upright position."

Asha glared at Ken and shook her head. "Whatever."

"Anyway," Ken said. "Do you want to sign the lease? I spoke to the realtor and he needs a decision by Friday."

Asha nodded. "Friday works. *Abbot*, do you see any issues with the lease?"

Abbot said, "I advise against such action."

That was a surprise. "Really? Why not? The place looks perfect."

"In accordance with your instructions, I have a standing order to do a background investigation on those you come in contact with."

"Did you find a problem with someone?"

"The taxi driver at the hospital."

Asha smiled and said, "I'm not sure how he is a threat to the lease. Can you explain?"

"He is of Asian origin."

Asha considered *Abbot's* words. "That's right. When I told him to never mind, I saw a Chinese newspaper on the dash. I figured he was from Chinatown, down by the river. But *Abbot*, not every oriental person is our enemy."

"I acknowledge that fact. But this particular individual is on the payroll of the People's Liberation Army."

"The Chinese army?" Ken asked astonished.

"That is correct. His name is Major Mao. He is a covert agent for the Second Department of the Joint Staff Headquarters in Beijing."

"What in the world is he doing driving a taxi? Is he spying on Asha?"

"Affirmative. It is a result of her association with you. After I detected Major Mao's identity, I did some additional research and discovered that both of you are the primary subjects of an investigation. The Chinese Intelligence Bureau has connected the development of *Monroe* to Riddle Systems. After your bankruptcy, they lost track of your activities but recently reacquired your location at Shaded Lair. They are very interested in your next project."

Ken gave Asha a worried look. "The last thing we need is for them to find out we're opening a war room to go after them. *Abbot*, how much information do they have on us?"

"That you are engaged in the creation of a new virtual reality video game. They are undecided if that is a cover for something more nefarious."

After a moment of consideration, Asha said, "We still need the war room. That's a given. Just because they know where we are doesn't mean we give up."

"I could have Cody create a shell company," Ken offered.

Asha's mouth turned down in a scornful expression. "I like Cody, but he's married to Maryanne, and she's married to the FBI, and the FBI can't keep a secret. I'll take the lease to Bernard. He has a big law firm behind him so they should be able to handle the matter without any problems. Do you have a copy?"

Ken pointed to his briefcase. "There's a PDF in my laptop."

"Email it to him, and I'll talk to him later." She looked at the sun rising over Lake Michigan. "First, I'm going back to bed and get another hour of sleep. You need to come up with a real video game. If that's what they think you're working on, let's make sure they keep believing it."

"I'm sleepy too," Ken said hopefully.

Asha replied, "Then I suggest you take a nap…in your own apartment."

* * * *

"You were going to sign this lease?" Stephenson asked disbelievingly, holding up a small sheaf of documents.

Asha nodded. "That's right. I like the property." She was sitting in his office in the now-familiar plush leather chair that faced his desk. It was a little after ten in the morning since her nap had gone longer than she expected.

Stephenson placed the package on the desktop and massaged his face. "Mrs. Riddle. Please, in the future, do not even think about signing anything until I see it. This is a boilerplate lease that is skewed entirely toward the landlord. You should never sign this type of document."

"Okay," Asha replied easily. "Can I just dump the entire thing in your lap? I want to move into the space, but as I explained, I don't want there to be any association between Ken and me and the new operation. I guess we need a phony business front. Is that legal?"

"We shall certainly keep it legal. One of our partners specializes in real estate. Do you have a preference for the charade?"

"Not really."

"Then I suggest a temporary employment agency. You said you will be working with teenagers?"

"That's right, for the most part. But we want to keep what we're doing under wraps."

"Then a temp agency would not look suspicious for young people to be coming in and out. But why are you trying to keep the activity secret? I can't help if you are going to be breaking the law."

"No, nothing illegal," Asha said innocently. "I just want to destroy China's ability to engage in cyberwarfare."

Stephenson's eyes widened momentarily. "I beg your pardon?"

"You heard me. It was the Chinese military who put me in the hospital. I can't afford to let that happen again. It's best if I take them out first."

"Mrs. Riddle, you cannot unilaterally wage war against a foreign nation! That is definitely against the law."

"Who says?"

"The government! Treaties. International Law. The National Information Infrastructure Protection Act of 1996 specifically states that it is illegal to access another person's computer without authorization."

"But that's what hacking is," Asha pointed out. "Everybody does it all the time. The Chinese blew up my eye, and I certainly didn't authorize it!"

"*Everybody does it* is not a legal defense."

"So, what then? I'm not allowed to protect myself? They almost killed me!"

"Of course you are. There are dozens of products on the market for self-protection."

"None of which can stand up against *Monroe*. And I know that for a fact because *Monroe* is part of my original AI."

Stephenson looked puzzled. "*Monroe?*"

Asha waved away his question. "Okay, listen. There is a software package called *Monroe*; it's mine. The Chinese stole it. That much is beyond dispute, and even Nigel Cherry acknowledges it. You're saying I can't disable my own software to keep them from attacking me again?"

"Hmmm. I agree, there may be some gray area there, but this is not an uncomplicated issue. There have been several congressional initiatives to allow what they call *hack back* by non-governmental actors, but none of them have passed into legislation."

"Then let's leave it at that; it's a gray area. But whether you help me or not, Bernard, I'm going to protect myself." She gave her attorney a warning look that said she would not remain a client if he turned her down.

He folded instantly.

"No, no. We are here to serve your needs, of course. A temp agency it is. What about the other matter you mentioned, something about an insurance company? Does this have to do with your Mr. Stuart?"

Asha's face hardened. "Yes. I want to sue those bastards out of existence. They deliberately withheld medical treatment until Scott died."

Stephenson sighed. "My condolences. Regrettably, this is not an uncommon practice in our country. I can do what you ask, but it is a lengthy and expensive operation. Legal fees can run into seven figures and there is no guarantee of the outcome."

"I don't care. I want it done, and I want to win."

"I understand. Fortunately, Illinois has what we call the Health Care Arbitration Act, which prohibits binding arbitration. Still, they will balk at every step, particularly in the disclosure process."

"What does that mean?"

"First, you can expect them to hide behind voluminous court filings, and second, any documents that show their true motive will be deeply buried. Our ability to find hard evidence is practically nil."

Asha pulled an Echo Dot out of her briefcase. "You are familiar with *Abbot*, I believe?" she asked, plugging it in. "My AI? This is the precursor to the one we just talked about."

Stephenson shrugged. "You told me it assisted you with the money laundering situation." He nodded at the plug-like cylinder. "My wife has one of those. I never found it very useful."

"This one is a little different. *Abbot*, can you hear me?"

"Affirmative," the AI replied.

"This is Bernard. I want you to help him with Scott's case."

"Of course. Hello, Bernard. How may I be of service?"

Stephenson gave Asha a skeptical look. "Well, it would be nice if he could locate the pertinent internal emails from the insurance company, but that's like asking for the moon. This is exactly what I'm referring to. The opposing counsel will not readily part with that kind of information, and in the unlikely instance that they do, it's often buried in a truckload of paper. It won't be easy to find what we really need to prove the case."

"Document found," *Abbot* said.

Stephenson's computer dinged with a new mail notification. Asha gestured for him to read it.

"What's this?" he asked.

Abbot said, "That is an email thread between the insurance company president and his Director of Claims Management in which they discuss their strategy for denying Mr. Stuart's claim. They reference a corporate policy titled *Exceptions for Special Cases*. That policy was updated during Scott's illness."

"How did you get this?" Stephenson asked, his face showing the faintest trace of surprise, which for him was the same as his jaw hitting the floor in astonishment.

Asha spoke to cut off *Abbot's* answer. "We know a guy who knows a guy. Can we leave it at that?"

Stephenson leaned back and closed his eyes in contemplation. After a moment he said, "All right. Let's assume that is true. The question of whether this was obtained legally, which I doubt, still remains. Although the exclusionary rule does not necessarily apply to civil law, evidence that is obtained in a manner that *shocks the courts* may not be admissible." He nodded toward his monitor. "This is rather shocking."

"What's that supposed to mean?" Asha demanded, a new flash of irritation on her face.

"It means the court endeavors to operate in an ethical fashion."

"Why is everyone so hung up on ethics all of a sudden?" Asha challenged. "I just want those guys dead."

Stephenson smiled paternally. "And that is the ethical response of a toddler. Which candidly, is not all that surprising since you are in effect less than a year old."

Asha glared at her attorney. "Are you sure you want to make this personal between you and me?"

Stephenson shook his head in a jovial manner. "I apologize, my dear. What I'm saying is the insurance company was probably operating lawfully, and that is one of our problems. They can change their internal policies whenever they desire. It's the same thing when politicians pass legislation to cover their own backside rather than representing the needs of their constituents. Unfortunately, there are far too many companies, attorneys, and politicians who, though they stay within the boundaries of intentionally toxic laws, operate far beyond what is ethical. Our task is to prove that point, and it doesn't help our case by being unethical ourselves."

"So, we let them get away with it?"

"Not at all. We simply have to be smarter than they are." He nodded at his computer screen. "This is valuable information. Now that we know it exists, our job is to force them to acknowledge it in court. We can do that without the testimony of *Abbot* or your so-called *guys*. I believe you have a reasonable case."

"When will you file the lawsuit?"

"First, we must get Mr. Scott's mother on board. You yourself have no standing in this case. Have you spoken to her?"

"Not really."

"That is the first step."

"Would you do that?"

"If you wish. Attorneys are not known as ambulance chasers without cause."

"Then you take care of it."

"Very well. Just so you are aware, I won't handle this case myself; I'm a specialist in divorce. But our firm is well equipped for this type of litigation."

"I don't care about the details. You are my attorney, and I expect you to keep me in the loop."

"That is understood," Stephenson said. Then he studied Asha's face with a look of concern. "Are there any other documents I might need to know about?"

Asha thought about it and shrugged. "I dunno. We did modify our disclosure form the other day."

"Why was that?"

"Because we discovered our research materially alters the brain structure of the teenagers we experiment on."

Stephenson visibly flinched in his chair at her statement. He took a deep breath and said, "Perhaps you could let me see that form and tell me a little more about what's going on."

288

Chapter 12 – The Wargame

"Here's my permission slip," Vonn said, handing Asha the newly revised disclosure form.

"Your mom was okay with the revised wording?" Asha asked, curiously.

"She said, don't stop what you are doing. She likes the new me."

He had a slight smirk on his face, thanks to the score on his most recent personality test. Raphael had found the descriptors worrisome; Vonn's results had changed from the one labeled Protagonist to that of Entrepreneur. Asha thought it was good, saying it basically described the same person but with a little less emphasis on the judgmental scale. She said the result only meant he was more thoughtful, which for a teenager had to be a good thing.

"Do you feel like a new person?" she asked.

"Not at all," Vonn replied. "I'm just glad we can get back to work. I really missed not being able to turbo-surf." He looked at Raphael hopefully.

"I guess we should get started," the doctor replied. "Lean back and put on the headset. The first thing we want to test is if you can enter the Internet unassisted."

He couldn't. After ten minutes of figuratively bumping his head against the wall, Asha entered the network and reached out to him. *"Like this, remember?"*

The simple nudge was all it took, and Vonn was ready to browse the Web.

Raphael stopped the test and made Vonn try again from the beginning. No matter how many times they tried, he could not connect to the network without help from Asha.

"This is discouraging," Raphael concluded. "I had hoped he could do this unassisted. Perhaps this is a good time to introduce him to *Sherlock*. If that doesn't work, Asha, you become a fairly large bottleneck."

"Okay," she replied. To Vonn, she said, "This is the surprise I mentioned last time. You ready?"

"Yes, ma'am. Who's *Sherlock*?"

"We're hoping that *Sherlock* will be your guide from here on. He's a special AI that I created for you."

Vonn looked crestfallen. "I thought you would teach me."

"I'll be here if you need me, but I bet you'll be happy with *Sherlock*. Here he is. *Sherlock*, see if you can connect to Vonn, and say hello."

"Good morning, Master Vonn," the British voice said, appearing in Vonn's mind.

"Whoa!" Vonn exclaimed. "He's in my head like you were that first time."

"That's right," Asha said. "I put a lot of effort into teaching him how to connect with you. From here on, he'll be your online partner, the same way that *Abbot* is my partner. For now, I want the two of you to go through a few exercises. We created a couple of virtual games that you'll enjoy. Tag and Hide and Seek."

Vonn gave her a skeptical look. "Sounds pretty basic."

"You may think differently in thirty minutes."

"Tag," Sherlock said.

"I felt that," Vonn said. "How did he do that?"

"I'll show you," Asha said. "Can you feel this?" She mentally stroked the top of Vonn's head. "Do you see what I'm doing?"

"Kind of."

Asha demonstrated several times until Vonn could return the gesture. "Be careful," she warned him. "Part of your grade is based on your control. When you start playing with others, I don't want anyone to get hurt."

"This couldn't hurt a person," he countered.

Asha mentally bopped him on the side of the head.

In his recliner, Vonn's body jerked. "Oww!" he whimpered.

"Don't argue with me," she warned.

"Okay. I see what you mean."

"Now, I want you to tag *Sherlock*. Watch me first." A few tries later, Vonn had the hang of it. Asha said, "Okay, this time *Sherlock* is going to evade you. Try to tag him and then it'll be his turn to chase you. Ready?"

Vonn nodded.

"Tag," the AI said, moving away.

Vonn took off after him in hot pursuit. Asha turned her attention to Raphael's monitor, which displayed a localized version of the worldwide threat map. On the screen, *Sherlock* and Vonn's locations were reflected by the flashing lines that zigged and zagged, first across the city, and then across the nation. With each exchange of tags, Vonn's body contorted as he tried to avoid *Sherlock's* touch. Within minutes their telltale traces were flashing around the globe. *Sherlock* stretched Vonn's abilities to their limit. After a quarter of an hour, Vonn was panting and sweating profusely.

"That's enough, *Sherlock*," Asha said.

"Program terminated," he replied mentally.

Vonn pulled off his headset. "Holy crap!" he wheezed. "That's worse than running sprints."

"I think it's time to call it a day," Asha said. "Let's hold off on the Hide and Seek until tomorrow."

"Sounds good to me."

Asha was surprised at his willingness to stop. "Are you okay? I didn't realize it would take that much out of you. Will you be ready to try again tomorrow?"

Vonn's smile spread across his face. "Oh, yeah. That was the coolest thing I've ever done. It's like paintball on a whole new level."

After Vonn left, Raphael looked at Asha with surprise on his face. "This is fascinating for several reasons. Did you go through that kind of exhaustion?"

"No, since I did everything at my own pace. It is a draining experience, there is no question. And when *Abbot* and I were doing our research on the money laundering guy, each night I went to bed pretty tired."

"Are we ready for the next subject?" he asked.

Asha checked the list of names on her clipboard. "I guess. Our young Mr. Rascal is next."

..*.*

"Thank you, Moth," Raphael said as he assisted the young man in removing his headset. "We'll be in touch if we decide to move forward with your training."

"Did I do okay?" Moth asked hopefully.

"You did very well," Asha replied, trying hard to keep the disappointment out of her voice. "You should be very proud of yourself."

Once Moth had left, she asked Raphael, "Can you explain it?"

They had gone through fifteen applicants in the last few days, and only three had been able to enter the Internet through the VR headset, even with Asha's assistance.

"I suspect it's age related," Raphael said. "At this age, the male brain is nearing its full development. There must be a narrow window where their brain is old enough to make the effort but not past the point it can't learn a new skill."

"What about Reaper?" Asha asked. "He's older than most of these guys. Wasn't he a freshman in college?"

"True, but if you noticed, he did not strike me as having reached physical maturity."

"A late bloomer?"

"That would be my guess. I think we need to concentrate on our younger applicants next week."

"Suits me," Asha said. "I had hoped we would have an army by now. This is taking a lot longer than I anticipated."

"That may be true, but let's not rush it," Raphael cautioned. "I'm worried that we're playing a high-stakes game without understanding the bet or even what the game really is."

"I have the same concern," Asha agreed. "And our new digs aren't ready yet, anyway. Ken says they are ahead of schedule. I guess that's one good thing. We're going to talk about it over dinner.

He wants me to look over some etchings the decorator found for our new office area."

Raphael looked up in surprise. "He wants you to look at some etchings? Seriously? That's what he said?"

"Yeah. Is that a problem?"

A slow smile spread across Raphael's face. "No, no problem at all. But I'm glad to see you two getting back together, that's all."

Asha shook her head. "No, no. That's not going to happen, I can tell you that for sure. We're only going to have dinner, and then he'll go home. I drew that line in the sand very clearly."

"Your place or his?"

"Mine. I told him I would cook something if he brings the drinks. I haven't really tried alcohol yet, so he's bringing an assortment. It should be fun."

Raphael nodded with a straight face. "I agree."

..*.*

So, this is what a hangover feels like, Asha thought miserably as she crawled out of the bedroom. Ken was still sound asleep.

Her emotions were all over the place. She was furious with her husband for spending the night. It was a line she had warned him not to cross. But she was angrier with herself because she had invited him to stay.

At least, that's what she recalled; most of last night's activities were fuzzy. Unfortunately, the memory of their bodies wrapped around each other was perfectly clear and absolutely mortifying. She could not bear the idea of saying good morning when he woke up.

Fortunately, she had gotten into the habit of taking an early jog around Avery Park. And right now, hangover or not, she needed to get out of the apartment.

By the time she made it to the jogging trail, her head was clearing. The sun was rising over the lake and the cold breeze made her feel human again. She pushed troublesome thoughts from her mind and concentrated on breathing.

Beijing, China

Major Wong hunched over the conference room table while everyone peered at their new virtual reality headset. With him were Lieutenant Soong and a newcomer, Captain Wie, the Second Department's leading expert in electronics. They were all present to give General Xiao and Colonel Chaing an update.

"Who got this for us?" Xiao asked.

Wong explained, "One of our covert agents, Lieutenant Li, posed as a student applicant and went through their selection process. While he was in the building, he managed to take this one from a storage closet. They may not even realize it's gone. If they do, they will most likely attribute it to one of the kids taking it home."

"It looks like a toy."

Captain Wei shook his head. "I wouldn't call it that, General. The outer shell casing is original, but the inside is heavily customized. The important aspect is the addition of twin lasers that focus on the retina and the optical processor. The design is oriented toward browsing the Internet as opposed to gameplay."

"What are the lasers for?"

"They measure the reaction of a certain type of ganglion cell and transform it into a digital command. They also added inward-facing photo sensors that act like microscopes. I suspect their goal is to turn the user into a human Web browser. I read the report about Mrs. Riddle's capability. If they crack the code on this, they could have an army of Mrs. Riddles."

"How did our lieutenant do?" Colonel Chaing asked. "Is he still in their program?"

"He never got a call back," Wong replied. "He did everything they told him, but evidently, he did not meet their requirements. It seems that not too many of their subjects do. We don't really understand the criteria."

"Anything in the headset exploitable?" Xiao asked.

Wong smiled grimly. "It appears they didn't learn their lesson with Mrs. Riddle." He turned to Wei. "The captain can explain this better than I."

Wei said, "The internal lasers are high-quality, medical-grade products with a tunable power output; they are top-of-the-line items."

"What does all that mean?" Xiao asked.

"It means the lasers have pulse lengths between six hundred and thirteen hundred nanometers and can actually see into living tissue. But for that specific use, the power setting has to be extremely low, only fractions of a milliwatt."

"And this uses that much power?" Colonel Chaing asked, nodding at the headset.

"If I can rephrase your question, sir," Wei said. "What is important is their *maximum* output. For example, even a typical office laser pointer can damage the human retina, and they only put out between one and five milliwatts. The ones the Riddles are using have settings over a hundred times more powerful. They were engineered for surgical applications where doctors require lasers rather than scalpels. These things can deliver up to six hundred milliwatts. That's enough to cause permanent blindness in less than one-hundredth of a second. And if you were wondering, I've already presented this device to *Monroe*. She was able to hack the headset without any problem."

"You are saying that *Monroe* can change the laser's power output inside the actual headset?" Xiao asked hopefully.

"Yes, sir, that's correct. And she can do it while it is in use. We tested dozens of different configurations, and each time *Monroe* bypassed the unit's main processor in less than a second. If we wait until they have twenty or thirty of those kids using their headsets at the same time, we could take out their entire cadre with a single strike. *Monroe* would fire the lasers at a maximum power straight into their eyes."

"That sounds painful," Xiao said with an amused twitch of his lips. "What kind of injury are we talking about?"

"At the very least," Wong said, "the lasers will burn out their retinas. Depending on alignment inside the headset, it could even inflict brain damage. I doubt it will kill the children…but it would certainly be fatal for their research program."

Xiao leaned back in his chair with a satisfied smile and said, "I love working against the Americans. They never see beyond the end of their noses. Imagine if the Riddles suddenly blind a dozen children."

Soong said, "We are preparing a simultaneous propaganda campaign on social media, to launch right after the incident. We'll spread stories about reckless endangerment and demand the Riddles be charged; American civilians are quite gullible. It would permanently remove any threat to Project Mobius."

"I like it," Xiao said. "The question is when to do it. I guess we should find out if or when enough of the kids wear the headset at the same time."

"We don't know about that," Soong said. "If you want us to find out, we would have to place someone inside the company. I can advise our Chicago field agent to work on it."

General Xiao chuckled and gave Wong a curious glance. Wong felt his heart sink. This was not what he expected.

"I've been studying your personnel file, Major. You have quite an accomplished background."

"Thank you, sir," Wong replied dully.

Xiao laughed out loud. "Don't be so downcast, Major. Take care of this problem and you can take your pick of assignments when you get back. You should think of this as a promotion."

Wong didn't feel that way. He was happy here in Beijing.

Soong was looking back and forth between the two officers with questions in her eyes.

"Your Major Wong was a field agent in his younger days," Xiao explained. "In fact, he was one of the best we ever had. He could penetrate any organization and find out any secret. He reminds me of me, in fact."

"I didn't know that," Soong said.

Colonel Chaing nodded. "His kind of expertise is hard to find."

"You want me to go to Chicago," Wong said. It was a statement, not a question.

"I think that's best," Xiao said. We have too much invested in Stunning Blow and Project Mobius. I can't afford for Mrs. Riddle to interfere, not at this point."

Wong schooled his features into one of obedience. The decision had already been made so he might as well go with the flow. Hopefully, it would not be a permanent change to field duty; the general was known as someone who kept his word. He said, "Of course, sir. It is my privilege to serve."

"You won't lose by it. I don't see this as a long-term mission."

"Thank you, General. I will do my best. Before I leave, however, might I offer a suggestion?"

Xiao nodded. "As long as it's not for someone else to go in your place."

Wong smiled grimly. "No sir. I just always believe that a backup plan is a good idea. If we can take out Mrs. Riddle in an unrelated fashion, even while I am there, maybe their little scheme will never get off the ground."

"Do you have something in mind?"

"If we examine the FBI's history with Mrs. Riddle, it's clear they don't trust her. I believe we could induce them to neutralize her themselves."

"That's true," Soong said. "One of Major Mao's sources reported a big stink within the Bureau recently. Evidently, she appropriated some reward money that had not been authorized. The story wasn't clear, but apparently, a few people weren't happy with her."

Wong added, "We should capitalize on their dissatisfaction. We have confirmed the US government is aware that we used their *Monroe* technology against NASA."

"That is correct," Soong said. "And word has gotten around that she is the inventor."

Wong glanced at Soong. "I suggest we push the idea that she's on our side. Don't we know someone who can spread that concept?"

Soong nodded. "Yes, sir. We have several contacts in the cyber division of their Homeland Security. That would be the best place to plant the idea. It would spread quite rapidly."

"I like that idea," Xiao said. "Make it happen."

Wong turned to Wei and added, "Do you have a *Monroe* unit of your own or are you borrowing ours?"

"Sergeant Ahn has been very helpful," Wei answered. "But if you plan to set up a strike force for Mrs. Riddle's private cyber army, I recommend dedicating several machines."

Before Wong could answer, Xiao interrupted. "Lieutenant Soong, I'm going to reassign you to the Strategic Support Force as the Deputy Plans Officer for Project Mobius. Captain Wei, you are going there too. You'll both work for Colonel Hsieh. Captain, you know more about these goggles than anyone else, so I want you to establish a specialized team to focus on addressing the issue. Interface with the Lieutenant to make sure all of your efforts remain integrated into the overall program."

"Thank you, General," Soong replied. She looked pleased with the new assignment.

Wong said, "Please be careful, Captain Wei. When Mrs. Riddle struck us last time, she took out five of our *Monroe* servers. Sergeant Ahn has not been able to probe the Americans without them realizing we're doing it, and yet Mrs. Riddle moves about invisibly. Your team must not advertise we still have *Monroe* working for us."

"Yes, sir."

General Xiao said, "And I guess this is as good a time as any." He pulled a small envelope from his pocket and took out a pair of captain's shoulder boards. Looking at Soong, he said, "The deputy position over there is a Captain's slot." He handed the insignia to Wong. "You want to do the honors, Major? Let's make her your contact while you're in Chicago."

"Thank you, sir," Wong said. He helped the smiling Soong replace her lieutenant's rank with the new epaulets.

"Congratulations, *Captain* Soong. Now *I'm* the one who has to stay on *your* good side."

Soong giggled with appreciation. "Thank you, Major. I owe you more than I can say. I will always be available when you call."

Congratulations were shared all around, although for Wong it was a bit tongue-in-cheek. He wasn't at all excited about his new assignment. After everyone left, it was just him and Soong.

"Sorry, Major," Soong said sympathetically. "I know you like living in Beijing."

"It happens," Wong said with a sigh. "We'll just have to work quickly to get it done so I can come back. In the meantime, you need to add a few pages to the Project Mobius plan. The team designated for Mrs. Riddle's warriors must be on alert because when I make the call, you have to respond instantly."

"I understand," Soong said. "We'll be ready."

"Be sure you are. Why don't we call your section Operation Bartimaeus? Do you know who Bartimaeus was?"

"Wasn't he the blind man that Jesus healed in Jericho?"

Wong was pleasantly surprised by his former subordinate's knowledge. "You are exactly right. The difference is, in our case, rather than healing the blind, we'll be making them that way. I will identify the time of the attack. Your goal is to take out Mrs. Riddle's teenagers all at once. We'll only get one shot at this."

* * * *

Grant Park, Chicago, Illinois

Did I jog before the accident? Asha wondered as she pounded along the pavement. A month ago, she was grateful for the exercise because it got her out of the apartment that first morning after Ken had stayed over. But now, their situation had evolved. He was essentially living with her, and so far, it was working. In the mornings, she didn't feel panicked, just comfortable he was there.

Apart from that, she still enjoyed her morning runs along the lakefront. She'd cross Roosevelt Road and then take the jogging trail under Lake Shore Drive. From there she ran along the waterfront to

Queen's Landing. Sometimes she would keep going, but normally she turned left to cross Grant Park, going around the stunning Buckingham Fountain, and then down Columbia Drive for the last leg. She was impressed the first time she saw the fountain shooting water a hundred and fifty feet into the air. This morning, however, the maintenance crew had it shut down for service.

In addition to her fellow joggers, other people were often scurrying around the park at sunrise, usually setting up tents and booths for one type of public gathering or another. Chicago had put on three massive music concerts since she had moved in.

Today, though, it was all about food. Dozens of vendors were getting ready for the Taste of Chicago festival. Tantalizing aromas from all over the world already filled the air. Ken had promised they would attend and she was looking forward to the evening's extravaganza.

Halfway down Columbia Drive, *Abbot* warned her that a government surveillance vehicle was present, hiding among the vendor delivery trucks. The people inside were monitoring her movement. The AIs description brought back memories of the US Attorney's battlewagon in Des Moines.

Asha spotted the nondescript white van on the other side of the street. There were more electronic signals coming out of it than the TV van at the Iowa governor's mansion.

Who is inside that thing? she asked.

Federal agents, he replied. *Do you want details on their individual identities?*

Asha didn't. Instead, she directed the AI to locate the Agent in Charge. Beyond confirming what agency was tracking her, she didn't care to investigate anything.

I had hoped we were past all that, she thought. It was a disappointing discovery. What were they interested in now? She would bet money this was related to helping out Nigel and his brother-in-law at NASA. She never should have done the man a favor.

It didn't matter. Whoever was crowded into the van, their eavesdropping was about to end.

All of the surveillance equipment was powered by the engine's oversized generator. Asha piggybacked onto one of their data feeds to get inside the van and found electrical continuity into the motor's computer systems, one of which monitored oxygen, air pressure, emissions, and most importantly for Asha's needs, the throttle position.

First, she disabled the overspeed governor on the van's idling engine, then she locked the throttle to full open. It was as though the driver had floored the accelerator while in neutral. The RPMs skyrocketed, way over redline, and within seconds smoke began pouring from the engine compartment.

The men in the back bailed out and began swearing at the driver who claimed he hadn't done anything. The front of the truck bucked once as the motor tore itself apart. Asha didn't even break stride as she jogged pass the ruined vehicle.

She was still in a bad mood when she got back to the apartment. She told Ken about the agents while he finished preparing their breakfast. When she sat down at the kitchen table, she put the incident out of her mind. It was time to focus on the day ahead, not dwell on events in the past. The government's reappearance, however, made it difficult, and her thoughts involuntarily drifted back over recent weeks.

A sudden thought came to mind and she slapped her spoon onto the table, startled by a realization. She looked at Ken in surprise.

"What?" Ken said.

"I just figured it out...you did that on purpose."

"Did what?"

"Got me drunk."

"That was a month ago."

"I know. But you've been sleeping over ever since. Oh my God!" In hindsight, it was painfully obvious that he had planned that evening with military precision. His well-executed strategy of *introduction to alcohol* hat gotten past her lingering resentment.

Afterward, he never asked about sleeping at her place; he simply assumed it.

After the first embarrassing morning, their continued close proximity to each other at the office grew more comfortable, and now, they often worked after hours on various aspects of their project, usually in her living room. And if she was honest about it, she didn't mind.

"That was your game plan from the very beginning," she nevertheless exclaimed in an accusatory tone. "Wasn't it?"

There was a trace of smugness on his face when he said, "We're married. These things happen between married people. They enjoy each other's company, share drinks, make love."

"It's supposed to be mutual."

"I thought it was. You were only drunk that one time."

Asha stared at him for a moment and then asked, "Why did I marry you, anyway? I could see it in your eyes that day with the investors; you remembered something."

"You're right. It was Robert, actually. When he spoke to you, I recognized him and a flood of those missing memories all came back in one big whoosh."

"You knew Robert?"

"No, but you pointed him out to me at the airport when we got back from Vegas. You wanted to talk to him on your own, to let him know about us, and I went for the car. You told me to pick you up in front of the terminal. And I did."

Asha searched her own memory but found no trace of what he described. "Then how did we meet in Vegas?" she asked.

"You were standing in front of a slot machine looking sad. I put a quarter in for you and pulled the handle. I told you to cheer up."

"What was I upset about?"

"Your parents. They had passed away a month prior. That got us talking and one thing led to another."

"Why didn't we use my name when we got married?"

Ken shook his head. "I told you about my idea to mislead Erica. You started pointing out all the flaws in the plan, like what would happen when I got back without a wife. We were pretty drunk, and you thought the whole idea was hilarious. Then you said you would play the role of Asha for a couple of days. It was all a lark."

"And we actually got married?"

Ken nodded. "Yeah, but we never considered it real. I bribed the guy in the chapel since we used a name that wasn't on your ID. We were going to come back, spend a few days and then you would leave on a *vacation* and that would be it. We didn't plan much beyond that."

"How stupid was that?" Asha asked rhetorically. The behavior matched what she would have expected after talking to Candy.

"We had fun," Ken said. "More fun than I ever had in my life. Just like last night."

Asha's face reddened. Last night had been spectacular, but he was not supposed to bring it up afterward.

Ken reached across the table and took her hands. "Listen, right now I could not be happier with our marriage. I want us to go on just like this for the rest of our lives."

Asha pulled her hands back, discomfited, but not sure why. "I do too," she said quietly, and then fled to the bedroom to get ready for work.

She was about to leave the apartment when *Abbot* announced, "Mrs. Dorsey has just been arrested by the Bureau of Alcohol, Tobacco, Firearms, and Explosives on a weapons charge."

"Who's Mrs. Dorsey?" Asha asked.

"Roadhog's grandmother," Ken said. "She raised him."

"Roadhog is one of our best students. I didn't realize he had problems at home. It didn't show up in our screening."

"Maybe he doesn't," Ken said. "*Abbot*, is this is a bogus charge?"

"Standby. I will investigate the situation."

Ken added, "If I remember correctly, Mrs. Dorsey is an older woman who has a housekeeping job. Not your typical arms dealer."

"So, what's going on?" Asha asked.

Abbot said, "You are correct. I have captured the security camera feed from the country club where she works. I will display it on the television."

The TV screen illuminated with a shot of the custodial staff's locker-room. An elderly, overweight woman entered the field of view. She had just arrived at work and put a huge handbag and her sweater into an employee locker. The clock on the wall indicated it was just before midnight.

The scene fast-forwarded to seven in the morning when a man entered. He opened her locker easily and took a handgun from a zip-top plastic bag. He then slipped it into Mrs. Dorsey's handbag. Fast-forwarding another hour, to the eight o'clock shift change, the woman came in, punched her timecard, and walked out.

The scene changed to a shot of the country club's employee parking area. As Mrs. Dorsey approached her run-down Chevrolet, two official-looking vans pulled up, and several ATF agents jumped out with weapons drawn. They cuffed the elderly woman and hauled her away in the back seat of one of their vehicles. The expression on her face was one of absolute shock and fear.

"They're trying to get to us through Roadhog," Ken said. "This has to be related to that tracking van."

"What is it with these people?" Asha exclaimed angrily. "If they have a question, why can't they just ask?"

"I imagine they're afraid to," Ken said. "As I recall, the last time Maryanne asked you to work for them, you told them all to take a hike."

"And this is why," she said, gesturing at the TV. "*Abbot*, please inform Bernard, and get someone down to the police station."

"Acknowledged. For your information, as a federal prisoner, Mrs. Dorsey is probably being held in the Metropolitan Correctional Center on Van Buren. Standby... Yes, I show her being processed in as we speak."

"Does Roadhog know about this?" Ken asked.

"Not as yet," *Abbot* replied. "Shall I advise him?"

"No," Ken said. "Let me take care of that. Is he at the office?"

"He will arrive shortly. He has a training session scheduled in twenty minutes."

"Call Raphael. Tell him to hold off and that I'm on the way." Ken gave Asha a quick hug and dashed out the door.

Asha said, "*Abbot*, find out who is behind this, and tell me where they are. And I want all the background you have. This is insane."

..*.*

Asha found Special Agent in Charge Nigel Cherry seated with another man at one of the round wooden tables inside the Potbelly Sandwich Shop on Michigan Avenue. They were working their way through a pair of huge sandwiches. Nigel had roast beef on a wheat roll, and the other guy was making a mess with his meatball special. A red splotch on his tie indicated he had literally bitten off more than he could chew.

Asha plopped down in an empty seat across from them.

"Hello, Nigel," she said. "I had hoped we wouldn't see each other again."

"Asha?" he responded, surprised by her sudden appearance. "What brings you here?" He looked around as though wondering if this was a chance meeting.

"No," Asha said, correctly interpreting his look. "I'm not here for you. I assume this is Special Agent Hugo King." She examined the other man's shirt and pulled several napkins from the wooden holder on the table. "I'm Asha Riddle," she said, handing them to him across the table. "I'll give you one chance to release Mrs. Dorsey with a written apology. If you refuse, I promise you will regret it. Nigel here can tell you that I don't joke around."

Hugo's expression showed nothing but contempt for the woman facing him.

"I'm not sure what's going on," Nigel said, "but I'd listen to her, Hugo." To Asha, he said, "What happened? Is this why you're here?"

"I don't respond well to threats, lady," Hugo said. "And you are coming this close to obstruction of justice if you keep on with your accusations."

"You are being set up, Hugo," Asha said. "The folks in the Homeland Security Cyber Security Division got some bad information about me and are using you to put pressure on me. That much is obvious. But I don't care about that. You are the guy who just picked up my employee's grandmother, and I won't let that go."

Hugo scowled and pulled out his cell phone to make a call. Asha rolled her eyes, not really surprised by the way he was totally ignoring her warning. Before he could dial a number, a text message appeared on his screen. Nigel's phone chimed as well.

"Time's up," Asha said. "I gave you a chance. You might want to look at that. I just sent you a link to a breaking news segment on WMAQ. They'll be the first to get it on the air, but other stations are picking it up. It will be a national story by this evening."

Hugo scowled at his phone, but Nigel clicked on the link to bring up the video.

An attractive reporter was saying, "We have confirmed these recordings are from the security cameras at the Durham Country Club. They conclusively show ATF agents planting evidence in the handbag of a senior citizen and then arresting her moments later. The suspect's attorney, Mr. Huey Warner, of the firm Hawley, Hepworth, and Kidwell, has issued a statement that they intend to sue the government, and will demand eighty million dollars for false arrest and damages due to pain and suffering. We'll have more on this..."

Nigel shook his head and looked at his colleague. "It's only going to get worse, buddy. Did you guys really do that?" Hugo didn't answer, but his face said it was true. "You need to put this fire out right now," Nigel advised. "Let it go and concentrate on damage control."

"She's a Chinese agent!" Hugo growled. "She sold restricted cyber tools to the Chinese. And she's still at it with some kind of lab over in Fuller Park."

306

"You better explain it to him," Asha said to Nigel.

Nigel shook his head at his colleague. "That's not what happened, Hugo. I can't reveal how the Chinese obtained the technology, but I promise you it wasn't Asha."

"I can tell you," Asha said blithely. "One of Nigel's guys seized a computer with those tools during a trumped-up raid and then turned around and sold it. That's how the Chinese got it. And when the Chinese started using it to attack NASA, I'm the one who shut them down! And now you are being suckered by the same enemy to do their new dirty work. If you had done any research at all, you would already know all of this. I'm not sure who it is on your side that hates me so much, but you guys are giving me a lot more trouble than the Chinese!"

Hugo's expression started to show doubt. To Nigel, he said, "Is that really what happened?"

Nigel nodded. "I have some history with Mrs. Riddle, and it's always been above board on her part. Unfortunately, we made some bad decisions and ruined the relationship. From the sound of it, you walked right into a self-inflicted disaster."

Asha stood up. "We're done. My attorneys will see you in court. Good day, gentlemen."

Chapter 13 – The Offer

Major Wong stood across the street from the construction site in downtown Chicago. This made a lot more sense. The strip mall was only a ruse.

Thank God he had come to Chicago himself. Before leaving Beijing, *Monroe* told him how Mrs. Riddle could easily detect electronic devices, including cell phones. For that reason, he decided to forgo standard espionage tech. Instead, he kept his ears open and worked hard at keeping one of the Riddles in sight.

After two days, he had the address of their new location. Within a week, he had the blueprints. The Riddles were building a cyber war room, one that was several quality steps above the ones in Pudong. And this one had dorm rooms for around-the-clock operation. Based on the location's size, Wong estimated a maximum force of thirty people. The only good news was that it didn't come close to the size of Project Mobius.

The entire first floor of the Riddle's new location was being fitted out with equipment that would make an expensive restaurant blush. The construction drawings called it an employee cafeteria.

But the best news for Wong was found by Major Mao. The Riddles were advertising for a chef, and cooking happened to be one of Wong's hidden talents. Mao had prepared a resumé for Wong and submitted it to the right people. He obviously knew the city well, because Wong had a job interview scheduled with the young woman coming out from behind the construction fencing. He stepped back into the shadows, not wanting her to see him between now and the interview. It was important for her to believe she was meeting him for the first time.

* * * *

Asha finished her site visit of the progress on the new location and made her way through the exterior mess onto the sidewalk. The build-out was going well and Ken said they would move in within the next two or three weeks. She was about to leave when *Abbot* contacted her.

Mr. Stephenson has an update on the insurance lawsuit if you would like to call or stop by.

The timing was good. *Tell him I'm on the way.*

Instead of catching the subway, Asha walked north for two blocks to Two Illinois Center. The local branch of Hawley, Hepworth, and Kidwell took up most of the twenty-second floor. Stephenson's secretary let her straight in.

"Hi, Bernard," she greeted him, taking her normal seat in front of his desk. His nod was minuscule. That meant there was nothing earth-shattering in his news. "Whacha got?"

"Hello, Mrs. Riddle. The insurance company is offering Chromite's mother three hundred thousand dollars to settle."

"Can we pay her that much and just keep on with the lawsuit?"

"As long as we follow certain accords, the answer is yes."

"Let's do it then. I don't think she is hurting for money in the meantime."

"That is correct. Your stipend was quite generous at the outset. Mrs. Stuart does volunteer work at the hospital three days a week and does not participate in the lawsuit unless necessary. Her deposition, by the way, was excellent."

"Are we going to win?"

"That is an ambiguous term at best. As I have mentioned, nothing is guaranteed. We have filed motions for disclosure, and they are fighting that. All I can say is the case is proceeding as expected."

Asha nodded. "I understand the process takes a long time, but I want to be sure it isn't put on a back burner. Keep pushing every day. Don't let them ask for another continuance."

"We didn't. We asked for a fast track, and so far, the judge is being accommodating."

"Sounds good. Anything else?"

"I received a call from Agent Cherry. He would like to meet with you."

Asha was immediately suspicious. "About what."

"My impression is that he wants to do some fence-mending now that the situation with Mrs. Dorsey is cleared up."

"It's not as far as I'm concerned. I want to make everyone in that camp regret they ever tried anything. Keep pressing."

"Are you sure?" Stephenson asked. "This won't make you any friends inside the federal government, and it's never a good idea to be on the wrong side of a machine that big."

"They were wrong!" Asha insisted. "That was about as clear cut as you can get."

"And Mrs. Dorsey will undoubtedly win the case if we continue, but why not talk to Agent Cherry first? See what he wants and is willing to give up."

"I know exactly what he wants. The same thing as always; a big favor in return for broken promises." Stephenson didn't respond. He waited patiently while giving Asha a long-suffering expression. Finally, she gave in. "All right. But you set it up. I'm not interested in any surprises. I want to see an agenda and a list of who is going to be there. And I want Ken to attend as well. He can give you the time and location."

Stephenson nodded. "That is a reasonable response. I will be in touch."

* * * *

Two weeks later, Asha was in Stephenson's office once more. He said, "Agent Cherry wants to issue a formal apology to Mrs. Dorsey. I contacted her, and she asked you to attend on her behalf. She doesn't trust them quite yet."

"I don't blame her. What about the lawsuit against them for false arrest?"

"They are offering a cash settlement of two hundred thousand. I recommend you accept in light of Agent Cherry's second agenda item."

"Which is?"

"They are interested in a written agreement. In other words, they would be willing to pay for your service."

Asha scoffed dismissively. "I've heard that before, too many times."

"Don't be hasty. If they are serious about a contract, it's worth listening to. They are not being specific at the moment because they're not sure what you have to offer. This would be a formal meet-and-greet type of meeting."

"Who would attend?"

"Agent Cherry, of course, and his boss up the chain, the deputy director from DC. Also, a Colonel Earl Roth, from the office of J3 of the US Cyber Command, and perhaps most importantly, Mr. Bill Ellis from the General Services Administration, who, I am told, is an expert in government contracting and managing compliance with the Federal Acquisition Regulations. Now, in case you didn't know, these are big dogs, all. If you take this meeting, you need to step up to the plate. This is not the place to throw one of your temper tantrums."

Asha was impressed. They sounded like big dogs indeed. "Ken will be interested," she said. "But I want to talk it over with him first. Let me get back to you…and I have never thrown a temper tantrum!"

* * * *

"What do you think?" Asha asked Ken over dinner after telling him about her visit with Stephenson. They were having their meal in the recently completed cafeteria of their new building. Asha wanted to show off the cooking skills of the new chef she had hired.

"I suspect Bernard's right," Ken said. "But he's got it backward. They're not going to offer anything. The government doesn't work that way. They want a proposal from us. I had a similar meeting

311

once. The request came out of the blue after I talked to some Air Force weapons guys. I had shown them a prototype of a new seeker head Rafe had developed. A week later, a crew from Lockheed and DOD showed up, and they just sat there waiting for me to make a proposal."

"Did you?"

"Of course. But it was the worst contract I ever made because I wasn't prepared. We need to be ready."

"And they'll sign it?"

"No, but if they like what we offer, they might issue a solicitation. Or maybe what they want is an *unsolicited* proposal. Except they can't actually *ask* for it because then it wouldn't be unsolicited, and that would be illegal. So, we have to have one ready to go."

"This all sounds very confusing." She glanced up at the chef as he served the dessert, a thinly layered ginger cake with wine-poached pears and cream. "Don't you think so, Tony?"

Major Wong gave her a friendly smile. "I have no idea about such things, Miss Asha. If Mr. Riddle says so, I'd have to go along with his recommendation."

Ken grinned and said, "Don't give him a hard time. This looks great, by the way, Tony."

"Thank you, Mr. Riddle. It's a family recipe from Mama Wong's deli in Chinatown, God rest her soul. I hope you enjoy it."

"Oh, my God," Asha mumbled around a dripping mouthful. "This tastes like heaven. Where have you been all my life?"

"Right here in Chicago, ma'am. Glad you like it." Wong polished the edge of the table with a quick swipe of his cloth and discreetly left the dining area.

Ken turned his attention back to Asha and said, "This is where it gets exciting. We need to imagine a world where you and I don't have to worry about a Chinese cyberthreat ever again. And then come up with a plan to get there."

"Doesn't the government have this kind of capability already? I'm not trying to save the world. I only want to teach China they're better off if they leave you and me alone."

"That's our starting point," Ken said. "But we have to think it all the way through to our exit strategy. Remember the presentation you gave to the FBI when you took out the money laundering guy?"

Asha nodded. "They seemed impressed."

"These new people won't be because that was for one bad guy on a long list. This time the briefing has to deal with an existential threat to the nation and include a solution that is verifiable."

"Is our ego a bit out of proportion?" Asha asked skeptically.

"Not in the least. The capability you and I and Raphael have developed is far beyond what anyone else has. This is why we need to let our imagination run wild."

"I have no idea what you mean."

"Remember a few months ago when I warned you getting even with China would be like Armageddon? If you want to take them on, you have to accept that it's a global undertaking. The good news is, maybe we get Uncle Sam to pay for it. This will be fun."

"You make it sound scary."

"It is. More than either of us appreciate. I need two more weeks to prepare for the meeting. Then we can give Nigel and his crew a demonstration that should make their eyes water."

* * * *

Asha and Ken met their visitors at the door of their new facility.

"Welcome to Chromium Plus, gentlemen," Asha said in greeting. "I'm Asha Riddle, and this is my husband, Ken. Please come in. Let's take the elevator up to our training area, and you can meet some of our team."

The second floor was a large open area, more like an executive lounge than an education center. It was filled with clusters of overstuffed leather couches and recliners. The back wall held a pair of large video screens, and six armchairs were lined up in front of them for easy viewing.

Asha continued. "This is Doctor Raphael Acosta. He is our miracle man who made all of our technology possible. Cody Anderson is our general counsel." She also introduced Ronny Santos, brought back to reprise his role from Riddle Systems as Chief of Operations.

"And here are three of our operators," she said, gesturing to a group of awkward teenagers. The youngsters shook hands and answered a few questions while the visitors treated them with amused respect. After everyone had shaken hands, Ken dismissed the teens who quietly left the room via the stairway.

Asha continued, "You'll get a chance to see them in action when we get into the demonstration phase. Now, Nigel. Who have you brought along?"

Nigel introduced his team in turn. There were five men and one woman. Their names went out of Asha's mind as soon as the introductions were complete and she was too embarrassed to ask them to repeat. Ken would remember them; he had that knack.

He got the visitors settled into the chairs facing the television screens.

"Let's start with Raphael," Ken said. "He will explain how we created this new technology. I imagine you are interested in how it works."

Raphael gestured to a photo of Asha on the main screen. It was a gruesome picture taken during her first few hours in the hospital after her initial car accident. He went on to describe the medical process used to give her sight back and discussed the unexpected ability she developed regarding the Internet.

"Don't ask me how she does this because I don't know and she doesn't either. All we can say is it works. Ken will discuss her accomplishments."

Ken briefed them on the initial hack of Riddle Systems by the Chinese and the devastating response she had retaliated with. He summarized her work with the FBI, in particular how she had shut down one of the world's largest money laundering operations. "And

314

by the way, that netted the government over a hundred and twenty billion dollars."

Next, he introduced the development of her AI bots, and the offshoots of the *Abby* and *Monroe* AIs. "The *Monroe* variant was in federal hands when it was stolen by the Chinese military. They used that very same AI technology to initiate their attacks on NASA. Any questions so far? Yes, Colonel Roth?"

Roth was the J3 officer from Cyber Command.

"I have a question," he said. To Nigel, he asked, "I heard it was the FBI who had the *Monroe* AI when it was lost. What were you guys doing with it?"

Ken interrupted before Nigel could answer. "That's beyond the scope of our discussion today, Colonel. Perhaps you could go over that with Agent Cherry at a later time. Anything else?"

Ken turned the discussion back to Raphael.

Raphael said, "Our most recent, and perhaps most important development, is that on a limited scale we have been able to duplicate Asha's ability. The young operators you met earlier now have that same ability."

That created a buzz of comments.

"We will demonstrate their capability in a moment. Any other questions?"

Roth spoke up again. "This is all very impressive, Doctor, but all I hear you saying is these kids can surf the Internet. I don't really care how they do it; every millennial in the world can do the same thing. I'm not sure what your fancy tech brings to the table."

"Let me answer that one," Ken said. "Colonel, you understand the value of a first strike in a military environment."

"Of course. If war is inevitable, it's the only way to go."

"But that's not possible on the virtual battlefield, is it? Before you can attack an enemy's computer, you have to infiltrate it with a virus, or a worm, or some kind of phishing attack."

"That's an oversimplification," Roth said, "but I'll accept your premise in a general sense."

"What we *bring to the table*, as you say, is that now we have true first strike capability in the virtual universe."

"How is that?"

To the other visitors, Ken said, "Speaking in broad terms, when one person is hacking another on the Internet, they are trying to deliver *malware* to that person's computer. Malware is what we call malicious software, and it is generally destructive in nature. Colonel Roth, for clarification, could you describe what happens during a generic virus attack?"

"I suppose," Roth said. "With a virus, the aggressor installs a piece of software on the target's machine."

Ken nodded. "That's the infection, hence the word *virus*. And to place that infection on the target's computer, the hacker will sometimes exploit what is called a zero-day defect in the target's operating system."

Roth said, "We also employ phishing, worms, and other methods."

Ken appeared to think about Roth's comment for a moment, and then asked, "In that case, when another country attacks us, why don't we just launch a counterattack? Why not go in, take down their systems, and disappear without anyone being the wiser?"

"Sometimes we do," Roth acknowledged. "But the trick is getting through the target's defenses. Zero-day options are rare, and can only be used once. Penetrating today's sophisticated computer security is quite difficult. That's why we use the other methods I just mentioned; like Trojans, bots, or maybe a honey pot. The Stuxnet worm is a famous example."

"And that is my point," Ken said. "The fact is, to attack an enemy's computer system, you almost always need their assistance in one manner or another. And that normally happens through a security failure on their part."

"Fair enough," Roth said.

"What's new here is that our operators don't need the target's help. They literally send their consciousness out across the Internet. They can penetrate any defense, stay there as long as necessary, and cause whatever damage they wish. And as of today, no one has the technology to stand against us."

Roth shook his head. "That's impossible. It doesn't work that way."

Ken smiled. "I guess my challenge today is to convince you that it *is* possible and that we can do it at will. Wasn't that the type of attack that was carried out against NASA?"

From the expression on Roth's face, Ken had touched a sore point.

"I can't say for sure," Roth caveated. "But yeah, the Chinese were getting through NASA's security like it was butter."

"And that is the problem we can solve," Ken said. "As we discussed, the NASA attacks were launched via the *Monroe* AI bot. My wife was able to shut them down. She has the ability to identify a *Monroe* bot and neutralize it. When she struck back, she destroyed a total of five *Monroe* AIs."

"Five?" Roth asked. "I thought they only stole one computer."

"You are correct, they did. And that means the Chinese have the ability to duplicate the code. We don't know how many of those bots they have, but I doubt Asha took out all of them."

"Can you find any that are left?" Nigel asked.

"That is our objective," Ken said. "So, let me make it clear. In a few minutes, we are going to give you an unsolicited proposal. The deliverable is not to engage in the standard back-and-forth cyberwar that goes on every day. Our sole purpose is to track down *Monroe*, however many there are, whether there are two or three or several thousand, and put them out of business permanently. I can tell you that doing so will have a significant impact on the Chinese military and China's economy in general."

"That's rather a large undertaking for such a small operation," Roth said, gesturing to the building.

"True, but our national security is at risk and will remain so as long as *Monroe* is around. We believe the threat should be eliminated, and the sooner the better. And with all due respect, Colonel, you simply can't stand up to that AI. You just admitted that. If we don't move against the people who are using it, and I'm talking about the Chinese government, our country is vulnerable."

Roth said, "I got that, but I'm a little uncomfortable having a civilian operation going after a world power in that kind of freelance, ride-'em-cowboy fashion, which, to be blunt, is what you are describing."

"Well, what would you propose?" Ken asked.

"That you provide us with the technology, teach us how to use it, and let us handle it through proper channels."

Ken smiled. "An interesting idea. And as it happens, our proposal includes that very option." He nodded at Asha, who held up a thick document. "But rather than getting into the details this minute, let's go down to our war room. I suspect you want to see a little proof of our claims."

* * * *

Asha and the group of visitors exited the elevator into the underground war room, which like the training room above, was furnished exclusively with comfortable recliners. Each one was positioned to not face another. A pair of two-hundred-inch television screens were mounted on the left and right walls. Three chairs near the center of the room were occupied by the youngsters they had met previously. They were fully reclined and wore VR headsets.

"These are our warriors, gentlemen," Ken explained. "As Raphael explained, those headsets allow them to literally enter the Internet, and go anywhere in the world. If you look at the multiplexed wide-screens, they show what each operator is seeing at this moment. The big monitor on the far wall is the current world situation."

The large display he referred to was similar to the one upstairs. It showed ongoing cyberattacks around the globe on in real time.

"We have a war room too," Roth said, looking at the luxurious furnishings, "but we have real workstations, and the techs are doing real work. This looks more like a high-end arcade for rich kids."

Ken grinned without taking offense but had to grab Asha's hand to stop her angry retort. "I'm sure you do," he said. "And we'll discuss that in more detail shortly. Over here on the right, this hallway leads to a dormitory area. We opened a few of the rooms for you to inspect."

Raphael hurried ahead and stood by an open door to act as a guide. "As you can see," he said, "each room holds two bunks. Nothing fancy, as the kids don't live here. These are only for sleeping when they need a break, or if the workload gets too stressful."

"Stressful!" Roth snorted. "My techs would die to work in a place like this."

"I'm sure they would," Ken agreed with a congenial smile. "Further down the hall, we have gym-style shower rooms, one for girls and one for boys. At the very back are storerooms and utilities. Any questions? Okay, let's find out what the kids are working on right now."

In the middle of the main war room area, Ken led his visitors over to one of the boys whose face was beaded with sweat.

"This is Fusion," Ken said. With a slight chuckle, he added, "Everyone has a nickname. Over there is Night Fury, and the young lady behind him goes by Tigress. Now, as I said, if you look on the side wall there, you can see the big screen is split into three displays where each square represents one of the operators. On the left is what Fusion is seeing."

The scene was of a crowded roadway in a foreign country, it looked like an Asian city, but the motion was so fast it was difficult to follow. The streets flashed by like the viewer was jet-propelled.

"If you are wondering," Ken said, "the answer is yes, Fusion overlays his location reference with Google's Street View. It gives him situational awareness in almost any locale...except for China, unfortunately, as the Communist Party is afraid of Google's kind of transparency. For our work on the Chinese mainland, the kids use a combination of regular Google Maps and China's Street View lookalikes, Baidu and QQ dot com. Asha, please explain what Fusion is doing at the moment?"

Asha pointed to the world map projection on the opposite wall. Dozens of attacks were streaming out of Sri Lanka, the large island off the southeast tip of India. Their targets included multiple countries and several locations inside the US.

"Sri Lanka is a common source of malware," she explained. "These are not military, per se. Most often they are criminal operations. Specifically, the one we're seeing right now is from an enterprise that employs Bujobot attacks. The Bujobot attaches nasty extensions to the victim's Chrome web browser. Those extensions communicate with computers owned by the bad guys. Once installed, they have a foothold on the infected computer."

"Seriously?" Roth asked with disdain. "You're wasting your time on backroom hackers?"

"Why not?" Asha responded with irritation. "I don't see anyone else trying to stop them, and these guys cause a lot of heartache. How much effort does Cyber Command spend on taking down *backrooms,* as you call them?"

Roth sniffed and said, "None. We concentrate on national security. I thought that's what you were doing."

"You mean like you did with the NASA attack?" Asha asked, equaling his condescension with her own.

"Now, wait a minute—" Roth started to snarl.

"Anyway!" Ken said, jumping in to stop the exchange before it became too acrimonious. "If you examine the map, you'll see Sri Lanka's attack has, in fact, generated a response from other countries. There it is."

Streams of light took off from multiple locations around the globe, including New York, Germany, the Netherlands, and others, all of them focused on Sri Lanka.

Ken explained, "Those counterattacks are probably from legitimate commercial operators. Many larger companies have their own war rooms, especially financial institutions. Whether or not it's legal is still debated in Congress. But contrary to what some might have you believe, these small-time criminal enterprises are not that small anymore. The cost of cybercrime exceeds a trillion dollars a year. And as you see, the counterattacks don't seem to be having much of an effect. Most of the bad guys have their own robust security setups in place for just that reason."

"So, what is the point of what Fusion is doing?" Nigel asked, gesturing at the displays.

Asha said, "There are a couple of answers to that question. First, Ken and I have developed a new AI bot that is specifically oriented to helping our young operators in this room. We call it *Sherlock* because it is primarily a detective. Each operator's *Sherlock* helps track down the actual location of our targets."

"They each have their own dedicated AI?" Roth asked.

"Yes. Between the pair, they make an effective hunter/killer team. The second point is that Fusion is not responding to a simple IP address. He and his *Sherlock* are looking for the actual building where these guys are operating from this very minute." She paused for a moment to let the display sink in.

The military woman accompanying Roth, Major Margaret Levy, asked, "So this is real time?"

"That's correct," Asha said. "It may not look like much from this perspective, but keep in mind that Fusion is wearing virtual reality headgear, so he is totally immersed in his environment. It might help you understand the experience if I switch this to full-screen. That way, you can appreciate the impact of what he is looking at, and why his expression is so intense."

The smaller inset display suddenly expanded to fill up the entire wall-sized digital screen.

It was like sitting on the front row of an IMAX theater during a chase scene. The government visitors were virtually yanked down crowded streets and periodically thrust up into the sky as Fusion followed the traced data packets. Then he would zoom down to a street-level view once more, always moving at warp speed.

Asha said, "*Sherlock* has now identified the source of the attacks. It's located in a business district in Colombo, the capital city of Sri Lanka. And it appears he found the actual address."

The Street View came to a stop on a narrow avenue facing a kaleidoscope of storefronts, each one only twelve to fifteen feet across. They resembled vendor stalls in an open market, except every shop was a separate tiny building. Several were multi-story structures, but the upper floors often looked like afterthoughts, added to the original ground floor by a series of successive owners.

The colorful signs above the doorways were illustrated in the curly Sinhala script, the primary language of Sri Lanka, and most included English subtext. The sign in the very center was labeled Kingdom Foreign Employment Agency. Above the first floor, the windows were heavily curtained.

The scene switched again, this time it was from a security camera in a small room. Two kitchen tables were pushed together and piled high with computers amongst a forest of tangled cords. Five young men of Sri Lankan descent sat around the computers, chain-smoking and jabbering at each other. They would periodically type on their keyboards and carefully examine the result.

Asha continued, "One nice thing about criminal overlords, even puny, third world ones, is they take security as seriously as the next guy. We love it when they use CCTV to monitor their employees. These are the men who just launched that attack against the US, and this is where Fusion will start to work."

A dialog box popped up along the left side of the main screen, and what appeared to be a contact list began to scroll. "Fusion is now hacking into their cell phones and capturing all the people in their address books. We'll sort through those later. While he's at it, he'll plant a bug so all of their future calls will be logged for later review. We'll find out who their boss is in a minute when they call to report their system is down."

Asha chuckled then and looked embarrassed. "And finally, we add pornography of other men to the photo gallery in each hacker's cell phone. When Fusion finishes his data retrieval, *Sherlock* will anonymously tip off the Sri Lankan law enforcement about this group. If he were to report them as hackers, the police would simply ignore it. But telling them they might be homosexual…well, in that culture, it's an entirely different story. Those guys can expect some difficult interrogations before nightfall, and if we're lucky, their hacking activities will also come to light."

Another screen popped up and Asha continued, "If that looks like a directory listing of system files on a Windows computer, that's because it is. Fusion is now hacking into each of the computers and deleting several of the more important DLL files. In about a second, those machines will turn into oversized paperweights. We ruin the hard drives, so whatever information they had on them is irretrievably lost."

Ken said, "Hard drives are an easy target, but if necessary, we can apply an overvoltage to just about any CPU, whether it's in a desktop PC or any other type electronic equipment. If it's connected to the Internet in any way, we can turn it into junk."

While Ken spoke, the Sri Lankan hackers started shouting at each other angrily.

"As you can see," Asha said, "it goes downhill pretty quickly. These guys are already out of business, they just don't know it quite yet. Now, *Sherlock* will ruin that location as a base of operations anytime in the near future."

The screen began hopping from one outdoor camera to another as the AI searched for the building's electrical supply.

Ken explained, "Most third world countries don't have anything like our power grid. Electrical service is haphazard at best, and often dangerous. Once *Sherlock* finds a vulnerable utility point, we'll take it out."

The scene fixated on a power pole across the street. After a moment, the transformer began to smoke and then burst into a shower of sparks.

"That's an example of what Ken just mentioned," Asha said. "Almost every piece of equipment has a processor chip in it. That building, and probably those nearby, just lost power."

In a disapproving tone, Major Levy said, "Inflicting collateral damage on innocent people is irresponsible, wouldn't you say?"

Asha scowled and replied emphatically, "Not in the least. What those men were doing is no secret to their neighbors. The local population actively supports this type of activity. To them, it's good business because the targets are rich Americans. Perhaps you don't care, but I see no reason to sympathize with Sri Lankan criminals."

"Well, I know that," Levy said. "But—"

"But nothing! A lot of the time, the real victims are senior citizens who live all over the United States. Most of them are not technically savvy and they can have their life savings taken away in the blink of an eye." Asha pointed at the street scene, and her voice grew more strident. "Yes, the neighbors of those hackers may have to replace a burned-out calculator, but it won't ruin their lives. American grandparents, however, have no way to recoup their lost savings because law enforcement doesn't think it's a problem." She glared at Roth for a second before saying, "So, no! I don't feel bad about it, and the fact that I have to explain it to a professional in cybercrime prevention boggles my mind!"

"Okay now," Ken said, jumping in once more, patting Asha on the back to calm her down. To the others, he said, "What we've shown you is an example of the kind of work we can do."

"Don't patronize me!" Asha growled and moved away from Ken and the others.

Ken gave her some space and continued with the explanation of their strike. "*Sherlock's* next task is to package up the data he collected and send it to the European Cybercrime Center. And to answer your other question, no, this type of activity is not our priority. For Fusion, this was a useful training mission that directly benefits our own citizens. For you, Colonel Roth, it's an opportunity to see our capability. What is your opinion at the moment?"

Roth nodded reluctantly. "It's impressive, I'll admit that. And I like that you're coordinating with the Europeans. We work with the ECC as well. You have a good operation. But those guys in Sri Lanka are really nothing more than petty crooks. And yes, I am aware there are bigger criminal enterprises out there who might also be susceptible to your tactics, but like I said, our focus is defending against military-grade threats. I heard about the attack on NASA, and now that we've reviewed what happened, I'm confident we can handle it."

Ken smiled and said, "Colonel, allow me to question that confidence of yours. Asha, what is Night Fury doing at the moment?"

Asha's voice suddenly came out of hidden speakers, although her lips never moved.

"I'll ask him. Matthew? What are you doing right now?"

Ken explained, "Asha can communicate with the operators mentally, through her wireless connection. For your visit today, she's putting the conversation on our intercom system so you can listen in."

A young man's voice responded. "I was about to shut down a ransomware operation in Russia. Should I hold off?"

On one of the recliners, the youngster Ken had called Night Fury had not spoken, and to all appearances might be napping except for the muscle tension across his face, and the giant video screen which Asha had switched to his viewpoint. He was racing down a boulevard between tall European-style buildings.

"Yes, please," Asha said. "I'd like to show our visitors what you and I talked about. Can you do that?"

"You want me to penetrate Cyber Command's secret war room?" Night Fury asked.

"That's correct. Don't damage anything. This is just for demonstration."

A bit of humor came through in his reply. "Yes, ma'am."

The screen's large display jumped off the streets of St. Petersburg and flew toward the continental United States at high speed.

Ken took up the narrative. "You will notice that Night Fury is *not* headed toward Fort Meade in Maryland, which is Cyber

Command's Headquarters." To Roth, he said, "You heard him mention your secret war room, I believe?"

Roth nodded, a worried expression on his face.

"Here he comes," Ken continued. "As you see, he's heading to Texas. His *Sherlock* is taking him to a newly constructed facility on a not-very-well-known military installation called Goodfellow Air Force Base. Goodfellow doesn't have aircraft, does it, Colonel? They train military firefighters and intelligence officers. But recently, they added a new mission, although that fact is not widely known."

Roth's face turned red, and he said, "You're playing with fire, Mr. Riddle. You try anything there, and you'll set off a thousand alarms. I won't protect you if you break the law."

The screen changed once again, this time showing the feed from a security camera overseeing a large, modern operations center. The room was arranged with oversized workstations in rows that faced a front wall featuring a digital display similar to Ken's world map but with much more information.

Young technicians sat in front of multiple monitors, typing away while coordinating with others in their workgroups. It was a very professional setting, the complete opposite of the Sri Lankan kitchen tables.

Ken said, "Well, I hope you won't consider this breaking the law. As you can see, in the time it took to think about it, Night Fury got past your network security, and has access to your entire operation."

Roth looked stunned but argued lamely, "The security cameras are not on our secure internal network."

"Fair enough," Ken replied. He opened the proposal he had carried down from the earlier briefing upstairs. Inside it, he drew a little sketch on the front page. It was a line drawing of the well-known *Kilroy Was Here* face, with a big nose and eyes, peeking over a wall. He showed it to Major Levy and said, "Would you write something on this drawing. Whatever you want."

Levy took her pen and wrote, "Pi=5.1417," under Kilroy's nose.

Ken looked at it with a smile, and said, "You know that's not the correct number for pi, don't you?"

Levy nodded. "I'm not sure what you're planning, but we all saw what I wrote down."

"Good enough," Ken said and showed the drawing to Asha. She studied it for a moment and nodded. Ken turned to the television screen and pointed to a networked printer at the end of one of the rows of workstations. "Keep your eye on that."

Seconds later, the printer kicked out a single sheet of paper.

Roth looked astonished and made a call on his cell phone. "Are you in the center?" he asked the person on the other end. "Go check the printer on row three, and hold it up to the security camera on the back wall... No, just do it. Now!"

A captain hurried into the war room from a side door and took a single page from the output tray. With a puzzled expression, he asked a question of the technicians nearby, but they shrugged and shook their heads. Then he walked over to the security camera and held it up. It was the exact same drawing with the wrong number for pi.

"How the hell did you do that?" Roth asked Ken angrily. Then he spoke into his cell phone again. "I want you to pull all the logs for the last fifteen minutes. You damn well better find something, and tell me who printed that, and how you're going to stop it from happening again." Roth hung up and glowered at Ken and Asha.

Very sweetly, Asha said, "You guys probably need a minute to absorb all this. And while you're at it, keep in mind that a few months ago the Chinese were operating in much the same way against NASA. They used the AI called *Monroe* and you could not stop them. *Sherlock* is far superior and is the only way to bring them down. Let's go back upstairs." She gestured toward the elevator.

"Good idea," Nigel said. He put a comradely arm around Roth's shoulders. "Come on, Colonel, you look a little pale. Believe me, I know just how you feel.

Chapter 14 – The Rejection

Asha stopped the elevator on the first floor and guided everyone into the cafeteria. "This is Tony Wong, our chef. He can prepare whatever you would like for lunch. Take a few minutes and talk amongst yourselves," she said. "Come on upstairs when you're ready."

Major Wong pulled out his ever-present pad and began taking orders. With his friendly banter, he managed to get the name of each customer.

Ken handed the proposal document to the GSA contracting officer, Mr. Bill Ellis, and then went with Asha up to the training area.

Once they were settled in one of the clusters of overstuffed furniture on the second floor, Ken gave Asha a quick shoulder massage and said, "You've got to throttle back, babe. I was afraid you were going to punch out the major."

"I'm sorry," Asha replied. "I don't know why I have such a short fuse with these people. I understand they are doing their due diligence, but everything they say makes me angry. Should I leave the building?"

"No. They're going to have questions, and I'd like to get that contract signed."

"You said that won't happen."

Ken sighed with disappointment. "That's true. Ellis will have to run it through his purchasing hoops. But we need more than an agreement in principle to be legitimate."

"That colonel doesn't like us. That's pretty obvious."

"We're stepping on his toes. Let's try to reassure him that we have no intention of intruding into his territory." They sat quietly until the elevator dinged. "Here they come," Ken said, and the door opened.

It was just Raphael.

"If nothing else," Rafe said philosophically, "they're enjoying the food. Tony is taking care of them. They'll be up in a few minutes, or so they say."

"What's the mood?" Ken asked.

"Major Levy is impressed but she's trying not to show it. I am afraid the contracting guy is going to be argumentative. Roth is wavering, which surprises me, quite frankly. When he got here, he basically thought we were a scam; now he's not sure. Nigel is on our side, but his boss wants to be somewhere else. He might take off."

"Who is that other man?" Asha asked. "The skinny one? I didn't get his name."

Ken said, "That's the NASA guy, Warren Booth. He's Nigel's brother-in-law. He's the person who got all this started."

"Does he like us?"

"Definitely," Raphael replied. "He said from NASA's perspective, the night you hit the Chinese, it was like flipping a switch. One minute he was being beaten down, and then nothing. He hasn't seen a problem since."

Raphael asked Ken, "Do you still want me to give them the bad news?"

"We have to," Ken replied. "If that's a deal killer, so be it. The worst thing we can do is make a long-term commitment that we can't keep."

Asha disagreed with her husband's strategy, but her arguments had not been enough to change his mind. Thirty minutes later, the elevator dinged, and she stood up, trying to compose her expression.

Nigel's boss had indeed taken off. Just five of the visitors were left.

"Welcome back," Ken said cheerfully, inviting everyone to have a seat. They all faced each other like UN diplomats. To the GSA contracting officer, he said, "Mr. Ellis, you appear to have some questions."

"I do," Ellis replied. "The first of those would be, what is it exactly you are proposing?"

"To protect American interests from the *Monroe* threat."

"You would have to turn over all of your software."

"We're prepared to do that. If you noticed, the specifications are in the proposal."

"I did notice," Ellis said. "Not too many people give away their intellectual property for free. Why do we need you if we have that?"

"Because none of it works without me," Asha stated.

Roth said, "You went to great lengths to prove your operators can operate just fine on their own."

"Let me address that," Raphael said. "When you read the medical section, you will find our biggest problem is the ability we give to these young people is not permanent."

"How do you mean?" Major Levy asked.

Raphael's manner became professorial. "We don't completely understand the medical science, but our guess is they grow out of it. The human male brain fully matures around the age of twenty-five. I've documented how our training materially affects their mind. It appears to me that it also accelerates their physiological maturation. The brain quickly reaches its full potential, and in doing so, they lose the ability to connect with the Internet."

"Couldn't you keep them going with drugs?" Roth asked. "Retard their growth?"

Raphael looked shocked and shook his head vehemently. "I wouldn't even try, Colonel. These are people, not experimental weapons."

"It can't be pleasant for them," Levy observed. "To have such a capability and then lose it must be difficult."

"It is traumatic," Raphael agreed. "One of our early successes, a young man named Vonn, was the first to reach that stage. He was a bit older when he started, and was devastated by the change. We've reduced the minimum age somewhat, but we can't really go any younger. I estimate we will average about twelve to eighteen months of operational effectiveness with each student. That's why we have an ongoing recruitment effort."

"We can do the same thing," Roth said. "The military is quite effective at convincing young people to join up."

"Yes, but you see, none of our operators have so far been able to connect to the Internet without first being taught how to do so by Asha. No matter how hard they try, she has to lead them by the hand, almost literally, on that first step. Afterward, they can do it with the help of their *Sherlock*."

"So, the contract here is actually to hire Mrs. Riddle's services," Ellis concluded. "A pay package of twenty-five million dollars, if I read that correctly, is a little steep."

"You didn't read it correctly," Asha said. "Yes, the proposal includes my time, but the money is to create a foundation for the students. We estimate a maximum of eighty students for this project. It will provide full scholarships to each child when they age out."

"Why so few students?" Levy asked. "If this goes on for a few years, you would go through a lot more than that."

Raphael shook his head a bit sadly. "That's not the case. Our biggest problem is Asha herself. You heard my discussion about her initial memory problems. The auto accident seems to have reset the same biological maturity process in her body too. I already see signs on her MRIs that she is going to age out as well. We do a cranial MRI on her every month, and at this point, I estimate she has six to eight months left before she too loses the ability to access the Internet. That trait within her brain, just as for all of our students, will die."

Raphael's pronouncement brought the discussion to a temporary halt while everyone considered the ramifications.

"So, this is not a long-term arrangement," Roth said finally.

"That is correct," Ken said. "And that is why we say time is of the essence. The moment you sign the agreement, we'll go after the Chinese hackers. We know where the *Monroe* entities are being developed for future attacks. We would like to get the contract executed immediately."

Ellis shook his head. "You were a government contractor yourself, Mr. Riddle. I'm sure you understand the contracting process doesn't work that way. If we push this hard, it's at least three months out, probably more."

"I have seen contracts done overnight, Mr. Ellis," Ken replied. "And for a lot more than this one."

"That's true. But those had political firepower behind them. Here, you are talking about actually attacking a foreign power, China, no less. That in itself will expose the country to retaliation. I can't sign off on something like that without approval from a much higher pay grade than my own."

Nigel's brother-in-law spoke up. He had a personal interest in having the protection that Asha offered. "Can you provide NASA with security while the contract is being processed?"

Ken shook his head. "I'm sorry, Warren, but no. The nature of this threat demands an all or nothing response. If we suddenly shield your organization, it tips our hand and invites retaliation against the rest of the country."

Warren looked over at Ellis. "You need to get this thing done, Bill. Damage from the last attack has already cost me eighty million dollars and counting. What they're asking for is peanuts. And what if the Chinese hit more than just me? What if they go after all of Roth's precious computers or all the servers in DC? This is a national emergency, man; that's what I'd call it."

Ellis shrugged. "I can elevate the request, but I'm not sure how it will be received."

Roth said to the group as a whole, "I don't like saying it, but I agree with NASA. This is not an expensive contract. I came here today as a skeptic; I still am to some extent. But I saw what they were doing to you, Warren." He turned to Asha. "The one thing we didn't see was your kids actually take on the *Monroe* virus. Any reason for that?"

"The Chinese aren't using it, that's all. I can set up an exercise for you, but it might alert the enemy to what we are developing. We're trying to stay under the radar as much as possible."

Roth nodded. "Understood. But I would like to make a request."

"What's that?" Asha replied.

"I want to assign Major Levy to this location as an observer while Ellis does his thing. At the same time, I'll lean on the contracting side of the house, and see if we can push it through."

Asha looked over at Ken. "What's your take? I'm not sure how to respond to that. It would probably be good for both sides, but if she tries to throw her weight around, it would be disruptive."

To Levy, Ken said, "Maggie, do you suppose you could stay out of trouble while you're here?"

Levy smiled. "I promise to be as quiet as a mouse."

"You can't wear a uniform. I don't want to advertise any connection to the government. You saw the sign above the door. Chromium Plus, a staffing agency."

"Not a problem. I can fit in."

"All right, Colonel," Ken said. "We'll take her on, but it doesn't change our position. Until we get the contract, we're independent."

Roth nodded and said, "I'd also like to get a copy of *Monroe* and let our guys see what makes her tick."

"That's already in the proposal. It's not something I'll put in the mail, but if you send me a courier, I'll give you a drive with everything we have. Just remember that when you see there is no documentation, we're not being cute. We don't have anything either."

"Nothing?"

"Nada. All it is, literally, is a piece of Asha's mind. She created her AI bots on the fly as it were, by just imagining them in the cloud. They come out fully functional in machine language. None of us understand how she does that. Raphael has some theories that I included as background, and I put in a few of my own, but there's nothing like normal documentation, let alone commented code."

"Very well," Roth said. "I'll take whatever you can give me. Ellis, this is the classic definition of a sole-source requirement. Don't put this on the back burner."

"I hear you," Ellis replied. "But I'm still concerned that Mr. Riddle is planning to target a foreign power on his own. That's a prerogative of Congress, and I don't see them waving away that authority."

"We're not talking about bombing raids," Roth argued, pointing at the world map display. "This is the same virtual crap we do every day. And so do a lot of the Fortune 100." As he spoke, dozens of attacks launched from within the continental US against Brazil, Ecuador, Viet Nam, India, and China. "The difference is what the Riddles are doing looks a whole lot more effective."

"That's my point," Ellis insisted. "Against a foreign power that is incredibly formidable in every other way."

Roth gave a quick head shake as though dropping the argument. "You do what you have to, Bill, and so will I. I'm going to elevate this the minute I get back." He looked around the group. "Mr. Riddle, do you have anything else to show us?"

"That's all. Here's a copy of the proposal. Do you want to take the hard drive with you?"

"No, I'll send someone. I want to make a run at the brass in DC before heading back to Fort Meade." Roth stood to shake hands.

"So, will you be here tomorrow?" Ken asked Levy.

Levy shook her head. "Probably a week to get orders cut and make my way back. Does that work for you?"

"Absolutely. Just come on in when you arrive. You'll find hotels all around here."

Asha and Ken escorted their visitors down the stairs and out the front door. After the last goodbye, they retired to the cafeteria, their favorite place for talking business. Their magician-like chef always had the perfect snack when they wanted a break. At the moment, he had turned the lights down low to give the room a cozy ambiance.

As if on cue, Wong appeared, notepad in hand to take their orders.

"How did your sales pitch go?" Wong asked once they got settled in one of the booths.

"A lot better than I expected this morning," Asha said, looking through the menu. "Roth impressed me the way he swung over to our side. At first, he was totally against us."

"He might still be," Ken said. "I can't tell if he's putting Levy here as a spy or an ally."

"What should we do with her? Asha asked.

"Treat her like a friend. Maybe she'll become an influencer for our side. It's clear these guys don't understand what's coming. This is as close to war as our country has been in a long time. Once we start our offensive, I don't know what will happen, but China won't sit back and take it. They've been getting ready for a confrontation with the US ever since Xi Jinping took over. I'm really worried, and not just about a few virus attacks." He closed the menu in resignation and glanced up at Wong. "I'll have whatever she has," he said.

"Something for dessert," Asha said. "And a cup of coffee if you have it."

"Yes, ma'am," Wong said, "I have just the thing. I'll have it right out."

* * * *

Major Wong waited patiently until Ken and Asha left the building. They were accustomed now to leaving him to lock up. Evidence of that trust was that he had free access to the storeroom in the back corner of the basement level. Wong kept most of his kitchen supplies down there.

Since starting work for the company, he had carefully studied the layout. The luxury and sophistication of the war room was almost frightening. If nothing else, Riddle knew how to set up an effective operation.

But Wong's excellence as a spymaster was due in large part to his patience. This was not the moment to strike. So far, he had only witnessed one or two students at a time using the main facility. Sometimes they gathered in small clusters upstairs, but never in the war room. He would wait for the opportunity to get all of the so-called operators at once.

Based on all the conversations today, that could happen in the not too distant future.

Wong locked up and took the Orange Line down to Chinatown. He wandered around for thirty minutes and finally entered the Daguan Tea Garden. An elderly woman walked by and placed a cell phone on his table. He slid it into his pocket. It was a weekly exercise coordinated by Major Mao.

Wong got back on the Orange Line and rode south. When no one was seated close by, he used WhatsApp to call Soong. The app's encryption would ensure no one could listen in.

"Captain Soong, here," she answered.

"It's me," Wong said. "Everything on your end ready for Mobius?"

"Not yet, sir. Colonel Hsieh is holding a simulated war game tomorrow. He divided everyone into red versus blue to make it as realistic as possible. He'll be completely operational in another week."

"What about Plan Bartimaeus?"

"Captain Wei is fully functioning but he's only staffed at thirty percent. In a week, he'll be able to carry out a strike."

"Good enough. The situation here is coming together more quickly than I anticipated. Riddle has a grasp of the world's state of affairs that most of his government doesn't appreciate. If I didn't know better, I'd say he had seen our own timetable for the Taiwan Strait encounter."

"Do you think he has?" Soong asked, concerned.

"No, there is no way he could. I overhear most of their strategy discussions; they treat the restaurant like it's a secure conference room. They really have no clue about operations security. At the moment, their focus is on convincing American officials they can take down the *Monroe* threat. They know we still have them."

"Did the Americans buy it? Should we go silent on our end?"

"It's not necessary," Wong said. "An officer from their Cyber Command acknowledges Riddle's ability, but I think the American military will be reluctant to give Riddle all the authority he wants. Everyone is concerned about their own territory. My guess is the government won't give Riddle a contract."

"Would he attack us, anyway?" Soong wondered aloud.

"I doubt it. He doesn't strike me as a particularly driven individual. He spends most of his time romancing his wife. Too bad. Either way, when this is all over, he'll take the fall when the US infrastructure starts going down. I couldn't be happier about the whole thing."

Soong laughed. "You are such an evil man, Major. You're not going to get stuck over there, are you?"

"I better not. Major Mao has arranged my extraction plan. I'll leave through Canada and be back before you know it."

"Sounds good. Both Mobius and Bartimaeus should be fully operational the next time you call."

"Thank you, Lieutenant. I'll buy you a meal when I return."

"I look forward to it, sir. Anything else?"

"Not at the moment. I'll call again in a week, or sooner if the Riddles get a contract. If that happens, it puts Stunning Blow at risk. Make sure Captain Wei knows that he must be ready to execute Plan Bartimaeus at a moment's notice, even if he isn't fully manned. I'll keep you posted."

"Yes, sir. I'll wait for your call. Good luck!"

When Wong got off the train, he disassembled the phone and threw away the pieces in a series of waste receptacles on the way to his flat. In a few days, the same elderly woman would provide him with a new one.

* * * *

Asha was in the cafeteria enjoying a cranberry orange scone when a familiar face came in from the street. It was Major Levy and she was sporting a new look.

"Well, hello!" Asha said in greeting. "You sure don't look military now."

Levy smiled and gestured at her outfit uncertainly. She wore a pink hoodie over jeans with an *I Love Chicago* T-shirt. "I haven't worn these in ages. Is it too awful?"

Asha laughed. "We didn't mean you had to dress seventeen, but it suits you. As long as you're comfortable, that's all we care about."

"Well, it beats a uniform, for sure. Sorry it took so long to get here. I really expected to be here last week, but the Colonel wanted me to brief the Pentagon planners first."

"Not a problem. But you got here just in time. We see an uptick in their activity. They started probing with *Monroe* last night. Let's go downstairs."

Asha took Levy down to the bottom floor, where three teenagers were sprawled out in recliners. The two women sat on a pair of empty chairs directly in front of the large display screen on the sidewall. The screen changed to show the world threat map.

"How does that work?" Levy asked curiously. "Do you change the display?"

"That's right," Asha replied, tapping her forehead. "I control the video multiplexer to display whatever we need out here. The various images are generated by different servers that Ken's people manage in the IT room on the third floor." She nodded at the screen. "Notice anything different?"

"You mean the purple lines?"

Several of the attack streams coming from China were a dark shade of mauve.

"Those are all *Monroe* probes," Asha said. "Looks like they are getting ready to try again."

Levy was alarmed. "But they're hitting so many targets. Are they doing that all at once?"

"They're not hitting anything at the moment. Right now, they are testing our defenses."

"Are you trying to stop them?"

"Afraid not," Asha said. "We still don't have a contract."

"A contract! Are you serious? They are about to attack our country. You have to intervene!"

"And we will, just as soon as someone on your end gives us a written agreement. If nothing else, this should add a little urgency to the decision."

"I can't believe—" Levy's cell phone chimed, cutting off her remark. She saw Roth's name and answered. "Yes, sir. Are you seeing this?" She listened for a moment, and then replied, "That's right. I'm talking to Asha right now and she said the purple means *Monroe*... No, they aren't doing a thing because they don't have a contract... I know! That's what I said but... Okay." She handed the phone toward Asha, but Asha shook her head.

"I don't need to talk to anyone," Asha said. "All I need is a signed contract. Otherwise, if this goes south, Ken and I will get blamed for everything."

Levy spoke into her phone. "Did you hear that? No, she won't speak to you. You want me to stay here or not?" She listened a moment longer and then hung up. "He said if you *don't* do anything, you'll get blamed anyway, contract or not."

Asha nodded. "Not exactly breaking news. The FBI treated me the same way on more than one occasion. I guess it's a consistent theme with Uncle Sam." She made herself comfortable and gazed at the screen. "See what they're doing? They're checking out all of our military installations. Ken is sure they're getting ready to launch a major strike against us."

"Right now?" Levy asked, alarmed.

"Not this minute. He said they'll do a new in-depth inventory of our hard assets and then develop a comprehensive attack plan. Right now, I'd say they're in the early stages. We've got perhaps a week."

"A week? That doesn't sound like a long-term planning phase."

Asha gave Levy a frank look. "What planet are you living on? I'm only a year old, and I can see that they've been getting ready for years."

"What are you talking about? According to you, they only got *Monroe* six months ago."

Asha shook her head. "*Monroe* is just a small piece of their larger plan. Look at how much money they spend on their military. Their defense budget has gone up ten percent every single year for the past two decades. And during that same period, they have

339

undercut everything the US has accomplished in the Pacific since World War Two."

"You actually believe China is going to start a war?"

"No. That's not their style. Ken said what they really want to do is humiliate us on the world stage—embarrass us publicly in such a big way the whole world will realize that *they* are the big dog now. It might include a few skirmishes, but they're ready for that too. Haven't you read about all the close calls in the China Sea? They build military bases, run their big ships up against ours or the Japanese, and say it was an accident. You watch; in the next day or two it won't be a bump. They'll do real damage, and people will get killed."

"So how does *Monroe* fit in?" Levy wanted to know.

"That's the critical part. To create confusion. First, they'll take out our military's command and control structure in the Pacific region. At the same time, they'll shut down our entire civilian communication network. Then, when they start pushing us around on the world stage, no one on our side will respond because whoever is in charge won't know what's going on. It will make our politicians look like a bunch of idiots—although honestly, that's not a tall order. But you get what I mean."

"You never mentioned any of this in your presentation! Why didn't you say that was why stopping *Monroe* is so important?"

Asha shook her head. "Maggie, think about it. If we had started talking global strategic policy, Colonel Roth would have walked out. This is way over his pay grade. All he wants is an answer for *Monroe* because cyber defense is the center of his universe."

Levy sighed. "That's true and that's even scarier. I swear, most of the time the people at the top have no idea about the rest of the world."

"Ken says that's politics at its best, but he doesn't mean it as a compliment."

They watched the threat map for several minutes. It had a doomsday atmosphere.

"How long have we got?" Levy asked.

Asha shrugged. "Keep an eye on their fleet in the South China Sea. That's where they want to make a statement. I'd say late this week or early next week. Now I understand why Ken kept calling this Armageddon. It really feels like it is."

..*.*

"Good morning, Maggie," Asha said when Levy came out of the elevator on the basement floor into the war room. It was Monday morning and she and Ken were studying the threat map.

"Hi," Levy said. "Did you guys even go home this weekend?"

"Not really," Ken replied. "That's why we have dorm rooms. We think the Chinese must be getting close because a new *Monroe* location went active last night, this time in Bangkok."

Asha nodded at the map and added, "And another one popped up five minutes ago."

A new mauve stream originating from Boise looked particularly out of place.

"Who is that?" Levy asked. "Is that really the Chinese?" A screen overlay appeared on the map with a downtown Boise address. "Why does that look familiar?" she mused aloud.

Asha said, "*Abbot* is tracking down who it is as we speak. It will only be a moment or two. This site came up just before you got here."

"Where is everyone?" Levy asked, looking around. The three or four operators that were normally sprawled out were gone, and only two of the young men were present.

"We've got them in crew rest," Ken replied. "If the situation is about to pop, we want everyone to get as much sleep as possible."

A second screen opened up with a familiar face. It was of Congressman Lou Carson, one of only two representatives from the Potato State. Below his image were the addresses of his state offices. The one in Boise matched the listing with the US-based *Monroe* bot.

"I didn't see that coming," Asha said.

"Oh, my God," Levy said breathlessly. "He's working for the Chinese? I've got to report this!"

"Hang on," Ken said softly. "Before we ruin the guy's career, let's do some research. I seriously doubt the congressman is involved in this. More likely, an employee or some idiot intern compromised his server. *Abbot*, find out who is operating the Boise server. Does the congressman have any ties to China, and if not, who does?"

"Acknowledged."

Levy's cell phone chirped. "It's Colonel Roth," she said before answering. "Yes sir, we're looking at it now. Mr. Riddle is checking to see who it is… Yes, sir, I agree… Okay, I'll call." She ended the call and said, "He wants to keep anything about the congressman quiet until you have proof."

"We don't talk, regardless," Ken said. "Our entire operation is confidential. Any word on the contract?"

Levy groaned. "I forgot to ask. Hang on; I'll call him back." She turned away to get an update on the potential agreement.

"Will this help our case?" Asha asked.

"One would think," Ken replied. "But how can it? They want to keep everything under the covers even more than we do. Don't worry. Our best bet is to—uh oh. There's another one. We probably need a special *Sherlock* to investigate any new *Monroe* that pops up outside of China. I would bet money these three won't be the only ones."

"All right," Asha said. "I'll go upstairs and work on it."

The more complicated the situation became, the more Asha needed peace and quiet when programming additional AI entities. When finished, she named it *Churchill* and returned to the war room.

"All set?" Ken asked.

"His name is *Churchill*. He'll track down all *Monroe* AIs outside of China and add them to our list of targets. I wasn't sure about the legality of hitting US-based locations, so those strikes will be limited to IT assets only; no public utility interruptions."

"That's a good precaution," Ken said. "It's always the little things that send you to jail. Anyway, a bunch more showed up while you were working on it. One in Florida, three in Europe, and a half dozen in India. I hope the Indian ones aren't State-sponsored."

Levy swiped off yet another call with Roth, and said, "Would you accept a letter of intent?"

Ken didn't hesitate. "Sorry, but no. Letters of intent are worthless; especially since the only reason he would sign one is because the government won't back him up with a real contract. And it wouldn't protect me in the judicial system."

"It's all he can offer right now," Levy replied. She looked at the global map. The mauve lines were multiplying by the hour. "It's obvious something is about to break, but he needs more time to get approval for a signed agreement."

Ken exchanged glances with Asha who shrugged, saying, "I don't know about stuff like this. We can ask Stephenson if you want."

Ken scoffed. "Bernard won't approve anything without a contract signed in blood."

"It's up to you, babe," Asha said. "I have a hard time trusting the government under any circumstances."

Ken sat down in one of the recliners with his head in his hands. After a moment he spoke to Levy. "First of all, this will definitely get ugly. We can see that on the map. The Chinese Army is about to launch a massive cyberattack, almost certainly preceded by an incident that includes physical aggression. If Asha and I are in the middle of it, we have to be standing on firm ground. A simple letter of intent won't do it."

Asha said, "What if they included a retainer with the letter? Stephenson is always saying that an exchange of money goes a long way to defining a contract."

"That's a good idea, actually," Ken said with a hopeful expression. He looked at Levy. "Could Roth come up with some cash? He's bound to have a contingency fund. What about ten percent? But the wording has to give us the authorization to act however we deem necessary. Otherwise it's a deal killer. I can't afford to have any second-guessing after the fact."

"I'll check," Levy said, and she hurriedly dialed her boss.

While Levy discussed the idea with Roth, two of the operators came out of the dorm area. Asha told them to go on duty and sent the two who wearing headgear to take a break.

Levy hung up and said, "He'll send the idea up the chain. He asked if you would take five percent? He can't stretch his budget more than that. The new sequester, you know."

"A million bucks," Ken said to Asha. "We'll never see another penny, no matter how the war goes. Would that be worth it to you?"

"Only if he pays upfront," Asha said. "Otherwise, it's just another broken promise and I've had enough of those."

Ken nodded and told Levy, "Okay, we'll take it, but the check has to accompany the letter. And the wording has to include full authorization for us to act."

"Got it," Levy said, calling again. A moment later, she sighed with relief and ended the call. "He'll try to have it to you this afternoon. Thank God."

Asha said, "I hate being so money-grubbing about national security."

"I know," Ken said deadpanned. "All defense contractors feel that way. We used to go to the big trade fairs in Las Vegas and complain that the government gave us too much money."

Asha rolled her eyes and glanced at Levy. "My husband has a knack for putting things into perspective. Suddenly I don't feel so guilty."

* * * *

The fax machine whirred to life and Levy jumped up. "That's it. He just sent me a text." She stood by the fax with a big grin while the first page slid into the hopper, and then the machine quietened. "Is that it?" she asked no one in particular while skimming the page. "Oh, no," she whispered. Then she handed the sheet to Ken and called her boss.

"Let's see what he's got," Ken said, and read quickly. When he finished, he laughed out loud. "So much for that."

"Not what you were expecting?" Asha asked.

"Frankly, it's exactly what I was expecting. It gives our dear Major Levy sole authority in decision making, on the condition her boss approves of any activity that might result in a diplomatic incident."

Levy swiped off her phone looking crestfallen. "Sorry," she said. "He thought they were going to approve the draft you saw earlier, but at the last minute this was all they would sign. What's this mean for you guys?"

Ken stood up and stretched, then he gestured toward the elevator. "That your work here is done. Maggie, it's been great *not* working with you. Let us know how it goes with you and Roth over the next few days. I suspect you guys are going to be very busy."

"Are you kicking me out?"

"I'm afraid so. We're shutting the place down; we don't really have a choice. I've already been through one bankruptcy because of the government and don't fancy doing it again."

Levy obviously hated to leave, but Ken forcibly shepherded her to the front door where he wished her well and said goodbye.

When he returned to the basement, Asha was waiting. She said, "We gave it a good try. You have to admit we were as flexible as we could be. But you were right. It was never going to work."

Ken shook his head. "If we had another year, perhaps they could put something together, but the timing just isn't there." He glanced at the threat map. "Ready to get started?"

"I guess so," she replied. The screen blanked out and was replaced with a live shot of a satellite feed. "*Abbot,* what are we looking at?"

The AI's voice replied, "This is a view of the Taiwan Strait from NROL-51, a Block 2 satellite in the TOPAZ program. The naval vessels traveling north are the *USS Mustin*, an Arleigh Burke Class guided-missile destroyer. It is part of the US Seventh Fleet based out of Yokosuka, Japan. The other is the *USNS Charles Drew*, a Lewis and Clark dry cargo ship. The two vessels are engaged in a freedom-of-the-sea maneuver in spite of strenuous objections from Beijing. This is a normal activity."

"Then why are we looking at it?" Ken asked.

Abbot replied, "Because of the three ships north of their location. They include the *Wenzhou*, a modern frigate with the People's Liberation Army Navy Surface Force, and two Chinese Coast Guard cutters. Their orders are to cause an incident."

"Is this going to affect us?" Asha asked Ken.

"I'm pretty sure it will," he said. "This is what we talked about. The ruling party in Beijing wants to push us around, and the timing is perfect. It's the middle of October and the general election is three weeks away. They would love nothing more than to shove the president's nose in the mud right now."

"How do you mean?"

"They're about to stage a confrontation at sea and damage one of our ships in the process. Everyone on our side can see it coming. But the president will flub the response because of all the computer glitches the Defense Department will suddenly have everywhere."

"So, this is the start of what you've been predicting?"

"I'd put money on it. *Abbot*, how long until the encounter?"

The AI said, "Between one and two hours at the vessel's current speed."

"Okay," Ken said. "The big question for us is, will they kick off the cyberattack before or after the naval incident?"

"I'd say after," Asha speculated. "They'll want word to get around to the international community that the US caused the problem. How long will that take, about an hour?"

"Less than that," Ken said. "Probably a few minutes."

"Okay, first the collision, then their diplomatic Twitter feed goes out, and third, their cyber hammer comes down, preventing a cohesive answer from the US government." Asha shook her head in resignation. "In the process, we—our country, that is—get our collective teeth kicked in by hackers who are operating from within our own borders and throughout Europe. Sounds like a good plan for them."

"Then let's start our timer. Have everyone in their seats in sixty minutes; call it four this afternoon. *Abbot*, tell the kids to get an early dinner. We'll put everyone on duty starting at four, and until something happens, start cycling them on and off shifts every two hours. We need to always have at least eight kids on duty."

Asha shuddered nervously. "This is really scary. It's exciting, but scary too."

"We've got a lot riding on it. Let's get something to eat before this thing kicks off. I wonder how accurate our guess is? This could still be a big nothing."

* * * *

Major Wong patted his back pocket for the twentieth time. His cell phone was still there. During his call to Captain Soong last night, she had sounded nervous.

Stunning Blow was imminent, although she could not get the timetable. She was, however, getting questions from General Xiao on a daily basis about the status of Plan Bartimaeus. Captain Wei's team was operational and had gone on a twenty-four-hour rotating shift.

After talking to Soong, instead of disposing of his phone, Wong took the battery out so he could keep it handy in case of an emergency. In spite of his worries, the overall plan was going fairly well.

Thanks to Wong's gracious manner, Major Levy had adopted him as a sort of unofficial confidante. Every morning she showed up for coffee and a pep talk before going down to the basement. Several times over the past ten days, she'd let slip that the Riddle's hoped-for contract had not materialized. He encouraged her to keep the faith and trust that something would ultimately be approved.

Wong periodically visited the downstairs storeroom to retrieve various food items; so many times, he worried his spying might become obvious. But during his reconnoitering, there were never more than two or three kids on duty at any one time.

It would be easy enough to execute Plan Bartimaeus but the propaganda team insisted that to get a sufficient backlash against the company, he needed to blind at least ten of the teenagers at once. As the days dragged on, he worried that continuing to wait for the optimum moment was a mistake. And now, from the look on Major Levy's face when Ken escorted her out of the building, it might be too late.

Her expression was not that of her usual cheerful self and her farewells had a ring of finality. She almost seemed frightened.

Two men came in from the street and spoke to the receptionist. They didn't look like routine salespeople looking for prospects, but she brought them into the cafeteria and told them she would let Mr. Riddle know they were here.

Wong offered for them to sit anywhere and they took a table facing the street. "Would you like a menu?" Tony asked. He waited patiently to take their orders while eavesdropping.

Before they could decide, Ken stepped out of the elevator with Asha. He was smiling but she looked worried. *Too many people are stressed out today*, Wong thought.

Ken came up to the table and said, "Hey, guys. Glad you could make it. Asha and I were about to have a burger. Have you had dinner?"

The quartet quickly agreed on four cheeseburgers with fries, depriving Tony of a chance to hear the reason for their meeting. Then more of the kids started filtering in, all of them wanting a variation of the same order.

By the time he could get back to the newcomers, Asha and Ken were getting up.

Ken turned to Wong and said, "Tony, I think we're going to be busy downstairs in another hour or two. Could you make arrangements to have about twenty pizzas delivered a little later?"

"Of course, Mr. Riddle."

"And if you need any supplies, you better get them now. I'm going to lock the place down when things start to heat up."

"I understand," Tony said, his internal alarm bells going off. This was not the right time to go downstairs. He needed access to the basement a little later, after everyone's meal, to verify exactly when the kids were all online.

"Let's go, then," Ken said, heading toward the elevator.

Wong followed, unconsciously patting his back pocket once more.

Five minutes later, he returned to the kitchen with a bag of frozen fries. While downstairs, only two of the kids were on their headsets. Several were going in and out of their dorm rooms. There was an air of anticipation.

He checked on the two men. They did not look like they planned to leave any time soon. Perhaps they were military observers sent by Major Levy. They had the look of understated strength. He should have asked Ken who they were.

Wong grimaced internally. This was not the time to lose control of the situation, but that's how he felt. The door to the stairway opened and three more of the young operators came up, all of them wanting a cheeseburger and fries.

* * * *

Thirty minutes later, Asha walked silently through the war room, stopping to say a few words to each of the boys and girls who made up their teenaged army. Their faces showed both excitement and worry; excitement at the prospective battle in which they were about to take part, and worry that they might get into trouble from their parents if it was discovered what they had been up to.

After giving each of them encouragement, Asha joined Ken, sitting in one of the two recliners reserved for them in front of the big screen. It currently showed a live satellite feed of the sea around the USS Mustin. The Chinese frigate and its accompanying cutters were still closing on the Americans.

"I've been thinking," Ken said as Asha settled into the plush chair.

"Should I be worried?" Asha asked.

"Probably. I'm wondering if we can shortstop their whole plan at the outset. Or at least delay it a few weeks. A close call might spring loose a contract."

"How could we do that?"

"Can you show me the most recent message to the captain of that Chinese frigate from their naval headquarters?"

"Let me check." Asha's eyes glazed over while she slipped into the ether. A few seconds later she said, "*Abbot*, display this page on the screen and overlay it with a translation." A military-style form appeared, filled out with Chinese characters that quickly morphed into English.

Several notations were routing symbols with unknown names and office symbols. In the center section, the body of the message read,

When your mind is strong, the enemy becomes prey; their mind shall become weak with fear in the face of our glorious destiny. An invisible thread connects you, our leaders, and our nation to our great ancestors before whom we will proudly stand!

"That's not a lot of help," Ken said.

Asha said, "How so?"

"I wanted something like 'sink the bloody Americans'. Not some Confucian philosophy."

"What are you thinking?" Asha asked. "To post the order on the Internet or something?"

"Not really. I just thought before we try to stop them, I'd like to see proof they plan to cause trouble."

"I'm not sure what you mean?"

"Well, historically, the Chinese navy will bump the vessels of other nations to intimidate them. I'd bet that frigate or one of the cutters plans to collide with the US cargo ship. See how our destroyer is staying between the Chinese and the cargo ship? The captain of the *Mustin* is trying to protect his wingman. The frigate won't mess with the destroyer because it can shoot back."

"And you want to keep any incident from happening?"

"It would be nice," Ken said. "Any way you could stop the Chinese from running into our vessels?"

"You mean take over their steering?"

"Yeah, if you can."

"Only if the Chinese vessels have Internet access?"

"Hmm. They probably don't, but the *Mustin* does. I read they stay online for command and control. It's through some highly encrypted electronic system."

"Where would I connect?" Asha asked.

"Try Seventh Fleet Headquarters. *Abbot* said they were operating from Yokosuka, Japan."

Asha took a deep breath and said, "Okay. *Abbot*, start recording; we'll need a record of everything for when Ken and I go to trial. I'm heading out now for Yokosuka." She closed her eyes, and the screen changed to a global view rapidly zooming toward Japan.

Chapter 15 – The War

Wong counted the kids as they came through for burgers. Right now, there were at least seventeen of them in the basement. But the important question was, were they on their headsets? This might be the perfect time for the Bartimaeus strike, but it could also be that everyone was just talking or goofing around. Before he called Soong, he needed to actually get his eyes inside the war room to ensure the kids were wearing the headsets.

He looked at his watch; in the Taiwan Strait, it was just after seven in the morning. If the PRC was going to launch Stunning Blow, they would likely do it early in the day. Although Ken had said the basement would be locked down, Wong prepared a snack tray as a pretext, piling it with granola bars and a giant thermos of coffee.

While contemplating how to unobtrusively get through the stairwell door, the receptionist appeared. She was escorting both Major Levy and Agent Nigel Cherry.

"Hey, Tony!" Cherry called in greeting. "Any chance of some of that coffee?"

"Of course, Mr. Cherry," Wong replied. "Two creams as I recall?" He prepared the coffee for Cherry and offered a cup to Levy who declined. She looked anxious, as though in a hurry.

"Thanks, my friend," Nigel said. "You're a lifesaver. You make the best coffee in Chicago. What brand is this? You need any help with that?" he asked.

Wong picked up the heavily laden tray and nodded toward the elevator. "No, sir. I have it. If you could just get the elevator door, please? This is a local grind; it's called Chicago Blend by Mud Pack Coffee. They're out in Franklin Park. I'll find their business card for you."

The receptionist swiped her card against the elevator button and the door slid open with a soft sigh.

"Great. Thanks," Nigel said. "I may look them up."

* * * *

The elevator dinged on the basement level and Wong stepped out with Nigel and Levy in tow. Ken got up to stop them from entering the war room. He motioned them to quiet with a finger to his lips.

Levy whispered, "The receptionist let us down here."

"She shouldn't have," Ken said with some irritation. "I told her no visitors today." He glanced at Wong and pointed to a side table. "Thanks, Tony. I'd take a cup, since you're here."

"Yes, sir. Coming up." While pouring the coffee, Wong counted the young people wearing their VR headsets; nineteen of them! The intensity on their faces meant they were actively engaged in online operations, possibly preparing to launch an attack against his homeland. He tried to hand the mug to Ken so he could get back upstairs and call Captain Soong, but Ken ignored him, focused instead on the two visitors.

Levy was explaining their presence. "Don't get mad at your receptionist. I told her Nigel had something for you."

"I brought you a contract," Nigel added.

"You did?" Ken was surprised.

So was Wong. This was the worst-case scenario. It meant Ken was about to get the all clear for aggressive action. It could also mean the kids might be able to deflect the Project Mobius thrust.

Maggie and Nigel glanced at the room, and Maggie gasped. "Everyone is here!" she exclaimed in surprise. "You said you were going to shut down."

"I lied because I wanted you gone. Things are about to heat up, and I don't want any government interference."

Nigel pulled an envelope from his coat pocket. "Maggie stopped by my office all worried World War Three might start any minute."

"I think it is," Ken confirmed.

"She told me the military didn't come through with their agreement."

Ken shook his head. "It was a long shot anyway. Asha's trying to intervene right now."

"Sounds like her," Nigel commented. "What's she doing?"

"Looking for an electronic pathway from the Yokosuka Naval Base to the USS *Mustin*." Ken gestured toward the filled war room. "Sorry, guys," he said to Nigel, "but this isn't a good time for visitors."

"A little too late for that now," Nigel said pointedly, his eyes wide at what was happening on the big screen. The scene was from a security camera inside a military command post.

"What did you say about a contract?" Ken asked, trying to shift Nigel's focus. He glanced at Wong standing close by with a full mug. "How about one for Asha too."

Nigel handed Ken the envelope. "Maggie was very persuasive. So, in my capacity as Special Agent in Charge for Chicago, I am giving you a fixed-fee, thousand-dollar contract to conduct counterintelligence operations. It's only a token amount, obviously, but Maggie said you needed at least something to seal the deal."

"That's true, I did," Ken agreed.

"Well, the FBI has been protecting the country from overseas adversaries for as long as we've been around, and I've seen what Asha can do. So, we'll consider this an extension of what she did on the NASA thing, but this time I'm throwing in a little cash."

Ken opened the envelope; it contained a check and a signed document. He scanned it quickly, and his eyes widened. He read aloud, "Chromium Plus is authorized to detect and counter any action of a foreign intelligence service or organization that employs electronic or other the technical means that may adversely affect our national interest." He looked at Nigel. "Seriously?"

"It's not much, but that's all I can offer at the moment."

"At least it gives me some cover. We accept. Thanks." Ken took the second coffee from Tony and then gestured toward the elevator for everyone to leave.

Nigel shook his head. "No, now that you've taken my money, I think I'll stay. What's going on?"

Ken hesitated and then gave in. "All right. But keep it down." He flagged one of the teenagers coming down the stairs. "Twilight, get a couple of chairs for our visitors, would you? Put them there next to Asha." He turned to Wong. "Tony, thanks for the coffee, but you're going to have to leave. You could get the pizza started, though. We may need it sooner than I thought."

"Of course, sir. Please call me if you need anything." Wong walked hurriedly to the elevator and the doors closed behind him.

* * * *

On the first floor, Major Wong raced into his kitchen, dialing Soong's number.

"Captain Soong, here."

"It's me," Wong said. "Now! Execute Plan Bartimaeus! All the kids are on their headsets. Even the FBI is here. Hurry!"

"I understand, sir," Soong said. Her voice mumbled to someone in the background. She continued, "I'm in the operations center. Is ten minutes good enough? Captain Wei's crew just went on break. Should I call them back in?"

"Yes!" Wong rasped sharply. "As quick as you can! What's going on with Stunning Blow?"

"I don't know the specifics, but the word is it will happen very soon."

"I think it's happening right this minute," Wong said. "Get your team up, and hit the kids as quickly as possible. We need twenty blind teenagers ASAP. This is it!"

"I understand, sir. Can you keep your phone with you for the next hour? Just in case I need to call you."

Wong had intended to throw it away, but at this point, it wouldn't make any difference. And Asha had her hands full at the moment. She would never know one of her employees had just called the Chinese Army's Second Department.

"All right; I'll keep it for another hour, but that's all. I'll call back to let you know how it goes." Wong hung up and started pacing rapidly back and forth until he realized what he was doing. This was not the time to act like an amateur. He picked up a cloth and went out into the dining room to wipe down a couple of tables. That would calm his mind.

First though, he should order the pizza. It was important to stay in character until he received a confirmation on the Bartimaeus strike. Still, he was worried about what was happening in the basement.

* * * *

Once Nigel and Levy were seated, Ken explained the situation. "Asha is looking for a way to keep the Chinese from hitting one of our ships."

"For God's sake, don't mess with our own Navy," Nigel urged.

Without opening her eyes, Asha growled, "You want to do this?"

Ken hushed Nigel's commentary. "Be quiet or leave. She has to concentrate. She's never tried anything like this."

The wall display changed to long lines of blazing light rushing by.

"I thought she saw automobiles," Nigel said.

"Not anymore," Ken said quickly. "Now, shut up!"

The screen jumped to a camera shot of a ship's bridge. It was a long thin room where two sailors manned an instrument-filled console that featured a smallish ship's wheel in front of a broad stretch of thick windows.

"I've reached the *Mustin*," Asha said. "There are a million data lines on this thing. Okay, I found an exterior camera; check this out."

The screen changed once more to a camera with a wide-angle view of the port side. In the distance, three other vessels were approaching.

"That's a small Chinese fleet," Ken explained to his two visitors. "They have orders to ram our cargo ship."

"I'm picking up some really strange signals," Asha said. "They're not like anything I've seen. Okay. It's the Chinese ship's radars. They are locked on to the *Mustin*. And the *Mustin* is locked on to them too. Hmmm. I wonder...Hang on..." She twisted back and forth as she lay in the recliner, her face in a grimace.

"Are you okay?" Ken asked urgently.

"Hang on," Asha repeated. "Okaaay... I've got it. I created a digital bridge through the radar signals."

The screen changed to another ship's bridge. This one had bigger windows and fewer instruments but looked crisp and modern, nonetheless.

Asha said, "This is a security camera on the Chinese frigate. Whups! They've got audio too. Here it is."

The war room filled with loud voices talking excitedly. The senior officer's voice carried over the others who answered in clipped tones.

"I wish we knew what he was saying," Ken said.

"I do," Nigel replied. "My wife is Taiwanese."

"Translate for us!" Ken said.

"They're talking too fast, but generally the captain is ordering one of the other ships—"

"The Chinese cutters," Ken said quickly.

"Okay...then one of the cutters to swing in front of the destroyer and hit the cargo ship from the starboard side."

"There he goes," Asha said. The TV screen split in two, to show both the exterior view from the *Mustin* and the interior of the Chinese frigate's bridge. The cutter on the frigate's portside accelerated and veered sharply to its left to pass well in front of the two American ships. The US Navy vessels began blaring loud horns warning the other ships to stay clear.

"I'm going to try something..." Asha said, almost to herself.

Nigel continued, "The Chinese skipper is telling his radioman to call in the collision the second it happens and to blame the Americans. Sounds like they've got this thing planned out."

"Are you recording this?" Levy asked. "At least you would have a record of it"

"Yes, but it doesn't matter," Ken replied. "Their media will scream bloody murder to the whole world. The headlines will say we invaded their territorial waters, even though we haven't." He pointed at the exterior view. "Something is happening there!"

The Chinese cutter was veering back to the south, so sharply that its starboard gunwale was almost level with the wave tops. "What's he doing? Is he going to hit the cargo ship head-on?"

"That's not where he's headed," Asha said, grunting with the effort. "This is really hard because the signals are so weird."

"What are you doing, babe?" Ken asked.

Asha did not reply, completely focused on the task she was engaged in.

Nigel said, "The Chinese skipper is going nuts."

The frigate's captain was shouting at his men and pointing at the cutter. He grabbed the microphone from one of his underlings and screamed into it.

"He's telling the cutter to veer off. Oh my God, look at that."

The cutter was now aimed directly at the frigate, bearing down at high speed.

The *Mustin* and *Wenzhou* both were now blaring their ship's horns. The men on the US bridge pointed in astonishment at the impending collision between the two Chinese vessels.

At the last second, the frigate tried to turn away, but it was much too late and only aggravated the impact. The cutter struck the *Wenzhou* directly amidships, partially caving in the portside hull. It left a gash that ran down below the waterline.

The collision was not like a car crash where both vehicles come to a sudden grinding halt. The *Wenzhou*, at almost five thousand tons, carried enormous momentum. Even though its captain called for emergency stop, the ship continued to glide forward. At cruising speed, the Wenzhou's stopping distance, even under emergency conditions, exceeded five ship lengths.

In spite of the deceleration, the cutter's nose, firmly embedded in the frigate's side, ripped an ever-larger wound in *Wenzhou's* hull, letting the sea rush in at thousands of gallons a second.

"That thing is going down," Nigel said.

"I lost the signal," Asha said. "I'm still connected to the *Mustin*. Do I need to stick with them?"

The US destroyer's captain also called for All Stop, ordering his crew to come about and render assistance. In the *Mustin's* camera, the *Wenzhou* was already listing heavily to port. The cutter finally separated from the frigate, its own survivability questionable with its bow crushed and a massive tear along its front starboard superstructure.

"Not necessary," Ken said. "Get out of there. Have *Abbot* make copies of that, and send them to TV networks all around the globe, especially any news outlet he can find in the Western Pacific. We might as well get our side of the story out there first. Make sure nothing links to us."

"Okay, CNN and FOX will have it in about a minute. Now what? Do you think the Chinese army will call off the cyberwar?"

"If they're smart, they will, but I don't think they are. If that radioman sent his signal before the ship lost power, all he probably got out was that there was a collision. The people on the other end will run with that, thinking everything happened as planned."

"So, what are you going to do?" Nigel asked.

Ken took a deep breath. "We'll wait for the first attack and then hit back with everything we have." He gestured to the teenage operators. "They are monitoring our critical assets at the moment. Also, Asha has set up fifty independent *Sherlocks* watching all the transoceanic traffic. If the Chinese launch a *Monroe* attack, we'll know it."

The wall display reverted to the standard global map. Over a hundred mauve lines were stretching out across the Pacific to the US. From Europe, dozens more probed America's eastern seaboard.

Asha opened her eyes to look at the screen. She said, "An actual attack changes the purple to red. As long as we don't see any red lines, we're okay."

Nigel nodded. "Then let's hope nothing changes color so—"

From each of the origination points across the Chinese mainland and Europe, all of the mauve streams suddenly turned bright red.

Abbot's voice filled the war room. "Enemy cyberattacks detected. Initiating cyber defense and targeting analysis."

On the map, blue tinted circles bloomed around the major metropolitan areas on both US coasts, expanding until a solid barrier was erected around the entire northern hemisphere.

"All bets are off now," Ken muttered. He glanced at Nigel. "Remember this moment if you ever have to answer questions. They struck first."

Every time a red line of attack from the *Monroe* AIs struck the US blue line of defense, the color changed from red to blue and rocketed back to its source.

"What's happening there?" Nigel asked.

"Asha created the equivalent of a suicide pill for all those *Monroe* bots. Every time one of them attacks North America they wind up getting a self-destruct command in return. It will take a couple of minutes to work, but after that, the *Monroe* threat will be over."

Abbot spoke up, "I am detecting a separate *Monroe* attack against this facility. The Chinese forces are hacking our operator headsets."

"Then we may not have much time," Ken said. "Put a list on the screen of all the locations those *Monroe* bots were reconnoitering. I'm concerned about our national infrastructure."

"Acknowledged. I am updating the map with China's intended military targets on US soil."

The threat map sparkled as practically every single military installation on the American continent appeared in bright white. "Now adding the list of civilian targets," the AI said.

A catalog of specific locations began to scroll in a separate window marked Utilities. It included Pacific Gas and Electric, Southern California Edison, Florida Power and Light, Consolidated Edison, Georgia Power, and many more.

When it was finished over twenty major utility companies were shown. Another window popped up, this one labeled Transportation. The major airlines' names came up, the big railroads, and ten of the largest trucking corporations. Sector by sector, *Abbot* listed the targets the Chinese had planned on hitting. When he was finished, including the military bases, over two thousand organizations had flashed across the screen.

Most concerning to Levy were all the military bases and especially the nation's command and control centers.

"Those guys are idiots," Nigel said. "Did they really think we wouldn't strike back for something like this?"

"If their attacks had been successful," Ken said, "we wouldn't be able to. They targeted all of our communications capability. Their big problem is they don't have a Plan B. That's going to become painfully obvious in a few minutes."

Abbot said, "Suicide pills are taking effect. Monroe attacks are diminishing."

The traces of red and mauve began to vanish from the screen.

"Okay, *Abbot*," Ken said. "Start converting our defensive shield to the planned counterattack. Queue up our operator targets. Tell the *Sherlock* assistants we want as much damage as possible."

Nigel looked surprised. "You've already identified counter targets? I thought you were just going to stop their attack."

Ken glanced at Nigel with an amused expression. "Why would I do that?" he asked. "They were out to destroy us. I'm not sure what their military plan was, but you know it wasn't going to stop with just ramming a single vessel. We're not tied into the Pentagon's monitoring system, but I'll bet those guys are freaking out right now because the Chinese probably went to high alert the second that frigate reported the incident."

Nigel glanced at the display. It had reverted to split screens showing each of the operators' individual viewpoints. The separate windows cycled every few moments as specific targets were hit and the operator moved to the next one.

"What exactly is happening?" Nigel asked, his voice filled with concern.

Ken took a deep breath and his voice became somber. "Just what *Abbot* said. For the last couple of months, he's been identifying all of the weak points inside mainland China. We divided up the most important into an array of preplanned counter-targets for each of our people. About three hundred of them. That's about fifteen apiece."

"Seriously? Do you realize the disruption that could cause?"

"Probably better than you. Did you know that in China this is Autumn Festival Golden Week?"

"Never heard of it," Nigel said.

"It's a weeklong national holiday. The government created them in early 2001 to let people travel home for family visits. The idea was it would improve the standard of living."

"I didn't know that."

"Family is important to their culture. My point is there is a lot of travel during the Golden Week. Last year it included almost a billion people."

Nigel looked confused. "You think messing with their holidays is an adequate military response?"

"Sort of," Ken said with a grin, "in a non-lethal way." He pointed at the display screen. In one window after another, internal security cameras of airport control towers were showing signs of bedlam. "We're taking down China's transportation system, starting with aviation."

"You're not going to crash airliners, are you?"

"Of course not. But we are destroying all the radars and radios in their air traffic control system. Roth wasn't listening when I said we can fry the central processor in any piece of equipment."

"I remember you saying that. I thought you were talking about desktop computers."

Ken shook his head. "Nope. Our capability is much broader. In the next couple of minutes, their entire aviation industry will be grounded until all those radios and radars can be replaced."

"I imagine they have spares," Nigel said.

"A few, sure. But most of their suppliers are overseas. It will take time. Think of all those families stuck at their parents' house or their equivalent of Aunt Bessie. How long would it take you to come unglued if you had to live with your in-laws for more than a day or two?"

"About ten minutes," Nigel said somberly. "But still…"

Ken said, "Apart from aviation, did you know that China has the second largest railway system in the world? And it all runs on computers? It's operated by the China Rail Corporation. That's a state-owned business and it has eighteen rail bureaus with over two million employees."

"You're not seriously going to…"

"Yep. The Chinese rail industry is coming to a halt as we speak."

"These twenty kids are doing all that?" Nigel asked, shocked by the scope of what Ken was suggesting.

"No, they are only hitting the highest priority targets. It takes a minute or two for each one. The other fifty *Sherlocks* that I told you about, are in the process of attacking about ten thousand lower level objectives. And we have another twenty *Sherlocks* actually stationed in China. A company called Sinnet Technology runs a cloud service operation." Ken grinned. "They're renting server space to us."

"What else are you doing?" Nigel wanted to know.

"The seaports are going to be tied up for a while. Do you have any idea how much computer power goes into keeping track of every single item in every single shipping container? All those computers are getting wiped clean. And that's going to slow up all the replacement parts I mentioned."

"I can't believe it. You are inviting a nuclear Armageddon by doing all this."

"I hope not," Ken said. "But keep in mind, it's not like their inventory comes close to ours. They have fewer than a hundred land-based ICBMs, and you don't launch those kinds of missiles by striking a match to a fuse. Night Fury over there is permanently disabling all their targeting and control systems."

"Are you sure about that?" Nigel asked.

"We're sure. That was an area of specific concern. We're disabling their submarines too. It will be a long time before any of their rockets can fly. Look there, second from the top. That's a shot of their highway system."

On one of the displays, the security camera of an expressway toll booth had lines backed up for miles.

Ken explained, "The Chinese highway system is about seventy percent toll road. Even though our AIs can't do much damage to pavement, we can cripple all their toll booths. The roads are getting blocked and it will take them a while to sort out."

"Is there any part of their system you're not messing with?" Levy asked.

"Not really. We have five dedicated *Sherlocks* screwing up the Shenzhen Stock Exchange. In the next few minutes no one in China will know who owns what. And the last thing, of course, will be their communications and power grid. China Telecom won't have an operable system; neither will the other two state-run phone companies. The last thing we'll take down is the coal industry and the nuclear power plants."

"If all this is true, you might as well have nuked them," Nigel said.

Ken shook his head. "I wouldn't put it that way. Yeah, we're having a big impact on the country…as much as we can. In another five minutes, those guys will be living in the middle of the last century. The most important thing though, is that we did it without mass casualties. Just think about it. If our military had responded and things went south, the fatalities could have been in the millions—hundreds of millions. And I'm not saying all of them would have been on their side. That's what we wanted to prevent."

Levy pulled out her cell phone. "I need to report this to Colonel Roth."

"You might want to think about that, Maggie," Ken said. "Right now, apart from my employees, you and Nigel are the only two people in the world who know about our operation here. Do you really want to highlight the fact that you were in the room when all this happened?"

Nigel carefully took Maggie's phone from her grasp and powered it off. "Ken has a point."

"But..."

Nigel shook his head. "Just let it be." He turned to Ken, and said, "What about the Russians? Won't they react to any of this?"

Ken smiled and replied, "If they so much as exhale in our direction, *Abbot* has a thousand Russian targets already lined up. Did you really think we've been sitting on our ass the last few months?"

One of the operators pulled off his headset and put his recliner upright. He rubbed his eyes and gave Ken two thumbs up. "Anything else?" he asked.

"Not at the moment. Sit tight for a minute and let's see what else happens."

One at a time, the operators finished their tasks and sat up straight. A few got up and stretched, and a buzz of conversation began amongst them.

"What about them?" Nigel said. "What if they try this on their own when they get bored on Friday night?"

Ken put his hand on Nigel's shoulder. "Don't be silly. They're teenagers. Why would a teenager get into mischief?"

"Are you serious?"

Ken chuckled. "Just kidding. They can't do anything without a headset, remember? And we keep them locked up. And in a few months, they're going to grow out of it, anyway. Relax."

Nigel nodded. "That's right. You mentioned that. But won't they talk?"

"I doubt it. They're good kids and they want to be part of our game development; we're still working on that. And being quiet is part of their scholarship deal."

"You've thought of everything, haven't you?"

"Wouldn't that be nice." Ken scoffed. "All we wanted was to stop the insanity that was coming our way. *Abbot*, give us a rundown. What's the status?"

Abbot replied over the intercom. "The operators completed three hundred and seventeen successful strikes on high priority targets.

The *Sherlock* battalion completed their assigned tasks on ten thousand and forty-five intermediate and lower priority attacks. Eighty-seven targets could not be struck before widespread loss of power. The Beijing government attempted to register a complaint before they lost transoceanic communications."

"What about our side of the ocean?" Ken asked.

"The Chinese government successfully placed seven *Monroe* AIs within the continental US. Although our response was almost instantaneous, we experienced interrupted service to two airlines and three utility companies. Those *Monroe* AIs were terminated."

"That's good enough," Ken said. "Good job, *Abbot*. And anyway, that gives legitimacy to our claim that it was a counterstrike in self-defense."

"Someone help me up," Asha called from her reclining position. "I'm exhausted." She held up a hand, demanding assistance.

"I'm not surprised," Ken said, pulling her to her feet and into a quick embrace. "You did good." He looked at the other teens in the war room. "You all did good!"

Everyone burst into cheers and a note of relief was evident in their voices.

"We ordered pizza before this started," Asha said. "Let's go upstairs. *Abbot*, call me if there are any issues."

"Any issues?" Nigel exclaimed. "Are you *kidding* me? There are going to be fourteen thousand issues in the next hour."

"Not for us," Ken said. "The politicians can sort all that out. If anything comes our way, we'll worry about it then. Want to join us for pizza?"

Nigel shook his head. "No, thanks. I want to get as far away from this building as possible." He looked at Major Levy. "If you're smart, you'll go back to Fort Meade, and keep this to yourself."

Ken laughed at the advice, and put his arm around Asha, pulling her toward the elevator. "You kids take the stairs!" he shouted over his shoulder.

* * * *

In spite of his best efforts to stay calm, Major Wong thought his heart would explode until he heard the faint screams filtering up the stairway through the locked door.

Thank God, he thought. It had taken longer than expected, but it sounded like Captain Soong's team had come through. It was time to put on an expression of concern for the injured children.

He heard them stampeding up the stairs. That in itself was a little surprising. He didn't think they would be able to walk after having their eyes burned out.

Then the door opened and they came out laughing and talking; jostling each other in comradely fun. They were in great spirits. Obviously, nothing had happened to their vision.

Had the attack on their headsets not worked? Was Soong too late? Had those idiots not come back from break? What was going on? He needed to call Soong for an update, but the kids filled up the cafeteria asking where their pizzas were. As if on cue, two young women from the next-door pizzeria came in, grunting from their heavy load.

The teenagers relieved them of their burden, and someone presented Wong with a ticket to sign; he scribbled his name.

Asha and Ken came in from the elevator and joined the festivities. Major Levy and Agent Cherry headed out the front door with downcast eyes. They looked like they were headed for a firing squad.

As the kids chowed down, Wong stepped out of sight behind the counter and called Soong several times, but she wouldn't pick up. He began to worry the celebratory reception he had anticipated on his return to Beijing might be in question.

* * * *

After an hour of noisy celebration, Asha sent the victorious operators on their way. "Stay close to a phone, just in case," she told them. "And unless you hear from us, don't come back here. Take off the rest of the week, and then check in at the office on Forty-Seventh Street next Monday. And remember, mum's the word. We don't want your parents getting in trouble for raising juvenile delinquents."

"Do we still get our scholarships?" Twilight asked.

"Absolutely," Ken said. "Each of you will receive a four-year, all expenses paid, college education. We'll send you paperwork with details. If you haven't already, you should start brushing up with a few SAT prep books."

That brought a round of groans, but relatively good-natured ones, as they flowed toward the exit.

Asha called out to one of them. "Tracer!" She pointed at the girl's neck. "Headset please, honey. You can't take those home, you know that." The youngster had it wrapped around her neck.

Tracer was appropriately apologetic. "Sorry, sorry." She pulled it off and handed it over. It was not the first time for the absentminded youngster. "Should I take it downstairs?" she asked.

"No, just give it here," Asha said. "Go on, you've done enough for one day." She looked around for Tony and found him standing near the cash register, a look of shock on his face. "Tony, can I get a Coke, please? I'm about parched."

Tony filled up a glass from the fountain and brought it over.

"Have a seat," Ken said, pushing out a chair. "You look done in too. We've all had a big day." He took Tracer's headset from Asha and handed it to Wong.

"What's this?" Wong asked numbly.

"That's our standard VR headset. If you notice, it's not all that heavy. I thought you might be interested to learn that the real ones don't have big batteries and lasers inside. The one your agent found, I think his name was Lieutenant Li, was one we had specially modified to throw you off track. Raphael spent a lot of time on the engineering to make it seem plausible. I guess it worked."

Realization dawned on Wong's face. "You know who I am?"

"Of course, we do," Asha said. "Why do you think we hired you? With you right here in the building, it was easy to keep track of what the Second Department was planning."

Wong looked at the headset, his face filled conflicting emotions. Asha didn't feel sorry for him.

"By the way," Ken said. "There's no sense in trying to contact Captain Soong. Beijing doesn't have cell phone service at the moment, nor any power, and they won't for quite some time. All the nuclear plants are dead. Don't worry; we didn't cause any meltdowns, but the main control systems are history. It'll take years to get them running."

"And the communication centers are down anyway," Asha added.

"Here is the good news, Major," Ken said. "We're not going to turn you over to the FBI. Or Major Mao either. It would highlight certain activities that neither one of us want passed around. But we did give all the information about you to Agent Cherry. He'll see it when he gets to his office, probably first thing in the morning. So that gives you a few hours' head start to get out of the country."

Asha added, "And you may want to rethink going back to China. I mean, it's going to be tough over there for a long time. With power and communications out, I'd be surprised if the government even survives. I'm just hoping they don't have food riots."

"We didn't touch Shanghai or Hong Kong," Ken said. "That might be a place to start over. Anyway, you better head out."

Wong stared at them for a moment with narrowed eyes. His face slowly transformed from their friendly chef to the deadly agent he really was.

The two men in the corner stood up menacingly and approached the table.

"Sorry, Tony," Asha said. "These gentlemen are from Pinkerton. Please believe me when I say they are very skilled in protective combat. Ken arranged for their presence just for this particular moment. So, you should ask yourself if a longshot at revenge is worth dying for."

Wong let out a disgusted sigh and with a threatening voice said, "I suggest you keep them on your payroll."

"Last chance to leave," Ken said.

Wong got up and left the building without looking back.

"I was worried there for a minute," Asha said.

Ken glanced at the bodyguards. "Can you guys take us home, just in case?"

"You got it, boss."

A limo was on standby and the men escorted the couple all the way to their apartment door before saying goodnight. Once inside, Asha settled on the couch, and said, "*Abbot*, put the TV on CNN."

One of the anchors was talking about the latest polls for the coming election. There was a brief mention of a widespread blackout in China, but details were scarce.

"Try FOX," Ken said.

A different anchor discussed a near tragedy at sea in the Taiwan Strait where a US Navy ship had rescued over a hundred Chinese sailors following an unexplained collision between two of the PRC's naval vessels.

There was no mention of cyberterrorism and counterattacks. After a commercial break, the newsman reported that First Energy Corporation had restored power to all customers after a brief interruption in the Cleveland area.

"Looks like a couple of their strikes got through," Ken observed. "It could have been worse."

"Turn it off," Asha told *Abbot* with a sigh. "Will it really be this easy?" she asked. "Did no one notice we almost went to war?"

"I have no idea," Ken said. "I'm surprised it's still this quiet, but we should stick with our plan."

"I agree," Asha said. "Better safe than sorry."

* * * *

A locksmith forced the doors open at Chromium Plus while Nigel stood on the sidewalk. He already knew what he would find inside; nothing.

He was right. The cafeteria was empty as were the two upper floors and the basements. All the furniture was still in place, and the computers were still in the IT room. Not even their hard drives had been wiped clean. The Riddles were clearly happy for the government to know everything.

Nigel's agents had found the same thing at the two apartments for the strange couple. It was like both husband and wife had disappeared from the face of the earth. Their clothes were even hanging in their closets and food was in the fridge. But the pair had vanished as if into thin air.

"They planned this out long ago," Nigel said aloud to no one in particular.

"You're paying for any damage to the front door," Cody said.

Nigel had contacted Cody through Maryanne at FinCEN, and the attorney had agreed to provide whatever assistance he could. It turned out to be nil.

"You could have given us a key," Nigel said.

"I would have if you had told me this is where we were coming. I told you they're gone."

"Where? You must have an idea."

"You're right, I should! And it pisses me off that I don't."

"Did they tell you they were leaving?"

"Of course. Ken had it all planned. But I wouldn't go with him because Maryanne won't leave, so he wouldn't tell me where they were headed. I assume they have an alias, but that's not a tall order when Asha can hack any computer in the world."

"And that's it?" Nigel asked. "They're gone forever?"

"No. Ken said when the heat dies down, he'll contact me. You're the only guy who knows when that will be. Or will it ever?"

"I don't know," Nigel confessed. "I'm taking enough crap of my own because of that damned agreement I gave him."

"That's why he wanted it. He hoped the people in DC would leave him alone if he were operating under contract."

"I'm not getting good vibes from Washington," Nigel said. "Just lots of second-guessing. My take is that no one can figure out if he is a saint or a villain."

"Then tell them to look at all the information he left behind. You have more information on our adversaries than ever before. Tell

Congress to study the whole thing to death. The longer it takes them in DC, the less impact in Chicago. Probably best for you too."

Nigel turned to leave. "Don't leave town," he said as he left the building.

"I'm not planning to," Cody replied. "I have to find a job."

* * * *

Two Years Later, Port Angeles, Washington,

Asha woke up early. She took her morning coffee onto the deck off the living room. After two years, she had not tired of the view. The sky was clear, and the Canadian city of Victoria was visible across the Strait of Juan de Fuca. It was a good omen for the start of the day.

The pillow next to hers had been untouched. Ken had not come home last night. He was consumed with the latest project at his new company. Hopefully, the new business would last longer than the last one.

In the months leading up to the almost-war, Asha had bought the out-of-the-way home so she and Ken would have a place to hide. It was a fifties-era ranch-style house in the small, blue-collar community. Located on the rising terrain of Washington State's northwestern coast, the topography meant that practically every home in the city had a spectacular view of either the sea or the mountains or both.

The area was called the Olympic Peninsula. It was populated by hard-working people who, by nature of their surroundings, loved the outdoors. It was a peaceful place to live, and since Asha and Ken's middle-of-the-night departure from Chicago, there had been no midnight knocks on the door from the FBI, the Chinese, or anyone else.

And that was why this was an important day. The question of their ever being able to return to the Windy City was supposed to be answered today. Asha wasn't certain what she wanted the result to be. She had come to love their new home. Maybe it was because she had grown up in a small community, the similarly sized town of

Bartlesville. Regardless, she had told Ken she wanted to stay where they were.

"That works for me," he had replied. "With this kind of work, it doesn't matter where we live. I just want to be sure no one is going to bother us."

It had been a recurring fear in the back of their minds. Would the government leave them alone or not?

Asha got dressed and drove down to Ken's workplace. It was a spacious building, once a local hardware store, located across the street from the waterfront.

Using a locally installed *Abbot*, Ken kept in constant communication with Raphael. Rafe had stayed behind to continue his research and work with the people at Shaded Lair. The government had questioned Raphael, of course, the same way they had Cody. Lots of questions but no answers because they honestly didn't know.

In the meantime, however, for Raphael's work to progress, he needed Asha's assistance. They collaborated frequently without exchanging physical addresses. Until just recently, he hadn't known where Ken and Asha had relocated to.

A few months ago, Asha had to bring Raphael into the secret to help him to identify new test subjects. They wanted young people who were just starting college.

"Hi, babe," Ken greeted Asha when she arrived at his new laboratory.

She said hello to her husband and three of his assistants. They were making painstakingly slow progress in unraveling the secrets of *Abbot's* mind.

"It's almost time," Asha said. "Any predictions?"

Ken shook his head. "I don't want to jinx it. Come on back."

Down a short hallway, they entered the video conference room. It had no windows, nor anything that could tip a participant on the other end about their location. They sat down, side-by-side, at a small table facing a large television screen. In the picture was an empty desk and chair, located in the same Forty-Seventh Street location in Chicago. After a moment, Raphael took the seat.

"Raphael!" Asha exclaimed delightedly. "I wasn't expecting you to be there. How are you?"

"Hey, Asha. Doing good. Stephenson is just arriving. I wanted to say hi and let you know that all the test subjects were excited to be selected as part of the experiment. How did the implants work?"

"I don't know yet," Asha said. "I'll find out later this morning. I read your reports. It seemed like everything went well on your end. I still can't get over your idea for bypassing the optic nerve."

"Sam came up with it. In retrospect, it was so simple. There are more cranial nerves in our heads than just that one. And the cochlear nerve has enough fibers that it can spare a couple."

"It's still a miracle from where I sit," Asha said. "This is going to be an entirely new chapter in our research."

"And the human condition," Raphael added. "I'm not sure how you convinced the school."

"All it takes is money. I set up an endowment and they agreed to it on an experimental basis. I didn't go into a lot of detail. I'll call you later today about how it went."

"I'll be waiting," Raphael replied. "Here's Bernard." He rose from the chair and moved out of the camera view.

Stephenson thudded into the seat, a scowl on his face.

"Hi, Bernard," Asha said cheerily. "Long time, no see. I hope you're doing well."

"I would be better if I was in my office. I detest this side of town."

"Ooh, poor baby," Asha teased, her mood unbroken. "What's the news? Don't make us wait."

Stephenson made the usual production out of opening his briefcase and sorting through papers before finally selecting one. Then he had to study it for a moment before speaking. "In essence," he said slowly, "all is forgiven. I have the document officially thanking you for your assistance in the War that Never Was. It includes an implicit caveat that you share whatever new technology you have since developed."

Asha squealed with joy, and Ken nodded with satisfaction. "Good job, Bernard," Ken said.

"Agent Cherry told me he doesn't believe Asha lost her abilities," Stephenson said. "Mostly, he just wants to keep closer tabs on whatever you two are up to."

"Can't fool Nigel," Asha said with a grin. "We're not coming back, but we will definitely work with him. Don't tell him where we are."

"I won't, but he would be glad to hear from you. He still takes heat for giving you that contract. But that was what finally cleared the way for the government to wrap this up once and for all, at least from his perspective. The State Department is still trying to deal with the Yangtze Breakup. South China, or I guess I should say the new nation of Nanjing, will be recognized by the United Nations later this week. Beijing doesn't recognize their independence, but there's nothing they can do about it."

Asha smiled happily. "Should I tell Nigel I've been working with Nanjing's new federal government?"

Stephenson paled. "You have? Mrs. Riddle, you put me in an impossible..." His voice trailed away, and he closed his eyes.

Ken covered Asha's hand with his. "Probably not a good topic for this morning," he said. "Let's take the agreement and be happy with it."

Asha sobered. "You're right. I take it back, Bernard. Forget I said anything."

Ken thanked Stephenson, and after mutual good wishes, terminated the connection. He stared at Asha, and said, "Have you really been talking to Shanghai?"

"I told you last summer that I was. It was after we found out Captain Soong had moved there. You said it would be a good idea to keep an eye on their recovery."

Ken shook his head. "I believe you, but I have no memory of that."

"All you think about is work these days." Asha patted her husband's shoulder. "That's okay. What you're doing is important."

"Well, that's true," Ken said. "At least I hope so. You better get out of here; it's time for class."

"Okay." Asha gave him a quick kiss and left the building.

* * * *

Thirty minutes later, Asha was at her desk, needlessly straightening her books. At the top of the hour, she stood up and introduced herself.

"Good morning, everyone," she said. "I'm Professor Kathy Huntingdon. Welcome to Peninsula College's Advanced Research and Data Analysis class, CLS 2450. Anyone in the wrong room?"

There were a few murmured responses of greetings, and several of the students touched the skin behind their right ear as though they had an unpleasant itch. Asha recognized several of the students; in particular, she gave a wink to Vonn Casey.

Asha continued, "Now, as I am sure you know, this class is experimental and had some unusual prerequisites. I'm going to administer a simple test to make sure you have successfully completed those requirements."

Asha closed her mouth firmly and sent a mental message into the Internet to be relayed straight into the brains of Raphael's latest test group. *Everyone who is getting this message, please raise your hand.*

The hand of every student in the class shot straight up.

The End

376

Thank You for Reading

We hope you enjoyed *The Cyclops Effect*. If so, please leave a comment on Amazon, even if only a word or two. It really helps.

Acknowledgments

Cover design by CJ Williams. Cover art includes images from ©Shutterstock. Thanks to my little sister Karen, a talented editor in the publishing industry, for her assistance. All products and brands included in the narrative are the property of and copyrighted by their respective businesses.

About the Author

CJ Williams is a husband and wife writing team. He was a military pilot, and she was an artist. Today, they live in Washington State, enjoy hiking in the Olympic Mountains, boating in the Salish Sea, and writing.

Other Books by CJ Williams

The Warlord Saga
The Commander
The Nobility
The Warlord

Science Fiction Novels
Effie
Galleon
D-Day
The Cyclops Effect

The Deep Mermaid Saga
Deep Trouble
Deep Anger
Deep Kiss

Mystery
Holding Hands (A White House Murder Mystery)

Author's Notes

In real life, state-sponsored hacking is a big problem. A Federal Grand Jury in the United States indicted five Chinese military officers, from PLA Unit 61398, located in Pudong, Shanghai, on charges of theft of confidential business information from U.S. commercial firms and planting malware on their computers. (Source: Wikipedia)

Made in the USA
Monee, IL
15 August 2020